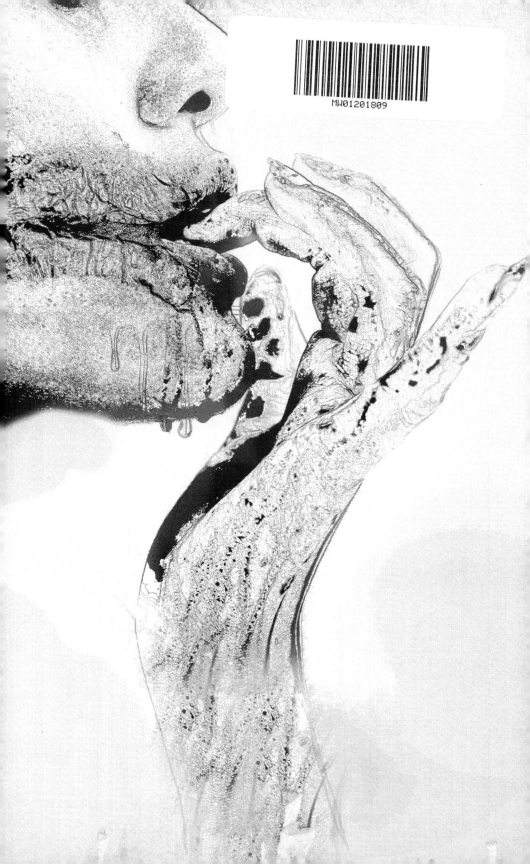

YEAR'S BEST
HARDCORE
HORROR
VOLUME 3

EDITORS:

RANDY CHANDLER
CHERYL MULLENAX

RED ROOM PRESS
WWW.REDROOMPRESS.COM

Copyrights Continued on page 313

Red Room Press

WWW.REDROOMPRESS.COM

Diabolically dedicated to all the hardcore and extreme publishers, editors, and authors.

TABLE OF CONTENTS

2017: KILLING IT DARKLY

INTRODUCTION BY RANDY CHANDLER AND CHERYL MULLENAX

It was a killer year for horror fiction of the harder kind. Authors, editors and publishers presented readers with some startling works of horrific imagination, stories graphic in the extreme yet with subtleties suggesting larger meanings, tales that explore humanity by plumbing depths of soulless inhumanity and, in some cases, outright depravity. The stories here represent the best of them, disturbing tales that dig deep and take you into the dark heart of horror itself, unrelenting and unapologetic.

You will no doubt notice that several of this year's stories edge into science fiction territory. This is not by thematic design; it just happened this way. Authors go where their stories take them, and then take us along with them. As you will see, Sci-Fi makes for very imaginative horror. The same can be said for fantasy, as evidenced by a few tales herein that border on fantasy while never betraying their horror roots.

Case in point, in our opening story "So Sings The Siren" Annie Neugebauer takes us onto a Dark Fantasy stage for a one-night-only performance of mythological torture. Then Ryan Harding's "Junk" gets right to the hardcore stuff with the ultimate dick-pic horror tale. Robert Levy's "The Cenacle" is a literary cemetery feast you may have a hard time stomaching (Tums won't save you).

Nathan Ballingrud's "The Maw" treads surefootedly on Sci-Fi ground, right up to the edge of the Maw itself in a tale of stunning originality. Luciano Marano made his first pro sell when he sold "Burnt" to *DOA III,* certainly one of the year's best anthologies, and the tale has it own fiery fetishistic twist.

"The Better Part of Drowning" by Octavia Cade treads waters of both science fiction and fantasy but it's pure horror at its biting depths. Tim Waggoner's "Til Death" is Lovecraftian Post-Apocalypse horror at its absolute best.

"Letter From Hell" comes with that special delivery you only get from Matt Shaw. Dani Brown gets down and very dirty in her "Theatrum Mortuum," which may be the most extreme thing you read all year. If the thought of torture porn scares or offends you, you may do well to skip this one.

Glenn Gray's "Break" is a hard-to-take anatomy lesson given to a man weary of doing hard time. In "Bernadette" Ramiro Perez de Pereda gets medieval in his tale of a djinn summoned by a desperate priest.

Brian Hodge takes you on a trip to Mexico you will never forget in "West of Matamoros, North of Hell." This story is a masterpiece of suspense, a grueling experience that may well leave you exhausted by the end. You might even feel like a vacation afterward, but we're betting it won't be to Matamoros.

Bracken MacLeod's "Reprising Her Role" takes us behind the scenes of a porno snuff film for a gut-wrenching reprisal and unexpected bonus footage.

The tension doesn't let up in our next offering. A real-life death threat inspired Doug Ford's "The Watcher" and we think it shows. "Scratching From The Outer Darkness" showcases Tim Curran's descriptive prowess and gives you a tale of hardcore Cthulhu Mythos.

Brace yourself when Adam Howe's "Foreign Bodies" takes you deep into the bowels of a nasty abyss—which might make a good echo chamber for the laughter Adam's patented black humor is likely to elicit.

Sean Patrick Hazlett introduces us to "Adramelech," an ancient demon with a taste for broiled children. Daniel Marc Chant's "ULTRA" jacks into a popular VR game called Slut Slayer. But what if it's more than a game?

Nathan Robinson takes us into the trees with a group of militant environmentalists who will discover a tree hugger of the deadly sort, entirely alien to their experience.

Scott Smith (*A Simple Plan* and *The Ruins*) wraps up this year's fat package of the hard stuff in a big bloody bow with "The Dogs." The canines in this tale are not Man's Best Friend variety, nor are they Woman's Besties, as you will see. But the story certainly is one of the best of the year, and not one you'll soon forget.

Thanks for coming along into this year's heart of hardcore darkness. We hope to see you on the other side.

SO SINGS THE SIREN

ANNIE NEUGEBAUER

From *Apex Magazine #101*
Editor: Jason Sizemore
Apex Publications

You can hold yourself back from the sufferings of the world, that is something you are free to do and it accords with your nature, but perhaps this very holding back is the one suffering you could avoid. —Franz Kafka

When the woman moved forward to order, the girl stepped within her shadow. "A vodka Sprite, please, and a bag of peanut M&Ms."

The girl tugged on her mother's brushed satin dress. "Mom, I'm thirsty too."

The woman glanced over her shoulder. "There's a water fountain by the bathroom, sweetie. I'm not paying six dollars for a bottle of water."

The girl returned her hand to her own dress of royal blue velvet, a fabric both heavy and soft. She liked to rub a fold of it between her fingers, feeling the nubby pile slip back and forth under her thumb. The dress's straps kept slipping from her shoulders beneath her sweater. Her mother bought it one size too big so she could wear it again next year. The girl didn't mind. It was the most beautiful dress she'd ever had.

The woman sat on an upholstered bench in the hallway, sipping her drink, but the girl couldn't sit still. She twirled to make her skirt flare, dancing back and forth across the hall as she crunched her candy.

"Hurry up, sweetie. We can't take those in with us."

The girl poured more M&Ms into her mouth, then spoke around them. "Mom?"

"Hm?"

"Will the siren have wings?"

"Yes, she should. I think they always have wings."

"What color will they be?"

"Whatever color her skin is, probably."

The girl twirled. "Will she have bird feet? And a beak?"

The woman smiled. "No. That's a myth. Stay here for a minute. Finish your candy." The woman walked down the hall and around the corner to throw away her empty plastic glass.

The girl rubbed her skirt between her fingers, tipped back the bag, and spun and spun and spun. She bumped into a man.

"Sorry," she muttered, glancing up at him. He was tall and crooked.

"That's all right," he said. "So much energy—best to get it out now. You'll be sitting still for a long time."

The girl glanced down the hall to where her mother had gone, then eyed the man warily. "How long?"

"That depends on the musician. The best ones can draw it out for hours."

"Hours?"

He wiggled his eyebrows. "Hours. Is this the first time you've come to hear a siren sing?"

She nodded, crushing velvet between her fingers.

"Is that your mom you're with?"

Another nod.

"Did you get seats on the floor or up in the mezzanine?" he asked.

She glanced to the corner. "We have a box."

"Oh, I see. Does it face the stage or the audience?"

Velvet specks stuck to the dew on her fingertips. "The audience."

"Ah." The man straightened himself. "That's a shame. You won't be able to see the siren's face that way."

"What does it look like?"

The man wobbled his jaw. "Her face is contorted in beautiful agony. Her pain is what draws the beauty of her voice in contrast. The better the musician, the more beautiful her song."

The mother hurried toward them. The girl asked the man, "What does he do to her?"

"Surely your mother told you that he tortures her."

"Yes, but how?"

"If you faced the stage, you would see for yourself. You would see the tools and methods he uses to play his instrument. He is a master, this man. A true artist."

Her mother took the girl by the hand and pulled her several steps away. "I have no desire to see his vulgar artistry, nor for my daughter's mind to be filled with such things."

The man raised his eyebrows. "The siren is willing. You don't respect the musician's work?"

The lights dimmed off and on. Crowds of murmuring people moved toward the auditorium.

"I respect the song itself, and the siren for sacrificing herself to give it. I respect the musician for drawing it from her, as is her wish." She raised her chin. "But I do not respect those who would watch the musician do his work rather than listen to the song. The musician is always a sick man. A mad man."

The man said, "Yes. He must have an exquisite sort of madness, to do what he does without breaking. Playing the song of a siren is not for the weak of will, nor the weak of heart."

The woman dipped her head in strained acknowledgement and turned to leave.

The man added, "What with the prying up of fingernails, the spindling of intestines, the flaying of skin. God forbid we see where the beauty is coming from."

The woman gasped, dragging the girl by the arm into the crowd. When the girl looked back, the man was shaking his head softly to himself. Then the cool, muted cave of the performance hall enveloped them. The brightest part of the room was the dim spotlight on the stage, where a beautiful but ordinary-looking woman sat on an empty stool in front of closed curtains.

"Where are her wings?" the girl whispered. Everyone whispered here. When her mother didn't answer, the girl tugged on her dress. "Where are the siren's wings?"

"Oh. They're down right now, sweetie. Closed like a bird, not out like a butterfly. They won't show until the musician spreads her arms."

"Mom, can I watch the stage when they start? Just for a little bit?"

Her mother didn't stop her path toward their box. "Not until you're older."

The lights flickered on and off several times, and the entire room sank into silence at once, seated but fidgeting. From her seat, the girl watched them in the darkness. An announcer introduced the musician, then the siren, who said in a soft voice that she was honored to be here sharing her art, that she could imagine no better cause for a life. Clinks and shifting from the stage punctuated long moments of silence.

Finally, the audience members grew still, the air grew thick, and a collective gasp charged the room. The siren began to sing.

It was unlike any music the girl had ever heard. There were no instruments, no lyrics, not even a melody to carry the voice along, but the girl knew at once that, somehow, it was still a song. She rubbed the nap of her skirt, leaning forward. The audience members' faces grew taut and full of emotions the girl couldn't name. The siren's voice grew and grew, filling the space with perfect clarity, slipping between notes in a way wholly unpredictable, yet perfect.

Some women fainted. A few couples got up and left. One man vomited into a bag even as he wept. Eventually, the girl closed her eyes and listened, crushing velvet between her fingers, and let the song fill her up with something she would someday learn was worth suffering for.

So felt the girl, that night. So sang the siren.

JUNK
RYAN HARDING

From *DOA III*
Editors: Marc Ciccarone & Andrea Dawn
Blood Bound Books

Nick didn't know where the impulse came from, but he followed it with vigor. It seemed to have been there as long as he could remember, like a post-hypnotic suggestion. Those moments were the only ones that mattered in his life. All the rest was simply preamble and postscript to the thrill.

The website was called InterphaZ. Nick thought of it as some kind of glory hole for casual conversation, a way to meet new people from all walks of life and forge some kind of friendship or perhaps even a relationship. A complete waste of time, in other words, but it hadn't taken him long to realize its potential for his own needs. That's when the fun began. And it hadn't let up in the past four months.

Virgins were the conquest—the ones who just signed up on InterphaZ and were more likely not to have had the random chat experience spoiled for them. New arrival HelKat84 looked promising, an attractive blond with hair tied up in two twists on her avatar. Like horns, he thought at first, but then realized they were supposed to affect cat ears. She must have liked what she saw from his avatar and profile (expertly crafted to present a charming and unthreatening persona after weeks of trial and error), because she accepted the chat request. Her webcam feed sprang up in the left corner of his screen.

He had it down to a science. As soon she accepted his request, he bolted up from his ergonomic chair and hit his mark like a consummate pro. The view of his maroon shirt and plain face—eyes too close together, nose too thin as if compressed by the nearness of his eyes, his fingers curled over his chin to suggest a pensive harmlessness—vanished in a flash, a smash cut leaving HelKat84 with a window to the bearded thatch of his scrotum. He lifted his shirt to allow her the unhindered view. And of course he was rock hard; how could he not be? This was the pinnacle. He could have run dick-first into a brick wall and crashed through like the Kool-Aid Man.

"*Ugh!*" HelKat84 grunted over the computer speakers. She recoiled from the image, eyes squinched shut like he'd proffered a photo of children blown to pieces in a drone strike rather than a pulsing boner. The resolution on webcams always left much to be desired, so it wasn't like she could see Rand McNally tributaries of veins spreading the good word about his arousal through the length of his girth, but if she wanted to act like it was the first time Cinderella went to ball, Nick was all for it. This was the kind of reaction he relished best.

HelKat84 finally realized she had the power to disconnect this live feed to genital horror, and she groped for her mouse with one hand. The other she kept in front of her eyes to block him, like he could glaze her face through the computer screen. E-facial, the next stage of human evolution.

"Sick bastard!" she shouted.

HelKat84 has disconnected this chat.

Nick sat down again, grinning ear to ear. Would she report him? It wouldn't be the first time. Nick changed his ISP address like some people changed their Facebook status. There were always ways around banishment.

He went ahead and blocked her. The prospect of a sequel down the line was amusing in theory—*just when you thought it was safe to InterphaZ . . .* —but it gave them time to process the encounter and reflect on what they should have said for maximum damage, a tirade against him and his ilk. They could run these little mental fire drills and assure his surprise reappearance (with a new name and profile) displayed the law of diminishing returns. Better to hit and run.

"Cock and awe, bitch."

This had been a good night with consistently satisfying reactions—disgust, horror, anger. Some nights were less fulfilling, prompting only indifference, boredom, and sarcasm. *Is that all you've got? My webcam doesn't have a microscope feature, little man.* Not tonight, though. They cringed, they shuddered. One even shrieked. The cross in her avatar suggested big time Christian beliefs. She was probably kneeling in broken glass and flagellating herself. Nick's personal project tomorrow during the misery of the call center would be to craft a more religious-friendly profile. That would be fishing with dynamite, something he should have considered long ago. Few were more predisposed to be forever haunted by the specter of Nick's throbbing gristle.

It was funny to think he would never have done something like this in different circumstances. On a crowded bus or in line at Starbucks, never. There were real world penalties for that, jail time from the cops, pepper spray, and sharp fingernails from the civilians. Doing it online in the privacy of his own apartment, though, may have been unwanted, but it was tolerated, the same as someone texting at a movie. You go to a theater, you expect to see the glowing screen of a smartphone during the feature presentation. You go online, someone's throwing a dick in your face. That was just the way of the world now.

He hadn't been thinking of doing it when he bought his webcam. He just expected to chat with different bitches who would get naked on their own cams every week, if not every night (law of averages), but it hadn't worked out that way. When the familiar disappointment shadowed his latest attempt to escape his incessant boredom in life, he was inspired by a new idea with a different objective. This one was working. He was winning.

A chime played through his speakers. New email alert. He clicked over to the tab. Another InterphaZ notification of his latest expulsion. *Failure to uphold community standard . . . conduct unbecoming . . . violation of membership agreement . . . blah, blah.* It meant about as much as dying in a video game. It was a fine paid with Monopoly money.

He frowned at the subject line of another new email: SAVAGE YOUR PENIS B4 ITS 2 LATE! That was a far cry from the usual promises of genital size enhancement and aphrodisiacs. Maybe it was supposed to pique his curiosity enough to read it (fail). It must work on someone out there, maybe the sort of person who thought they'd been personally selected to play cash mule for the Prince of Nigeria.

Nick marked the junk mail as spam, for all the good it would do, and closed the tab.

His preferred notification of a chat request from InterphaZ—the quaint sound of a ringing phone—brought him back to the mission at hand. This was surprising since Nick was supposed to be locked out again and had expected the need to switch to a new ISP and profile, presto-change-o before another chat encounter. The notification came from user nerXam83, the avatar a photo of some primo jailbait. She might have handled more dicks than a porn set fluffer or maybe the only cramming she did was for the SATs. (Or as a popular meme once said, why not both?) It was hard to tell these days. The 83 was questionable, but it didn't necessarily mean year of birth. If it was just some creepy guy, he could pull the plug easily enough.

Nick accepted. The window appeared in the same sacred place where so many InterphaZ users of yore found themselves blinded by a wall of his junk.

Nick's eyelids vanished in comical surprise. NerXam83 was definitely a man, a man who had bested the master of Cock and Awe at his own game. There was a twist to his version of surprise scrotal maneuvers, however. NerXam83 was *afflicted.* Like something out of a medical textbook passed around in a macabre parlor game to see who puked first. Pustules spread across the shaft of the dick, filling his chat window in a formation like bubble wrap. Perhaps it was the delay from the feed where a second here and there was lost, but Nick would swear the fleshy growths pulsated as he watched. Unfortunately, the resolution of this window to repulsion seemed mysteriously like Blu-ray quality to better disgust him with its palette of moist reds and yellows. Some nodules were blood blister-like, while others oozed with a custard syrup in milky tributaries he could see gradually advancing over and between the protuberances of inflamed skin like time lapse photography. NerXam83's presentation front and center on the world's sharpest webcam opened the coral reef of penile rot currently festering inches away.

In Nick's shock he looked far longer than reason dictated, both grossed out and engrossed by this abomination, the same as he would have been by an animal with two heads. Perhaps more so because this was the same species . . . someone who even shared the same pastime.

"*Ugh!*" Nick finally groaned and disconnected the chat without looking directly at it another second, lest he turn to stone. He needed his own eye wash station.

Some distance from the computer seemed like a good thing, so Nick made his way to the bathroom down the hall. An afterimage remained. What could have caused that? Did he bang some leper whore with syphilis near Chernobyl? Nick didn't think he could have shown his face to the world after contracting something so hideous, much less the spoiled genitals that were part and parcel of it.

It had to be fake. Dude could just be some special FX wizard looking to freak people out, that was all.

Sicko.

Mystery solved, he intended to relieve himself and then get back to the business of flashing his junk in the faces of unwary women on InterphaZ.

Another bone strike of Cock and Awe, that's the ticket.

He unzipped his pants, then forgot all about his special FX theory and plans for scrotal domination as the burst of pain ignited at the release of his bladder.

"*Ow, fuck!*"

He twitched like a frog hooked up to a car battery, the entirety of his world condensed to an inch of blazing fury at the tip of his organ. It was like pissing napalm and he had failed to fireproof his dickhole. His keening wail accompanied this slow eternity of urination, unself-conscious about the thin walls between him and his neighbor. Right now all that mattered, all that existed, was the geyser of molten lava. The last drops singed as well, as if they had claws slashing through membrane on the way out.

Nick had shut his eyes tight against the onslaught and now opened them to a world blurred by tears of pain. His aim was scattershot from the spasms, leaving splashes of red across the seat of the commode, the roll of toilet paper, the floor, the wastebasket.

That's blood, he thought dumbly, cold sweat beading in his scalp. *All of that was blood.*

He tenderly shook off, grimacing at the wetness on his fingers. He already dreaded a couple of hours when the call of nature forced him through this process of torture again. The first time might have only been a warm-up—

His train of thought derailed.

Wetness on his fingers? He didn't think he'd somehow sprayed himself even with all of his cringing a moment ago, but expected to see the same bloody excretion when he examined his hand. It wasn't, though. It still had traces of blood, but more suggestive of pus. A runny wax not unlike what he saw on the computer a moment ago.

He laughed with barely suppressed hysteria because the cause and effect was so impossible. Even if nerXam83 was one apartment over instead of another state or continent altogether, it was no more logical. Nick only looked at a computer screen.

It went viral, he thought and almost laughed again. It made an ominous sense, however crazy it was, especially when he considered the circumstances. Banned by InterphaZ but still able to receive that one request from the site. Now this.

Nick's guts double and triple knotted as he stood in front of the mirror and examined his penis. Perhaps it was largely psychological, but now that he knew the infection was there, his shaft felt tingly and hot, as if he could sense new pustules forming on a microscopic level. He held his length gingerly by the head, inspecting the column with mounting horror. Several sores had burst already from his tightened grip during the throes of anguish. A cobweb of stringy flesh dangled on the underside, having peeled off from the base. The layer revealed was raw, crustacean red.

Nick met his own stricken gaze in the mirror, mouth agape, his sickly pale reflection commiserating: *Are you seeing this?*

Unfortunately he was, and no reset from a universal do-over restored the integrity of his genitalia.

He had some gauze in one of the bathroom drawers. He didn't know what else to do but wrap himself up. Smear the bandages with some triple antibiotic (assuming quadruple antibiotic didn't exist) and pray for a miraculous return to its pristine state while he went through life in the meantime looking like a stunt dick for Claude Rains.

He reached for the drawer, and that was the point when the corona of his cock seemed to lose solidity and adopt the texture of a sponge. His index finger and thumb pushed trenches into either side instantaneously. He shrieked and withdrew his pincer grip, but the caverns remained. A piece dislodged within the crumpled pillar and dropped to the counter.

Nick looked around frantically, as if a bottle of Acme Dickhead Skin Regrowth OintmentTM would magically appear somewhere. It didn't.

The impulse now was to call for an ambulance, but what would he say? *My dick is rotting before my fucking eyes because of some freak's webcam. Hurry!* When they finally accepted it wasn't a crank call and actually sent someone, what could they do?

SAVAGE YOUR PENIS B4 ITS 2 LATE.

Yes, that was what the strange email said. It seemed no more coincidental than nerXam83's request. He gingerly walked back to the bedroom, stripping off his shirt so it didn't catch his groin and exacerbate the damage. He launched his email again, heedless of the rancid juices left behind on the mouse and keys and the pitter-patter of droplets on the carpet from his sores, like melting icicles. The nausea in his stomach churned with greater urgency.

At last he found the email in his spam folder and opened it. The sender name contained the word InterphaZ (and "no-reply"). There was no text, only an embedded .GIF file of a man with his sex organs on a flat table surface as he swung a meat cleaver at the scrotal pouch, an unsettling smile on his face. An animated balloon obscured the actual hit, filled with the word THWACK!

That was savage, all right. Not exactly the most tempting prospect for a potential cure.

B4 ITS 2 LATE.

2 late for what?

He looked forlornly at the disgusting thing attached to him, which had been perfectly normal not ten minutes ago. The disease progressed like an old school werewolf transformation with superimposed special FX, a process rapidly achieved.

"No," Nick said. "Oh God, no."

The sac of his scrotum showed burgeoning, bloated pearls emerging between the furrows. Hundreds of them, like mutant spider eggs primed to hatch an adipocerous offspring. The burning, tingling sensation erupted in full, with tiny needles prickling every millimeter of skin. The sensation was maddening.

There could be no doubt—it was spreading. Within minutes it had already done this much to him. By the time paramedics arrived, it could be far worse.

B4 ITS 2 LATE.

Nick hurried to the kitchen, the droplets now more poignant against linoleum. As he reached for the electric carving knife, he assuaged himself with the countless miracles of modern medicine. People lost body parts all the time and had them sewn back, although Nick of course didn't want his "gangroin" reattached. But with practical advances in technology, they could basically spin straw into dick, couldn't they? He wasn't out of options, as long as he survived this. The solidity of the carving knife handle reassured him. It featured a slide button rather than a trigger, so it would keep cutting if he passed out.

He called 9-1-1 first for an ambulance, reporting massive blood loss from a carving knife mishap. He claimed it was his fingers since they probably wouldn't get here any faster anyway. They assured him someone was coming and he hung up, his eyes blurry again.

He revved the carving knife as he took hold of everything in his other hand, cupping beneath his testicles with the palm, his fingers and thumb forming a C-shape. Any doubts about the necessity of his course of action were neutralized in short order with one last humiliation of the flesh. The patchwork of pustules slipped beneath his fingers like some kind of revolving cylinder, both on his dick and the sac beneath. Skin barely adhered to the organ now. It pulled loose from the stalk with ease, lasagna-colored meat beneath. The loose rope of dangling flesh slid away, abracadabra. It sloughed as a shed snakeskin, popping and bursting in the few places still attached, liquid tendrils stretching like taffy to reveal shimmering tissue. The underside tore with it in a burst as if something had detonated beneath. The sac detached in tandem like a wet rubber glove in his palm. The testicles and cords dropped like dead jellyfish, oysters in a Jell-O mold upon his quivering hand. The emptied pouch hung limp like a flap of torn curtain, the penile skin like the empty husk of some insect draped in his palm. It all clumped wetly to the floor. He watched it go like a soldier unable to hold in his own intestines. There was curiously no pain, other than the trauma of the sickening sight, the nerve endings perhaps jellified now. Clinging contents of the pouch sagged like syrup, halfway to the floor. His actual penis was but a strange glistening tendril apart from the head, which still had its skin and something of its shape save the trenches left from his fingers. Otherwise he beheld something virtually skinless, corroding.

On the plus side, he had much less he'd need to cut now.

Nick engaged the carving knife again. Whatever whimpers he made were drowned out by the whirring blades. He locked in on his target, a miraculous sliver of pale flesh at the base of his organ. There was pain at the root where the true skin remained, but far less than he expected. Perhaps that was the silver lining to an impromptu session of unlicensed surgery to rid yourself of your liquefying fuckmeat. He screamed anyway, for this insanity that had dethroned the natural order of his life. The blades shredded through the tissue effortlessly, an explosion of crimson giblets blown across the kitchen counter and sink, the refrigerator, his stomach, thighs, and feet. He held his other hand up to block the blowback before he gave new meaning to "facial tissue." In seconds it was over—barely longer than his webcam session with HelKat84.

Nick left the carving knife grinding, the circuit breaker in his mind so overloaded he couldn't remember how to turn it off at that moment. He looked at it as if he'd never seen such a thing before and didn't know how it wound up in his hand, but finally connected enough dots to see the slide button and remember its function as "on/off." Simple, sane. He was placing his thumb over the button when the awful tingling suddenly lit up across all the fingers of his right hand—the one with which he'd held himself in the bathroom. Even within the spatters from his operation, he saw the blisters forming like islands in a bloody ocean, felt them shifting beneath like tectonic plates.

B4 ITS 2 LATE.

His 9-1-1 call would be truthful after all.

Unsure if he heard an approaching siren or if it was just the grinding serenade of the blades, Nick withdrew his thumb and guided the carving knife over to his fingers, trying not to think about all the places now covered in his fluids.

AUTHOR'S STORY NOTE

I'm part of the last generation who remembers a world where cell phones and Internet were not so commonplace. It is a strange phenomenon where these advances have reshaped our reality so drastically in the last 20ish years, which has somehow resulted in something as primitive as a lot of guys on an endless crusade to share pictures of their genitals with as many unsuspecting women as possible. As technology and vocabulary evolve (although with the latter, "devolve" might be more appropriate), I started thinking about something going "viral" as a more physical manifestation in its own evolution. Other terms like "leaked" and "hacked" seemed to fit in quite nicely. I love the body horror of David Cronenberg and it was fun to explore an idea that seemed so Cronenbergian, however tangential—or in the case of "Junk," tan-genital.

THE CENACLE
ROBERT LEVY

From *Shadows and Tall Trees Vol. 7*
Editor: Michael Kelly
Undertow Publications

The widow waits for the service to be over. The incomprehensible liturgy of atonal Hebrew gutturals, millennia of meaning resonant for so many but not her. She'd never learned the language of her ancestors, never considered that her supposed faith might lend her any comfort until now. Her husband's coffin thirteen feet away and sunk six more, the pine box lowered south from the light of a sun invisible behind dreary February clouds. She can't face the hole so she stares down at her feet in the mud-dirtied snow, stockinged legs like sticks beneath her long coat. Everyone in black, from her stepdaughter to the rabbi to the cemetery attendants and scattered among the Brooklyn gravestones, the land blotted out by the unyielding blizzard that had buried the city in its own white grave. Even still the snow swirls.

She waits for them all to leave. From her awkward brothers to her overattentive coworkers, she nods as they go, each one in turn, moving on to the luncheon, then later *shiva*, and finally to a peaceful sleep she herself could never bear. She is an *onen*, in a state of mourning beyond reach. "I'll be along, I'll be along," she says, "I just need some time to myself." A deception. She wants no time alone, not ever. What she wants is her husband back.

Her husband's daughter, born of his previous marriage, is the hardest goodbye. "Why did he have to die?" the girl sobs, her wet face pressed against the widow's breast; the girl's mother keeps a safe distance, frozen beneath a denuded elm far from the plot. "Everyone dies, my love," the widow replies, and strokes the ten-year-old's strawberry hair, her wedding ring snagging in the girl's tangled mess of curls. "Only some go sooner than later."

She waits until the sun sinks behind the horizon of distant buildings before she admits to herself that she's too cold to remain here forever, that eventually the attendants will return to usher her from the premises, tell her she can return in the morning, some widows do, day after day after day. Darkening sky and she moves from the gravesite at last, shuffles through the snow until she's back at the road that snakes through the cemetery in one long and intricate seam.

She steps onto the path, and movement catches her attention: a dark shadow in the distance, hunched and shuffling along a mausoleum-dotted hillock overlooking the snow-caked grounds. The figure progresses slowly across the landscape, shreds of gauzy black cloth flapping like clerical vestments in the wind as it reaches with sickled arms to touch upon each tombstone as if blind and feeling the way forward. The stranger stops and cocks an ear to the side, nose threading the air, a bloodhound seeking a scent.

The widow is chilled by a bitter wind. She lifts the neck of her coat against it, the furred collar tugged up to her eyes as the figure turns toward her and lifts a hand in acknowledgment, the scraps of what seems to be a shawl shifting in the breeze. An elderly woman by the looks of it, hunched in a manner that suggests a kyphotic spine bent by defect or age.

The stranger turns and lowers her head once more before soldiering on, trudging through the scattered stones and disappearing around the side of a large rotunded mausoleum. The widow waits. But when the stranger fails to appear she makes her way up the hill, drawn to the crypt as if toward an answer to an unspoken but persistent question. Her shoes brown with mud as she slides against the wet earth, the still-falling snow. She rights herself, and she climbs, until she reaches the twin doors that announce the entrance to the crypt.

The braided door handles have been wiped clean of frost, and she takes hold of their cold iron and pulls. Softly at first, but then she puts her weight into it, leaning back as she yanks until the doors groan open, just wide enough to pass. Within the slash of muted light an interior wall is visible—much deeper inside than she'd expected, given the vault's outward dimensions— and it's only upon entering the antechamber and daring to ease the doors shut in her wake that she makes out the dim illuminations of candle flame flickering farther inside the crypt. That, and the pleasing smell of cedar smoke, as well as the vague susurrations of voices, just as they fall silent.

She takes care not to trip upon the raised step leading into the main rotunda of the tomb, and she treads forward, broaching the arched entryway as she comes to a halt beneath the rose marble lintel.

Seated in an approximation of a semicircle are two women, one quite old and another young, along with an elderly man. Lit only by votive candles burning upon the crypt's every ledge, the three are dressed in funereal black and huddled about a raised granite slab. Upon the stone surface are a further arrangement of votives, pale wax dripping and pooling into gray swirls along the floor of the rounded tomb.

"Hello, dear," the old woman says from her place between the others, eyes bright in the candle flame as she draws her shawl with a wrinkled hand, brown fingers sparkling with gold and azure rings. "Would you like to join us? We're just having a spot of dinner before it gets too late." The hunched woman casts a hand across the stone block: inside the circle of candles a pile of smoked fowl is laid out, picked at with tiny bones jutting from charred skin upon a bed of unidentifiable berries and roots. The widow knows she should be repulsed but her stomach lurches for a moment like a dog jerked on a chain, and she's shocked by her sudden hunger.

"Who are you?" she asks. "What are you doing in here?"

"What are *you* doing in here?" the old man says, his voice a scratched-vinyl rasp. "We're in this together, aren't we?" He gestures for her to sit. She stares down at her feet and the puddle of melted snow they've left upon the flagstone, and she regrets not stamping the ice off them before entering.

"Come," the old woman says, "don't be shy," and so the widow lowers herself onto the near side of the slab. "Excellent, excellent. Happy to see you're joining us here today. We're always looking for a decent fourth."

"Bridge numbers," the old man says. "I tried teaching them rummy, but there's really no convincing these two."

The old woman laughs, then covers her mouth. "Sorry. Bad joke, I'm afraid. We're not really much for bridge."

"What are you, then?" the widow asks, and turns to face the young woman, who remains quiet and still.

"Ah," the old woman says. "Well. I suppose we're many things, of course, no person being just *one* thing. But mostly, we're the ones left behind."

"Left behind by who?"

Even as the widow asks the question, however, she knows. For what is she now, but left behind herself? The young woman's light blue eyes swell with such alarming compassion that it makes her want to weep in recognition.

"How long have you been here?" the widow asks.

"Some time, now," the old woman replies. "After a while, you lose count of the days. You just . . . Stay." Her expectant face shines, incandescent in the flickering candlelight reflected upon the granite slab. "You'll stay, won't you?"

"I . . . don't think so." The widow makes no move to leave, however. Shadows dance about the curved walls as dusk's last light evaporates beyond the surprising warmth of the stone shelter. "I have to go."

"There's nothing for you out there," the old woman says. "Not anymore."

"I have a stepdaughter," the widow says. "I have friends."

"We'll be your friends now. We'll be your family too."

"I should go."

"We're the only ones who can care for you."

"I should go."

"We're the only ones that can know you."

"Let her go already!" the old man barks, spittle flung from the corner of his mouth as he waves her away. "Let her see for herself what it's like out there, now."

They fall silent. The widow begins to back away from them and toward the doors, but makes it no farther than the step leading to the anteroom when she stills, all the while her eyes on theirs. She has a stepdaughter; she has friends; she drinks two cups of coffee in the morning as she does the crossword with a ballpoint pen. But she had a husband, then. So none of that could now be so.

"Perhaps I will stay," the widow says. "For a little while."

The old woman smiles. "Good," she says, and nods in eager approval. "Good."

So she stays. For a few minutes, and then for an hour, for the evening and then overnight, sleeping beside them beneath an oilskin tarpaulin on the cold and damp flagstones that pave the floor of the crypt. They wake her at dawn and lead her to the evergreen hedges abutting the high flat stone of the cemetery walls to collect chokeberries, which grow there in red clotted bunches, a gift of winter. They show her how they use barbed wire as snares to catch sparrows and pigeons, starlings and other birds too stupid or slow to fly south for the winter. She keeps expecting someone to come looking for her—her family, her friends, the police—but no one ever does.

She spends the day with them, and then another night, another morning and a new day, spent occupied with the daily business of acquiring food, of learning from the others the customs and rules of their strange and insular world. They melt frost in marble cisterns and drink from ornamental urns, the accoutrements of the dead refashioned for the needs of the living. But isn't it all for the living? The widow casts her eyes across the snow-blanketed graves. The coffins and tombstones, the ritual pyres and monumental obelisks . . . What do the dead care, anymore?

Most wonderful of all, there's no need for the widow to speak of her husband, for any of them to speak of their husbands, or the old man of his wife. It's enough for them to be together in their grief. Their simple companionship abates the pain of her loss more than she would have ever thought possible.

Early on the morning of the third day, they finish stealing candles from the small chapel near the gates when they come upon a pair of parka-clad workers digging a fresh grave on the south side of the cemetery. The widow, exposed to them in the bright light of day, scuttles behind the obscuring limbs of a weeping willow, but the others continue undaunted along the path toward the mausoleum that is their home. The gravediggers fail to acknowledge them, and after some time she realizes that the workers take no notice of them whatsoever.

"Why don't they see us?" she asks the others once she's caught up with them.

The old woman shrugs. "They don't want to see us, I suppose. It's too . . . difficult for them."

"They don't have any skin in the game," the old man says, and hocks a dark yellow loogie into the thick paste of snow. "They might as well work at a bank."

"Once the funeral is over, they move on. Everyone does. But not us." The old woman smiles her bright warm smile, but this time there's something sorrowful in it, which feels just right.

By the seventh day, the end of *shiva*, the widow rarely thinks of the life that awaits her at her former home, doesn't even remember more than a vague outline of what she ever did with her time. Where did I work? she wonders. Was it at an office building? Or was it some kind of school? By the ninth day it's like walking through a waking dream: she no longer recalls her stepdaughter's age, or the color of her hair, and soon the girl's name is lost to her altogether, along with the general features of her face. All she remembers now is her husband, and she clings to his memory like a talisman, a lantern in the dark of night. It's all she has left to hold.

She knows it's because of her new friends. They understand her, in a way others are unable, and she knows this to be true because she understands them the same way. The widow knows that by staying with them—by haunting the hallowed grounds of the cemetery and living off what grows here, and alights here, and is fed by the flesh and marrow of the departed—that she needn't move on, not ever. Because some people never do.

By the tenth day in the cemetery, however, the pain of her husband's absence returns unabated. It surges like a cresting wave and crashes over her, bringing her back to that awful phone call, that moment that ushered her unwillingly into the midnight realm of unmitigated despair. I can't breathe, she thinks, I'll never breathe again, and she runs the familiar distance from the crypt down the hill to the family plot, where her husband's grave, as with the rest, is buried in white. Her chapped pink hands dig at the wet ground, her tears pocking the snow. It's only once she's made her way to the hard dirt below that she stops to wonder whether she's trying to dig her husband out of his resting place or make a grave for herself to crawl into, where she can lie down and pull the earth around her like a shroud. Even the accusation of her stepdaughter's face begins to return, the dark almond eyes the girl shared with her father, the single dimple in her right cheek. She has abandoned her husband's daughter, as she herself has been abandoned. She wants to die.

And what truth this is! As true as the aim of the steering column that had impaled her husband in his twisted metal cage, the one they needed the Jaws of Life to free him from, though there would be no life for him, not anymore. Twelve days gone since the phone call from the police, the race to the hospital to bear witness to his mangled body, her knuckles white against the steering wheel of her own car as she tried to wish it undone the way she had wished Tinkerbell back to life as a little girl, one among many at a crowded matinee clapping her hands at the screen so hard she was sure her numbed fingers would bleed.

Has it been only twelve days? Impossible. Surely it has been months.

Twelve days? No. She couldn't do this. No. She could not. Never.

"You can," the old woman says at her side, all three of them here now, her friends. "You will."

"How?" The widow wipes away tears and peers down at the pathetic little pit she's carved. "How can I keep from wanting it to be over, every second of every hour?"

The old woman looks to the man, who slowly nods, just once, his head drooping so that his pallid chin touches the immaculate Windsor knot in his tweed necktie. He looks to the young woman, who nods once herself, the air crisping with electric tension.

"We have a trick that helps." The old woman steps closer, her stale breath carried on the wind. "Would you like us to show you?"

That night after their rounds they trail back inside the crypt, back to the central round chamber, the widow entering last of all. The young woman lights the arrangement of ledge candles, one after the next, as the temple-like room takes on the eerie half-flame of a winter hearth. The old man clears their last meal's detritus from the granite slab to help the old woman as she lowers herself down upon the tomb.

The old man and the young woman gather on either side of her prone form, the pair tugging back the old woman's tatty black shawl. They unbutton her blouse and lower it, unfasten her nude-colored brassiere and shimmy it out from beneath her, peeling off the rest of her mourning attire until she is naked upon the slab. The old woman crosses her arms over her breasts and closes her eyes, as if she herself is laid out in death's final repose.

All along the woman's body are painted intricate black circles. Of varying size and shape, the patterns run up and down her sides in erratic intervals, appearing to spot her the way a leopard's coat is spotted, dark swirls patching her sagging and distended skin.

Mesmerized, the widow steps forward. Inches away now, and she can see at last that they aren't inked-on designs, but are in fact suppurated wounds, the size of bite marks. Just as soon as she realizes this fact a festering smell hits her, and she staggers back gasping from the slab.

"What is this?" the widow asks, and covers her nose and mouth with a trembling hand.

"This," the old man says, "is the trick."

The widow stares at the young woman, who remains silent as ever, only nodding gravely as she lowers herself to her knees beside the older woman's prostrate figure. Without taking her eyes off the widow, the young woman lifts the older woman's arm, brings it to her mouth, and sinks her teeth into its spongy flesh, the aged brown parchment of skin bruising and blooding a deeper shade of red.

"My God," the widow whispers. "Why?"

"This is our sacrament," the old woman says from the slab, eyes still shut though her parted lips quiver as if jolted by an electric current. "This is the holy of holy, the flesh that binds us together."

"Take of her," the old man says, so close his rotted breath masks the scent of the old woman's wounds. "Take of her flesh and blood, so that you may strengthen grief's resolve. It's the only way, now."

"I . . . can't. I can't." She wipes away tears and retreats for the doors, wedges her chaffed fingers into the narrow space between them and wrenches them open, ready to flee into the darkness. No one tries to stop her.

But looking out at pale tombstones that litter the dim night like scattered teeth, she hesitates. It's because she knows she cannot face the outside world, not anymore. She cannot face anyone who had ever known her before. She needs to be with her own kind, now.

The widow eases the doors shut, a whinnying grind of iron on stone as she turns back to face them. A thrill prickles her skin, an admixture of terror and fascination as she walks the length of the antechamber and back inside the domed sepulcher, where they wait for her in their strange tableau.

She lowers herself beside the slab. "Show me how it's done."

The young woman wipes her mouth and points with a blood-flecked finger at the old woman's free arm. The widow lifts it, bringing the hand toward her. The smell of the old woman's lesions is gone now, replaced by that of snuffed-out candles, as well as a holier scent, sandalwood, perhaps. The widow finds an unblemished section of skin along the inside of the old woman's papery wrist, brings it to her lips, and sinks her teeth into the flesh.

The taste is revolting, and also extraordinary; it reminds her of her first taste of tomato, of being a young girl and plucking one from her grandmother's garden vines, sliding its tough membrane across her lips before biting down. How surprising the spurting of its contents, the strong perfumy taste of lifeblood and liquefied meat, and she retches now as she did then.

But even as she raises her head from where she is sick beside the slab and stares up at them—the looming old man, the wide-eyed young woman, the mutilated older one whose death mask of a face remains still, save the tears spilling from her closed eyes—even as she wants to scream and run from them and die from anguish and sorrow and the guilt of abandoning her stepdaughter, she knows that she will not.

She will not scream. She will not run away. She will stay, and she will eat. And she will live. Without her stepdaughter, who is better off without the burden of the widow's annihilative grief. She will live without her husband. But for him. For him.

"Think of him as you eat of me," the old woman whispers, her eyes still closed tight. "Think of him, and the pain begins to slip away, like braised meat off the bone."

The widow grimaces, a trickle of blood leaking from the corner of her mouth as she swallows back a bit of fleshy gristle, the taste of it like tomato skin. She lowers her skull to the old woman's arm, and bites down again, more.

This she could do. Yes. She could. Forever, even. Yes.

On the seventeenth day, they take of the old man. Of his chalky white skin and sinewy flesh, his tough hide and enlarged veins, a thin cord of muscle snagging in the widow's teeth before she manages to swallow it down. He doesn't remain still the way the old woman had, but rather hums and rocks from side to side as the three women feed upon him, their shadows expanding and contracting against the curved walls of the crypt like their own set of dark wounds. "Think of him as you eat of me," the old man whispers and groans, the scent of sandalwood permeating the musty air. "Think of him. Think of him."

And so she does. Of her husband's coppery thick beard and wire-rim spectacles, his swollen gut that he used to take in his two large hands and cradle as if it were a baby. The old man's blooded flesh travels fast through her system, and she feels a calm she hasn't known in memory.

On the twenty-fourth day, they eat of the young woman. She whimpers as the old woman suckles at her thigh, her little hands pressed over her mouth as if trying to keep something down herself. The widow feels a tremor of unease. But didn't she see for herself how the young woman had given herself over? Submission is a precept of faith, the old woman had said, what the widow's own people would call a *mitzvah*, or even *tikkun olam*. Think of him, she reminds herself, and crouches beside the old man to taste of the young woman's bony shoulder, the meat soft beneath its warm baste of blood. Think of him. And she does.

The thirtieth day arrives. The end of *shloshim*, the traditional period of mourning, the one her mother had practiced, and her mother's mother before her. Back from the chokeberry shrubs she walks weaving through the maze of gravestones, the snow reduced to patches, the sun bright overhead with a faint blossoming scent in the air. Spring is on its way to Gravesend Cemetery at last.

Just as she reaches the turnoff to the crypt, she catches the unmistakable sound of liturgy on the wind, and she slows, a small service taking place on the other side of the road. A Greek one, she believes, the priest droning on in his own devotional recitations, the way her rabbi had in his. A few dozen mourners are arranged around the priest, around the square hole dug into the earth and framed by too-bright astroturf meant to conceal the fresh grave dirt scattered upon the soft ground. None of them see her standing there. Not the priest or the cemetery workers, the mourners or even the dead. She is but a ghost among them, something so raw and terrible the brain stutters upon sight of her, the eye failing to alight before it quickly flits away.

But then one of them looks up, and she starts: a salt-and-pepper-haired man not terribly much older than herself, but with the prematurely aged face and shocked hollow expression of a widower. His glazed eyes narrow and blink, and they stare at each other, the world falling silent of prayer. I see you, she thinks, and nods slowly before she moves on. I see you. She wonders if he'll be lucky enough to find his way to the crypt, or if the outside world will force him into its plastic and deadening embrace, all platitudes and hopeful falsities. Sometimes it's better not to be seen.

She smells the incense the moment she opens the doors to the crypt, that same perfumy scent that seemed to arise from nowhere each time they took of one another. It was as if the very act had caused some unaccountable pheromone to be secreted from beneath the skin, either the consumer or the consumed. Today, she thinks. It must be the day for me to submit to them, so that their own pain might be eased in turn. Today.

But when she passes through the narrow antechamber and enters the main room of the crypt, she's surprised to see the granite slab is already taken. A large figure lies upon it, swathed crown to toe in a *tachrichim*, which reminds the widow of nothing so much as a last-minute Halloween costume, someone playing at being a ghost.

The others are gathered around the slab, their eyes upon her, watchful. You see me, she thinks, and steps forward to join them.

"Go on," the old man says, and chins toward the head of the shrouded figure. Who else has joined us, then? It never occurred to her before that there would ever be five of them. The widow leans over, and begins to unwrap the dressing.

Even before she has the linen undone, she knows. But still she must see to be sure. She pulls down the folds of the shroud to find his coppery red hair, and only a bit more, only a bit, his skin a dead and dark shade of charcoal around the sunken pits of black and unidentifiable matter where her husband's eyes once were, but no longer are. She finds she cannot breathe.

"You must take of him." The old woman's voice is like a rock hurled against the widow's breast. "To be bound to him forever. The way you've been bound to us."

"This is the night feast," the old man says, "the feast of last partings. The final sacrament of the oldest funerary rites, passed down but occulted from one culture to the next. We have set the table in the sacred space, so that you too might become a part of greater things. This is our gift to you, in the manner we have been gifted by others."

"No." The widow pulls the cloth back over her husband's too-bright hair. "No. I won't do it. Not to him." She looks to the young woman, who only bows her head, whether in prayer or shame it's unclear.

"There must be a feast," the old woman says. "And there must be one tonight." The kindness gone from her wizened face, she rears up from the floor and takes hold of the shroud in two clawlike hands and begins to tug it away. The widow pulls her husband toward herself, and the old woman pulls him back, the corpse rocking between them as if undecided.

She finally reaches over the slab and shoves the old woman, who stumbles against the wall of the crypt, toppling a shelf of candles, the shroud still grasped in one fist. The uncovered body goes with her. It tumbles from the back of the slab, only the briefest glimpse of its hideous decomposition as it falls mercifully into the shadows with a dull thunk.

The widow hurries toward the doors. The old man and young woman are soon upon her, however, dragging her back by her hair and wrestling her toward the slab as they pull away her long coat, her own shroud of winter these past thirty days. The old man thrusts her down onto the cold granite, her head slamming against it so hard she blacks out.

But not for long enough. She awakens moments later to a nighttime sea of imagined stars, dancing about her mind. There is a disturbing sensation of icy breath across her naked belly, followed by an acute stabbing upon her inner thigh, where they're already beginning to take.

"Move over, move over," the old man mutters in the near dark. The three are backlit now, the candlelight and shadow a long distant dream; everything looks darker from the slab.

"Give it here," the old woman says. "You're not doing it right!" The woman takes the widow's hand, sinks her sharp teeth into the soft white flesh of her arm and the widow cries out, the worst pain she's ever learned. No, not the worst: even this blinding curtain of agony pales next to that phone call, a month gone. It's still not enough. So that's what she thinks of, the phone call that ended her old life. That and the back of her husband's freckled and sunburnt neck, his wavy red hair as he runs laughing from her and down to the sea on some past and distant shore. Sand whips all around them as she hurries and fails to keep pace, his sunhatted daughter trailing behind them both, a bright yellow bucket dragged in her wake.

The old woman grunts as she chaws her way up the bloodied and spasming arm, and the widow's own mouth goes agape. She forces herself back to the greater pain, her loss a worried scab that's been prized open anew.

They take of her, and they think of lost loves, and it should be enough for them all. She will survive this.

Think of him.

"Help me! Help!" she screams, and the old man hurries to mount her, bends leering over her and lowers his skull in an open-mouthed kiss. He finds her tongue and fastens his brittle teeth to it, blood spattering his glasses and rushing down both their throats as he silences her. Her tongue severed now, the old man turns his head to spit it slippery and wet against the curved wall of the crypt. The old woman scrambles after it, a starved dog after a scrap of meat, the widow gurgling in protestation as she continues to drink of her own blood. Now she knows why the young woman never speaks.

Help me!

She screams in silence, as they continue to devour her.

Think of him.

A distant shore, a laugh. It should be enough.

His face!

She sees him, again.

His face!

At last, she smiles.

AUTHOR'S STORY NOTE

Over the same weekend, my great-aunt and great-uncle (my grandmother's sister and her brother-in-law) died two days apart from each other. Due to the close timing, as well as various mourning customs, our family had two separate viewings, two separate burials, and two separate wakes, all at the same locations but spread over the course of a week. This occurred amidst a frigid and epic blizzard that blanketed New York and the cemetery, complicating everything from the service to the actual burial arrangements; we could barely make it to the gravesite. Needless to say, death and snow both weighed heavily on my mind.

I'm also a big fan of Mahalia Jackson, and one day I had her song "In the Upper Room" in my head, which I've loved since high school. It struck me that I actually didn't know what the upper room referred to, so I looked it up and discovered it's the room where the Last Supper took place. Another name for the upper room is the cenacle, and a secondary meaning of cenacle is a small group or clique. The dual meaning of this word, coupled with the aforementioned personal background, provided me with the main ingredients for my less-than-wholesome stew.

THE MAW

NATHAN BALLINGRUD

From *Dark Cities*
Editor: Christopher Golden
Titan Books

1.

Mix was about ready to ditch the weird old bastard already. Too slow, too clumsy, too loud. Not even a block into Hollow City and already they'd captured the attention of one of the wagoneers, and in her experience you could almost clap your hands in front of their faces and they wouldn't know it. Experience, though; that was the key word. She had it and he didn't, and it was probably going to get him killed. But she'd be goddamned if she'd let it get her killed too.

She pulled him into an alcove and they waited quietly until the thing had passed.

"You need to rest?" she said.

"No I don't need to rest," he snapped. "Keep going."

Mix was seventeen years old, and anybody on the far side of fifty seemed inexcusably ancient to her, but she reckoned this man to be pretty old even by those standards. He was spry enough to walk through streets cluttered with the detritus and the debris of long abandonment without too much difficulty, but she could see the strain in his face, the sheen of sweat on his forehead. And a respectable pace for an old man was still just a fraction of the speed she preferred to move while in Hollow City. She'd been stupid to take his money, but she'd always been a stupid girl. Just ask anybody.

They turned a corner and the last checkpoint, a little wooden shack with a lantern gleaming in a window, disappeared from view. It might as well have been a hundred miles away. The buildings hulked into the cloudy sky around them, windows shattered and bellied with darkness. The doors of little shops gaped like open mouths. Glass pebbled the sidewalk. Rags of newspapers, torn and scattered clothing, and tangles of bloody meat lay strewn across the pavement. Cars lined the sidewalks in their final repose. Life still prospered here, to be sure: rats, roaches, feral cats and dogs; she'd even seen a mother bear and her train of cubs once, moving through the ruined neighborhood like a fragment of a better dream. The place seethed with it. But there weren't any people anymore. At least, not the way she used to think of people.

"Dear God," the man said, and she stopped. He shuffled into the middle of the street, shoulders slouched, his face slack as a dead man's. His eyes roved over the place, taking it all in. He looked frail, and lonely, and scared; which, she supposed, is exactly what he was. Despite herself, she felt a twinge of sympathy for him. She followed him, took his elbow, and pulled him back into the relative shadow of the sidewalk.

"Hard to believe this is all just a few blocks away from where you live, huh?"

He swallowed, nodded.

"But listen to me, okay? You gotta listen to me, and do what I say. No walking out in the middle of the street. We stay quiet, we keep moving, we don't draw attention. Don't think I won't leave your ass if you get us in trouble. Do you understand me?"

He disengaged his elbow from her hand. At least he had the decency to look embarrassed. "Sorry," he said. "This is just my first time seeing it since I left. At the time it was just, it was . . . it was just chaos. Everything was so confused."

"Yeah, I get it." She didn't want to hear his story. Everybody had one. Tragedy gets boring after a while.

Hollow City was not a city at all, but a series of city blocks that used to be part of the Fleming and South Kensington neighborhoods, and had acquired its own peculiar identity over the last few months. Its informal name came from its emptiness: each building a shell, scoured of life, whether through evacuation or the attentions of the surgeons. The atmosphere had long turned an ashy gray, as though under perpetual cloud cover, even around the city beyond the afflicted neighborhood. Lamps burned all the time, but not in here. Electricity had been cut off weeks ago. Nevertheless, light still swelled from isolated pockets, as though furnaces were being stoked to facilitate some awful labor transpiring beyond the sight of the surrounding populace.

"There's things coming up that're gonna be hard to see," she said. "You ready for that?"

The old man looked disgusted. "I don't need to be lectured on what's hard to see by a child," he said. "You have no idea what I've seen."

"Yeah, well, whatever. Just don't freak out. And hustle it up."

Mix did not want to be here after the sun went down. She figured they had five good hours. Plenty of time for the old bastard to find who he was looking for, or—more likely—realize there was no one left to find.

They continued along the sidewalk, walking quickly but quietly. The rhythmic squeaking of unoiled wheels came from around a corner ahead, accompanied by the sound of several small voices holding a single high note in unison, like a miniature boys' choir. Mix put out her hand to stop him. He must not have been paying attention, because he walked right into it before stuttering to a halt. She felt the thinness of his chest, the sparrow-like brittleness of his bones. Guilt welled up from some long buried spring in her gut: she had no business bringing him here on his stupid errand. It was doomed, and he was doomed right along with it. She should have told him no. There were other ways to make money. Another client would have come along eventually. Except that fewer and fewer people were paying to be escorted through Hollow City, and those that were tended to be adrenaline junkies, who were likely to get you killed, or—worse—religious nuts and artists, who felt entitled to bear witness to what was happening here due to some perceived calling. It was a species of narcissism that offended her on an obscure, inarticulate level. A few weeks ago she had guided a poet out to the center of the place and almost slipped away while he scribbled furiously, self-importantly, in his notebook. The temptation was stronger than she would have believed possible; she'd fantasized about how long she'd hear him calling out for her before the surgeons stopped his tongue for good, or turned it to other purposes.

She didn't leave the poet, but she learned that there was an animal living inside her, something that celebrated when nature did its work upon the weak. She came to value that animal. She knew it would keep her alive.

This sudden guilt, then, was both unexpected and unwelcome. She set her jaw and waited for it to subside.

The prow of a wheelbarrow emerged from beyond the corner of the building, followed by its laden body, the wooden wheels turning in slow, wobbling rotations. The barrow was filled with the grey, hacked torsos of children, some sprouting both arms, most with less, but all still wearing their heads, eyes rolled back to reveal the whites with little exploded capillaries standing in bright contrast to the gray pallor, each mouth rounded into an ellipse from which emitted that single, perfect note, as heartbreakingly beautiful as anything heard in one of God's cathedrals. Then the wagoneer hoved into view, its naked body blackened and wasted, comprised of just enough gristle and bone to render it ambulatory. The skin on its face was shrunken around its skull, and a withered crown of long black hair rustled like straw in the breeze. It turned its head, and for the second time that day they found themselves speared into place by a wagoneer's stare. This one actually stopped its movement and leaned closer, as if committing their faces to memory, or transferring the sight of them via some infernal channel to a more distant intelligence, which might answer their intrusion with punishment.

Her gaze still fixed on the wagoneer, Mix reached behind and grabbed the old man's wrist. "We have to run," she said.

2.

The dog was gone. Carlos realized it at once, and a gravity took him, a feeling of aging so suddenly and so completely that he half expected to die right there. He looked at the kitchen floor and wondered if he would hurt himself in the fall. Instead, he pulled a chair from the kitchen table and collapsed into it, settling his head onto the table, his arms dangling at his sides. A great sadness moved inside him, turning in his chest, too big to be voiced. It threatened to break him in half.

Maria had been with him for fifteen years. A scruffy, tan mutt, her muzzle gone gray and her eyes rheumy, they were walking life's last mile together. Carlos had never married; he'd become so acclimated to his loneliness that eventually the very idea of human companionship just made him antsy and tired. It was not as though he'd had to fight for his independence; his demeanor had grown cold and mean as he aged, not from any ill-feeling toward other people, but simply from an unwillingness to endure their eccentricities. He had a theory that people warped as they aged, like old records left out in the sun, and unless you did it together and warped in conformity to each other, you eventually became incapable of aligning with anybody else.

Well, he'd grown old with Maria, that grand old dame, and she was all he needed or wanted.

When the tremors had started in Fleming, and the nights started filling with the screams of neighbors and strangers alike, he and Maria had huddled together in his apartment. He'd kept his baseball bat clutched in his thin, spotted hands while Maria bristled and growled at his side. She'd always been a gentle dog, frightened by visitors, scurrying under the bed at a loud knock, but now she had found a core of steel within herself and she stood between him and the door, her lips peeled from her yellowed teeth, prepared to hurl her frail old body against whatever might come through it. That, even more than the screaming outside, convinced him that whatever was out there was something to fear.

On the second night, the door was kicked in and bright flashlights sprayed into his apartment, the commanding voices of men piling into the room like something physical. Maria's whole body shook and snapped with fear and rage, her own hoarse barking pushing back at them, but when Carlos recognized what they were saying, he wrapped his arms around his dog and held her tight, whispering in her ear. "It's okay baby, it's okay little mama, calm down, calm down. Calm down."

And she did, though she still trembled. The police, one of them sobbing unashamedly, loaded them both into a van parked at the bottom of the apartment building, not giving him any grief about taking the dog, thank God. He cast a quick glance down the street before a hand shoved him inside with a few of his terrified neighbors, huddled in their pajamas, and slammed the door behind him. What he saw was impossible. A man, eight feet tall or more, skinny as a handful of sticks, crossing a street only a block away with eerie, doe-like grace. He was a shape in the sodium lights, featureless and indistinct, like a child's drawing of a nightmare. He was stretching what looked like thin, bloody parchment from one streetlight to another; suspended from one end of the parchment was a human arm, flexing at the elbow again and again, like an animal in distress.

He looked at his neighbors, but he didn't know any of their names. They weren't talking, anyway.

Then the van surged to life, moving with ferocious speed to a location only a mile distant, behind a battery of checkpoints and blockades, and rings of armed officers.

Carlos and his dog were provided with a small apartment—even smaller than the one they'd been living in—in tenement housing, with as many of the other residents of the besieged neighborhood as could be evacuated. The building was overcrowded, and the previous residents received these newcomers with a gamut of reactions ranging from sympathy to resentment to outright anger. The refugees greeted their new hosts in kind.

No one knew exactly what was happening in South Kensington and Fleming. Rumors spread that a tribe of kids, homeless or in gangs or God knows what, had started charging people to go in looking for people or items of value left behind, or sometimes even chaperoning people to their old homes. Though some minor effort had been made to quell these activities, the little industry managed to thrive. It disgusted Carlos; someone was always ready to make a dollar, no matter what the circumstance.

It was thanks to them, though, that news bled back of the old neighborhood transformed, stalked by weird figures pushing wheelbarrows or hauling huge carts of human wreckage, strange music drifting from empty streets, the tall figures—surgeons, some called them—knitting people together in grotesque configurations. Buildings were empty, some completely hollowed out, as though cored from within, leaving nothing but their outer shells. The kids sneaking back inside starting calling it Hollow City, and the name stuck. Which was just one more thing Carlos hated. The old place had a name. Two names, in fact. There was a history there, lives had been lived there. It didn't deserve some stupid comic book tag. It had belonged to humanity once.

A gray pallor hung over the place, slowly expanding until most of the real city was covered. Carlos believed it was responsible for the way people acclimated too quickly to the transformation of the old neighborhoods. Apathy took root like a weed. Police kept up the blockades, but they were indifferently manned, and the kids' scouting efforts grew in proportion. The Army never came in. No one in the tenements knew whether or not they were even called. There was nothing about this on the news. It was as though the city suffered its own private nightmare, which would continue unobserved until it could wake up and talk about it, or until it died in its sleep.

Carlos was resigned to let it play out in the background. He was nothing if not adaptive, and it did not take long for him to accept his reduced surroundings. It was noisy, chaotic, the walls were thin, but these things had been true of his old apartment, too. Sound was a comfort to him; he might not have friends, but his spirit was eased by the human commotion. He would have died there, as close to contentment as he might get, if only Maria had stayed with him.

He knew Maria was gone almost instantly, well before he hobbled out of bed and saw the apartment door ajar. He could feel her absence, like a pocket of airlessness. And he knew immediately that she'd gone back to her old home. What he didn't know was why. Was there something there that called her? Was she confused? Did the place mean more to her than he did? Her absence almost felt like a betrayal, like a spade digging into his heart.

But she was Maria. He would go and get her. He would bring her home.

Everything had gone lax at the border to the old neighborhood. The checkpoints seemed to be devoid of the police altogether; only these kids now, living in makeshift shacks, sleeping on mattresses harvested from local housing or perhaps from the afflicted area, living out of boxes and suitcases and school backpacks. Carlos knew he ought to be grateful for it, because it would only help him get back inside, but a part of him couldn't help but despair for the continued decline of responsibilities and standards in the hands of this privileged youth. It's good to be old, he thought. I'll be dead before they've finished their work on this world.

It took a while to find anybody willing to give him the time of day. He knew they considered him too risky: old, slow, fragile. But eventually he found one who would: a girl with a shaved head, dressed in a dark blue hoodie and jeans, who called herself Mix. Ridiculous name; why did they do that? Why couldn't they just be who they were? She considered the three crumpled twenties he offered her, and accepted them with poor grace. She turned her back to him, reaching into a box she kept by her sleeping bag and jamming it with bottles of water, a first aid kit, and what looked like a folded knife. She interrogated him as she packed.

"What are we looking for?"

"Maria," he said.

She stopped, turned and looked at him with something like contempt. "You know she's dead, right?"

"No. I don't know that at all."

"Do you know anything about what's going on in there?"

He flashed back to the tall man—one of the surgeons, he supposed—stretching the twitching human parchment between streetlights. "Sure," he said. "It's Hell."

"Who knows what the fuck it is, but there's no one left alive in there. At least, no one that can be saved."

A swell of impatience threatened to overwhelm him. He would go in alone if he had to. What he would not do was stand here being condescended to by an infant. "Do you want my money or not?"

"Yeah I want it. But you have to follow my rules, okay? Stay quiet and stay moving. Keep to the sidewalks at all times, and close to the walls when you can. They mostly ignore stragglers, unless they're traveling in big groups or making some kinda scene. If one of them notices you, stay still. Usually they just move on."

"What if they don't?"

"Then I make it up on the fly. And you do exactly what I fucking say." She waited until he acknowledged this before continuing. "And whenever we realize this Maria or whoever is dead, we get the fuck out again. Like, immediately."

"She's not dead."

Mix zipped up her backpack and slung it over her shoulder. "Yeah, okay. Maybe you think you're the hero in a movie or something. You're not. You're just some old guy making a bad choice. So listen to me. Once *I'm* sure she's dead, I am leaving. If you come with me I'll make sure you get back out safe. If you stay behind, that's on you."

"Fine. Can we go?"

"Yeah, let's go. Where are we looking?"

"Home. She'll have gone home." He gave her the address.

She sighed. "Old man, that building has been cored. There's nothing inside."

"That's where she is."

Mix nodded, already turning away from him. Already, in some sense, finished. "Whatever you say."

3.

She yanked him around, as close to panic as she'd been in weeks, and they walked briskly back in the direction they'd come. She wanted to run, but either he couldn't or he wouldn't. It wasn't until he wrenched his wrist free of her grip, though, that she considered leaving him there. The animal inside her started to pace.

He stood resolutely in place, rubbing the place she'd grabbed him. Behind him, in the dense gray air, the wagoneer still watched, its lidless eyes shedding a dim yellow light. The thin choir of dismembered bodies held their sustained note. She'd been glanced at before, but none had ever stopped and stared until now. She thought about the knife in her backpack. An affectation. So stupid. Unless she gutted this old man right here and ran while the things fell upon him instead.

"Where are you going?" he said. He wasn't even trying to be quiet anymore. His voice bounced down the empty street, came back at them like a strange reflection of itself.

Out, she wanted to say. We're getting out. But instead, she said, "We'll go around. A detour. Hurry." She wasn't a dumb kid. She had a job. She would do it. She could handle this.

"Okay," he said, showing her a little deference for the first time. He joined her, even picking up his pace. "I thought you were going to leave me."

"Fuck you, I'm not leaving." She could hear the tears in her voice and she hated herself for it. Stupid girl. That's what they called her. They were right all along.

They doubled back, turned a corner, pursuing a longer route to the address. Mix glanced behind her often, sure they were being followed, but the wagoneer was nowhere to be seen.

The streets had continued to transform since last she'd been here. The wagoneers hauled their cartloads of human remains, coming from some central location and depositing them in moldering piles throughout Hollow City, where the surgeons continued to stitch them together into grotesque, seemingly meaningless configurations: there were more torsos like the ones they had just seen strung like bunting from one side of the street to the other, each one tuned to a different pitch; great kites of skin flapped tautly in similar fashion, punched through with holes of varying sizes and patterns, as though a kind of Morse code had been pierced into them with an awl; skeletal structures made from the combined parts of a hundred rendered people loomed between the buildings in great, stilled wheels, fitting together like cogs in some grotesque engine. The bone wheels had been hastily assembled, still wet with blood and dripping with rags of meat. The eyes of the workers boiled with furnace-light as they toiled, and the air grew steadily colder.

Mix stopped, hugging the corner of what had once been a 24-hour drug store. Blood splashed the interior of the picture window now, obscuring whatever was inside. She plotted their course in her head, and realized with a buckle of disbelief that the address they were going to—the building she knew from reports of the others had been cored from the inside—seemed to be the center of the wagoneers' activity.

If Carlos was impatient with her stopping, he gave no sign. He was leaning against the wall too, breathing heavily. His eyes were unfocused, and she wondered how much of this he was taking in.

"You still alive back there?" she said.

"I think so. Hard to tell anymore." He made a vague gesture. "What is all this?"

"Shit, you're asking me? It's just another bad dream, I guess. You're the one with all the life experience, you ought to recognize one by now." When he didn't respond, she said, "So, you seen enough now?"

"What do you mean?"

She pointed ahead, to where his old apartment building hulked into the sky a little over a block away. The desiccated bodies of the wagoneers came and went from inside with a clockwork regularity. "There's no one left in there, old man. That's fucking grand central station."

"No. She's in there."

For a moment, Mix couldn't speak through the rage. The degree of obliviousness he was displaying, the absolute blind faith in an impossible outcome, had just crossed the border from desperate hope to outright derangement. He was crazy, probably had been for some time, and now he was going to get them both killed. Or worse than killed. The thing inside her paced and growled. She was ready to let it out at last.

She felt a curious dread about it. Not at his fate—he'd bought that for himself—but at the simple act of walking away, and at the border she would be crossing within herself by doing it. It was one she had always taken pride in being ready to cross, but now that the moment had come, she was afraid of it, and afraid of the world that waited for her on the other side. She pressed her forehead against the wall, closed her eyes, and listened to the strange sounds the new architectures of flesh created around her: the gorgeous notes, the flag-like snapping, the hollow tone of bones clattering in the wind. It reminded her of the various instruments in her school band tuning themselves before a concert. She heard him breathing beside her, too, heavily and quickly, as he expended what she knew were his final energies on this suicidal quest.

"So who is she, anyway? Your wife? Your daughter?"

"No. She's my dog."

It was as though he said something in a foreign language. She needed a moment to translate it into something she could understand. When it happened, the last beleaguered rank of resistance inside her folded, and she started to laugh. It was quiet, almost despairing, and she couldn't stop it. She pressed her face into the stone wall and laughed through her clenched teeth.

The absurdity of it all.

"She's my dog," Carlos said, a little defensively. "She's my only friend. I'm going to bring her home."

"Your home is gone," she said, the thin stream of giggles reaching its end, giving way instead to a huge sadness, the kind that did not seem to visit her but instead emerged from within, as much a part of her body as a liver or a spleen. She wanted to hate the old man but what she felt for him wasn't hate. It was something complicated and awful and unknown to her, but hate was too simple a word to describe it. If she had ever loved a child still innocent of its first heartbreak, she might have known the feeling. But she wasn't a parent; and anyway, she couldn't remember love.

"A dog," she said.

Carlos stood beside her, the aesthetic of Hell manifested around him, an abyssal acoustic being built by its wretched servants, and he looked like what he was: a slumped, fading old man, lonely in the world but for one simple animal, and fully aware of the impossibility of retrieving it. His speech was defiant but his mind had already recognized the truth, and she could see it erode him even as she watched, like a sand dune in a strong wind.

Somewhere in this bloody tangle of bone and flesh, maybe even some still-muttering faces affixed to a wall with an unguent excreted from the lungs of the surgeons, were her parents, their cold anger still seeping from their tongues, their self-loathing and their resentment still animating the flayed muscles in their peeled faces. She could hear them as clearly as ever.

Stupid girl.

God damn them anyway.

"All right," she said. "Let's go get your dog."

4.

The girl was careful, but there was no need to sneak. What could they do to him? Death wasn't shit. Carlos knew he should tell her to leave—it was obvious he wasn't going to be coming back, with or without Maria—but it was her choice to make. Life was long or short, and it meant something or it didn't. It wasn't his business to tell her how to measure hers.

The walls of his old apartment building bowed slightly, as though some great pressure grew from within. The doors had been torn off and the windows broken, though, and he could see nothing inside but shadow. Pacing the perimeter of the building were three dark-robed figures, their heads encased in black iron boxes. They exuded a monastic patience, moving slowly and with obvious precision. The lead figure held an open book in his left hand, scribbling busily into it with his right. The one in the middle swung a censer, a black orb from which spilled a heavy yellow smoke. The scent of marigolds carried over to him. The figure in the back held aloft a severed head on a pole, which emitted a beam of light from its wrenched mouth.

Carlos waited for these figures to pass before approaching the doors as casually as if he belonged there. Mix made a sound of protest, but he ignored her. A surgeon emerged from the doors just as he reached them, stooping low to fit, but though it cast him a curious glance, it did not interfere with him, or even break its stride. It stretched itself to its full height and walked away, thin hands trailing long needles of bone and bloody thread. It moved slowly and languidly, like something walking underwater.

He moved to enter the building, but Mix restrained him from behind and edged in front of him instead. She held her left arm across his chest, protectively, as they crept forward; in her right she held the knife she'd stashed in her backpack, unfolded into an ugly silver talon. He didn't know what had changed her mind about him, but he was grateful for it.

Though barely enough light intruded into the building to see anything by, it was immediately obvious that the girl had been right: the building's expansive interior had been scooped clean, leaving nothing but the outer walls, like the husk of an insect following a spider's feast. A great, wet hole had opened in the earth beneath it, almost as wide as the building's foundation. The hole looked like a gaping wound, raw and bloody, its walls sloping inward and meeting a hundred feet down in a moist, clutching glottis. Above it, the walls and ceiling had been sprayed with its meaty exhalations, red organic matter pasted over them so that they resembled the underside of a tongue.

Bodies of residents who'd been unable to evacuate were glued to the far wall with a thick yellow resin; even as they watched, one Carlos recognized as a young cashier at a local take-out was peeled from his perch and subjected to the attentions of a cleaver-wielding surgeon, who quickly quartered him with a series of heavy and efficient chops. The cashier's limbs quivered yet, and his mouth gaped in wonderment at his own butchering. But instead of a cry or a scream, what emerged from him was a pure note, as clean and undiluted as anything heard on Earth. Tears sprang to Carlos's eyes at the beauty of it, and ahead of him Mix put her hand over her lowered face, the curved knife glinting dully by her ear, a gesture of humility or of supplication.

"Maria," Carlos said, and there she was, snuffling through piled offal in a far corner, her snout filthy, her hair matted and sticky. The laborers of hell walked around her without concern, and she seemed undisturbed by them as well. When she heard Carlos call her name, she answered with a happy bark and bounded over to him, spry for the moment, slamming the side of her body into his legs and lifting her head in grateful joy as he ran his gnarled fingers through her fur. Carlos dropped to his knees, heedless of the bright pain, of how difficult it would be to rise again. His dog sprawled into his lap. For a moment, they were happy.

And then Carlos thought, *You left me. You left me in the end. Why?* He hugged his dog close, burying his nose in her fur. He knew there was no answer beyond obvious, constant imbalance in any transaction of the heart. *You don't love me the way I love you.*

He forgave her for it. There really wasn't anything else he could do.

5.

Mix watched them from a few feet away, the knife forgotten in her hand. She knew why the dog had come here. She could feel it; if the old man would leave the animal alone for a moment, he would too. The sound coming through that great, open throat in the ground, barely heard but thrumming in her blood, had called it here. She felt it like a density in the air, a gravity in the heart. She felt it in the way the earth called her to itself, with its promise of loam and worms, so that she sat down too, beside them but apart, unwelcome in their reunion.

Stupid girl. You weren't invited. You don't belong. You never did.

The sound from the hole grew in volume. It was an answer to loneliness, and a call to the forgotten. It was Hell's lullaby, and as the long tone blew from the abyss it filtered out through the windows and the doors and it caught in the reedlike parchments of skin and set them to keening, it powered the wheels of bone so they clamored and rattled and chimed, and it blended with the chorus of notes from the suspended bodies until the whole of the city became as the bell of a great trumpet, spilling a mournful beauty into the world. Every yearning for love rang like a bell in the chest, every lonely fear found its justification.

The clangor of the song kept rising, until it filled the sky. Their ache stretched them until their bodies sang. In dark fathoms, something turned its vast head, and found it beautiful.

BURNT
LUCIANO MARANO

From *DOA III*
Editor: Marc Ciccarone & Andrea Dawn
Blood Bound Books

Fire gets all the glory, but the real action happens beneath the flames. It's a secret spectacle. The blaze itself is just a side effect of matter changing form, a simple chemical reaction. Something transforming into something new. The change is what's important. Combustion is the product of just the right amount of oxygen, heat, and fuel. Fuel being something that will burn. Wood. Cloth. Flesh. Actually, flesh alone isn't flammable enough to begin a conflagration. You have to start with something else first. An ignitor, the professionals call it. The pretty flames we love—the mood lighting of many a romantic dinner, fluffy carpet fuck fest and cozy campfire—are just the calling card of transmutation.

Watch wood change as it burns. You will see it char and then whiten as the flame advances across it like a shiny wave, a brilliant blanket. That's a sexy dance. It's hard not to love a spectacle like that. But it's all style, no substance.

Fire isn't even necessary to burn something at all. Hot water will affect skin in much the same way. So will steam, radiation, and even long enough exposure to sunlight. That's why they call it a sun*burn*. Flesh burnt badly enough will literally die while still attached, a patch of blight on an otherwise healthy organ, and become like sun-bleached leather, waxy to the touch. Or it might harden into coal-black scales, otherworldly armor.

Watch. The skin reddens, then blisters. Fatty bubbles begin to appear like soap on the surface of still water. Small at first. Then they grow. They swell, balloon up, ready to bloom like the bulbs of some strange fleshy flower, waiting to burst open in a shocking display of new life. When they do, the freshly revealed skin is the glistening newborn result of that flickering, feverish passion.

Watch the pretty skin. See it change. It will whiten, melt and pool, reassemble into a great and terrible new visage. Striking. Compelling. A human recreated, not in the image of a kindly God, but by the design of heat. Burn wards are Satan's art gallery. The figure in each bed a grotesque new rendition of an alien vision for the human form, an interpretation of the old flesh. Beauty reimagined. Not beholden to the constraints of symmetry, or even function, the new flesh splits through the old, rending violently through to breathe and touch, to be touched, in a dizzying display of a striking new aesthetic.

Losing her face was the best thing that ever happened to Vicki's mother.

Every year, deep fryer accidents are responsible for about five deaths in America. Catherine was almost one of them, but she lived. They didn't think she would and, at first, she wished that she hadn't. Recovery was slow and arduous, indescribably painful. But the best experts in the country were consulted, all of them eager to attach their name to such a sensational case study, and they were able to save one of her eyes, replace her lips—sufficient enough for her to speak—also reconstruct enough of her ears so that she could eventually wear large stylish sunglasses.

The scar tissue, smooth and leathery, enveloped her head like the hood of a wetsuit. Thick crimson tentacles snaked down her neck in both the front, curving sensuously between her breasts, and also in back, like the seeking appendages of a parasite. The division between the new burned area and the old pale skin was a rough barrier of scale, like the hide of a primordial beast, surrounded by a tender, pinkish outline.

Catherine took to wearing scarves and hats, wigs sometimes, but she loved masks most of all. She had an impressive collection by the time Vicki's father left. He couldn't look at his wife anymore. He couldn't stand the thought of touching her. It was almost funny. Before the accident he never cared if she was in the mood or not. When he wanted her affection, he took it. She eventually learned not to struggle.

Now Catherine wanted it all the time. She was ready, positively in heat. She strutted around the house in her wigs, her masks, and not much else most of the time. In a carnival disguise or a domino mask and scarf, lace panties peeking out from under a sheer teddy or riding low beneath a bustier, she moaned and writhed yet to no avail. What's the saying? She couldn't get laid in prison with a handful of pardons.

Dad hadn't been around much before the accident, so it wasn't a hard adjustment for the kids when he split. Vicki's older brother Gregory was upset at first, but even he got over it soon enough. Besides, there were plenty of men at the house after that. There were other things for him to be upset about too.

Deliverymen were easy. So was the plumber, the handyman and the paper boy. And when Catherine couldn't think up a job to bring a new man over, there was always the Internet. The lawsuit settlement with the deep fryer manufacturer paid the doctor's bills and left Catherine with plenty of cash and plenty of time at home to be available for entertaining. Though it hadn't been true for Dad, most men will overlook almost anything in the face of a guaranteed score. If some lonely slut wanted to wear a mask, or a wig and maybe do it only from behind, what did they care? They got off just the same.

Vicki heard her mother often in the bedroom with her men—and in the living room and in the bathroom and in the garage—encouraging them, urging them, commanding them. Harder. Faster. Deeper.

It was as if along with her face the boiling oil had relieved Catherine of the person she had been beneath it. Where once she was meek, now she was in control. Where once she was passive, now she was insatiable; once sad, now gleeful. As her new face had torn free in a violent eruption of steam and blister flowers, so had the person she was meant to be.

And when it got really lonely, when she couldn't get anyone else to tend to her, Mom could always tiptoe down the hall to Gregory's room. He was fifteen by then, after all.

"Such a big boy," Vicki would hear her mother coo from inside her brother's room at night. "Mommy's big, sexy boy."

"No," he said. "Don't. I don't like it!"

"But look here," Mom would giggle. "That means that you do, baby. Looks to me like you like it a lot."

He eventually learned not to struggle.

It was Vicki who found her mother dead in the bathtub.

She was naked. Really naked. She hardly ever wore much, but she was not wearing a mask or wig either. Her wrists were severed. She'd been serious, too, cutting up and down, not across. Determined to die. Every mirror in the house was broken, smashed to bits, and she'd used one of the biggest pieces to gouge the deep, moist slits into her skinny forearms. Vicki had heard the glass breaking the night before, lying absolutely still in bed. She had been terrified, but she knew by then to stay out of Mom's way. When Mom was in a mood, it was best to lay low.

Catherine had tried to fuck herself back to life. It didn't make sense to Vicki then, but later on she began to understand. Her mother's plan had worked, for a little while. She'd filled herself with a Naval fleet's worth of cock, and enough jizz to float their ships on, but it hadn't been enough. She could never feel desired enough, be wanted enough, to look at herself for very long. For just a little while though, she had been happy. But Catherine couldn't embrace the change. She got caught up in the surface. All style, no substance. The change is what's really important, and that happens below. It happens within.

Gregory was eighteen and out of the picture by then. So Vicki was alone when she called the police. She was alone as she watched TV and waited. She was alone when they finally arrived to take her mother away forever.

Years passed.

Vicki didn't often think about her mother. Though, in another way, she never really stopped thinking about her. It wasn't so much a case of thinking or not thinking about her, really. The memory of her mother coated every feeling she had, every action and thought, like a layer of dust that she couldn't wipe away.

Tonight, once more, she had her hands full of hair. Beautiful strawberry blond hair, beneath which her roommate Andrea spat and sobbed into the toilet. Devastated by another man, the comely petite girl from Minneapolis had again tried to assuage her feelings with vodka—a lot of vodka—and now she suffered on her knees before the pitiless porcelain goddess.

Sitting on the side of the tub, leaned forward with elbows on her thighs, Vicki gathered up the sad girl's hair into one fist and slid her other hand to her roommate's heaving back. She rubbed small, comforting circles.

"It's OK," Vicki said again. "It's all going to be fine," for the hundredth time. Then she said, "You're better off." Vicki searched for what usually came next in the speech. She came up blank though and went back to rubbing and shushing instead.

Tomorrow would come the hangover, brutal and debilitating but a necessary period in the depressing run-on sentence that was Andrea's love life. Then the slow recovery, until her next paramour and the accompanying, almost assured, infidelity, dishonesty and mistreatment.

Andrea was a beautiful girl. The broken ones almost always are. But it did not make her happy. Vicki felt bad for her. She felt a lot of things for her. She'd watched Andrea for the three years they'd lived together, watched her very closely. She'd seen her desperately squeezing herself into the role dictated by the world, killing herself at fitness classes and starving herself to slip into seductive clothes. Still not happy. Andrea wanted to be the girl she thought she should be so badly. So many long, painful hours, so much time standing before mirrors analyzing and adjusting. So many trinkets, tricks, powders, gels and sprays. And she was still not happy.

Vicki had watched Andrea alter herself for every man who came along. Hair, interests, mannerisms, they'd all been changed easier than underwear if the next willing cock in her life had seen fit to encourage, or forbid, something. They were never real changes, though. Just a surface disguise. A mask to hide behind.

"Shh," Vicki said in her friend's ear. It was stretched and punctured by many heavy, twinkly, eye-catching baubles. "It'll be OK. I promise. I love you."

"Thanks," Andrea said, staring down into the toilet, head on her forearm. "I love you too, Vick."

Andrea didn't really mean it. Not like Vicki did. It was just one of those things heartbroken girlfriends say to each other. Fueled by sorrow and Smirnoff, it was an easy thing to say. But Vicki could pretend, just for a moment at least, that her friend's words meant more than that. In the darker private places of her mind she always did. But all she said was, "I'll always take care of you."

*   *   *

Moans and whimpers are the crickets of the nighttime burn ward. Occasionally, a lone shriek would pierce the relative quiet the way a wolf's howl might ring out over an otherwise hushful landscape. Vicki moved like a silent specter in her white scrubs among the still aberrations displayed in uniform rows, their mutations thinly veiled beneath hospital blankets and stark patches of alabaster gauze.

Vicki often worked shifts for other nurses. She liked to be at work—especially late at night when there were less people around—and she was qualified to work in many departments. Her primary duties were in the burn ward, though. It was a specialty she had chosen without much conscious thought. It just felt right.

Regardless, it was an excellent fit for her, and a position that not many others could handle. The doctors were all impressed with her unflinching coolness in the face of the horrors effected on humans by heat, and her attentive hands-on approach to each newly warped victim. Vicki had advanced quickly, and she enjoyed her position at the hospital. It was where she had first met Andrea.

She paused at the foot of the bed of a man who had earned his new countenance in a car accident. Third-degree burns are more serious, more often fatal. But second-degree burns are more painful because the nerves survive. This man was covered in the latter variety, and he cried in his semiconscious, drug-induced haze. As she slipped the thin sheet down to reveal his wrecked body, Vicki absently wondered if he even knew was crying.

Dangling tubes descended from high on metal arms to penetrate his tumescent skin and deliver medications and liquid food. The man had become swollen, saturated with the dripping sustenance like waterlogged driftwood. His insides strained against the confinement of his own skin, like something left in the microwave too long. Rips had begun to show, and crimson fat split though the growing fissures.

Vicki ran a finger along those lines and remembered her mother's husky pleas—the soundtrack to her own budding sexuality. The man's scrotum had ballooned up to cartoonish proportions, and Vicki lightly prodded him there too. He made a pathetic little mewling sound—*I don't like that! I don't like it!*—and she imagined the strong calloused hands of working men caressing perfumed scabs. The man's eyelids were bulgy, like rotten fruit. Vicki poked them gently, imagining they might pop.

Tomorrow, she knew, they would cut him. As the pressure choked off blood vessels, the man's skin would suffocate and die. He would rot from the outside in. So the surgeons would cut him free by slicing vents in his constrictive skin casing.

She'd seen it done many times, including the long gashes sliced into her mother's neck and shoulders. Like tiger stripes, she'd thought at the time. Or gills, like the kind a mermaid might have.

Vicki rested a hand on his plump tummy, guts tightly corseted in over-cooked leather wrapping. His entire body lay engorged beneath her touch, pulsing and warm. Like he might burst at any second.

She reached into her pocket, took out a tiny digital camera and began to photograph the extraordinary specimen before her, all fevered tension and mounting pressure. The man made a babyish keening noise. It leaked out from between his bloated lips like air escaping from a balloon.

Vicki crouched lower for a close-up. She wondered what the man had been like before his accident, and what he was becoming beneath his hardened cocoon.

Days later, Vicki returned from a double shift at the hospital to the sound of Stevie Nicks. Today, she'd been subbing in pediatrics. It had been tedious and boring. She had no interest in children and it was Andrea's day off, so Vicki could not even look forward to catching a glimpse of her roommate while making the rounds or sharing a meal break.

Inside the apartment, she found Andrea bopping near the stereo, drink in hand, wearing tiny gray shorts and an old Metallica t-shirt that was too big for her, a comfy relic of a long-gone boyfriend. She was devastatingly sexy. From the doorway, Vicki watched her dance for a moment that seemed to last forever.

"Vick!" Andrea cried, turning to face the entrance as Stevie Nicks sang. "Vick, Vick-ay! How was your day, slut?"

Vicki groaned, playing her established part in their domestic act. She dropped her bag near the couch and kicked off her white sneakers.

"Yeah." Andrea made a pouty duck face, nodded sharply and turned back to the stereo. "Fuck work. Slip out of them scrubs. There's margaritas in the kitchen and pizza on the way. Fingers crossed we get the blond delivery guy with the neck tattoo."

"You seem to be feeling better." Vicki headed to the kitchen, dragging her eyes away from Andrea's legs and reaching for a glass.

"I'm fucking great," Andrea said, sauntering in behind her for a refill. "Come on, shed the work clothes and get with the party. You're off tomorrow and I know you got nothing planned."

It didn't matter if she did or didn't have plans. Vicki knew she could never disappoint Andrea. She never would. She poured herself a glass of the frozen booze concoction, topped off Andrea's and headed off down the hall toward her bedroom.

Alone, Vicki stripped down and tossed her clothes into the hamper by the closet. She saw herself in the mirror above her dresser. She eyed herself dispassionately with a professional, clinical gaze, then opened the bottom left drawer and took out a mismatched pair of fluffy socks. One was bedecked in dolphins, the other a pattern of cherries. She rubbed them between her fingers and ran them up and down her bare legs. Goosebumps broke out over her entire body. They were Andrea's socks. She had taken them from the laundry, one at a time, over the course of the winter. Slob that she was, Andrea hadn't even noticed. Vicki held them both to her face, inhaled deeply.

She set the socks on the bed and, from the same drawer, took out some red lace boy shorts, also pilfered from the laundry. She ran them likewise over her legs, then caressed her stomach, gliding them up to her breasts, tickling herself. She held them close to her face and licked them daintily.

From the living room, Andrea called, "Pizza's here." There was a lot of giggling; she must have gotten the blond guy after all. Stevie Nicks played on.

Vicki pulled the underwear away from her mouth. "Coming."

She stepped into her roommate's panties, grabbed some sweats off the back of the door and dressed. Steve Nicks now sang "Talk To Me."

Andrea caterwauled along with Stevie. With her blond hair, and having retrieved a black wide-brimmed hat and scarf from her room a few drinks ago, she looked the part more and more. An obsession with the gypsy rocker was one of the things that Vicki loved about Andrea. It was an unapologetically corny thing they shared. Vicki sipped from her glass. It was only water now and had been for a while. She let Andrea drag her off the couch, gave in and danced along. She couldn't let Andrea down, even if she wanted to. And she never did.

Vicki felt, as she always did when she heard this song, like Stevie was talking for her, like the lyrics were written for her. She watched Andrea sway and stumble near the record player, sloshing more margarita than she was drinking, with a smoldering American Spirit stuck between her flawless lips and her hat tilted way back. Buzzed enough to be brave, Vicki came up close behind Andrea and danced a little slower.

Andrea suddenly fell away from Vicki's grasp and caught herself against the entertainment center, the record skipping and scratching over Stevie's haunting voice.

"You okay?"

"Sorry," Andrea slurred. She shuffled over to the couch on unstable legs. Vicki followed and kept her hands on Andrea's toned obliques, helping to guide her.

"It's OK."

"Just need a rest." Andrea sank into the couch, her limp arm hanging over the edge, smoldering filter inches above the carpet. She was instantly asleep.

Andrea could be happy. She just needed some help. She needed freeing from her cycle of disappointment.

Vicki thought about this while sitting at her computer an hour or so after Andrea passed out. She was angry, frustrated and disappointed. She was also excited.

She scrolled through the photos in a desktop folder labeled "Research." Some she'd taken herself at the hospital, others she'd been sent in trade. Most came from a man who claimed to be a paramedic in Nevada, including the ones in front of her now. Her favorites.

The blackened, twisted form of a woman in a number of lewd poses bared itself for her. A life-sized sex doll the man said he'd found in the remains of an adult shop that burned down. He liked to send Vicki pictures of the things he did to her. The poses he put her in, the clothes he made her wear. She sent him back suggestions.

The aberration is the attraction.

That's what he'd written. She'd never put it into words before, the slippery thing that coiled deep inside her, but it was true. Pouty lips blistered just right. A coquettish smile stretched and smeared into a novel, unreproducible expression. The world's full of pretty girls. But real carnage? That's rare. Before the fire, this doll had been like any other. Just one more on the shelf. Ignored. Not special. Licked by flame, assaulted by the inferno, though, she was divine. Special. She was saved.

She and Andrea could both be happy. They deserved to be happy. It had almost worked for her mother. It would have worked, if she hadn't been so alone. Vicki was older now. She finally understood. She would be there for Andrea, and she would make sure it *worked*. She would comfort and care for Andrea. She would sate her. She wouldn't leave like Dad had. Like Gregory.

Vicki crushed sleeping pills into a glass of water and managed to wake Andrea long enough to gulp it down. "You'll feel better tomorrow if you drink this now," she said.

"Thanks, slut," Andrea mumbled. Then she was out again, slumped on the couch and sleeping more soundly than ever.

Vicki gathered her tools, then waited.

An hour passed. The harsh blinking digits on the microwave clock told her it was almost three in the morning. She splashed the face of her comatose love, her very own sad Sleeping Beauty, with the last of the tequila and tucked the soaked scarf securely around Andrea's face. Vicki lit a cigarette from Andrea's nearby pack and pressed it to the sodden silk.

Watch her pretty skin. See it change from pink to crimson, then darken still further. See it crack and rupture. Fatty bubbles begin to appear. Small dots. Then they grow. They swell and bloom like the bulbs of a fleshy flower, a bloody bouquet.

Vicki gazed down with wide, unblinking eyes as it happened, a great secret show, just for her. She knew that Andrea's once smooth skin would melt and pool, and reassemble itself. A beautiful new flesh would eventually burst free, split through the old. She would be changed, permanently this time, and for the better.

Andrea woke, a guttural scream swallowed by the fire. She pawed at the molten cloth sticking to her face. She tried to roll off the couch, but Vicki was there. She wore thick rubber gloves pulled up to her elbows and grabbed hold of Andrea's flailing wrists and held them tight in her determined, sober grip. She pounced on Andrea's stomach, pinning her to the couch, and held her hands far away from her burning face.

Vicki watched, tears running over her smiling face as she listened to the wails, as Andrea's lips pulled back so far the budding blisters tore open. Her skin ripped and curled, peeling back like worn paint, and she bucked wildly between Vicki's legs like a live wire.

Finally, Vicki let go and leapt onto the floor. She grabbed the fire extinguisher—the one she would tell the police she ran to get from the kitchen—and let loose the cool white foam.

Later, from the chair beside her love's hospital bed, Vicki stared longingly at the bandaged figure lying silently before her. She stroked Andrea's arm above one of her gauze mittens. The doctors were confident they could save her hands. They had not been so badly burned as her face. Her eyes too, they thought, would probably be all right. Though the scarring would be severe.

Thank God, they'd said, that Andrea had the good fortune to have another nurse for a roommate—a burn specialist, no less—who was on hand when she passed out drunk with her lit cigarette. She must have spilled tequila on herself after Vicki went to bed. It happens. It happens every day. This could have been worse, they all agreed. She could have died.

Vicki nodded, but of course she had known that wouldn't happen. She would never allow her friend to die. Andrea would probably not remember Vicki's part in her accident. She had been very drunk, and mixing alcohol with sleeping pills . . . the trauma of seeing her new face would be devastating to her memory too.

Vicki moved a hand under the bleach-smelling covers and ran her fingers up Andrea's bare leg. Yes, she knew that Andrea would need to feel encouraged and supported. She would need to feel loved. Her fingertips moved up over Andrea's knee to her thigh. Unlike with her mother, Vicki knew what to do now. She knew how to help. Her hand moved under Andrea's paper gown and found its way between her legs. Beneath the bandages, Andrea moaned. It was an ambiguous sound, painful arousal.

"I know," Vicki whispered. "First it will only hurt. But it will get better. Soon, you won't even remember why you were so afraid."

Vicki worked her fingers. Andrea stirred and moaned louder. She squirmed and tried to pull away. Vicki grabbed her arm, dug her nails in hard and shushed her.

"I'm right here," she said. "I'll never leave you alone."

It was true. That was another way that Andrea would not be like Catherine. She couldn't kill herself even if she wanted to. Vicki would see to that. She would be around all the time and she would give Andrea what all those men, what even her own brother, could never give Catherine: affection without end. Idolatry.

She leaned close, put her lips to the thick gauze covering what was left of Andrea's ear and sang softly. Stevie Nicks, of course. Their music. She playfully licked the fabric cocoon covering her love's mouth, exploring her own damaged doll. Vicki felt herself get wet inside Andrea's stolen, red panties.

"I'll help you change," Vicki whispered. "I'll take care of you."

AUTHOR'S STORY NOTE

"Burnt" was the first story I ever published. I always wrote short fiction as a hobby, but I'd been looking to get some of my work out there for about a year by then, based on the advice and encouragement of some trusted friends. Alas, I was hip-deep in form rejections. Then, I came across the call for submission for *DOA III*, and, having enjoyed the first two volumes, thought I'd try to work up something appropriate. My only goal was a *personalized* rejection. But, the editors were very kind and encouraging and wrote back with a few suggestions. I took another stab at it with their thoughts in mind, and the result is the story as you know it now—that is, much improved.

The genesis of the plot itself was this: I'd been on a reading kick, seeking out the novels that inspired some of my favorite movies. I'd finally gotten to J.G. Ballard's *Crash*, and his mingling of grotesque and alluring imagery really impressed me. Simultaneously, the news here was full of coverage about a local firefighter who had been horribly burned while working at a California wildfire site. The details of his arduous recovery cemented what I'd always thought: Being badly burned is the worst *physical* thing that could ever happen to me. So, I decided to pull a Ballard and see if I could imagine the worst experience I could think of in a fetishized light. The response has been extremely gratifying.

THE
BETTER
PART OF
DROWNING
OCTAVIA CADE

From *The Dark* Magazine
Editors: Silvia Moreno-Garcia & Sean Wallace
Prime Books

A lix was never sure what kept the groaning rickety-spider of a dock up, unless it was the mussels that swarmed over the piles, turning them to hazards that could slice a swimmer open. The divers were allover scars from waves and mussels, always being pushed into shell sharp as knives and leaving their blood to scent the water.

"You kids be careful you don't draw the crabs!" If she heard that once a day she heard it fifty times, and each time she had to smile over the slicing pain and wave up, because coins weren't thrown to kids who wailed. Wailing made her choke if she tried to dive anyway, and there were always kids enough to squabble over coins so tears did nothing but anchor her to surface and starvation and blind her to the sudden scuttle of predation.

Don't draw the crabs, they always said, and smiled as they said it, because it was entertaining to see kids dive in crab beds, and entertaining to see the bloodshed when they were slow enough for catching. Alix didn't blame them for that. She'd never been able to look away either, no matter how much bile rose in her throat, the metal taste of panic.

Crabmeat, crabmeat. It was their own little circle of carnivorism, the smallest crabs providing one and the smaller kids the other. Not that the biggest of the scuttlers couldn't take a man full-grown, but usually the bigger you got the more sense you had, and the more the habit of watching claws kept them away from bone.

Alix had long since learned not to feel resentment for the crab-call—"Don't draw the crabs" was always sung out in the whistle-tones of scuttlers—but it was the call for sharks that made her shudder most, because she didn't understand it and the fin-man knew it and sang anyway. "Don't draw the sharks," he sang in crab-tones, but his business was sharks and if Alix didn't draw them then he'd starve.

"I've never seen no sharks," she called up, sulky in the water because his call never came with coins, or small pieces for trading. "Crabs must have ate 'em all, mister."

"Course there's sharks here," he said, hanging over and his mouth empty of teeth, the words rounded off like shoreline glass. "Don't you see them hanging?"

There were dried fins hung from the last dock shop but one, the Street of Endings, stretched out over ocean, but they could have come from anything. "Where do you think I get them from, if not from you kids?" said the fin-man. It struck her that if sharks swam after all, then she was basically being used as bait, and for more than crabs.

"Course we're not," said Toby, at fourteen the oldest of the divers and impatient with ignorance. "There's no such thing as sharks. Not anymore. You want to know what those fins *really* are?" he said, leaning close. "They're *us*. If he catches you he skins you and folds you into fins."

"You're making that up," said Alix. "He's got teeth hanging there too, strings of them. Kids' teeth don't look like that." She'd spat her milk teeth into the sea as they came out, until another of the divers told her she could sell them for grinding and teas, traded the knowledge for a day chiselling mussels from the nearest dock support. After that she'd examined each tooth carefully before selling it to the apothecary for salve to harden her fingers against shellfish and a charm to keep the crabs away. It wasn't as good a protection as the small tattoo that Toby had between his shoulder blades, the crab-sign that blurred their sight enough for slowness, but it was all her milk teeth could support.

Toby scoffed at her. "Teeth last *forever*," he said. "They're a thousand years old, those old teeth, like as not. I bet he got them handed down to him, from his da."

Alix chewed her lip, considering. "He *is* pretty old," she admitted, in doubtful tones. It was difficult to think of the fin-man having a parent. Parents died when you were a babe, mostly, or just beginning to toddle. The fin-man would have come diving with the rest of them then. "Maybe there were sharks when he was a kid."

If he ever was a kid. It seemed unfathomable that a person who spent so little time in salt could be so wrinkled.

"If you're not careful he'll come and eat you up," said Toby, trying to sneak an arm around. He was always trying to do that now, was a lot more patient with her than he'd been only a year since, and it wasn't as if any part of her was rounding out for pinching yet.

"Bugger off," she said, slipping out from under and swift-kicking. "Go try your scary lies on some other girl." But she said it smiling, because he kissed her sometimes and sometimes she kissed him, when the weather made poor sport of diving and she wanted to taste something other than starvation.

She didn't believe him. Not in broad daylight with the sun on the water making it look less murky from surface-side at least. Then Toby washed up with his back flayed off, his eyes and lips eaten away by little fish, and all Alix could do was drag him up out of the water-scum of surf and leave him.

"That's not all you can do," said Perette, grim. "The 'pothecary takes more than teeth." They didn't have a knife between them so she traded a kidney and half of a spleen for the use of one and got to butchering.

Under the knife he looked very young. Then he stopped looking like much of anything, and when Perette was done she loaded up Alix with the organs they had left to them, the usable ones, and left the rest for crabs.

"I'll never eat crabs again," said Alix, but when the offal was traded away Perette bought them steaming bowls of chowder and there were little red legs in it from baby crabs too young for sugar and singing.

"Get that down you," she said, and it was kinder than it could have been. "Look, those ones died last week, like as not. The meat's on the edge of turning. They didn't have time to munch on him."

"S'pose." She still felt weird about eating it. But that was more from politeness than scruples. Not that the hungry little eyes watching from beneath the edge of dock bothered her. If you shared what you got you starved. They'd be better working than eating and there was always opportunity for coins once word got round that a diver had died. People liked to play at ghouls then, it gave them a thrill to come throw coins into the murk and watch kids bleed and drown for them, get snipped apart by claws thick as thighs.

It still seemed a bit off to gorge on the death of someone who'd been friendly. But the crab meat was rich and it was sweet, even on the verge as it was, and most of all it was warm. She licked the bowl out when she was done, didn't leave even a scrap.

"I'm so full I'll sink like sugar," she said, and Perette smiled fondly from deep in her own bowl and warned of cramps.

"I'm not some nitwit baby four year," Alix scoffed. "I know my business." It was a simple business, easily remembered: dive and eat again, or stay in hammocks tied up close under the dock planks and think of death and crabs, just out of reach of either.

There was competition in the water, but she was older than most of the others now, and cannier with it. She did her best to look shocked and helpless over the mate she'd eaten at one remove, but the smaller kids cornered the market there and she had to push them away as coins were thrown to them, as crab-shells were thrown, old meat and fruit and melting biscuits, little pieces of scrap, empty bottles, cloth weighed down with stones. The sea didn't ruin much if you got to it quick enough, even the biscuits were still edible though they made the lips pucker and felt like wet sand in her mouth.

"You kids be careful you don't draw the crabs!"

There was nothing to do but smile and wave, and to dive in the places away from fish hooks because they were let down sometimes by the fin-man, embedded in the piles between mussels and she lost blood enough to shellfish without sacrificing to iron and teeth as well.

Besides, there were better places to dive under than the fin-shop. Nothing came down from there but cartilage. She'd snaffled one once, a thin leathery piece that she had to boil for hours with bladderwrack to be able to stomach. Better than nothing, but there were other things to dive for and other things to sell, and the fin-man was so parsimonious in his hanging that anyone waiting for a windfall would be waiting a long time.

Loot was different beneath each shop. The bakery was the best, and not only because the baker gave them bread each night, the last of the loaves that didn't sell, and sometimes little sugar cakes that Alix thought she kept aside especially on feast days. There were times, floating beneath, when the smells made her nauseous—the richness of the sugar, the sickly scent of caramel—but the caramel overflowed sometimes, bubbled through floor-boards and into the ocean. It was no good hooking it as it came down, soft still and plastic in fingers, the salt water improving the flavour a little even as it made the caramel gritty on the tongue. It had to settle, to sit on the bottom and be covered in sand until the crabs came for it, until the sugar turned their shells to thin and sweetened wafer crisps.

"It's magic," Alix told the younger kids, same as she was told when she was four and learning to dive. "Magic sugar. If you eat it it'll turn to iron in your belly and *drown* you." The words had a bitter taste she was long used to, and the small starving faces turned up to hers had lost any appeal they might once have had in the shadow of her own hunger. Those sugary lumps might make a meal, if a scanty one, but a sugared crab small enough to be caught and sold would feed the seller for a day and there was no time nor pity for little ones who couldn't learn and gobbled the sugar instead.

They tended to learn quicker when it was drowning on the menu, drowning come with sugar and consequence. She'd learned to make the descriptions as vivid as she could, gurgling and choking, turning her own face blue with held breath. It was a stupid lie, but if they didn't grasp it they *would* drown, pulled under not by weight of caramel but by the bigger kids, the ones with a vested interest in keeping the story going.

Alix had only done it once, held a kid under but she'd cried all through it and made it longer than it needed to be. One of the other divers had taken over, called her soft and scorned her twelve year old muscles, more suited for sunbathing than sugar work he said. A year ago it was, and she still felt shame in remembering, still felt the weakness in her arms and the disgrace of needing help to finish it.

It had been Toby who'd done it for her. His skinny-strong arms had held the little one under, and one hand about her wrist had made her help with the holding too, so she wouldn't look even weaker.

He'd sat with her afterwards, under the darkest corner of under-dock and thrown stones at the big crabs to keep them away while she bawled into wood. She could still feel the piles under her arms, the big logs that kept the dock from drowning—the whistle-chant of the crabs as they circled round, the clacking of claws a punctuation to notes.

"It's shit, I know," he said.

"It'll be better next time," he said, and Alix wanted to scream at him, to pummel him with her shell-scarred hands and make him promise there wouldn't be a next time, but he'd done her the courtesy of truth-telling and to throw that back might have seen him leave her to crabs and she wasn't that far gone yet.

"Big bastards under here," he said, over the scuttling and the clack-clacking, the crustacean hunger choir, but Alix could hear the tension in his voice, the way that he turned as the crabs circled round and she didn't put them in danger of staying longer than the stones held out. The largest of them was bigger than she was, almost, with a curved shell the size of her chest and it didn't circle, that one, just stayed still as stones and watched, the stalk-eyes glaring, the claws coming together too softly to hear and that made it worse, as if it were waiting, conserving itself for the final rush and feeling the hunger rise within it. It looked at Alix as she looked at chowder—intelligently, as if she were something to be devoured, and the soft crab-crooning that came from it raised hairs all down the length of her.

"It was stupid to come down here anyway," she said, scrubbing at eyes turned small and red.

"Don't ever do it by yourself," said Toby, and she'd rolled those small red eyes at him.

"I *know*. I'm not a baby." But the truth was she'd forgotten, had run at once for the darkest place when the drowning was over and hadn't one thought for the crabs with claws thick as her arm and how they'd slice her up easy enough, the carnivorous crawlers, if they ever cornered her alone.

Now those crabs were going to eat Toby up, if they hadn't already. The useless bits of him, the kissing bits and the stoning bits, the ones that couldn't be dried and powdered up for drugs and trade.

"Perette," she said, turning over in the hammock they shared in the early morning—sunrise and sunset the only time they were able to share body heat, being on different schedules as they were, diving and fucking requiring different levels of light. "D'you think the crabs took his back?"

The other girl was silent for long moments, her body shaking with the effort not to cough. She'd had the cough for a long time and Alix worried for her, pretended not to see the effort it took to settle, the choking ropes of bloody phlegm. "Crabs don't skin that ways," she said. "It were knife work, and good work too. All the cuts were clean."

They knew what they were doing, was what she didn't say.

Perette was aging out of diving and into fishing of another sort. "It's still going down," she said, pretty-mouthed, and Alix brought her salt water to rinse with. She was lucky in that she was straight up and down still; less fat made the sinking easier and no-one was going to mistake her for a mermaid, anyway.

"What about sharks?"

"Mermaids are more likely than sharks," mumbled Perette.

"What are the fins then?"

"Dunno. But I'm not going to find out and neither are you." That, of course, was enough for Alix to risk another theft—sheer perversity, and they boiled it up together on a night so cold that there was no-one willing enough to spend coin in watching them freeze.

"Wonder if we'll grow fins now too," said Alix. It wouldn't be the first time, on the Street of Endings, with another of the shops above full of goldfish that were human, once. They fell through the cracks sometimes when the dock shifted and she'd even eaten one, when she was small, before she knew what they'd been.

Now that she knew she still ate them, given half the chance. The fish were sweet and plump and they wiggled going down, and she could say they escaped for true, take the fallen fishbowl back up to the woman who owned the place and say, honest enough, that she couldn't find the fish in the ocean no more.

"It doesn't bother me if you eat them," said the Lady of Scales one day, as Alix was slipping out the door with a fistful of small coin in her hand for the return of glass. "It's the risk they take," she said, and Alix had promised herself then not to eat any more that came down in the winds. Fearful enough to let yourself be turned into goldfish—and she understood escape, she did, but some bargains were bad no matter what you were running from—and worse to be dumped from bowl into ocean and unable to get back. Worse still to be eaten up by some starving brat—but to have the woman who'd transformed you praise the eating made the scales sour in her stomach.

"They say it was eating the goldfish turned the crabs to singing," she said. "All the souls crying they couldn't come back."

"I should think they'd know better than to go after kids then," Perette scowled. "Could be their own or near to it."

"I think someone should be sorry for them," said Alix, but Perette was less certain.

"I'm more sorry for me," she said. "If you don't want to I will." She liked to roast them on a stick over burning driftwood, char the little gold bodies until the flesh was burnt and sweet. "It's them or me," said Perette, "and if them were me they'd understand. Fish-folk know about bargains better than anyone," for if there was one thing Perette understood it was trade. "You put your body on the line, you'd best be willing to accept what that means," she said, coming back of a morning with a black eye, sometimes, or just walking funny. "It'll break your heart else," she said, and Alix would come up out of the water, wrap her in the driest blanket they had and sit with her 'til she fell asleep, even though it took hours sometimes and that was time she wasn't diving for coin or sugar or any of the other falling treasures.

"I bet they thought they'd get to be human again one day," she said. "But maybe it's better to be a crab than a goldfish?" Crabs at least were hunters, and they sang so pretty sometimes, especially when sugared up.

"D'you think they get souls from more than goldfish?" she said, not wanting the answer, not really, because they'd only left the useless pieces of Toby for the crabs and any soul they got from those was bound to be a bitty shredded thing.

"You don't know they got souls at all," said Perette. "How many goldies have we guzzled?"

Between them it wasn't many. The Lady of Scales kept a close enough eye above for all; it wasn't gimlet, but even a few should have seen a change and Alix felt no different after swallowing. If there were more souls than one sloshing about in her tummy with chowder and little bones then they'd never said nothing to her.

"Maybe they only stick if there's nowt there to begin with," she began, but Perette started coughing then and it took her too long to stop, her chest allover spasms.

"It's too damp down here for you," said Alix, tucking her spare shirt closely around the other girl and trying not to mind the shivers herself. "We'll go to the fin-man's shop." She'd learned the trick of sneaking in and there was a warm corner at the back where he dried the fins, where the remains of shark flesh hung in hundreds of triangles, in thousands of them. The trapdoor over the water was always bolted from the inside, but a board was loose at the back and Perette was not round enough yet to get caught between if she held her breath tight enough to suck in.

"I'm *'fraid* of him," the older girl whispered, but Alix had drowned before for less whining than that and she had no pity. Just hoisted her up, slid under an arm and heaved with legs used to kicking, to dodging crab-claws.

"Just to warm you up. He'll never know if we're quiet"—if they could be quiet, but Perette's cough was more silent wheezing than hack, the cough of a girl who spent too many nights outside and found it hard to get air enough for the chill in her lungs—"and he's probably not there anyway."

Lies, but learning to lie was the first step in learning to dive, before holding your breath even. Lies that said you'd come back up again alright, lies that said the crabs wouldn't get you. Lies that their singing was an ugly thing.

But the board was loose and the shop warm and Perette's lungs came easier and lying had made that happen, so Alix was all for lies then, and theft as well. No sense hiding in strings of food and starving, and the newest fins hung above, still sweating from being packed in salt for the first stage of drying. "There's too many for him to miss," she whispered and hooked one down with her fingers like crab claws, pinching the fin between. "Can't see a place for soaking, but maybe it's soft enough still," she said, and would have tried it with her teeth if she hadn't seen it in the folds: the small ink of crab-sign, and her own sight blurred around her.

"If he catches you he skins you and folds you into fins."

She hadn't believed him. No-one had, because kids were taken by crabs all the time and if there was one monster circling round there were bound to be others and there weren't much of a difference between teeth and claws when it came to meat.

Her sight stayed blurred as she pulled Perette back to the hammock, the Toby-fin tucked into her shirt. It stayed blurred as she found the kid with the knife, the one who traded Toby-parts for the use of it and she gave him the fin for a second borrowing because dead was dead and the living had to eat, regardless.

She'd eaten fins before, too.

The knife brought the world back into focus, and Alix sneaked back into the fin-shop on silent feet, let the fins brush against her as she made her way to the stairs, avoided the teeth in case they rattled. And the shark teeth *were* shark teeth, she thought, because none of hers ever looked like that but teeth lasted forever. Flesh didn't, and if the sharks were gone then no-one would know that shark fin wasn't shark fin but stitched and folded flesh, and kids were eaten all the time.

Diving was quick and silent and keeping alert, trying not to draw attention so when Alix stood over the fin-man she wasn't some small and stupid kid who'd never seen crabs up close before. She didn't make the mistake of muddying up the bottom, causing disturbance to draw the crabs. She just cut across his throat quick as pincers. Not quite deep enough, but it'd do the job if Alix left him to bleed though it didn't seem right somehow—those that never learned better should drown, and she'd been taught to drown.

"Don't draw the sharks," she sang, bending down to look in rolling eyes as he choked on his own blood. "Don't draw the cra-a-abs."

Dragging him down the narrow stairs to the trap was harder, but she managed it. Heaving him through was harder still, and when he caught hold of her ankle, one last wheezing strike, she fell through with him into shallow water, and the crabs gathering round.

Alix could see shadows of them in the dark, circling, moving, the little clicks and the beginning of song. So pretty, almost enough to lull her into stillness and she had no stones, nothing to bargain with except a body which they'd have anyway, and she knelt on the fin-man's back, held his head under to the sound of sugar shells and harmony.

There was nothing else to do when the movement stopped beneath her. Nothing but to try not to cry and wet herself as the crabs moved closer and she failed even at that when the biggest crab dragged itself through the water to loom before her. On her knees as she was, her eyes were on a level with its own and Alix recognised it then, the crooning and hungry, considering look she'd seen before under dock, the first time she'd drowned a person.

She'd left the knife in the shop, had nothing but the charm round her throat and that was a cheap thing with none of the force of ink. As the harmonies rose about her, echoed under dock, all Alix could hear was crab-song and her skin shuddered with it, with the sight of those massive claws only moments from her face, only inches from her flesh.

Then the crab began to cough. The big crab, the queen crab, and out of its mouth and into the water between them plopped a goldfish. It sank to the sand like a stunned soul and Alix caught it up, pressed it to her chest and the crab stumbled for a second, and when it righted itself it was more crab than she had ever seen, the intelligence gone and only crustacean-cunning remaining.

She threw herself backwards as the crab hurtled forward, and it would have sliced her in two with one snap of a powerful claw but the body of the fin-man was between them and the crab hesitated . . . and began to feed.

Behind Alix the smaller crabs were waiting. Still big enough to slaughter, to snip her between their claws, they nonetheless moved apart, left a small path to the nearest post. The souls of the dead, she thought. The souls of the kids who were divers, the kids who were shark-bait. Toby-souls, all wretched and ragged and she didn't know what was left of them but they recognised the fin-man, and that gave her grace from pincers even if only briefly.

Alix stuffed the goldfish into a pocket, shinnied up the post and wooden wharf supports towards the trapdoor as the crabs moved in to feed. The mussels sliced her all open, her hands and feet and stomach and her blood ran down the pole into the water below, and the smaller crabs began to gather. Staring up and singing their hunger-song, and Alix knew that if she fell again there'd be no second chance.

She didn't fall.

Instead she hauled herself over the lip of the trap, hands lacerated until they looked like so much raw meat. She set the goldfish in a chamber pot she found under the fin-man's bed, and went to wake the Lady of Scales.

"My granddad stole it," she said, lying through her teeth. "He's real sorry; gone away for a bit. A pilgrimage or some such bloody thing. Said I should mind the shop for him."

"Your grandfather," said the Lady of the Scales, taking the goldfish and decanting it from chamber pot to tank. "No-one's going to believe that, child."

Alix let herself rest on the side of the open door, too dizzy to stand straight and with her own blood slicked down her, skin from a drowning man under her fingers. "I brought your fish back," she said, trying not to cry and the Lady sighed.

"They'll believe me," she said. "I suppose he came to apologise himself. For the bad example he set to kin. I promised to keep an eye on his estranged . . . grandchild, was it?"

"It'll do," said Alix, sniffling, and reaching up one red hand to wipe away warm snot.

"It's the risk they take," said the Lady of Scales, and drew her in for bandaging and breakfast.

It was a good breakfast, but Alix learned to cook better. While her slices healed up Perette hauled in the fins of the shark shop, stacked them in the back where they'd be out of the way until needed for bait, and scrubbed until it shone clean enough for cauldrons.

"I feel bad, still, about eating them," Alix said, of the crabs that found their way to the pot. "Isn't a bit of soul still a soul?"

"Souls are only good for vengeance, far as I can tell," said Perette, standing over the pot and stirring before the lunch crowd came in. "They might have let you go for the fin-man, but there are still kids getting munched."

Alix wasn't a diver anymore, and Perette had stopped her fishing nights as well. They still heard the cries and crunching, and if they still heard the calling down from people with too much coin and too little . . . well. It wasn't as if Alix never tossed things down herself. The shop was enough to keep the two of them with only a tiny bit left over, and she might have left the rest of the kids behind but they still had to eat.

She never said it, though. At least not to them.

"We need more meat for tomorrow," said Perette. "You want to do it or shall I?"

"I'll do it," said Alix, making for the trap. She wasn't as skinny as before, but Perette was still a bigger draw for customers, and seemed to mind their pinching less. Alix had no patience for it, not after the night under dock and the memory of claws all around.

"Don't call the crabs," she sang, but crab-calling was easy enough with blood and flesh, and she had one and the shop the other. Palms pressed against the mussels beneath the trap, and it stung for only a moment, a slicing she was used to and her palms were tight with scars anyway, most of the feeling gone. Blood over the fins, the remains of kids she'd known and forgotten and Alix didn't think they'd have grudged her, their skin folded over and lowered down on chains and she hoped that all their souls were gone, wherever they were, because the giant crabs that came back up, clinging to iron and gorging on child-skin were headed for nothing but an iron spike to the brain and cooking pots.

"They're so *sweet,*" said Perette, over the pot and stirring. She sang as she stirred—a kid song, a crab song, one that they'd learned early from diving—and didn't cough anymore.

Of course they were, Alix thought, remembering the falling caramel, the lumps of boiling sugar falling from above. The crabs were scavengers too.

AUTHOR'S STORY NOTE

"The Better Part of Drowning" was first published in *The Dark*, November 2017. It's part of a series of stories I'm writing in the same setting, some of which have also appeared (or are coming soon) in *Kaleidotrope* and the *Mother of Invention* anthology from Twelfth Planet Press.

Kids have a history of being used in dangerous labour. Whether they're being sent down mineshafts or forced to dive for pearls and pennies or exploited for sex work, they have less opportunity to protect themselves than adults . . . and frequently, they have fewer options. "The Better Part of Drowning" is a story of a society of kids, literally living under the homes and housing of the adults. There's a vertical hierarchy here, one with predators above and below. There's also, for the kids, very little choice. It's risk themselves or starve, and in a world defined by that risk they develop their own ways of managing, and their own means of enforcing order. They take the slivers of power they get and use them for survival—but surviving the monsters below, the monsters they become in order to live, gives tools as well as torture. And sooner or later, those kids are going to take those tools and start looking up, because the knives that work on crabs and children work on adults as well, and they are by far the most complicit.

TIL DEATH

TIM WAGGONER

From *Never Fear: The Apocalypse*
13Thirty Books LLC.

Audrey pushed the shopping cart filled with metal odds and ends along the cracked sidewalk, her husband Edmund trailing behind her, struggling to keep up. Sweat beaded on her upper lip, despite the slight chill in the air. The temperature never varied in the World After, never grew colder, never grew warmer. But Audrey was seventy-three, and even though she worked every day and was in good shape for her age, pushing a full cart took it out of her. She had no idea how long she'd been working. Time didn't operate the same way it had before the Masters' arrival. There was no day or night now. The sky was a perpetually hazy sour yellow like diseased phlegm with no sun or moon ever visible. Audrey didn't know if there even *was* a sun or moon anymore. For all she knew, the rest of the universe might've ceased to exist once the Masters came to Earth. Without day or night, Audrey had no sense of time. She could've gathered metal for five hours or fifty. There was no way to know. She only knew that she was tired all the way down to the bone.

The thrall mark on her forehead hurt like a fresh sunburn, and her head pounded with a rhythm that almost felt like language.

BRING, BRING . . .

Maybe it was her Master's voice, maybe it was her imagination. It didn't matter. Either way, she had to make her delivery—so much depended on it. She stopped pushing the cart, released her grip on the handle, and turned around.

Edmund, her senior by eight years, was twenty paces behind her on the sidewalk. He was naked, his parchment-thin skin drawn close to his old bones. His limbs had been rearranged, so he could only move by crab-walking backward, and his head was turned 180 degrees so he could see where he was going. Not that his cataract-covered eyes could see much. His sparse body hair was wiry and snow-white, but his head was bald. Instead of a beard, thick worm-like growths grew out of his chin and cheeks. The fleshy tendrils were tipped with oozing pustules, and Audrey thought of them as pimple-snakes. They writhed with independent life, and Audrey couldn't look at them without nausea twisting her stomach. His mouth hung upon, jaw slack as if the muscles no longer functioned, and perpetual lines of drool ran from his mouth to moisten his pimple-snakes.

He didn't talk—or maybe he *couldn't*. Either way, Audrey was grateful. She had no idea how his mind functioned these days, but whatever distorted thoughts might spark and sputter inside what remained of his mind, she was glad he couldn't share them. He did make sounds from time to time: strange mournful hissings and tremulous bleats. His penis was always erect, so filled with blood it was purple-black, and a clear fluid that smelled like ammonia leaked from his ass. A line of the foul stuff trailed behind him on the sidewalk. In some ways, his body odor was the worst part. He stank like unwashed cock and balls that had been slathered in shit, and his breath was a sour-sweet reek that reminded her of rotting fruit.

Edmund hadn't always been like this, of course. Like so many things about the world, he'd changed since the advent of the Masters. So had she, just not outwardly.

It took him a while to close half the distance between them, but when he had, he stopped, gazed at her with eyes dull and lifeless as glass marbles, and lowered himself to the sidewalk. Audrey gritted her teeth in frustration. She *hated* it when he did this. She wanted to yell at him, shout that he should get his lazy ass moving, but she knew it wouldn't do any good. He understood so little these days. Not that he'd understood much in the last few years before he'd changed. She knew of only one way to get him going again, and while she was reluctant to do it, it was vital they made their delivery today . . . before she lost her nerve.

She hesitated a moment, uncomfortable about leaving her shopping cart unattended. She'd worked hard to gather this much metal, and she didn't want to risk another thrall stealing it while she was trying to coax Edmund to get moving. Then again, the longer she remained in one place, the more she risked being noticed by another thrall. Or by one of the deadly creatures that roamed the World After.

Damned if you do, damned if you don't.

She once thought she'd understood that phrase, but she hadn't known shit.

She started walking toward Edmund.

*   *   *

In the first days after the Masters' advent, and the remaking of the world, Audrey had often thought it a blessing that Edmund's mind had been mostly devoured by dementia. He remembered her—more or less—but otherwise he wasn't aware of much. In a way, she envied him. She wished she was insulated from the World After with a comforting blanket of mental oblivion.

After the Arrival, she estimated they had remained in their home, doors locked and curtains drawn, for nine days before their supplies became dangerously low. Water was the biggest issue. Something still came out of the taps, but it was thick as tar, smelled like a mixture of cinnamon and turpentine, and had a corrosive effect on both metal and porcelain. She didn't want to know what it could do to flesh. Their only food was one nearly empty container of oatmeal and a few boxes of pasta. But she had no water or electricity to prepare any of it.

One evening—or perhaps morning, it was all the same now—she lay in bed, curtains closed so she wouldn't have to look at the phlegm-colored sky outside . . . or at whatever hideous abomination might go lurching past. Edmund lay on the bed next to her, so motionless he might have been dead.

She couldn't remember the last time she had slept, was certain that she wouldn't drift off no matter how long she lay there, but sooner than she expected, her eyes closed and sleep took her. She hadn't dreamed since the Masters' arrival, but she did so now.

In the dream, she stood on a patch of bare earth enclosed by a high wooden fence with barbed wire all around the top. The white paint on the fence was old and peeling, the wood beneath gray and weathered. Mounds of scrap metal were piled at the corners of the fence, each taller than she was. In the middle of the enclosure was an open pit, ten feet in diameter, she estimated, maybe fifteen. The edges were smooth, almost as if the pit was a natural structure, though the perfect roundness of it argued against that. She stood several feet away from the pit, but she still had a good view of the inside. All she could see was darkness, so black, so deep, so *absolute*, that it seemed to actually be absorbing light, pulling it into itself and swallowing it.

Gazing into the pit caused unreasoning atavistic fear to well within her. She couldn't move, couldn't think, could only stand and watch, heart pounding rapidly in her chest like a small bird caught by a predator's mesmeric gaze.

She heard the Master's wordless voice for the first time then. It asked her a question, offered her payment for her service—unquestioning, unwavering. She spoke a single word in reply.

"Yes."

Fiery pain seared her forehead then, as if an invisible branding iron had been pressed to her flesh, and she screamed herself awake. Edmund woke too, confused and frightened. He began to shout and then to cry, and Audrey held him for a time, comforting him while her forehead pulsed with pain. When Edmund fell back to sleep, she took a flashlight from her nightstand, went into the master bathroom, looked into the mirror over the sink, shone the beam on her forehead, and saw her thrall mark for the first time. Along with the mark came knowledge: the location of the Master's lair and what was expected of her. The Master wanted her to get to work immediately, for it hungered. There was just one problem, one that she hadn't considered in her dream.

She fixed her gaze on the thrall mark's reflection, as if by addressing it she could communicate with her new Master. "I can't leave Edmund alone for long. He's not strong enough to work, and his mind . . ." She trailed off, uncertain how best to explain it. But before she could speak again, she heard

Edmund scream, a high-pitched shriek so intense it sounded as if he were tearing his throat to shreds.

She dropped the flashlight and ran back into the bedroom. Edmund writhed on the bed as his body reformed itself, bones breaking and resetting into new configurations. The transformation wasn't swift and it only became more painful as it continued, but when it was finished, Edmund had become a monstrously twisted thing, a creature strong enough to accompany Audrey while she worked. Her Master had done this somehow, she realized, in order to help her. It was, to the Master's alien mind, an act of kindness and generosity.

Audrey swallowed her rising gorge and forced herself to whisper, "Thank you," all the while unable to take her gaze off the horrible thing her husband had become.

*   *   *

The Masters had come from elsewhere. Space, another dimension, a different time . . . no one knew for certain. Some believed the Masters had ruled Earth in the far distant past, perhaps even created it to be their plaything—or feeding ground—and long ago they'd left Earth for unknown reasons, but now had returned to reclaim what was theirs. They had no individual names—at least, none that humans were aware of—and no one had ever seen a Master. No one who'd ever lived to tell about it, anyway. Most believed they possessed no physical form, not as humans understood the concept. They lived in separate lairs and worked through thralls and monstrous servants of their own creation. Thralls were rewarded for their service with food, clean water, and electricity in their homes, and while wearing a thrall mark didn't protect you from every danger in the World After, it usually gave predators—both those human and those not—pause.

A thrall's main purpose was to feed his or her Master. Sometimes this meant capturing other humans and bringing them—kicking and screaming, if need be—to the Master's lair. But Masters didn't always feed on human flesh. From other thralls, Audrey had learned of Masters that fed on blood, human waste, and specific organs such as pancreas. Some fed on inorganic objects such as used clothing, books, electronic devices, CD's, and DVD's. Some dined on more abstract fare: people's memories, emotions, or fantasies. All Audrey's Master required was metal. Any kind would do, although it was particularly fond of copper. Audrey had no idea exactly what happened to the metal after she threw it into the pit that served as her Master's lair, but she'd never heard it hit bottom.

Even though their Master gave them food and water—somehow made it materialize right in their home—Audrey was thin to the point of emaciation, as was Edmund. Masters might reward thralls for their service, but they were far from generous. They gave just enough for their servants to remain alive, and not a scrap more. And for this, thralls risked their lives day after day. But what else could they do? It was the only game in town.

*   *   *

In the World Before, Audrey's therapist had warned her about something called compassion fatigue.

It happens to long-term caregivers, she'd said. *Especially those whose loved ones suffer from conditions like dementia, which only worsen over time. You become emotionally exhausted, and—if you're not careful—that exhaustion can turn into feelings of resentment. Even hatred.*

That hadn't happened to Audrey. Not *before*, anyway. But now? Now it was hard to think of the loathsome thing that followed her around like some freakish dog as the man who had been her husband. She wanted to be free of Edmund as much, if not more, as she wanted him to be free of the nightmarish existence she'd inadvertently cursed him with.

The first time she'd tried to kill Edmund, she'd done it during a scavenging run, when she'd been picking through the ruins of a downtown office building. She didn't know what had caused the building's collapse. There was no sign of fire, no sign that something had struck the building. No wood rot, no crumbling concrete, no fatigued metal. It looked as if the pieces of the building had simply detached from one another and fallen into a jumbled heap. Edmund stayed away from the debris, guarding the shopping cart and watching as she walked through the odds and ends, searching for choice bits of metal. If anyone—or any*thing*—came near, he'd let out a loud hissing sound. She had no idea if this was a conscious warning on his part or merely an instinctive reaction. Either way, his warnings came in handy.

As she searched among the debris, she came across large shards of glass, pieces of a window that had been broken in the building's collapse. A couple of shards were the right size to hold in one hand, and one of those was the basic size and shape of a butcher knife blade. She gazed at the glass knife for a long time before finally crouching down to pick it up. She gripped it like a knife, carefully not to squeeze too hard so she wouldn't cut her hand. She was surprised by how heavy it felt, almost as if it were a real blade instead of merely a piece of broken glass. She gingerly touched the finger of her free hand to the pointed tip, then ran it along one of the shard's edges, again careful not to press too hard.

After a time, she stood, turned, and began making her way toward Edmund.

He watched her approach, no awareness showing in his milky eyes. His erection bounced several times, like he was a dog wagging its tail upon his master's return. He didn't react when she knelt next to his head. Didn't flinch when she touched the glass shard to his throat. Didn't do more than let out a soft hiss of air—was there a hint of surprise in that breath?—as she drew the shard across his neck, the sharp edge parting flesh and severing veins and arteries, bringing forth a gushing flood of crimson.

He turned to look at her then, blood dribbling past his lips onto his pimple-snakes. No expression, no recognition. And then he slumped to the ground and continued to bleed out.

She stood and stepped back to avoid the worst of the blood, but it was too late. It had spattered her clothes, slicked her hands . . . so what did it matter if the widening pool on the ground touched her shoes?

She watched her husband die, surprised by how long it took for his erection to subside. But subside it did, and Edmund let out a last choked gurgle and stopped breathing.

Heart pounding, she stepped forward and pressed two trembling figures to the side of his neck. No pulse.

She stood. She felt mostly relief, although there was some sorrow and guilt as well. She contemplated what to do with his body. He was little more than skin and bones, but he was still too heavy for her to lift. She couldn't get him in the cart, and even if she could, what would she do with him? There were no funeral homes anymore. She supposed she could bury him in their backyard, but something had happened to the grass. The edges of the blades were sharp as razors, and if you got too close they emitted high-pitched cries that sounded like tiny voices screaming. She wasn't sure it would be safe to try to dig there. Maybe if she just took his head . . .

She heard the first predator then, approaching in the distance. A simian *hoot-hoot-hoot* accompanied by a leathery sliding, as of something large dragging itself across asphalt. The scent of Edmund's blood had drawn it, whatever it was, and she knew it wouldn't be the last. At least she wouldn't have to worry about what to do with Edmund's remains now.

She dropped the glass knife, took hold of the shopping cart's handle, and began pushing it away from her husband's corpse as fast as she could.

*   *   *

She didn't have any metal to deliver to her Master that day, and her reward for her failure was an excruciating headache brought on by her throbbing thrall mark. Even so, when she got home she slept well for the first time since the Masters' arrival.

She woke to the sound of pounding at the front door. As she stumbled down the hallway, she already knew what she'd find waiting for her. She unlocked the door, opened it, and stood back as Edmund—who didn't have a mark anywhere on his body, including his throat—crab-walked inside. A thought drifted through her mind. *The cat came back . . .*

*   *   *

She tried three more times. She used an iron poker to cave in Edmund's skull. She jammed a pair of socks down his throat to block his airway. Finally, in desperation, she took a screwdriver, rammed it through his left eye into his brain, stirred it around real good, and then did the same to the other eye.

He healed each time.

She had no idea if Edmund healed because of some quality his transformed body possessed or if her Master specifically healed him each time as a way to torment her. Whatever the reason, she knew she couldn't kill him by ordinary means. To end his travesty of a life, she would need *power*. The same kind that had transformed him in the first place.

She began to plan.

*   *   *

The skin on Audrey's right hand was raw and blistered. Pushing the cart hurt, but she couldn't manage it with only one hand, so she endured the pain. Edmund followed behind her on the sidewalk, moving a bit faster now, with a decided bounce in his step. She'd jacked him off, and it hadn't taken him long to come. It never did. But while what shot out of his quivering cock looked more or less like semen, it was an unhealthy gray, stank like sulfur, and was boiling hot. Getting Edmund off was a sure way to motivate him. He'd be in a good mood for hours—but she only did it when nothing else worked, for no matter how hard she tried, she always got some of his cock lava on her. Usually on her hand, but if his orgasm was particularly strong, he'd blast like a firehose, and there was no telling where she might get hit. Today, she'd been lucky. Only her right hand and a small spot on her left wrist had been burned. Painful, but nothing that would slow her down, and now Edmund was trotting behind her like an eager puppy, cock already swollen purple once more.

Audrey didn't look down as she walked. She knew better than to gaze at the cracks in the sidewalk. Something—or many somethings—lived inside and whispered the most awful things. If they caught you looking down, they'd whisper louder. They'd urge you to do things to yourself and to others, and the longer they whispered, the harder it was to resist them. Better to not set them off in the first place.

The town's population was sparser now. Many people died during the early days after the Masters' arrival, and many more had died since. Some had been sacrificed to Masters, some had been killed by the new monstrous predators that roamed the world, and some died at the hands of their fellow survivors, people who'd been driven mad or had turned savage during their struggle to stay alive.

Because of this, Audrey saw few people along the route to her Master's lair, and those she did see were sitting in alleys or on front stoops, heads down, sleeping or—just as likely—gone deep into their minds to try to escape the horrors of the World After. Every now and again one of them would look up as she passed, and she always made sure to turn her head toward them so they could see her thrall mark. That was usually enough to make them look away and lower their heads once more.

She was aware of other creatures, moving swift and silent between buildings, or crouching on rooftops and watching, motionless and hopeful. At times she even had the sense that something was looking down at her from above, but when she looked up, she saw nothing in the sour-yellow sky. The land was filled with predators now—some large, some small, all deadly in their own ways. Her thrall mark would keep them at a distance, especially close to her Master's lair. She hoped.

Audrey had never had cause to visit the Third Street Iron and Metal Company before the Masters' arrival. She didn't live particularly close to the place, either. She had no idea why the Master who laired there had offered to take her on as one of its thralls. Maybe it had broadcast a general call and she'd answered. Maybe she'd been chosen for a specific reason, one she'd likely never know. Whatever the truth was, she'd come to wish she'd never accepted the Master's offer. If she hadn't, she and Edmund would've been dead by now, probably from lack of fresh water, but that end would've been preferable to what their lives had become. Serving as a thrall was a mistake, one she intended to rectify now.

The word *company* seemed too grand for this place. A high white wooden fence surrounded the property, with the business' name painted in red letters on one of the outside walls. A section of a wall served as a sliding door which could be closed and locked, although it was always open when Audrey came here. Since the only thing that could threaten a Master was another of its kind, there was no need for simple physical boundaries like doors and locks.

Audrey's thrall mark burned hot as fire. Her Master knew she was close, knew the *metal* was close, and it was losing what little patience it had. Audrey had heard about what happened to thralls that displeased their Masters. It made what had been done to Edmund look like little more than a mild swat on the hand.

She began pushing the cart once more, Edmund crab-walking obediently behind her.

The instant she set foot on the barren earth inside the fence, she felt the Master's power wash over her. She was officially in its lair now, the place where it was strongest. The air here seemed to ripple, like the distortion created by waves of heat rising off hot asphalt. Edmund made a small bleating sound when he entered. He was never comfortable in the Master's presence, but he always accompanied her inside anyway. She was counting on this—habit? loyalty?—now.

The ground was smooth, the path to the pit well worn, and the squeaking wheels of the shopping cart rolled easily over it. Normally, Audrey would push the cart up to the pit's edge—not *too* close—and then start lifting out pieces of metal one by one and tossing them in. If the Master was especially impatient and the cart's contents not too heavy, she might try to dump the entire load in at once. She would do neither of these things today, though.

Her Master's impatience, its lust to feed, filled her, made her thrall mark feel as if white-hot coals had been slipped beneath her skin. She gritted her teeth against the pain, gripped the cart handle tighter, and started to run. She was seventy-three, malnourished and dehydrated, but fear, anger, and determination fueled her, and she ran with the strength and speed of a much younger woman. The cart's wheels squeaked so loudly they almost seemed to be screaming. The sound of the wheels combined with the sound of her heart pounding in her ears, and she couldn't hear if Edmund continued to follow her, if he too had picked up speed, his bare hands and feet *slap-slap-slapping* the earth as he fought to keep up with her. She hoped he was.

At first, she felt only her Master's all-consuming hunger, but then she detected a hint of puzzlement. Why was this thrall approaching the pit so fast? But before the Master could command her to stop, Audrey felt the front wheels of the heavily laden cart roll over the edge of the pit. She held tight to the handle as the cart tipped forward and fell into the darkness, pulling her with it. She looked back in time to see Edmund fling himself after her, and she smiled. The Master might prefer to eat metal, but she hoped it wouldn't mind an offering of flesh. *Two* offerings.

Audrey and Edmund tumbled down through black nothingness.

*   *   *

Audrey had no idea how long they fell. She'd lost her grip on the cart somewhere along the line, and she had no idea where it was. Edmund was close by, though. She might not have been able to see him, but she could still *smell* him. More, she sensed his presence the same way she'd sometimes wake in the night and know he was lying in bed next to her without having to reach over to confirm his presence.

The vertiginous feeling of falling had subsided around the time she'd lost contact with the cart, and she couldn't tell if she still continued descending. Without so much as a speck of light, she had no way of telling which way was up and which way was down, if such directions even meant anything in this dark limbo. For all she knew, she was hanging motionless in this void, and she might remain so until she died. Or worse, she'd stay like this forever, never dying, always awake and conscious. How long could a person exist like that before going completely insane?

She tried to speak but was unable to tell if her mouth produced any sound.

I'm so sorry, Edmund. I didn't know something like this would happen. I thought we'd die.

No reply from her husband. For once, she was glad his mind was gone. If they were trapped in this place, he wouldn't go mad. After all, he was already there.

After a time—how long was impossible to say—she sensed another presence, enormous and terrifying. It was as if she were floating in a sea and a silent ocean liner had drifted close without her being aware of it until the massive craft was almost on top of her. She knew she was now truly in her Master's presence.

She felt a wave of curiosity roll forth from the Master. It wasn't a word, wasn't even a human concept, but Audrey interpreted it as a single-word question.

WHY?

She didn't have to ask why *what*.

I couldn't let him go on living like he is. And I couldn't leave him.

She sensed only continuing curiosity, now tinged with confusion, coming from the Master.

He's my husband. We belong together.

The Master's confusion and curiosity vanished, followed by a sense of satisfaction, which Audrey interpreted as a single word.

UNDERSTOOD.

Pain exploded throughout her body as her bones, muscles, and organs began to shift and rearrange. She let forth a soundless scream, but she felt a hand clasp her shoulder—Edmund's hand—and she knew that, whatever horrible thing was happening to her, at least she wasn't alone. And then she felt Edmund's fingers join with her flesh, their skin flowing together like liquid putty, and if she could've produced sound in this non-place, she would've screamed louder.

* * *

Audrey and Edmund shuffled slowly into an abandoned building. The sign out front said the place once had been a nightclub called Spinners, but since neither of them could read anymore, the letters were only meaningless nonsense. They moved on four hands and four feet, two pairs of eyes scanning the debris inside the club for any metal. Poking out from beneath a splintered table, they saw a thin half circle of what looked like . . . Could it be? *Copper!* Once, Audrey would've recognized this object as a bracelet, but now she only saw it as her Master's favorite delicacy. Audrey and Edmund were excited to retrieve the bracelet, but their combined anatomy made it difficult to move the pieces of broken wood. Yes, they had four hands, but their arms no longer bent the way they once did. Edmund carried a silver serving spoon they had found in a restaurant a couple blocks away, and he put it on the floor. The two of them then took hold of the table fragments with their teeth and slowly, painfully dragged them off the bracelet. When the object was fully revealed, Audrey leaned her head down to it. She used her thorn-covered tongue to lift it into her mouth, and then she gently gripped it between her serrated teeth. Audrey and Edmund couldn't operate a shopping cart, and so they were limited in what they could gather for their Master, but hopefully their meager offering would still be pleasing. Their Master would understand. After all, hadn't the Master made them this way?

Edmund retrieved his spoon, and they left the bar. Because of the tangled arrangement of their limbs, they scuttled and lurched instead of crab-walked, and they were more awkward than either of them had been on their own. But they'd learn to make due. Everything would be all right, just as long as they had each other. Once outside, they turned left and began heading in the direction of the Third Street Metal and Iron Company.

Together.

AUTHOR'S STORY NOTE

I originally created the World After for my novella *The Last Mile*, and I've returned to it several times since in short stories. The setting grew out of a single idea: when Lovecraft's malign alien gods finally returned and reclaimed the Earth, what would the planet become? And how would people survive in this new hellish world? I was sure at least *some* people would make it. After all, one of humanity's great strengths is our ability to adapt to different environments, no matter how harsh or unforgiving. But for those few humans who continue to live—or maybe I should say *exist*—in the World After, at what cost have they purchased their survival? Is an existence of madness and degradation better than death? Not that denizens of the World After have much time for introspection. They're too busy scrounging, fighting, maiming, and killing for their inhuman Masters, all in hope of being rewarded with one more breath of fetid air.

LETTER FROM HELL
MATT SHAW

Published by Matt Shaw

Dear Mrs. Williams,

You do not know me and I can but only apologise for this unwelcome intrusion during these difficult times for you. With the News channels hounding you and constant police activity buzzing around your home, I can only imagine you wish to be left alone—not welcoming further intrusion from people unless to do with what happened to your young daughter, Hayley.

I have been watching the events unfold via journalistic sites on the world wide web, television broadcasts and—of course—in the papers. Something like this to happen is shocking wherever it takes place in the world but, somehow, it feels worse given the fact it has occurred in our own little community. I cannot begin to imagine the stress and worry you are currently feeling and wish there was a way for me to take away the pain for you. I do not have any children so know not of the bond between parent and child but—when little Keith Bennett disappeared, murdered by Ian Brady, I felt the same feeling of empathy for his fretful mother that I feel for you. And—to this day—I can picture Jamie Bulger's mum running around that shopping centre frantically searching for little Jamie, hoping to find him somewhere. I wonder, had she found him, would she have hugged him tighter than she had ever done so before or would she have stood and berated him for wandering off? My guess is a mixture of both. An outward display of anger brought about by the relief of finding him and her own stupidity for taking her eye off of him, if only for a minute.

A minute is all it takes.

Anyway, like I said, I do not like the idea of you sitting at home and waiting by the telephone in the hope that someone rings with news. With that in mind, perhaps if I tell you my story, you will manage to find some kind of peace?

My name is Laurence Tope. I am seventy-three years old but sometimes feel as though I am older. Times were different when I was young—we used to go out without feeling the need to lock the front door, children used to play unsupervised in the streets and neighbours knew one another. Nowadays, kids can never stray far from the parents, doors and windows are double-locked and everyone is too busy with their head in their phone, computer, or other electronic device to know the names of the people living on their street. It was a simpler time when I was growing up and—in some respects—all the better for it. That is not to say it was always easy though. Companies struggled and people were continually being laid off. My own father, a man named Norman, lost his job leaving our family of six living in poverty. He was a hardworking individual, a good man. It was not his fault what happened—just one of those things. We went from having three meals a day to just two and—sometimes—one of those was nothing more than gruel without even crusts to mop up the plate. Father's mood changed for the worse the longer he remained unemployed. Daily he would go out seeking work and daily he would return home rejected. The once loving family unit became fragmented as he used to take his frustrations out on us. First he would shout and then he would hit. My brothers bore the brunt of the beatings. I guess that's one of the good things about being the youngest but it did mean my brothers grew to resent me, looking upon me as the favourite child.

I was not the favourite though. I believe father would beat them first for no other reason than they could take a harder beating than I. He was a big man and I was not only the youngest but also the skinniest. The runt of the litter, you could call me. One punch from him and I would have probably gone down, never to stand again. My father was a frustrated man, he was not a fool.

As the weeks turned to months, father was no longer able to afford the rent of our modest home and we were forced to move to new abodes. My brothers and I were crammed into the one room and my sister slept in the bed with my parents. My sister—like me—avoided the beatings. If any of the children was to be labeled as a favourite, it would be her with the way father seemed to dote upon her. Yet even so we could often hear her crying during the early hours of the morning but she would never discuss the reason. Most of the time she would even go so far as to say we had imagined it, my brothers then started teasing me saying that the new home was in fact haunted. Years later I can guess what had really been happening during those early morning hours.

Despite the new home, we were still living on the poverty line. Father was bringing in money only occasionally with odd-jobs here and there. The jobs could have been anything—painting, decorating, gardening, whatever it took to bring in some much needed income and put food in our bellies. Every night, before we ate, he would make us say a prayer. *Thankful for what we were about to receive.* We all joined in with the words but the sentiment was never there. How were we to be thankful to a God who had let our family sink to such depths? Surely we should only be thankful if father turned to us and informed us of a new full-time job, a better pay and—pushing our luck—the right to move back into the home we all missed? It didn't seem fair, or right, to thank a God who had forsaken you and yet we lied, if only to keep the beatings at bay.

As time went on, father seemed to stop seeking full-time employment. He had gotten used to the late mornings and ability to be his own boss. There was no one telling him what to do, there was no one he needed to answer to. For a man who had worked his entire life, since a young child, it was blissful—although I only truly appreciated this since retiring myself. I collect a pension but, like my father before me, I also still keep fairly active with the odd job here and there for my neighbours—people I took the time to get to know despite a weariness, or reluctance, on their part to begin with.

The money that came in—from my father's odd-jobs—was never the same as what he had received when working for a company but at least it was something. We could tell mother wasn't happy—so could father—but she never outwardly said anything. Their relationship, once warm and full of love and life, grew cold and dark. As time went on, in an evening, father would cuddle with sister as our favourite shows played through on the wireless as mother kept herself busy in the kitchen—always pristinely clean. This was our life now and—just as we had lived a life before—it was one that we seemed to settle into. There were differences, yes, but we were still a family.

Weeks turned to months, months to years. Father managed to keep the roof above our head doing his little jobs here and there. My oldest brother moved out, joining the forces, and that also helped to ease the pressure as it meant one less mouth to feed. It did have a knock on effect that meant, if a beating was due, I was now in the firing line too. I was still a slight man compared to some but was now, at least, big enough to take a beating should father have so desired. And sometimes I did, often through no fault of my own. I just happened to be there.

Occasionally father would bring a little extra home in his pay packet. With the extra money came a story that he had won it gambling. His bloodied knuckles hinted towards another, darker, alternative as to how he had secured the extras though. Again, no one said anything. For one—it meant there was more income for the house and—for another—no one wanted to accept the beating for daring to question his word. It wasn't just money that he brought home either. Sometimes he would bring us the freshest of breads, the juiciest of fruits and—occasionally—the tenderest meat imaginable. Those were good days where, with the extra food, he would also walk in with a beaming smile across his face. For a moment, if only for the evening, our old father returned to us.

I clearly remember father sitting at the head of the table as mother brought in the luxurious food for us. He would engage us, recounting stories of how he came by such culinary delights. The baker had needed the windows cleaned and, along with the usual payment, he had offered bread fresh from the ovens. The grocer needed some sanding to be done and did as the baker—first the money and then the fresh fruits of father's choosing. The butcher needed a hand with deliveries and—on days where they were heavier than usual—father would be permitted to choose a choice cut of meat as a reward for his hard work. It was never expected from his point of view but, and you could tell by the mood he returned to us in, it was always appreciated. *People looking out for one another.* Something else you tend not to find in this day and age.

Those nights—when everyone was happy and laughing, enjoying foods we were no longer used to receiving due to rising costs—those were the nights that helped to shape me into the man I am today but not for the reasons you may believe. You may believe me to be a kind, gentle soul with empathy and compassion for others but that is not the case. You see—what father said had been a lie. The hard work and the kindness of others within the community did not line our table, or stomachs, with the goods we feasted upon during those happier times. The baker, the grocer, the butcher—they did not give further reward to father for a job they had already paid him to do. We gorged because my father took. He stole for us what our family was missing. Luxurious foods that we had long since forgotten sat in our bellies due to my father breaking the trust of those he worked for. They would leave him to his task and he would fill his bag with whatever fitted. The laughter at our table—usually dark and full of despair and unanswered woes—were there due to ill-gotten means just as the laughter at my own table in recent weeks . . . Echoing through my house through similar means. My father stole to make our family seem happier. Following his lead—and not for the first time—I stole to make my own home brighter. And, for a time, your daughter did offer me a brightness of which I thought I would never tire.

Hayley was a beautiful girl. From the moment I saw her playing in the park, smiling at her friend, I had been truly captivated. Her eyes dazzled with life and intelligence and—for her age—she was well spoken and polite. A credit to you and your husband. I knew, from the moment I first saw her, I had to have her.

She was not hard to take. A little white lie, told when you popped across the road to the shop to fetch a drink, that you needed her and I was to take you to meet her immediately. She didn't know you were only across the road with your last words to her being that you'd be right back, and not where you were going. For all she knew—you had popped back to your home to fetch something. In her defence she took a little prompting to get into the van. Some reassurance that I was a friend of the family and was only doing as you had asked. She didn't even get me to tell her your name. Apparently knowing her own name—thanks to you calling it—was enough to prove I knew you.

Poor little Hayley did scream when she realised I had lied. I promised her though, if only to silence the screams, that I would be letting her return to you after an evening with me. I told her that I was lonely and wanted some company and this was the only way I knew how to get it. I didn't explain this to her but watching the way my father treated my mother—it had damaged me for my own relationships in years to come and when I did manage to find one, it never lasted long.

Hayley eventually calmed soon after. I guess it was the thought of going home, back to you and your husband, that filled her with a sense of hope. We spent the evening together and I must confess, I kept her up way past her bedtime. I made her tell me jokes and stories about your family (and it does sound as though it was a lovely family to be a part of). The way she told them, even through the fear, made me smile.

I know she has been out of your life for a couple of weeks now and I know you are missing her terribly but please rest easy in the knowledge that her suffering lasted no more than an evening. The day I took her, I have already told you that I kept her up past her bedtime. We were talking and she was making me laugh. I think it is important for you to know that I did not have sex with her. She died a virgin. That's not to say she had it any easier though.

As the evening progressed, she kept asking when she was going to return home. My answer was always the same: I would free her in the morning and—at the stroke of midnight, a new day, I did free her. I placed my hands around her neck and started to squeeze. Her eyes were wide with fear and she scratched and clawed at my hands with those tiny, dainty fingers—her nails drawing blood from my own flesh. Wounds that, even as I type, are still etched onto my skin. Your daughter, as young and fragile as she may have appeared, put up a fight. Know this though, she went home choking, crying, and scared. Had I not cut off her voice, I believe she would have been calling for you right up until the last minute. The way she spoke of you beforehand, she loved you greatly.

That night I laid with her in bed. I did not touch her. We were simply in the same bed. I stayed up for most of the early morning hours, looking at the beauty that would never age and never become ruined with the harshness of the world we live in. You may not feel so, but I did your daughter a favour. And you: I did you a favour too—not having to watch your child grow and become corrupt through outside influences of which you have little to no control.

The following morning was when I took a sharpened blade to her flesh, cutting it into manageable chunks which would be stored in both refrigerator and freezer.

Tonight, as I finish this letter, I will also finish the last of her—saving the best until last; her tender derriere. Not a single part has been wasted although, being perfectly honest and open with you, some sections were certainly tougher to stomach.

As stated at the start of my note, I told you that I wanted to bring you some peace and I truly hope that this letter does just that. You now know what happened to your little baby girl. Eight years old and forever innocent. You can stop looking now, she sleeps with the Angels—as will I by the time you read this.

I have grown weary of this world and recent news from the doctor has suggested my remaining years (if I was "lucky") are to be painful and heavily medicated with little chance of beating the poison within my body. I see little point in carrying on, stomach full of tablets and radiation flooding my weakening system. Seventy-three years is a good innings.

As I write my final words to you, I have already prepared the pile of tablets which will send me on my way. Your daughter went to the other place in a panic: Squirming, kicking, scratching, desperate. I shall venture there peacefully in my sleep.

Until our paths cross in the next life, I wish you nothing but the best and—again—hope that this letter brings you some kind of peace. What was done was not for personal reasons against you and your family. What was done was out of a need.

Kind Regards,

L. Tope.

THEATRUM MORTUUM

DANI BROWN

From *VS:X: US vs UK Extreme Horror*
Editor: Dawn Cano
Shadow Wrok Publishing

X turned on her hands and knees, offering her arsehole to any takers. Her lips brushed the floor, puckered for a kiss. If another injection didn't come soon, her arsehole would become unavailable.

Already, the first shakes of withdrawal had made her unstable. Her eyes turned up without lifting her head. If a Dragon caught her, there wouldn't be anything to get her through the night. It didn't matter anyways, none were here—unless they waited in the shadows that her eyes couldn't penetrate.

A boot came down on her shoulder blades, forcing her teeth to the floor and crushing her nose. The people sitting on plastic-covered thrones in a ring were at liberty to do whatever they pleased to her. The survival rate for the ordeal was higher, or estimated to be higher, than the death rate. X didn't have a say in it, nor was she allowed to argue her case against any act.

Hands pried apart her arse-cheeks; they were less flab and more loose skin these days. It wasn't so very long ago that they filled out even the largest of plus size clothing, thanks to her days spent having a date with the local fast food restaurants, drowning her sorrows in grease.

The land whale could sing. She would sit there, waiting for the next meal, and sing everything from metal, pop music, country, and even opera. Promises of stardom lured her away from her seat.

A nail ran down her arsecrack. It had to break through her loose-hanging dry and damaged skin before it could draw blood. Rapid weight loss brought with it folds and many layers to get through.

A foot in a pointed PVC shoe was shoved between her chin and the floor, picking up her drool for that extra bit of shine. If X looked, a distorted reflection of herself would stare back at her.

Noise from the party upstairs travelled down to the first basement. X had been up there not long ago, when she was still Xanthe and didn't know what happened in the basement. She wanted to scream out for the people upstairs to go home but knew she wouldn't be heard. And even if she was, it would be heard as part of the soundtrack—a mystery scream to get the party going and make the drugs flow.

With the shoe holding and pinning her jaw closed she couldn't scream or sing, only moan low in her throat. A titter came from above, some sinister demon in human clothing cloaked in the darkness and damp of the basement.

Plastic covered the thrones so they could be washed in bleach. When patrons were invited to bring guests, no one knew what diseases could be lurking and who might shit themselves.

When X wasn't paraded on stage as Xanthe, she was scrubbing the club from top to bottom with a toothbrush. The cum flakes on the floor—the sea of unborn babies—giggled in the dark as she washed the floors with her tears and sweat, kept from withdrawal by hourly injections.

It was attention she filled herself with when she couldn't get the greasy food. All those holes blasted in her mind needed filler to stop the memories from joining together and haunting her sleep. Standing on stage in front of an audience so large she couldn't make out the back of the auditorium, seeing them standing and applauding, made her burst with something that might have been joy or pride when she hit the final high note. The high kept the holes filled for hours after, but by the time it wore off, drugs were in place.

The director needed her to lose weight. The wardrobe department complained about the cost of fabric. Even with patrons and a paying audience, theatres were a costly business. Those extra metres of fabric could be spent elsewhere.

The cost of having the excess skin removed once the weight was gone was Xanthe's problem. She wore the skin flaps like a skirt but without any pride. Self-consciousness covered her in an aura of nervousness and shame. The skin folds were hard to keep clean and often itched with infection.

A groan, but not from her, echoed across the basement. The room in which she found herself was large and clean with low lights and curtains cutting it off from passages to other rooms and basements below—a murmur circulated among the performers. The groan could have come from anyone.

X didn't have to clean down here until a VIP chose to play with her above everyone else in the club upstairs. She knew the basement existed and that more lurked underneath. She knew nothing of what happened apart from there being an underground lake to carry her away on romantic daydreams.

The VIP rowed her across water in her best pink lingerie with real ostrich feathers. Created by the wardrobe department, it was a reward for losing weight. Skin flaps were easy to tuck in and required a lot less fabric to wrap around.

After-hours attention was another perk of the job. It kept the old memories from trying to rebuild themselves and patch the holes together. The first time she reached orgasm, she thought she might piss herself, but no one seemed to care. In the theatre, she was free to explore her sexuality, but only if she was being directed by someone else.

The performers lived together with the production staff like nurses did in years gone-by. They dined together. They played together. The theatre was used for the most raucous of parties, like the one going on above X's head.

No one ever talked about what went on in the basement. Even if X had known, she wasn't given much of a choice. Once the object of someone's sexual fantasies, the performer had no say in whether they took an active role in acting in them.

The VIP spread her legs and removed her tampon. He made it clear she was chosen for her monthly blood and not her looks when he ground the disposable cotton between his teeth and swallowed. With so many women living together, there should have been more than one on a heavy flow. That first trip to the basement, it was only X bleeding alone.

There was just enough light to see the act. The sucking sound was hidden beneath the faint waves. It might have been a figment of her imagination, until she received confirmation during act two. He forced his tongue into her mouth and she could taste the copper and uterine mucus.

She wasn't bleeding. She was close to shitting herself. Dignity had been almost completely flushed away over her stay with the theatre company. One act after another, forever stretching her limits. There wasn't much point in hanging onto that last thread of dignity. And yet, despite the variety of ways the people in the PVC thrones prodded her, she maintained it. Her arse shook. She didn't know if the vibrations travelled to the outer layers of skin for the people sat in the thrones to see. Warm air blew up her arsehole. It didn't help matters. The last thread of dignity held, and pulled tight.

X needed the ordeal to be over with. It ceased being an exploration of sexuality and became sexual assault when her tampon came out on the trip across the lake. Attention kept the blank holes in her head filled up. But this sort of attention only created new bad memories to replace the old ones.

She wanted to roll into a ball in a dark corner with the spunk. She looked up. Her first VIP was in the circle. She wasn't bleeding. He shouldn't be there. He seemed to express special affection for her, as much as someone can express affection for somebody they viewed as an object.

She forced her arms straight to look him in the eyes. He wore a mask, they all did, but she could tell it was him by the blood on his fingers and dripping from his chin. Jealousy tried to sink its claws in.

She shook. She managed to get an inch or two closer to him before being dragged back by her loose arse skin. It was dry enough to tear. Not even the infections kept it moist. They emitted an odour which made X choke on bad days.

The air pressed against her insides. She couldn't keep them as insides any longer. The last thread of dignity leaked out of her with the liquid.

Laughter travelled around the circle. X would be the one to clean the mess in the morning, once the Dragon paid a visit with her fix.

Footsteps echoed off the floor. X fell on top of her steamy mess. It would find the tightest folds of skin and fester in there overnight to make her gag in the morning.

"She's had enough now."

Salvation came. Skin on the back of her knee was pulled back. A needle connected with her vein. Warm relief swept outwards, enveloping even the furthest skin folds. There was always a knight to rescue the damsel in distress.

Bright stage lights shone into her eyes. The audience wouldn't be able to smell the puke or last night's bellyful of semen, but they'd be able to see the stains if a stagehand didn't hose her down. X still smelt ripe, even to her own heroin-dulled nose.

The fat lady was on and ready to belt out the final note. X's Dragons came disguised as people in evening wear to the night's performance. A better performance meant better drugs.

The tint of vomit surrounded her, and with it a hint of withdrawal. She needed that needle in her vein all the time. But she hit the high note without exiting stage left to puke.

She was bundled away back to her dressing room. A lesser Dragon held a needle in his hand, ready to inject her. She was new and fresh to this game.

Trackmarks decorated her arms right next to the old scars from the razor blade. The veins still welcomed the drug—there was no need to search her groin or beneath her toenails. It hit her system. It wasn't as strong as what was dished out at night, the shit that made her forget.

"That's a good girl."

X aimed to please, there was still some Xanthe hiding in her after all. Her smile spread with the heroin coursing through her system.

"There's been a change of plan for this evening."

The voice was distant, not attached to anything at all. X slumped in her chain. If only her neighbour could see her now. Some part of Xanthe locked away inside took control of a nerve centre and crossed her legs.

"The party is going to be held on the stage."

A string inside her snapped. Warm wetness rushed from between her legs.

"Wardrobe isn't going to like that."

The door slamming sounded like it was one million miles away. X was alone.

Voices haunted her and shadows danced across the wall with the flickering light. It was hard to say if she was truly haunted, or whether it was the poor quality of the drug that made her think she was. It came down to the same thing.

Her thoughts were lost in a swirling dance of green, with demons dropping in and out to say hi or simply hiss. There was shouting from outside her dressing room. It was real. X had the headache to prove it.

"There's a body in the lake."

Movement outside her dressing room found the centre of her head and shook it around a bit. Her stomach tied itself in knots. Until she learned how to source and cook her own fix, she was at the mercy of the Dragons.

"Party's still on."

A man barged into her dressing room. She didn't know who he was until she saw the tips of his fingers. Under the harsh lights, it looked like they were stained with the crimson glow of countless visits with Aunt Flo.

"Take your clothes off."

He stared her down.

"What did you do? Piss in these?"

She cringed against his loud voice and harsh words. Xanthe made an appearance when there wasn't the correct amount of H running through her system. He made a reach for her sleeve.

"Take it off."

He sounded like the whining man-child he was. They all were, the company—even the patrons.

"You're fucking disgusting."

The air of poshness and snobbery in his tone made the hairs on Xanthe's body stand up. There was too much skin hanging from X for this to register in the outside world.

X pushed herself out of the chair. There was no way to know how long she'd been out for. There was no way to mark the passing of time even without drugs, except when she was on stage.

The VIP pulled off her costume. The things were designed to be ripped off with speed and ease. Bandages held her loose flaps of skin in tight bounds to return a bit of her lost bulk.

"Take those things off."

He never gave her the chance before his bloodstained fingers started to pry at them. His nails drew droplets of blood to the inner skin folds. He noticed and went in for a taste.

"Not as good as your period."

X could've done without the assessment. He was a patron of the theatre; she had to keep her mouth shut. She'd never had a voice to begin with. Promises and assurances meant nothing when the words didn't carry over into reality.

He tore away the rest of her bandages leaving her with scratches and her stage undergarments. The wardrobe department needed to work on their laundering skills. The white had turned grey thanks to stretched elastic and a good case of crabs. They itched worse than what the neighbour had given her just when her pubes were starting to come in. Patrons still came to see them after hours. They seemed immune, like they could control who the crabs bit.

X knew better than to cross her arms over her breasts as he stripped off her bra. It was larger than her actual cup size due to the excess skin. Her nipples were nothing more than brown dots, only meeting the air on occasion.

"Take off your own underwear, fucking pig."

She bent down, digging it out of skin flaps. The smell of urine hung over them. It burnt her eyes like cat piss. Her underpants were damp, leaving her to conclude that she'd wet herself a few hours ago. Had it been more recently, there would have been a puddle beneath her and the clothes would have been saturated.

Xanthe raised her head. She wanted to throw the pissy underwear at the VIP. If he liked menstrual blood, then he should like golden showers and underwear damp with infected piss. X sent her back to her box and nailed it shut.

"Lift up your flaps like a skirt and turn around."

Her face went red. On the humiliation scale, this was up there with freezing her used tampons for his inspection.

"All the way."

He made a twirling gesture with his fingers. All X saw was the red. She wanted to feel special, but the stains indicated she wasn't his only one. He was the sort to keep different women, with different cycles locked in a dungeon so he had a continuous supply to meet his vampirical needs.

The theatre manager assured she was kept waxed and fresh down there, but everything passed in a blur of hazy green and vomit. She couldn't remember the tampons, only see them in her personal freezer, wrapped up in clear plastic just for him.

Her VIP reached with his bloodstained fingers. He had to move back her loose skin, because even down there had been fat, before he could shove a finger inside and lick. Her skin would suffocate him if he attempted to suck out her vaginal discharge.

Xanthe spent childhood as a big girl. Drowning her memories of the neighbour's wandering paws in grease had been her only escape.

One time, her mother caught her covered in dog food in a backyard paddling pool. She claimed she had been eating it, but really her neighbour had forced his Rottweiler to lick it off her. The dog's snout had penetrated her anus, resulting in a shart which he filmed. Videos like that attracted big bucks on the black market.

X didn't think any of the activities with the VIP were filmed, but it didn't make the experiences any less humiliating. No one at the theatre had made her eat dog food until she puked yet, like her mother had done. She shuddered beneath his probing fingers at the memory of lapping up the puke as her mother laughed. She'd even invited the neighbour over for a cup of tea and front-row viewing.

He slapped her skin. For loose bits, it had a lot of nerve endings. She knew better than to cry. She'd learned that lesson long ago. Tears only brought out anger in those around her.

"Hold yourself apart, you stupid whore."

X obeyed, finding the flaps of her vagina and all the excess skin they hid behind and pulled them apart until her clit and hole were kissed by cold air. She focused on the noise outside her dressing room.

"Who was it?"

Fast-moving footsteps echoed out there, taking her to a different place as the VIP risked a lick. X could kill him now, could let her skin fall and hand the victory to Xanthe. Someone was already dead, if the shouting was to be believed. Another person wouldn't matter. But this person was a patron. She would lose her Dragons along with her job and the cheering crowd that filled her up.

Her former neighbour was still out there somewhere, probably forcing dogs to lick food off her mother. She should save her loose skin for him. If anyone deserved to die between her thighs, it was him.

The VIP paid for the privilege to do as he wished. His fingers were so cold that if they hadn't been stained with monthly blood, they would have probably been blue. X could feel a circulation problem. She inhaled to stop from flinching against them.

He inserted another before pulling out and deciding his fist might be better able to determine where she was in her cycle.

"When was your last period?"

The sound of his voice came beneath the echoes from outside the door.

"Answer me."

He punched her cervix.

"You fucking junkies are all the same, why can't you stupid hoes keep yourselves clean."

He punched her again. It took all of X's willpower to stay standing. Xanthe peeked out of her box, checking to see if the coast was clear. Xanthe took the additional punches without a murmur. She didn't want X to lock her away again. She would save them both.

The door to the dressing room opened.

"Everyone needs to be accounted for. On the stage now."

Xanthe grabbed X's dressing gown. She would scrape back all the lost dignity and shove it down the VIP's throat with such force that he would also end up belly down in the lake. Xanthe had no great fear of it but some of the more superstitious performers did. Subterranean lakes were creepy. That was a fact. But their natural creepiness didn't produce the element of the supernatural, only fear did that.

It wasn't possible for her vagina to feel more open after her first three months with the company. Fisting was part of the game. Her cervix didn't appreciate the punches. It gave her a stagger as she walked.

The VIP stopped her from stumbling. As they walked he lifted her dressing gown and drooping skin. Xanthe sighed with the thought of more humiliation until the kiss of the needle and the warm embrace of heroin coursed through her again.

Xanthe faded into the background of her mind and let X have overall control. The theatre, the drug, the sex—it was X's world. If Xanthe had remained free, she could have made a run for it, dragging X kicking and screaming into the arms of a cold-turkey withdrawal.

The VIP carried her. With all the weight loss, she was considerably lighter, but the skin would have made it difficult. It was her responsibility to have it removed but the theatre didn't pay her. It was impossible to do something like that without money. Even backstreet plastic surgeons required it.

The next thing X/Xanthe was aware of was waking up on the cold, hard surface of the stage. Her dressing gown was gone. Once again, people surrounded her. This time, however, they were all men. With her skin rolls on display, she must have looked inviting.

Everywhere there were raised arses, with penises shoved violently in them. Xanthe sunk down into the depths of X's mind where she couldn't see or feel. X could handle it. This was her world, her dream; the sacrifice made for stardom.

"Who died," she whispered.

The man sweating into her shoulder and dripping warm sticky drool onto her chin heard.

"No one knows."

He went back to her pumping action. People tried to join the company every day, despite there never being an audition. Some new hopeful must have broken in and had an accident in the lake. Xanthe piped up then from the place she was hiding, *you know that's not what happened.* X's eyes went wide with understanding.

Her skin was heavy with cum shots. She wondered how many she took while she'd been passed out and how many more were to come. There was a party around her, past the pumping men. No one would miss her once they were bored with her skin rolls. X laid back and took the spunk.

Xanthe didn't want to let her in. There were plenty of dark spots in her mind to hide, blasted holes left by memories blown away by heroin.

X's eyes opened to the catwalk above. She was sure to project everything she saw into Xanthe, along with the warm sperm looking for an exit from her skin folds and the explosive display of diarrhea from the night before. Someone, most likely the theatre director, had pulled the body out of the lake and strung it up there. X had learned to never question and always accept early in her career. Existence was easier that way.

The body's glassy eyes stared back at her. It had a bloated stomach and death's erection. Xanthe closed her eyes but X could reach right into the centre of her brain to give her a taste. Even in death, the man could be used. Nothing went to waste in the theatre.

Fluid from above dripped on her. It seemed cold. Xanthe piped up with declarations of the chill being her imagination—*the fluid could very well be warm cum and the cold of withdrawal.*

X knew better. She watched the drop fall from the man's nose. Another came off his belly and yet more from his cock. Whoever had strung him up, facing the stage, hadn't bothered to dry him off. X supposed he had been hung to dry.

Another man joined the circle fighting for a place to fuck her skin. The smell from the new guy travelled through X's nostrils and straight to Xanthe. It transported her back to the smell of rain-soaked dog and the cackle of her mother's laughter. X was just a figment of Xanthe's imagination back then. She could be turned on and off. It wasn't until the heroin that she took over.

The man didn't fuck, he licked and nuzzled, pulling Xanthe out of her hole. X immediately filled the spot, leaving Xanthe to confront her past head on. She looked out of X's eyes, not feeling the withdrawal of heroin. The men around her looked up from their skin fucking, sensing something was different.

Xanthe couldn't force the shakes. They noticed. She could feel it coming out of their pores and the cocks of those who came. They didn't stick around for round two (or possibly three or four). There were plenty of other things to do on the stage. Xanthe could hear the noises.

She tried to focus on the girl screaming and the body above her. Anything to rid her mind of the man wearing socks over his ears like puppy-dog ears. His eyes peeked above a plastic snout. They had the penetrating glow of all she'd tried to run away from.

She banged on the door to X's cell demanding to be let in. X opened the window to flip her off before slamming it shut again. Xanthe needed to face her demons for them both to be free.

It didn't seem possible for it to be a coincidence. Her mother was of the sort to sell her secrets to the company. The other men finished up, covering her in semen.

"Come back, please come back."

Xanthe's voice sounded foreign to her own ears and small. Even her

VIP with his crimson fingers had left her alone with Dog-Boy.

She thought she heard barking but that could have been a backing track blaring from the speakers beneath the stage, put there by her mother. She couldn't see out into the auditorium past the golden circle. There were many shadows for her to watch, and to be watched from.

Cold, wet meaty chunks were dumped on her. The smell of dog food embraced her. Tears streamed down her face.

"Now, now beautiful Xanthe, don't cry."

She cringed against his touch on her cheek.

He shouldn't have been able to get it up any longer, but she could feel his erection pressing into her skin folds.

The shakes and stomach cramps of withdrawal reached Xanthe. She'd been the first one to take the drug. She needed it now.

A drop from above landed on her forehead and dripped down, mixing with her tears. The dead guy was better than Dog-Boy. Withdrawal was better than Dog-Boy.

He held something in his hands and affixed it to her ears. When he glued rubber to her nose, the outside scents were dulled. The result was dizziness.

She focused on the dripping body's dead erection and bloating stomach. She thought she saw a cockroach crawl across him. That might have been her imagination conjuring something to distract her mind, if not her body. Stress and withdrawal were never a good combination. She thought, what with the body hanging belly-down, it would have made more sense for the cockroaches to crawl across his back.

Dog-Boy was turning her into a dog. Her stomach wouldn't be able to handle a doggy-style pounding. Dignity meant nothing to her if by shitting herself she wouldn't have to feel him inside. Her stomach stopped turning with the thought. Typical—just her luck.

"Why are you crying sweet Xanthe?"

She didn't respond to stupidity.

He licked meaty chunks from her pale body. Some sank into her folds of skin and wouldn't be seen again. The smell would remind her when they began to rot. He went in for a kiss, still with a mouthful of dog food. She threw up in her mouth but that didn't put him off.

He looked up and noticed the body for the first time. Xanthe held the vomit. She was waiting for the best time to spit. Dog-Boy stared at the corpse. She wanted the puke to hit his eyes. The sounds of fucking reached through her muffled ears, along with Dog-Boy's panting breath.

The sound of creaking from above was loudest of all. It was said people weigh more in death than when they were alive. Whatever he was bound up there with was starting to snap.

Everything in the theatre was cut-price. Heroin, even with the special deal with the Dragons, was expensive. Despite how much money each performance pulled in, most of the money went to keeping the actors compliant.

The dead man's arm fell first, dropping fluid and cockroaches onto Xanthe and Dog-Boy. At least it hadn't detached from his body.

She pounded on X's door. There was no response, not even a cackle of laughter, from her creation. Parts of her brain blasted away, filled up with painful old memories and set a display of remembering. It wasn't safe in there either.

She kneed Dog-Boy in the groin. It was an action she'd wanted to do for a very long time. Although X/Xanthe never remembered them, it featured in her most pleasant dreams.

"Feisty, are we? I like that."

A dead man falling on them would be worse than being covered in dog food. She had to make her former neighbour realise it. The chance of building a life for herself, away from the theatre, heroin and orgies, depended on it. She couldn't have life if she died beneath the dead man's falling weight.

"Look up you fucking child-raping idiot."

She didn't lose a drop of vomit but instead, held it under her tongue.

"Hit me, here."

He pointed to his cheeks. Xanthe spat her puke at him.

"Is that the way we're going to play it?"

He held his small member in his hand. She couldn't see it throbbing but knew it was. Another arm came loose from above, dumping with it cockroaches and liquid—a combination of blood and the water from the lake.

Xanthe was never one for sticking fingers down her throat and puking up the excess grease she ate in her former life. She tried now though. Her gag reflex was strong, but not strong enough.

She squirmed beneath the weight of her former neighbour. He splattered her in a spray of cum. That was enough to make her vomit with such violence she was forced to sit up. Dog-Boy tumbled off her.

"Put up a fight like you used to, before you accepted it."

She wasn't putting up a fight for his pleasure. It was pure self-preservation. The old self-harm scars and loose flaps of skin kept the trackmarks hidden, but that didn't mean Xanthe wanted to die. Being crushed to death by a falling body was not the way to go out even if she did. With escape, there was a chance of a future.

She pulled her legs out from under Dog-Boy, even as he was trying to climb back on top of her. He took the opportunity to pull on the skin covering her ankles, putting his hands in some other guy's cum.

Xanthe pissed herself. After a month of after-hours parties, she could pee on demand. The urine did nothing to lube up the floor and aide in her escape. Dog-Boy laughed, bent over and lapped it up.

Xanthe threw herself from side-to-side, trying to get away. The next time she looked up, the body was dangling by one leg. She looked around. Everyone was too high on drugs and pleasure to notice her struggles and the body above them.

"Let me go."

She was screaming. If anything, the struggle should attract the attention of the theatre director. When he came over to punish her into submission, she could point out the body. He was nowhere in sight, most likely otherwise occupied. There was no knight in shining armour for Xanthe.

Dog-Boy pulled flaps of skin around her vagina looking for entry. Xanthe screamed. He hurt. She needed the attention of someone who could save her.

He forced dog food inside her and into her skin rolls. The centre of her attention was seized by the sound of cords snapping above. If X wouldn't let her in, she would project their death to her with extra concentration.

Dog-Boy couldn't hurt her again. He panted on top of her and dripped his drool all over the loose skin protecting her breasts. There would be some cushioning from the falling body.

Dog-Boy's dick was so small, she could hardly feel it at all. A long time ago, it was the source of the blood of her cherry-popping. She'd wanted to lose it learning to show jump like all of her friends, but the neighbour had had different plans. She hadn't even met her Aunt Flo and only had little rosebuds to grab onto. She'd been a skinny thing before drowning her sorrows in grease.

His cock had been so large then for someone of Xanthe's frame to take. It was the first she'd seen, so had had no comparison to one of average size.

Xanthe found herself laughing. Dog-Boy really was a nasty old man, even back then. Now somehow, he seemed worse, if only for his patheticness. She thrashed beneath him.

"I like that baby. I like that real good."

Could he get anymore creepy? She kicked. She threw up her knees to hit his pumping arse. She still couldn't feel his cock—not inside her, not in any one of her numerous skin rolls either.

"You want it harder."

It wasn't a question, more of a statement. It sounded like he was trying to make dirty talk. All he did was make her laugh harder.

X opened the peephole of her cell. It could have been a ruse designed to lure her into taking his seed. She rolled backwards in hysterical laughter. This was the neighbour that had caused her creation? He was outright pitiful.

She opened the door to her cell and joined Xanthe on top—two sisters united in mind as well as in body. They twisted Xanthe's hand around, catching the loose skin on the floor of the stage. It was in the way.

They yanked his balls as he pumped away on top of her. His drooling tongue licked the loose skin hanging from her face.

He was obviously feeling something Xanthe wasn't, until suddenly his pupils dilated and he let out a howl. He scrambled off her, trying to free his scrotum. She tore her nails in. He scratched at her hand. His nails had been shaped into dog's claws. Xanthe couldn't feel them and neither could X.

They were aware of the body swaying above. A second after they released Dog-Boy's balls, they rolled over and the body crashed down. It didn't splatter and landed with its erection facing up. X was the one to take in the information.

Xanthe usually remained in her hole except when they were on stage. She wouldn't know what could be done with a dead man's erection in a place like this. X pulled them to their feet. She knew the theatre better. Clutched by the stomach cramps and shakes of withdrawal, she was going to get them out of there.

She managed a few steps before she was tackled by her former neighbour, panting in her ear as he pulled her down. He pulled back the skin protecting her anus and shoved his cock in. She couldn't feel it. It was too small. She pulled herself on her elbows with him humping her and, she assumed, deriving some sexual pleasure from his actions.

"I love it when you squirm."

X/Xanthe didn't care. She pulled herself right over to the shiny shoes of a patron. She tried to move out of his way but it was too late, she was spotted.

"My, my, what do we have here?"

He snapped his finger and a Dragon appeared out of a curtain, needle in hand. She didn't have any choice. The drug won every time. She tried to conjure up the will to wave the hand away. She couldn't. It hit the system before X/Xanthe's shared bowel turned to liquid.

Dog-Boy was pulled away by the Dragon and patron. X/Xanthe was dragged to her feet. She couldn't walk. Her toes dragged along the floor, picking up splinters. Stage varnishing was something the male performers were responsible for. They didn't do a very good job.

She focused on the splinters to clear her mind. It was of no use. She kicked. She didn't want to be anywhere near the theatre, being dragged back to the body. The two men picked her up under her arms and grabbed her ankles. She could squirm, but in the air, all it did was sway the skin flaps.

Eyes burrowed into her from all around the stage and below in the golden circle. It looked golden tonight. Someone had covered it in blue tarps and filled it with water from their bladders. X/Xanthe focused on that.

They were in this together. A golden shower, or bath, in this case would be preferred to the body.

"No, no, you can bathe afterwards, if that's what you want."

A third man joined them—her former neighbour. He pulled flaps of loose skin away from her vagina as the other two planted her. She could feel the dead guy's erection. It was cold and not throbbing, but as large as a novelty dildo.

The men stood around her, pulling her, pushing her, making her ride the cold hard cock. They forced her head down and her eyes open to look into death's eyes staring back at her. They were empty, just like everything else and all the promises made.

Clammy hands with fur cuffs grabbed her arse skin and pulled it away from her anus. The snout bounced off her shoulder as Dog-Boy jumped onto her, scoring a direct hit for what might have been the first time in his life.

The cold hard cock in her vagina filled her up and pressed against the wall. It meant she could feel the former neighbour's cock for the first time since she was a little girl and he'd set his Rottweiler on her.

With two other men directing her actions, she wasn't allowed to reach around and grab his balls. To throw him off would mean being an active participant in riding the corpse. X/Xanthe tried to conjure another personality to take it but none of the half-formed creations took the bait.

Another needle found a vein. Her body fell over onto the dead man. Dog-Boy's thrusts became faster and then he collapsed on her, pulling his dick out. The other two men left her slumped over the body as they pulled him off and threw him into the golden circle with a splash. It was too far away for the piss to reach X/Xanthe and revive her.

For once, her mind stayed awake whilst her body slept. The two of them together shared control, but neither could move her pelvis enough to release the dick.

She watched the men's feet as they moved back. Black shoes polished to a mirror shine and snakeskin boots. The snakeskin belonged to the Dragon, to match his personality.

"We got rid of the wannabe furry for you, we deserve a reward."

X/Xanthe was pulled to her feet. She swayed. She couldn't hold herself up.

"Watching that gave me the biggest hard-on of my life."

"She's in no position to suck anyone off."

"Well I don't want her pussy after it's ridden that corpse."

"Well I don't want her arse after that guy went in. He had fucking fleas."

The shadow scratched at its arms. X/Xanthe listened to flakes of skin falling off above the noise of the party all around her.

"Her skin's had too many cocks tonight."

A new shadow joined the floor from behind Snakeskin Boots. X/Xanthe knew what it was from the shape. She'd seen enough of them in her life.

"I have something better for her."

He pressed the knife against her spine. She couldn't feel the pain of her skin being sliced away.

"But first, we need to get rid of some of the excess."

She watched him place it in neat little piles on the floor.

"Don't step on it. I want a mask."

She tried to roll away. The men performed the skin removal surgery she'd never been able to afford, but this wasn't going to end well. She could feel it on the air.

She couldn't move at all. Her own death would be slow. Slower than the man found in the lake. Drowning took a matter of minutes. X thought they'd be there for hours. Xanthe agreed.

"This is fucking disgusting."

Liquid dripped on her from her own skin. It could have been anything.

"It's mouldy."

"Oh my god, there's new fucking life forms in there. We should send a sample off to a lab."

More footsteps echoed off the stage. People were coming over to view the happening, or maybe join in. If anyone offered help, something worse would befall them.

"Now what?"

"Roll her over, there's more skin."

They used their hands to turn her. X/Xanthe thought they'd have used their feet. Hands were too tender, like a lover's kiss. But shoes that shiny and expensive didn't want to be damaged.

Slicing away skin on the front went much in the same way as slicing it away from her back and sides.

"She still isn't clean."

"We aren't going to fuck her."

The knife pressed along her belly button, which hadn't seen the light since heroin found her. The blade cut into it and sliced along. Warm hands pulled back that final layer of skin.

There was no pain. Not even when searching hands rearranged her organs. They found what they were looking for and pulled. Her small intestine was pulled out but only so far.

"Bring me a sheet."

Footsteps scurried away. A minute later they returned. The sheet created a small breeze as it fell to the floor. X and Xanthe were at peace with each other and themselves. They found joy in the breeze reaching and caressing her skin. It had growths on it, yeast infections and mould, but it was freer now than it had been in years, if ever.

The sheet was placed next to her.

"You there, and you, help us put her on it. Be careful of her guts, we don't want her to die just yet."

Hands reached underneath her. She was lifted into the air and took in the pleasure of feeling it between the growths. She was placed onto the sheet. She felt the weave of the fabric. It didn't have a high thread count—nothing in the theatre was as good as it appeared. Everything except the after-hours parties were built on illusions.

"Careful now everyone."

She was wrapped in the sheet and lifted into the air again with her intestine hanging out. Black dots appeared over her vision. It wasn't enough to claim her. She didn't move as the sheet was carried up various flights of stairs, up into the rafters. Even if she'd wanted to, she wouldn't have been able—paralysis and disembowelment did that to a junkie.

More black dots had formed into smudges by the time she was laid out on the floor. More of her intestine was yanked out of her midsection. Her eyes caught sight of the end being tied to a railing between black dots and clearing grey clouds.

A boot kicked her over an edge. Her intestine unravelled. Grey clouds and black stars claimed her eyesight.

X and Xanthe held onto each other as they tumbled through her mind to the cell. They locked themselves in. If pain came at the end, they didn't want to feel it. They didn't want to know what was happening as the body shut itself down.

Together, they conjured up a beach in some sunny climate but it wasn't all that it seemed. The water washing on the shore was golden, not with sunshine but with piss. The sand was dried cum. The rocks, shit. Shells, hollowed-out preserved shit. They weren't left for the hermit crabs but for the crabs that had formed themselves together into one big creature with itching on its mind. Even death's fantasy couldn't offer Xanthe release.

Together X and Xanthe prayed for the reaper to show up, holding each other and holding their noses shut. When they were in her mind, they didn't share a body. The darkness finally embraced them and carried them away together.

AUTHOR'S STORY NOTE

I had the character X in my head, a weird tribute to *The Story of O* (a book

I never liked) with the name, but not the character. I started the story a few times, but it never flowed right. I left for the day job, after yet another morning of moving the sentences around on the page. I was in a particularly foul mood. This foul mood impacted how I tortured that character. I wanted her to die. If I could have brought her back and killed her again, I would have.

I was at the day job for sometime between fifteen minutes and half an hour, when the story decided it was ready to be written. It was the body in the lake bit, which appeared first. The rest of the story worked around that. I held that image in my mind until I arrived home.

Luckily, it was one of the days I was only in for two hours and close to home. I had to stop at the supermarket on the way home, as I did plan on eating that day. I'm not a very good runner. I'm a pretty overweight person. I don't run. I can't run. I don't think anyone has ever seen a fat woman in a dress skipping and twirling down the street (sober, by the way) as quickly as I was. I didn't bother to put away my groceries and stopped at a sandwich shop for my lunch, premade and to take away. I sat down at my computer. I didn't bother with the thousand or so words written already, those were closed, never to be looked at again. The story poured out in one afternoon. I cleaned it up the following day. I don't know at what point X's personality split into two. It wasn't X and Xanthe when I left for the day job.

I was aiming for most extreme in *Vs Extreme*. I don't know if I obtained it. I was pretty nervous sending this one in. I'm usually not nervous about writing; two things could happen—it'll be accepted, or it won't be. So, that was unusual. I don't think I realised what I had written until it came down for my round to be judged and I won. I don't often win anything and I've never actually addressed my own fears of not being a particularly good writer.

BREAK

GLENN GRAY

From *Hard Sentences: Crime Fiction Inspired by Alcatraz*
Editor: David James Keaton
Broken River Books

The first self-inflicted fracture was the middle phalanx of the right fifth digit, but that was just a test. It didn't matter because it would have nothing to do with the job. Bone snapped easily with just a slight jerk, as if cracking a knuckle. It fractured swiftly and effortlessly, and surprisingly without much pain. I'm no stranger to fractures. A good part of my childhood was spent in hospitals and doctor's offices, showing up with bones broken due to forces that seemed no greater than a strong gust of wind. It started early on, as a toddler, and continued into my teens until things got sorted out. I always figured my bone issues were probably why I chose to become a doctor in the first place, thinking it would give me some kind of control, of which I had none.

I was born with a mild form of *osteogenesis imperfecta*, better known as "brittle bone disease." Genetics gave me bad collagen. Fractures were a regular occurrence, a routine part of my life, and the whole thing didn't make for a particularly active or happy childhood. I probably shouldn't complain too much because children born with more severe forms of the disease typically don't make it past their first month.

And it turns out, my brittle bones, in conjunction with my medical knowledge, became quite useful when I arrived at Alcatraz in July 1941. I laugh sometimes thinking my bones were also why I was there in the first place, angry at the cards I was dealt, huge chip on my shoulder. But that's a horse of another color. This story, the one about the prison, won't be found in any history books or newspapers, but it should be because I'm the only person ever to escape from Alcatraz and survive.

Well, sort of.

*   *   *

The first key was that the warden took a quick liking to me. My appearance was unintimidating, and I could be charming and affable when I wanted. My face had the classic physical features typical for the disease: triangular in shape, with a broad forehead and mild mandibular prognathism, or subtle underbite. The whites of my eyes had a blue tinge. But if you passed me in the street, you would think I was sort of funny looking and probably carry on, forgetting you ever saw me. I was average height, only achievable with mild forms of the disease. And due to prior fractures, my arms and legs had slight angulation deformities. My chest also had a barrel shape. And I possessed mild thoracic kyphoscoliosis. All in all, a perfect storm of impediments.

The next key was that I was a well-respected physician prior to incarceration, albeit with an anger issue. I made sure I was a model prisoner and behaved myself, easy with the "yes, sirs" and the nods and smiles. As a result, the warden singled me out. Not infrequently, he called me to his house in order to attend to minor medical issues for him and his family. He seemed to value my opinion much more than the prison docs that were usually just out of training, and besides, they never lasted that long, running back to the safety and tranquility of civilian life at the first hint of danger.

The real reason he requested me was his daughter, Mindy. Most people weren't even aware that she existed. It was obvious to me the warden was ashamed of her and kept her hidden. I was often called to treat her physical ailments, like pressure sores, contractures and bouts of mild pneumonia. She was twenty-one when I first met her. Her body was ravaged by childhood polio, but I thought she was beautiful. The first time we met, I saw nothing but warmth, and I knew right away she felt the same for me. It was as if we connected through our deformities, our ugliness a response to the world at large.

*   *   *

Apart from the bones, I had other medical issues, things I didn't divulge. I didn't want any unnecessary attention or questions, but I also had celiac disease, an intestinal malabsorption disorder. As a result, my intestine had problems absorbing calcium and vitamin D, a double whammy with the brittle bones, but a blessing and a curse, as I later discovered.

The celiac disease was also the main contributor to my pale, anemic coloring, a lack of vitamin D and B12, adding to my odd appearance. Because of my unusually white skin, I was referred to as Casper the Doc by fellow inmates, like the cartoon, or sometimes "Doctor Ghost." Eventually it was shortened to just "Casper."

I had been taking phosphates, vitamin D, and calcium supplements for years, in order to help prevent fractures. That and exercise, mostly walking and swimming. But when I arrived at Alcatraz, I stopped taking my supplements and cut out any dietary sources of calcium. I avoided the sun at all costs, wrapping myself up like a mummy anytime I was in the yard, as sunlight was necessary for vitamin D activation, something I was now denying my body. Everyone thought I was weird and quirky, which was perfect. Inmates kept their distance, and the warden thought I was a harmless loner, but my overall goal was two-fold:

I would lose weight and allow my bones to revert back to their tragic, weakened state.

*   *   *

As I sat in my cell and fractured my pinky finger, it dawned on me that I was ready. Sitting there on my cot, I shifted the fracture fragments back and forth, embracing the sense of freedom this new motion signified. It was the dead of night, and I glanced at the dinky sink, metal toilet, the 5x9 foot space and thought, *20 more years? No way.*

Pinching the middle phalanx on the opposite hand, I gave it a swift twisting jerk. There was a soft snap and another new motion.

The fragments, now as free as their brothers, glided right past one another.

I noted a subtle skin bruise at the fracture site, much less than normal, likely because the bone had diminished vascularity, and as a result, less oozing.

I stood. Shuffled to the bars. Grabbed cold metal with both hands, evaluated the width once again. Turning sideways, I passed my arm through to the shoulder and assessed the depth of my barrel chest. Turning forward, I pushed my face into the space between the bars, the metal squeezing my skull and my head stuck at the junction of the frontal and parietal bones, just above the squamous portion of the temporal bone. This was good.

The horizontal cross bars were a definite nuisance and created a dilemma in that the overall height of the space was cut in thirds, so I would have to squat and straddle my body to get out. Options were going out headfirst, front-way, or legs first and backwards. I needed to think about that. I put a leg through sideways until the bars met my pelvis. Anteriorly, the pubic symphysis would be an issue, so I made a mental note of the width of my pelvic girdle.

After full analysis, I sat back on the cot and set about doing some serious fracturing. Each night for two weeks, I fractured the same bones over and over, not allowing them to fully heal, but instead building a soft bridge of callus. I fractured the fourth through eleventh ribs on each side laterally, resulting in a vertical line from the armpit down. Each snap was easy, a short push with a fingertip, sometimes three pushes, each time a little harder than the last, right before the pop. These fractures allowed the front half of my rib cage to ride over the back half, like some kind of bony piston, and narrow my thoracic cage significantly.

The pubic bones required multiple fractures, two spots on each side, given the osseous configuration of a pelvis was akin to a pretzel, so it wouldn't normally deform. I had to fracture both the superior and inferior pubic rami. This allowed the front half of the pelvic girdle to ride past the posterior portion, and, like the chest, narrow the front to back dimension. These fractures were hard to achieve given their location. I couldn't just push like with a rib. I found the best way was to squeeze between the bars and force myself in until the cracking started. First on the left, then right.

The hardest part was the skull.

I only did it once, to make sure it worked. I had to be careful the fracture line didn't extend into the squamous temporal bone and lacerate the middle meningeal artery. The result would be catastrophic, ending up with an epidural hematoma, death almost instantaneous, my head probably outside the bars straddling my neck when I was found cold and stiff in the morning, like I'd hung myself between the metal. Embarrassing. I was not suicidal.

The skull fractures needed to be horizontal and high, so the inferior bony plates would push in under the superior plates, narrowing the key part of the calvarium. I did this by sitting alongside the cot, pushing the mattress away to expose the metallic edge, then imagining a line along the calvarium. I whacked my head sideways into the metal edge over and over, like some kind of desperate mental patient, of which I was neither.

It was the hardest fracture of all to achieve. The calvarium, even diseased, is thick and built to protect from exactly what I was doing to it. Eventually, it fractured. While banging the opposite side, in my excitement, I knocked myself unconscious on the fourth and final blow. I woke up on the cold floor in a daze, staring at the ceiling, just in time to crawl back in bed before the guard's perimeter walk.

*   *   *

The final key was Mindy. I said we connected immediately, but it was much more than that. We were in love. I knew from the moment I was called over to treat a decubitus ulcer on her lower back. Her left leg was paralyzed, the right partially, and she had poor sensation from the waist down, so she often developed pressure sores. One of her arms was severely spastic, causing her elbow and wrist to curl forward. Surprisingly, she was able to walk well with a cane, despite the bulky metal brace on her left leg.

When I arrived that first time, she was on her stomach, and I evaluated her gaping wound. Bad decubiti are typically hard to look at, even for a doctor. The smell, the pus, the dead skin and exposed flesh and bone. But when she rolled over though, our eyes met and it was glorious. All I saw were her eyes, wide, stunning, symmetrical orbits, full of wonder. She gazed at me and our line of vision was awkwardly locked in place, like a tightly tethered clothesline, until the warden, who was standing nearby, cleared his throat. He knew right away what had happened, and I believe he was pleased. He must have been, because I was asked back, again and again, and my love for Mindy deepened each time. We shared only one furtive kiss when we were alone for nine glorious minutes, but that was enough.

Over time, I whispered to her my plan to escape, and we spoke about spending the rest of our lives together once I was free. But first, I needed her to do one thing. I needed her to hide a raft and life vest at a particular spot along the shore on a particular night. She resisted at first, but ultimately agreed. After many evenings in the library, I became an expert on every current, tide, and weather pattern around San Francisco, and, specifically, around the Rock.

When I finally chose a week, a day, and a time, I was so excited that I almost risked cracking my knuckles.

*   *   *

On the night of the escape, I fluffed and arranged blankets and clothes in my cot to appear as if I were sleeping. Approaching the bars, I put my right leg through and shifted until my pelvis stuck. My original plan had been to go through legs and pelvis first, then chest, and head last, but I changed my mind at the last minute. I would put my arms through first, as if diving, then my head, then squiggle the rest of the way through. If I was able to pass my skull through first without a problem, then I figured I would be fine, and the rest of my body would follow me to freedom.

Withdrawing my leg, I got on my knees. I extended my straightened arms out, palms together, and slid them through the bars. I twisted sideways, but turned my head so that I was face out. My skull met the bars and stopped. Snug. I was able to bend my arms back and grab the bars from the outside, to get some traction, and I shifted my legs so that my feet were on the floor, bent as if at a track meet, ready in the starting blocks. Firming myself up, I waited a moment and took a deep breath. Closing my eyes as I exhaled, I pushed and pulled and heard the crackle of cranial plates, and a lightning bolt of pain flashed through my head as my brain squished inward. I actually felt my brain pulse, as if it was drawing breath, as I grew dizzy.

A dribble of saliva leaked from the corner of my mouth right before I passed out.

I woke a few minutes later, I think. I couldn't tell how long I'd been out, hanging there between the bars, but I hadn't been discovered, arms and head dangling, my worst fear. I regained my bearings and returned to work. I shimmied sideways so my sternum pressed against one bar, and my back, at the mid thoracic level, was at the other. I braced myself with arms and feet and pushed until I couldn't move anymore, and with a victory grunt lurched forward. With loud snaps, crackles, and pops, the anterior and posterior halves of my rib cage shifted over each other and choked the air from my lungs, compressed my heart so I was lightheaded again, and short of breath, pulse stuttering like a backfiring car. I thought of Mindy, and my heart grew tight as a fist.

And as I passed through the bars and the rib cage retracted outward, the air pulled in with a great whoosh and rivers of blood re-expanded my heart and it sped back up like a jackhammer. I hung there, slumped sideways up to my mid abdomen now. It took me a half hour to regulate my body and convince my organs to stop their revolt and regroup.

Eventually they agreed. We were all in this together.

Needing to work fast now, I wriggled and heaved my pelvis in between the bars, locking it in place. This awkward position made it harder, didn't allow for a good thrust from my legs, still thrumming in their starting blocks. I would have to rely more on arm strength, of which there never was much. And there was new pain growing in my chest with each movement.

I managed to get a hand around a bar, the other palm flat on the floor, and I inhaled and exhaled deeply as I yanked forward. The bones didn't move. I rested a moment and tried again. This time I tried harder, and I heard a crunch, but it wasn't enough. I waited a moment and sensed something, and when I looked around, I saw the prisoner next door glaring at me in horror. I brought a broken finger to my lips, imploring him to remain quiet, but something like a boat motor erupted from my mouth. He just shook his head at the ghost suspended between the bars, maybe a sight not unfamiliar to a prisoner after all.

I drew in a deep breath and knew that this time it had to work, as men were waking up, and I was running out of time. I thought of Mindy again, and pulled with all my might. I couldn't get a short quick pull, which was preferable, only a long, drawn-out motion, but I didn't care, as I heard the crackling and grinding of bone on bone and the shift and thud which compressed my bladder and sigmoid colon. Urine and stool leaked from my body as I passed through with a triumphant but protracted groan.

I fell to the ground with my ankles draping the cross bar, the not-subtle smell of bodily fluids seeping upward into my nostrils, mercifully jarring me awake like smelling salts. My breath hitched and coughed, each inspiration accompanied by shooting pains into my chest. But I couldn't let that bother me. I clambered to my feet, clutching the bars for assistance and stood tall a moment, gathering myself, the prisoner on the other side of my cell now wide-eyed and agape.

I started to stumble towards a sliver of sunlight and the promise of vitamin D activation in the distance, pelvic bones clicking with each step, wobbling like a damaged puppet, limping, grasping the bars for support. Up ahead, a guard walked away from me, headed toward the cell that housed the staff restrooms at the end of C-Block. I quickly turned and started the other way, toward one of the two doors that would release me forever.

And when I got to the barred door, I repeated the whole procedure again.

It was so much easier squeezing through the bars this time, given I was warmed up and the bones were freshly broken. But what really helped, besides that flicker of sun, was the adrenaline pouring through my body, endorphins streaming and dampening the pain.

Eventually, I made it outside, dazed, and I slowly staggered down towards the water, my body drinking in the sun. I saw the tumble of boulders up ahead. Then I saw the yellow raft and an orange flash of the life vest Mindy had hid amongst the rocks and brush. I dragged the raft toward the water and could smell the sea salt as the cold air slapped my face. I found myself at a small ledge, a drop-off of about three feet to the sand and water below.

"Stop!"

I turned and saw two guards a couple hundred yards away, moving towards me, guns drawn.

I reacted instinctively, thinking I could kick out in the raft far enough into the fog before they got to the water.

And I jumped.

Under normal circumstances, this would not have been a problem for anyone. But in my condition, it always was. I knew I'd made a mistake as soon as my feet left the ground, and the split second before I hit felt like an eternity.

My knees shattered simultaneously, followed by both tibia and fibula, fracturing and collapsing in multiple sites so my kneecaps plunged all the way down to my feet. Both femurs drove upward, first breaking above the knees as they hit the ground and subsequently pushed up through the acetabuli, with the femoral heads jutting up above the iliac crests, resulting in two grotesque soft tissue bulges at the low back, to join the new distortions pulsing at my hips.

My torso folded forward, like a closing book, multiple ribs splintering as my chest hit the ground, finishing up in a heap at the water's edge. Sand rode a wave into my mouth as my face hit, and overwhelming pain seared my body. I struggled to move an arm, my hand reaching out to the icy water lapping at my fingertips.

When one of the guards ran up, he stopped abruptly, befuddled at the contorted, gnarled pile of flesh and bone sprawled on the sand. He was unsure of what he was seeing, and it took him a moment to process. And after a tense pause, he uttered, "Mother of God." I caught a glimpse of the raft riding off without me, and I closed my eyes to block out the sun. Traitors all.

*   *   *

Technically, I escaped from Alcatraz on an emergency medical ferry, and I was hospitalized for a year. My body was hideous to most, deformed beyond belief and beyond repair. And given the situation, what I had tried to do, my case was never given top priority. I remain bedbound and contorted, catheterized and diapered.

But because of Mindy's petitioning, along with her father's begrudging fondness for me, my contorted form being possibly the closest approximation he'd ever had to a son, I was granted something like a pardon, essentially paroled early, which didn't matter because I wasn't going anywhere fast in my condition.

Mindy and I lived together as she took care of me, and we both hid from the sun out of habit, but, truthfully, we no longer had any need for it. This went on for twelve years, until recently, when she passed due to complications of pneumonia. The warden had died several years before after a major stroke, but for as many days as we had, Mindy and I loved each other dearly.

It is only now, with both of them gone, and the island and its crumbling, cold fortress relegated to a tourist hotspot, that I am able to reveal this story as per an agreement with the warden. Not a legal agreement, but more of a gentleman's agreement, which I respected. I have no doubt I should be in the history books, somewhere next to Houdini, who died from suffering far fewer injuries than my own, and even the warden believed this to be true. But it's okay. My body doesn't hold a grudge. I can't even hold a pencil for very long. And all the anger drained from my skeleton and muscles long ago. I lived and loved, and I was happy for a while. But more importantly, I escaped.

AUTHOR'S STORY NOTE

"Break" started with a call for submissions to an Alcatraz themed anthology (*Hard Sentences*) that was to be published by Broken River Books, with David James Keaton putting it together. I really wanted to be part of it. I tossed around a few ideas but nothing panned out. That is, until DJK posted a list of potential concepts in the guidelines. One of them was, "a story inspired by that Russian guy in the news who squeezed through the food slot in his prison cell." I was like, huh? And it didn't take long to find the video online. I stared at the screen, grinning, thinking, hell yes; we just may have something here. Things were getting visceral. I watched this lanky naked dude wriggle through the food slot of his cell like some kind of oversized slippery fish. Taking his time, bending, pushing, pulling, wriggling. He finally disgorged himself and plopped down to the floor on the other side of the bars, pulled on his clothes and nonchalantly walked out of view. Now that was very cool, but how could we ramp it up? What if there was no food slot? Could someone squeeze through the bars? What would stop you? Bones. If we had no skeleton, it'd be so damn easy. I started thinking about diseases, anomalies, syndromes, anything that could help. And for me, the medicine has to make sense. It can be fantastical but it has to be based in some real medicine or disease. And the anatomy has to be perfect. I had some diseases in mind, did more research, settled on osteogenesis imperfecta, and knew I had something workable. I never imagined it'd be in a year's best anthology. Mucho thanks to DJK, Randy and Cheryl.

BERNADETTE

R. PEREZ DE PEREDA

From *Shadows And Teeth*
Editor: R. Perez de Pereda
Darkwater Syndicate, Inc.

It is far better to have loved and have lost, than to have recovered and regretted the cost.

A letter from the Monastery of San Millán in La Rioja, Kingdom of Castile, dated the seventeenth of August, in the Year of our Lord 1224.

My dearest brother, it is my sincerest hope this missive finds you well and healthy, though none would fault me for presuming the worst. As I write this, it has been four years since you set sail in the employ of those damnable Venetian merchants. Word has since reached home that your ship foundered near Ephesus. Would that by the grace of our Lord Jesus you return home safely. By His grace, too, I pray you find it in yourself to forgive me, as I have perpetrated a terrible offense against God and you.

I fear for your daughter, Bernadette.

Truth be told, I loved her—I loved her like the daughter I never had. If I had not found my calling in the service of the most high, I so would have wanted to raise such a demure young lady as your daughter was.

I loved her. That is why I have decided she must die.

Do not judge me a murderer, for a killer I most certainly am not. Bernadette is not dead. More precisely: your daughter Bernadette will not stay dead.

No doubt you must think me mad. With all that I have witnessed since your departure, I can only wonder how I am yet to lose my faculties. But no—I am of sound mind; I am sane and not a murderer, as the account in this letter shall demonstrate. By means of this letter also, I entrust to you the two distasteful yet obligatory labors that must be undertaken once you have read these pages.

First, I pray you have mercy on me. I have not long to live, and the thought of dying with this guilt weighs heavily on my soul. I leave this, rightfully, within your discretion, and I will understand and accept your decision regardless of your choice.

Second, Bernadette must be killed. There simply is no other way. Now that the Holy Father has decreed I live out my days in a Castilian monastery, I am too far removed to make it happen myself. She must be killed, if not for the sake of her immortal soul, then for the safety of countless others residing in Aragon.

Your daughter is a monster. She is beyond sense, beyond reason. Do not be fooled by her appearance should you cross her. While she is the very image of your daughter, it is merely a ruse. The person behind her eyes—if indeed it is a person—is not the child you reared and loved. Take note of her gaunt features, her drawn face, her pallid skin, and the way her eyes dart about like an animal that hunts knowing it too is hunted.

I realize now I owe you more than an apology. I owe you an explanation, and it is well and good that you should have one. My hope is that it shall serve you in your task.

We shall start at the beginning.

When your ship did not arrive from Ephesus, your wife immediately suspected the worst. Clara donned the mourning veil, and yet a part of her kept hope that you would return. She took it upon herself to visit the docks every morning and inquire about you. Each time she received the same response, and it seemed to kill her a little more each day.

With you missing, the family's savings dwindled to nothing. Your wife was a daily visitor at my parish. I was still residing in Barcelona at the time, and whenever she came to my church I offered her hospitality, making sure I saw her home with food and, on occasion, some money. And yet, despite my efforts to keep your family fed, with each passing day she seemed to shrivel up into herself. When one day she did not come for her regular visit, I knew she had died. I went to your house and found her lying on her cot with a simple wooden crucifix between her folded hands.

And then your daughter came home. She was twelve at the time. Clara had sent her off to buy some bread, and Bernadette had returned with a small round loaf in her arms. I moved to block her view of her mother lying in state and ushered her back out the door with the promise of candied almonds. Back at the parish church, I told her what had happened to her mother, though I never told her about the deadly monkshood flowers I found crushed between Clara's teeth.

Clara was a good woman. May she rest in peace.

I soon encountered a quandary. It would have been unseemly to allow Bernadette to stay in either my home or the parish rectory—what would the townspeople think seeing this girl taking residence with the men of God?—and yet I could not in good conscience leave the child to fend for herself in the street. The only solution was to have her reside at a nunnery.

Bernadette took well to cloistered life. Indeed, I daresay the child found her calling. After three years living with the nuns, at fifteen she took the vows. During that time, she blossomed into a pious, beautiful young woman wise beyond her years. But alas, her service to God was short-lived. Smallpox tore through Barcelona a few short months afterward. Neither a life spent in prayer nor the convent's walls could spare her from her fate. In mere days, her skin was studded with pustules that looked like grains of rice, except they were red, yellow, and white. These inflammations swelled on her flesh, growing bigger as they claimed more ground, and bursting with foul water at the slightest touch when the skin was stretched too taut. They caused her burning pain. I prayed on my knees that the Lord God would restore her to health, but as her illness progressed it became apparent that her recovery would not be His will. Before long, she was bedridden. Sensing how ill she was, I administered her last rites. I knew she was not long for this world.

That night, while I was returning home, I pondered why it was that this child of fifteen summers ought to suffer and die while cutthroats and thieves grew fat and wealthy. The Lord did say that the kingdom of heaven belonged to those who follow the beatitudes, but it did not make the circumstances seem any less unfair. I resolved right then, that if it was God's will that your daughter should live, then I would be the instrument through which her life might be saved, even if that meant resorting to unconventional methods.

Instead of retiring to my home, I went instead to the house where my deacon lived. It was well past nightfall by now, and he was understandably apprehensive when he answered my knock at his door.

The parish deacon at the time was Rosario Dieguez al-Maqdisi. He was a *Morisco* from Granada. Reared in the teachings of Mohammed from an early age, he became a follower of Christ in his adulthood. Indeed, he was zealous in the defense of the Church, having fought in the Fifth Crusade. It is said that, when he was captured and brought before Sultan Al-Kamil, Rosario spat in the heathen king's face. For that, his right hand was lopped off at the wrist, which got him the nickname "*el manco*," or "the maimed one," though no one ever said that to his face.

Swarthy, well-built, and stern, Rosario cut an impressive figure. The man could split a block of granite just by scowling at it. And when a glower failed to get his point across, the gleaming hook that took the place of his missing hand was often more than convincing.

While these qualities did little service to him as a deacon, they were perfect when he served as the parish inquisitor—which was, ultimately, how he devoted the majority of his efforts. The man worked like a hound that had scented blood, seeking out occultists, devil-worshippers, and wrong-thinkers with ardor. On occasion, his raids would turn up stockpiles of heretical books. Most of these went to the pyre except for a choice few, which I kept hidden in my study. Rosario knew I kept these books, but he also could keep a secret, which was another reason he was so good at his work.

The inquisition had left me with no want for esoteric books. Before long I had amassed a small library. I thought at first I would keep them as trophies of past exploits, but the more I collected, the more curiosity gnawed at me. Heavens, what wondrous things these books promised, if their methods actually held any water. It was all nonsense. Spells to make the crops grow, or the rain to fall, or to find a lover. However, one book in particular stood out from the others in my collection. Vividly I remember setting it on my desk, a smile on my face as I prepared to roll my eyes at the foolishness that no doubt awaited me within its pages. No sooner had I opened it than my smile was swept clean off, and my body took on a slick sheen of cold sweat. Rosario had seized a grimoire—an *actual* grimoire—and what it spoke of could not be dismissed as mere tricks to fleece the feeble-minded of their coin.

He had gotten it during a sortie into the Pyrenees. Having heard rumors of a Basque witch living in the woods, he sallied out with a group of armed men and found her. Now, the Basques are an ancient people, older than the Visigoths and the Romans, and they are possessed of certain knowledge that was old when the world was new. This much Rosario could appreciate, for he knew the value her grimoire would hold for me. That, too, was why he spared the book even as the witch's cottage went up in flames, with the witch herself nailed to a chair within it.

This was a true book of witchcraft. It bore all the signs of legitimacy. I would not be surprised if the legendary Witch of Endor who summoned up the shade of Samuel at King Saul's behest had a copy of the book that lay open before me.

Judging by the handwriting in the book, the same person had copied each spell into the tome, but the spells themselves each came from different sources. I myself can read Castilian, Latin, Greek, and Aramaic. It is through my familiarity with these languages that I was able to spot translation errors—errors that would have been made by people with some working understanding of the source languages, but not true fluency. The translations from Latin could be understood with effort, but the Aramaic passages were nearly unintelligible. The written symbols resembled Aramaic, but looked as though they had been copied down merely by sight by someone with no understanding of what they stood for or how to properly shape them. Still, the fact that the book contained portions in Aramaic spoke of its age. This book was no hoax. It might not have been a stretch to believe some of these passages had been penned by a certain mad Arab from the burning sands in the east.

Standing at Rosario's doorstep that night, I explained what I intended to do about Bernadette. I would be lying to you if I said the stolid man did not flinch at the notion, but Rosario was as loyal to me as he was devout, and offered his support in my endeavors. Together, we weaved through Barcelona's darkened streets, arriving at my house, where we ascended the stairs to the study to consult the Basque witch's tome. What horrors it contained . . . it does not bear repeating in detail. Nonetheless, in its pages we found an incantation we thought would serve our purposes.

It was a very old spell. Many a candle we burned through the night as we attempted to parse the poor quality transcription, rendering it from Aramaic to Castilian. It was instructions on how to bind a djinni.

Rosario's jaw dropped in mute shock when he heard that word. It instantly recalled tales from his youth, when he was being brought up in the worship of Allah. As I was unfamiliar with the term, he explained that a djinni was a creature of smokeless fire, a very old and very powerful being. He related stories his father would read him from the Qur'an about how King Solomon the wise managed to trap one and make it do his bidding. A djinni could perform feats thought impossible—constructing palaces overnight, becoming invisible to the eye, and even, perhaps, curing one of a mortal illness.

Armed with this knowledge, we set about gathering the necessary ingredients. It took us all of the following day, but we located them surely enough. What they were, and how we prepared them for the ritual, is of no consequence; let it suffice that by the following evening we were ready.

Nightfall found Rosario and me in my study. In with us were four burly peasant men. As I had no idea what to expect should the djinni be summoned successfully, I figured it wise to have extra men on hand in case the entity was hostile. The men were plain folk, possessing more by way of arm and back than brains and wit. They had the sense to agree when offered gold for their silence, even without first telling them what they had gotten themselves into.

Rosario bolted the door shut and stood with his back to it, he and the knife on his belt ensuring that no one would leave without his saying so. Meanwhile, I went about lighting the candles in the prescribed pattern. Strangely, as each candle was lit, the room appeared not to brighten but instead to grow darker. All we could see were the outlines of our faces and the tiny coronae of light dancing atop each candle. The peasant men grew uneasy, some anxiously shifting their feet and others murmuring snippets of the Lord's Prayer.

I lit the final candle. I ignited the bowl of powdered ingredients. Then I stood back and said the words. Nothing happened. Then the floor was rent asunder in the middle of the candles and a plume of smoke burst from it, as though hell itself had breathed into the study. A mighty gout of fire shot to the ceiling in a constant stream of blazes, resembling a pillar as wide around as a large man's grasp. The room shook, and several men and I were knocked to the floor; Rosario just barely kept his footing by hanging onto the doorknob. Throughout all this, I thought I heard myself shout, "Dear

Lord, save us!" although I cannot be sure, as the noise was deafening.

But no sooner had I called out than the manifestations ended, and a voice answered me: "Your god is not here."

I stood up from the floor looking in the direction of the thing within the circle of candles, and yet unable to set my eyes upon it. My eyes simply could not be compelled to shift in its direction. Each time I tried, they moved away of their own volition.

"Dare thee to gaze upon me, humans?"

Its voice—if you could call it that—was a snake's hiss and a bass drum's boom, and louder than a church organ. Its mouth did not produce any sound, rather, the djinni instilled images, words, and speech into my mind. This was communication on an intimate level, deeper than what could be achieved through spoken language. Every idea the djinni put in my head was smoldered indelibly into my memories as if with a cattle brand. I cannot forget any of these alien images, ideas, feelings—though I wish I could. They are now forever a part of me, and this is what makes them so terrible. Such is the price for communion with djinni.

"Answer me!" it bellowed, shaking the window shutters in their frames.

I lowered my arms from my face. Standing in the ring of candles was the very epitome of the human form—a beautiful bronze man with chiseled definition and frosty blue eyes. It was perfectly hairless and plainly naked as it hovered with the tips of its toes grazing the floor. Its form constantly changed. Its burnished orange body seamlessly shaped and reshaped itself before my stunned eyes, parts of it becoming feminine as others grew more masculine, and running the circuit through all points in between. First it had two bare breasts, then many along its belly like a pregnant dog, then none, then one that grew from out of the top of its shoulder, and when that one receded back into the skin it sprouted again from the flesh of its penis.

I . . . I find it hard to confess, but . . . my heart leapt in my breast at how beautiful it was, and I—forgive me—I gripped my erect manhood with both hands and wept, falling to my knees, wanting only to surrender myself to this sublime being and forever be its own. Whatever it would have asked, I would have given. Did it want my eye or my ear, or all my skin, or perhaps to know me sexually? Oh, what I would have given to be called its favorite among however many wretches like me it had conducted into its harem. Harem? Ha! That presumed too much of myself. All I wanted was to ever be at its side like a lapdog with its master. I would have committed any number of disgusting atrocities for the slightest look of approval. I wanted right then to die, and would have died happily, if it meant spending forever with my glorious golden god.

My body crumpled forward, my forehead resting on the floorboards.

I would have remained this way, if I had not been roused by a shout from behind me. Rosario roared and shook his head like an enraged bull, stamping his feet and frothing between gritted teeth. He clutched his temples and shook his head, and when he had gathered enough clarity of mind, he leveled a penetrating stare at the djinni and yelled, "Enough!"

All around Rosario, the peasant men stood frozen as though they were statues, eyes on the djinni. Clenching his jaw, he staggered forward a step, inadvertently brushing against one of the men. The man instantly spilled to his knees in supplication, droning, "I adore thee, oh my lord!" in such rapid succession that the words were hardly perceptible.

Scowling with rage at this irreverence, Rosario let fly an uppercut swing with his hook. The metal flashed in the dim candlelight and caught the man in the crook of his lower mandible. The man did not so much as scream, so overawed was he by the djinni.

Rosario raised his arm aloft, lifting the man fully erect, looking like a fisherman with a prize catch. Then he tore his dagger out of his belt with his opposite hand and plunged it into the side of the man's neck between the skull and the shoulders. The skin at the peasant's neck pulled apart, opening his throat as though his shoulders were yawning wide, until at last the weight of his collapsing body snapped his head off his neck. The body slumped to its knees and spilled headlong, gushing blood in spurts from its severed arteries.

Something like a sigh came from the djinni. Then it said, "Man is a foolish child who calls many things gods. Man knows not the gods."

Its skin seemed to dull, losing some of the magnificent radiance it exuded, and I found that I was no longer overawed in its presence. Rosario helped me to my feet and together we addressed the djinni. The remaining three peasants all were unconscious, seemingly asleep on the floor.

"In the name of the most high, I command you to speak your name, djinni!" I yelled, thinking it could be cowed in the same manner as a demon might.

The djinni's eyes widened. If it had eyebrows, they would surely have bobbed at my effrontery. Its eyes narrowed into angry slits that contained all the deadly chill of a winter snowstorm. "Hadst thou instead come to visit me, I would have attended thee in the manner befitting of a guest. I would have filled thy mouth with rotten pus until thy belly were full. Thou wouldst have told me a great many wondrous things of thy life, and I, having learned such, would have sent thee home with an anus so full of scorpions the trail of blood behind thee would stretch for miles."

The images each word represented, along with the concepts and sensations those phrases conveyed, flashed in my mind as the djinni spoke. They are as vivid now as then—by God, *I still taste the pus!* These images are always in the forefront of my mind, constantly playing out before my eyes, and it is hard to focus on anything else except through purposeful concentration.

"Wherefore hast thou brought me here?" it asked.

Seeing how my last attempt at communication had failed, I bowed my head and spoke in lowered tones. "Djinni, we have called you to ask a favor."

"Indeed," it cut me short, "it is always so when mortals call upon the djinn. Impudent humans! What boon seeketh ye? Be it pleasure? I shall show ye such pain that the greatest pleasure would be anticipating its end! I ask again: wherefore disturbest me thou?"

It was then I explained we sought to spare your daughter from the ailment that would surely take her, and requested the djinni's succor.

The djinni sighed, if otherworldly beings can be said to sigh. "Alas, thy mortality is a concept thy limited intellect can only dimly grasp." It looked down at the floor as it considered this, then raised its gaze to make eye contact with me. "What wouldst thou have me do? The child is already dead."

An image of her flashed in my mind's eye. I was there, in the room with Bernadette as she languished in her bed, delirious with fever. The eyes I saw her with were not my physical eyes, as they saw more than human eyes could ever hope to detect. Bernadette's body was like a red-hot fireplace poker, glowing orange from her core. The glow collapsed on itself, giving way to lifeless, cold black, shriveling into her center like a bonfire shrunk to embers. I knew she was dead when the light faltered and snuffed out, leaving nothing but a dreadful stillness in its passing.

Brother, do not think for a moment that so terse an account of your daughter's death should mean I was hard-hearted about the matter. Nothing could be further from the truth. She was my niece, and—by God!—my only living relative; that is, save for you of course, if ever you should return to read this.

Her passing crushed me. It opened wounds in me, wounds that weep much as my eyes might weep. And while time has dried my tears, it has done nothing to soothe the ache of missing her.

I was flashed back to my study with the djinni standing before me. The realization that Bernadette was dead weighted my body; I crumpled to my knees and collapsed to all fours.

All of this, for naught! Frustration churned the searing bile in my stomach. "You must be able to do something," I pleaded.

The djinni cocked its head to one side. "Thou hast misunderstood. I can do a great many things."

"You could not save her!"

"Thou didst not ask."

My mouth went dry on realizing it was right—I had not asked it to save her from the disease. "Save her!" I blurted, figuring this was as good a time to ask as any.

"I cannot. She has died."

I plunged my fingers into my hair and clawed at my scalp. "Quit speaking in circles!"

"I speak as plainly as I can. Ye men possess little aptitude for understanding."

"If you cannot save her, then . . ." I stammered. At the time, I did not know why I had broken off; I was only aware that I had stopped mid-sentence. I had found that strange, especially since I had already deliberated on what it was I wanted to say before saying it. In retrospect, I think I know what halted my tongue—some combination of my conscience and divine intervention giving me one last chance before I could commit a heinous sin.

"Then . . . bring her back," I finished my sentence.

"It is already done."

I blinked, and then again, looking upon the djinni in mute shock as its words sank into my mind. Was Bernadette alive? When had she been brought back—when I asked, or sometime prior? Had she even died? It was not lost on me that the djinni could be lying, but before I could ask any questions, it said, "Thy niece lies upon her deathbed. Lay her body down in this circle before moonrise tomorrow night, and thou shall have what thou seeketh."

A thought occurred to me then that I wanted to give voice to, but I stopped myself. To even reflect upon it sent shivers down my spine. What might the djinni want of me in exchange?

As if it had sensed my thoughts, the djinni said, "Thou wonderest what thou must offer to uphold the bargain. Rest assured, human, thy debt is paid in advance."

I was about to ask what it meant, but suddenly I felt compelled to look over my shoulder. Behind and to one side of me was Rosario, standing rigidly at attention with his arms straight and shoulders squared. His eyes were locked on the djinni. Then, as if in a daze, his neck swiveled slowly to face me. His eyes never moved in his skull; they stared forward at nothing in particular as though they were fixed in place with carpenter's nails. I returned his gaze, looking him in the eyes, those empty, glassy eyes that saw for miles and sweeping miles and yet saw nothing.

His mouth popped open with the tiniest exhalation, then hung open as his jaw dropped as wide as it would go. He stuck out his tongue—I almost laughed at how out of place this was. And then he threaded the point of his hook through his tongue like a fisherman baiting a fishhook.

I screamed and toppled over onto my backside, wanting to shield my face from the horrible vision playing out before me, and yet I could not turn away, I could not close my eyes.

Rosario rotated the hook so that it was point-up. His head rocked one way, then the other, as though he were admiring the pulpy red muscle at the end of his hook. Then, like a man giving a mighty yawn, he pressed both arms to his chest and stretched them out in a wide arc. The tongue stretched, then tore, then came right out of his mouth in a fan of spurting blood. More blood churned out from between his lips, drenching his neck, soaking into his tunic. Rosario was oblivious to it all, a sleepwalker trapped in an inside-out nightmare.

I wish I could say that was where the carnage ended.

Next, Rosario raised his hook to eye-level. He brought it in close to inspect it, and on noticing it was covered in his blood, he dutifully buffed it to a gleam. Once it was shiny again, he raised it to his eyes, as if to admire his reflection in it.

Then his eyes shifted, and his gaze was upon me. He was smiling—smiling! Never, for as long as I have known Rosario, had I seen him smile, and I had thought him incapable of it. But now his mouth was open in a wide grin befitting of a madman. When his lips pulled back, what looked like a quart of blood spilled out from between his teeth.

And then he spoke to me. His lips did not move, but I heard his voice in my mind. I heard him clearly, despite his lack of a tongue. Uncharacteristically cheerful, he said, "Tomás, my friend! I will say nothing of this night!"

My gorge rose when I sensed what he was about to do. "No, please don't . . ." the words left my throat as feeble whispers.

"And that is because . . ." he went on, smiling like a loon, "I *saw* nothing!"

His right arm swept across his chest from right to left as though he were performing the most vehement sign of the cross in history. Then the arm came back across, leading with the elbow folding as the hook flashed in the dying candlelight. He buried the hook point-first in his temple. As it raked across his face, the hook sent airborne both his eyes and the bridge of his nose, cutting a rectangular swathe into the front of his skull. His brains became unanchored from within his head and they sluiced down into the window he had just cut, stopping only where the organ was too big to pass any further. Then his body went slack and he pitched forward, landing on where his face would have been. His brains hit the floorboards and burst in a muffled splatter of blood.

I screamed.

I screamed, and screamed, and screamed.

I could do nothing else.

The candles all went out at once, flooding my study in darkness. I did not awaken until the morning light that entered my window shutters was too bright to be ignored.

The djinni was gone, leaving behind only the lingering scent of burnt cedar. The fissure in the ground was gone too.

As my groggy mind struggled through the haze of restless sleep, a realization struck me just then. I lay in a room with an occult sigil drawn on the ground—enough evidence to get me excommunicated—and five dead men fanned out around me—proof enough to get my neck stretched by an executioner's rope. But with the dawning of this knowledge came a single-mindedness of purpose: I had risked so much for Bernadette that it would be senseless to give up now.

Rushing downstairs and out the door, I went to the parish rectory across the footpath from my front stoop. The two novitiates seated at the table eating breakfast were put off at my sudden appearance. Before the first could even say, "Good morning, Father," I ordered them to retrieve Bernadette's body and bring it to my home. Their faces went milk-white in alarm.

"Go! Do it now!" I urged them, and like stubborn mares goaded into action, they got up from their seats and set off running in the direction of the nunnery.

I cloistered myself in my study to await the return of my novitiates. Sitting in the rear corner with my knees hunched to my chest, I gazed upon the carnage wrought the night previous. I was as good as dead—the sheriffs would be coming for me soon, and there would be no explaining my way out of this. I nearly leapt out of my skin at the sound of an urgent knock at the door.

They're here! I now recall thinking, believing the sheriffs had arrived. I shook these paranoid thoughts from my head and peered out my second-story window. Down below in the street were my novitiates with a wheeled cart, within which lay your daughter's remains.

"Take her upstairs," I said to them from the window.

I could hear their heavy footfalls coming up the staircase. I timed their steps, waiting until they had nearly reached the second floor before cracking the door to my study open just a sliver. The novitiates carried her by the arms and ankles. Judging by how supple her body still was, rigor mortis was yet to set in.

"Leave her on the floor by the stairs," I said.

The lead novitiate's face wrinkled in concern. "But Father . . ."

"Do as I say!" I roared, pressing my face to the gap the door. They set her down, and I added, "Now leave, and do not disturb me!"

I slammed the door to my study to emphasize that would be the final word. Then I pressed my ear to the door and listened. The novitiates' footfalls grew quieter as they tramped down the stairs and to my front door. I listened as the door to the street creaked open and shut. To make absolutely certain they had left, I peeked out my window to watch them amble down the path back to the rectory and their already-cold breakfasts.

Once I had convinced myself that I was alone in the house, I pulled open the door to my study. Bernadette lay on the ground, looking more asleep than dead. The novitiates had had the tact to set her down in a tasteful position—legs straight, arms folded on her breast.

I hooked my arms beneath her armpits and dragged her to the circle as the djinni had instructed. Nothing. The thought occurred to me that perhaps I had forgotten something, but as I took stock of last night's events, I became more certain that I had done all that was asked. There was, after all, only one instruction: bring her to the circle before moonrise. I had accomplished that with time to spare.

I waited for a quarter hour, and nothing happened. Bernadette was still quite deceased, djinni's promise to the contrary notwithstanding. That was when I suspected something must not be right.

The circle of candles had gone inert—that had to be the reason nothing was happening. Whatever sorcery had brought forth the djinni had since faded. Therefore, in order to call that sorcery back into my service, I would have to repeat the ritual that summoned the djinni.

Working quickly, I removed the spent candles and replaced them with new ones, being ever so careful as to place them in the exact same spot as their predecessors. I prepared another mixture of dry ingredients—we had made sure to gather more than enough. Once everything was set, I lit the candles, burnt the mixture, and said the words.

This time, there was no earthquake, no pillar of smoke and fire. Instead, Bernadette leapt and jerked in the circle, her body wracked by violent convulsions. Her spine arched backward at a steep angle as her hands groped and punched at the air. I watched, horrified, as she thrashed her legs, spilling the candles into the air. Her foot crashed into the bowl of smoldering ingredients and sent it flying, scattering burning ash to all points on the compass. The fire caught on my bookshelf of occult "trophies," spreading quickly to the thatch roof. In an instant, my house was ablaze. My stunned gaze swept from Bernadette to the bookshelf to the flames to Bernadette again, and I saw that her body was still.

Had the ritual worked? There was no way to tell. She lay motionless and completely unaware of the peril that surrounded us. I knelt beside her and sat her up, then cradled her like a bride being carried across the threshold. I was about to stand with her in my arms when I felt her breath on my cheek.

She lived! She lived, and she was rousing as if from a nightmare.

I set her back down, this time face to face before me. I shouted her name, she didn't respond. Her head lolled drunkenly from one shoulder to the other. I shook her, repeating her name. Her eyes opened. They danced in their sockets, looking all about but at nothing in particular. I slapped her hard across the face, and she stirred, her eyes taking on a keenness that had been absent until now.

She looked at me, and my blood ran cold. Her eyes were no longer those of a fifteen year old girl. They belonged to a predator. Those eyes spoke volumes. In them was a primeval savagery, one that demanded to hunt and that would never be sated.

Bernadette leapt from the balls of her feet and pounced, knocking me onto my back with her sitting atop me. Her hands clawed at my eyes, flailing like a mountain lion subduing its kill. I crossed my arms before my face in a feeble attempt to shield myself.

Not one to be deterred, she dove with her jaws splayed wide, her teeth aimed for my throat. I shifted away at the last minute, and her mouth clamped down on my ear instead. She reared her head back and her whole body followed. Blood traced a solid arc in the air from my head to the ear in her teeth. In the same movement she knocked her head back and swallowed my ear whole.

In a blind panic I managed to get my hand around the mixing bowl, and swung for her head as she rushed in for another bite. The bowl hit her temple—it was cast-iron. I fully expected her skull to shatter under the force of the blow. Instead she rolled off me and recovered, landing on all fours and snarling like a wild animal, looking none the worse for wear.

The house shuddered, threatening imminent collapse. Bernadette, sensing this, leapt from all fours out the window and landed on the ground below like a housecat. I ran to the windowsill to watch her, too stunned was I by what I had seen to do anything else. Running on twos and occasionally on fours, Bernadette sprinted up the path at beastly speed. She did not break stride when she got to the churchyard wall—which is easily as high as a man is tall—and vaulted over, disappearing behind it into the streets of Barcelona.

The following days were a blur of activity. I hardly remember them except in snippets. The fire destroyed my home and, thankfully, any evidence that would conclusively brand me a murderer. Still, I was hard-pressed to explain why five adult skeletons were discovered in the rubble. Even harder to account for was why the skeleton of my deacon, Rosario, was among them. His remains were easy enough to identify—the hook-hand was a giveaway.

There being insufficient evidence to send me to the gaol, I was exonerated in the court of secular justice. Even so, the whole affair sat poorly with my superiors in the Church, who—without saying so—had begun to suspect that I was an occultist. Here too, they lacked evidence to proceed against me formally, but they did not let that stop them. I was neither excommunicated nor defrocked, but it was clear I was being punished when orders came from Rome that I should be relieved of my post as pastor. Without so much as a day to pack my things, I was carted off to this faraway monastery in Castile, from which I write you today. And while I am treated well enough, there exists an unspoken truth between the brothers and me, that never again shall I set foot outside the monastery grounds.

My former novitiates write me from Barcelona on occasion. Their letters speak mostly of life at the parish, but every so often they pass along word of unexplained deaths along roadways at the parish's outskirts. They attribute these deaths to wild animals or highwaymen, but I know better. Wild animals lack the intellect and nerve to ambush an entire traveling party and leave no one alive; highwaymen know better than to leave the scene of a crime without first taking whatever loot they can carry.

Sometimes their letters tell of a strange howl that rises from a throat no one can identify as either man or beast. On clear evenings when the wind blows just right, I can hear them even from as far away as Castile—mournful, hungry cries, that sometimes sound like my name.

Your daughter must be stopped. She has killed before, and will continue to do so, until she, herself, is killed. I wish you nothing but success in this gruesome business, though I am at a loss for what to do to help you, assuming I could do anything at all. Here, in this monastery, I am useless. When she stood before me, and I hit her as hard as I could with that iron bowl, she did not so much as flinch. It was a blow that would have dashed a man's brains out. Perhaps one who has already died cannot be made to die again, although, for all our sakes, I pray I am mistaken.

Godspeed, and may the Lord have mercy on us all.

Your brother,

Tomás Martín Maior

AUTHOR'S STORY NOTE

If there's anything you come to appreciate as you grow old, it's history. Young folks study it to see where they're headed (because history repeats, you know); whereas for old folks like me, it's more a matter of keeping track of where you've been. I guess I'm an old soul then, as I've always been a history buff, particularly when it comes to medieval Spain. It was a time of religious and political tension the likes of which society today can surely relate to, and it lays the perfect foundation for a historically accurate horror tale.

The story, Bernadette, for me represents what happens when moral duties clash. When people are willing to circumvent what is right to correct a perceived wrong, sometimes, the solution turns out worse than the problem, as was the case for our protagonist. What I like best about it is that the protagonist wrote this missive in the hopes that his brother has safely returned home to read it. Neither the protagonist nor the audience will ever know if the letter was read, and this adds a certain desperation and gloom to the narrative. In a way, too, the style makes you, the reader, a character in the story—you're holding the letter outlining the parish priest's thoughts; how did you come into possession of it?

All things considered, I hope you enjoyed my story, and had as much fun reading it as I had writing it. Until next time, adios.

WEST OF MATAMOROS, NORTH OF HELL

BRIAN HODGE

From *Dark Screams Volume Seven*
Editors: Brian James Freeman & Richard Chizmar
Hydra/Random House

t was the photographer's idea, get some shots of the band in the city before heading west into the countryside. He'd done his homework. Good for him. Good for Olaf the photographer. He'd read up on how one of Mexico's biggest shrines to Santa Muerte was here in Matamoros. So they might as well take advantage of that, right? The shots they'd already planned for, they wanted afternoon light for those, didn't want that glaring vernal sun directly overhead. There was time.

Sofia thought it was cheesy and wasn't shy about saying so. Sebastián was all for it, but then, he would be. More pictures meant more pictures of *him*. Enrique didn't care either way. You choose your battles wisely. No point in getting into one here inside the airport terminal.

And see? The idea was a done deal anyway. Olaf had run it past the PR guy on their flight down from L.A., so Crispin had arrived presold. Crispin was all about the enthusiasm. That was his job: make cheesy things sound like a good idea. The label must have paid him well for enthusiasm.

Besides, Crispin reminded them, they had to stay in town long enough to find a *carniceria* for the pig's heart. There had to be one close to a Santa Muerte shrine. They practically went together, right?

Crispin turned to Morgan, who looked all of a hundred pounds, half of it hair and the rest of it camera bags. "Maybe we can put you on that."

She looked queasy and stammered something about not speaking the language.

Olaf wasn't having it anyway. "If you want an assistant, maybe you should've brought your own."

So. These three in from L.A. Plus the crate they'd shipped along in cargo. Plus Enrique and Sebastián and Sofia, fresh off their puddle-jumper flight up from Mexico City. Twenty minutes later, all of them were packed into their driver's SUV. This was how it was going to be for the rest of a very long day. At least it was a long SUV.

Crispin sat up front, taking the only other bucket seat for himself so he could play captain, give the orders. After a few moments of idling beside the curb as their driver scrolled his phone, Crispin slapped his fingertips on the back of the man's headrest, bap-bap-bap-bap-bap. "Come on, let's get rolling. We're not paying you to check Twitter."

"Yeah you are," Enrique said. "Back home, all you got to check is traffic reports. Where we are now, before you go anywhere it's a good idea to check that you're not gonna be heading into somebody's shootout."

"I'm sorry, señor," the driver said. "He is correct."

Sofia perked up from the very back. "Crossfires don't ask to see your passport."

Hector, that was their driver's name. A middle-aged guy, big thick moustache, and you could just tell, this spotless SUV meant everything to him. It wasn't all that long ago Enrique would've laughed at the idea of a guy like Hector, where Hector found his pride. And had, probably more times than he wanted to admit. It took awhile to grow up and find the respect again. The man was somebody's father.

Hector spent a few more moments on his phone, then looked up happy and put the SUV in gear. They were rolling.

Next to Enrique, Morgan was still looking queasy, but in a whole new way, like she didn't know what she was doing here and was two seconds from jumping out and running back into the terminal. They'd ended up seated together in the middle because he was so big and she was so small, so they evened out. And what was wrong with this Olaf guy, anyhow, he does his homework but doesn't bother telling her what to expect.

"It's okay. We'll be okay." Enrique leaned in close, kept his voice to a soothing murmur. "Just a little precaution, that's all. Nothing bad is gonna happen."

She took a deep breath and smiled at him. Tried to, at least.

"And remember this: *Tiene usted un corazón de cerdo?*" he told her. "That's how you ask for a pig's heart. Just in case."

*   *   *

Growing up, Enrique knew who Santa Muerte was. No secret about her. She was around. You just didn't see much of her, not then. She was a back room kind of saint, for the kind of altars you never got to see as a kid, because they were private, kept by people who fucking meant business.

Now, though? Now you didn't have to look hard at all to find her. Santa Muerte was everywhere, never more so than during the last decade, ever since the cartel wars erupted into a never-ending series of bloodbaths and massacres. Saint Death, Holy Death, had really come into her own.

In hindsight, it seemed inevitable. There were things you took for granted as a kid that took being an adult to see how strange they really were. That, and being lucky enough to gain perspective, to see past your own borders. And he had. Enrique had seen enough of the world to know now. The band had given him that much. Every tour made it that much clearer:

Here at home, people found death a lot more interesting than life.

Santa Muerte—she might look different in a hundred details, but was always the same simple figure: a skull in a dress, a skeleton where a woman used to be. She might look like a nun. She might look like bride. She might look no different from Santa Maria, except for that face of bone. Sometimes she might be holding a scythe. Always, she held your fate.

Here in the southside neighborhood in the Colonia Buenavista, Enrique knew they were getting close without anybody having to say a thing. It was the population explosion on the other side of the SUV. People on their own. Families. Mothers and fathers carrying sleepy babies, crying toddlers, to introduce them to the Saint of Death. The slow-goers made it up the street on their knees, not because they had to, but to show humility and devotion. They brought offerings. They brought photos and needs. They brought sorrows no one would ever hear about except the saint.

It wasn't a proper sanctuary, not like a church or a mission. The shrines never were. It just happened, grew up here like a tree from a seed. Some family starts it in their home, puts up the saint in their front window, and that's all it takes. They built it, and people came. Eventually they moved the saint farther inside, where there was more room, once their shrine took on a life of its own.

Hector wheeled as close as he could, then cut over to the side of the street and shut down. He stayed with the SUV while the rest of them went ahead, stepping out into the clamor, the laughter and the tears and the numb despair of people who didn't know where else to turn.

Along the way, Crispin bought a bouquet of droopy flowers from a kid on the street. "Why not?" he said, and waggled them at Enrique and Sofia and Sebastián, petals sifting to the street. "Maybe we can get her to bless this next album."

Sofia perked up again. She was like that—you never knew when she was tuned in and listening. Looked hard and wiry and ready for combat, muscles like taut cables, drummer's muscles, her thoughts a thousand miles away, yet she was onto you. She shouldered past to squeeze up close to this PR guy who was always coming off like the band's biggest fan, like he'd never heard genius until he heard Los Hijos del Infierno.

"Don't joke," Sofia told him. "I know you're only joking, but don't, okay? You stop a minute and think what it takes to push people, good people, everyday people, to revere what's inside there. It makes sense the *narcos* would pray to her, sacrifice to her. She's made for men like that. But these folk? Jesus and Mother Mary . . . people still believe, they've just given up. Jesus and Mary don't deliver anymore. Or they can't. Or maybe they stopped listening. But Santa Muerte does. She's the one who listens now. She's the one who loves them. She's the one they look to for healing. So remember where you are and think what it's taken to do that to them."

Crispin was a clean-cut Anglo who looked beyond shame, but he wasn't above looking chastened. Good to see.

Did these people in the street know who they were? Many looked, some stared. A few, maybe, might have recognized them. The six of them weren't your average half-dozen people out here, that much was blatant. Three gringos and three Mexicans, but even as locals, more or less, he and Sebastián and Sofia stood out. The black clothes and boots, the hair. No other guys out here had a need for eye makeup. Sebastián drew the stares most of all, the way a front man should—a head taller than most, crazy thin, with a spiked black leather pauldron belted over his left shoulder, like a gladiator on his way into the arena.

Equals, though, in spite of it all. Death turned everybody into equals.

The closer they got to the pink shrine house, the more crowded it got. After a minute of conferring with Olaf, Crispin squeezed his way inside and found the owners, used the power of dollars to get them to close off the inside for a private audience. After passing through a couple of arched doorways, the walls close and the ceiling low, they had the place to themselves.

Santa Muerte came in all sizes, and this one was as big as a live woman— on her pedestal, even a little bigger than that. She wore pale patterned robes, purple and white, with a sky blue cowl over her head. A wreath of dried-out flowers circled her brow. Her scythe was enormous, the blade oversized and stylized, six inches wide in the middle, curving over her head from outside one shoulder to past the other. It was way bigger than anything you'd want to swing in the fields, with a smaller skull mounted where it angled away from the wooden shaft.

Her teeth were white and even, her eyes a pair of empty voids.

She swam in wavering shadows, lit by a forest of candles. The rest was like every shrine he'd ever seen, gaudy and colorful and beautiful and sad. Flowers, from fresh to withered, lay everywhere, more bouquets than they had vases. A plate of tortillas sat at the bottom hem of her robes. Petitioners' notes were pinned to her robes. Pictures were taped to the walls, propped against the candle jars, stacked on tables—the sick and the dying, the dead and the missing, and somewhere in between them, the lost. Those who were simply lost.

Morgan was on it, in her element now, setting up a tiny, stubby-legged tripod with the efficiency of a soldier field-stripping a rifle—a tabletop tripod, but down on the floor. She set out a couple of Nikons, then unfolded a pair of circular reflectors, one silver and the other gold, and put them off to one side, and then went scurrying about with a light meter.

Olaf moved the three of them around, had them hunker and squat while he sprawled in the floor with his camera mounted on the pygmy tripod, the lens angled at them, shooting up from below. You could see his bald spot from here, a circular patch the size of a drink coaster missing from his white-blond hair.

He sounded happy with what he was seeing.

He'd positioned Sofia in the middle, the way photographers often did. Balance, Olaf was probably after, but there was something else he may not have been consciously aware of. The way Sofia looked, her features were a hybrid of the polarities on either side of her. In Sebastián, what you saw was a fine-boned European strain, the face of a Spanish conquistador. In Enrique, the broad peasant face and long, coarse hair of what the conquerors had found waiting for them, like he'd stepped out of some arid canyon that time forgot.

You looked at their faces and saw the whole of Mexico's history in them.

And now, behind them, Santa Muerte looming over them all.

* * *

A couple hours later and one pig's heart heavier, the SUV rolled west out of Matamoros, through that zone where the city frayed apart and unraveled into the countryside, a stark land seared by the sun and sprinkled with small farms, small ranches, tiny hovels. Twenty miles into it, Hector hooked a right onto a dirt road and headed north, until they were only a mile or so from the river. One mile away, Texas, but still, a whole other world.

Hooray for GPS. It wasn't like there were signs pointing the way here.

They stretched their legs again across the scrubby, hardscrabble ground and listened to Crispin be confused.

"There's nothing here," he said. "I thought there'd at least be some buildings left."

"Not for a long time," Sebastián told him. "After the investigation, the police brought in some *curanderos* to cleanse the spirit of the place, then burned everything."

"Then what's the point, may I ask? For all that's going to show in the photos, you could shoot them literally anywhere."

"Because the point is here. *Here* is the point." Bas sidled up to him and threw an arm around Crispin's shoulders, a rare moment of salesmanship for him instead of flat-out telling how it's going to be. "You can't cleanse away something like what happened here. You can't get it all. You don't feel it? You will. It'll come through." He patted Crispin on the back. "The fans, it'll mean something to *them*. They'll appreciate the effort. This place called to us. We heard it loud and clear, and we had to answer."

"What's this *we* shit?" Sofia muttered, only loud enough for Enrique to hear.

She was right. This was totally a Sebastián thing. Not a bad idea, necessarily, as image went, because image mattered, but still . . . this was kind of out there even for Bas.

"Half the songs on this next album are about here, and what came out of here. What they did here opened the gates to Hell and the gates never shut. If you don't get that, you don't get us." Sebastián, closing the deal with their alleged number one fan. "Where else *could* we shoot?"

Rancho Santa Elena, this place had been called, back when it was somewhere that somebody wanted to live. A generation ago it was the headquarters of a family business moving marijuana from the south up into the States. Different era, same old shit. Problems with the DEA, problems with rivals. They'd hooked up with this good-looking Cuban guy out of Florida who was making his own religion—part voodoo, part Santeria, part Palo Mayombe, and the rest, his own sick craziness. An isolated spot like this, with an outbuilding to repurpose as a temple, nobody close enough to hear the screams, human sacrifice seemed a reasonable price to pay for keeping their traffic routes safe. Eleven shallow graves' worth. Body parts for their cauldron, necklaces out of bones. There was power in it. It made you bulletproof. Made you invisible.

And nobody knew, nobody cared, until the Cuban decided he needed the blood of a young gringo who would die screaming. So they nabbed a college boy down on spring break, he and his buddies coming over the border for a change of scenery after they got tired of things on South Padre Island. Poor guy went off for a piss and never came back. They gave him twelve or so really bad hours before they got down to the serious business and took off the top of his head with a machete to get at his brain.

Enrique had to get a little older to learn the less obvious lesson: where he and his parents and sisters and everyone he knew ranked in the North American scheme of things. If it had been another dead Mexican, those people would've kept getting away with it. You want to wreck your shit, kill a gringo. That's when people start noticing.

By now, Hector had opened up the SUV's back door, and they moved in to help slide out the long, bulky crate that had flown cargo class from L.A. Real wood, you didn't see that much anymore. Pride in your work, right there—the props company had packed this thing for *survival*. Hector took a tire tool and pried off the lid, and after they pawed aside the foam peanuts, they lifted the thing free.

Plenty of *wows* and *holy shits* all around. Those props people knew their stuff, how to take fiberglass and make magic. The statue was lighter than it looked, sturdier than it felt, and even when standing right next to it, looked exactly like stone that had weathered for centuries. They'd even painted it with stains.

"What is it?" Morgan asked, the only one of them who didn't know.

"It's called a *chacmool*," Sebastián told her. "It's a really old design, pre-Colombian. Aztecs, Mayans, maybe even older. Up at the top of a pyramid, that was one place they might go. See that platter in the middle? That was for holding sacrifices." He grinned, a needling meanness behind it. "Didn't have to be a heart, but if you got one laying around loose, why not."

The same as the likenesses of Santa Muerte, *chacmools* might differ in little details, but the core was always the same. A strange design, blocky, the way so much of that ancient Mesoamerican sculpture was carved. The basic template was a man, feet flat, knees up, leaning back on both elbows, while balanced on his middle was a receptacle to receive offerings—could be a platter, could be a bowl. His head was turned to the side, like he was challenging anyone who approached him to give until it hurt.

For their replica, they'd opted for a platter. They all three liked the look of the bowl better, but its sides would have blocked the view, in pictures as well as onstage. Sebastián's idea—for the next tour's stage show, he was going to mime a self-sacrifice three songs in, cut out his own heart with a fake obsidian knife and present it to the audience on the *chacmool*. It would continue beating the whole time, and eventually start gushing blood again.

Every tour, the show just got messier.

And why shouldn't it. So was everything else in the land of their birth.

Olaf and Morgan and Sebastián conferred on where to set up for the shots. Crispin kept trying to offer suggestions and was tolerated, but otherwise got frozen out. Looked like it would be awhile, so Enrique wandered the property, scouting for clues as to what might have happened where. Where was the temple, where were the graves?

It was easy to be distracted in a cluster of people bickering and chasing the best light. Get off by yourself and you could feel the weight of what had happened here.

No . . . not *happened*. That made it sound like an accident. Everything that went on here had been *done*. It had occurred to human beings to *do* this to other human beings. Sodomize them. Chop them up. Lop off the top of their heads. Scoop out their brains. Wrap wire around their spines before they buried them, and leave the end sticking out of the ground so that after the worms and beetles and decay had their way with the corpses, they could pull the wire and haul up a nice new spinal column to use for making necklaces. Save them the trouble of digging again.

Shit like that did not just *happen*. Something got inside you, or was there all along and got loose from its cage, and told you that doing these terrible things was a good idea. Told you that was how business needed to get handled from now on. Same as it told the Aztecs: This is what it takes to keep the corn coming up in the fields, to keep the sun moving across the sky every day. This is what it takes to keep your world intact. Blood, and lots of it.

"You feel it too, don't you?" Sofia, coming up behind him.

"It leaves a stain, you know?" he said. "Like it's sunk in. You'd have to dig this place out fifty feet down and haul the dirt to an incinerator, and maybe even then you wouldn't get it all. It's like, whatever the *curanderos* thought they were doing, all they managed was to sweep the porch."

Somebody had died here. Right here. On this spot. He was sure of it. The whole plot of earth, saturated with fear and betrayal. Maybe it was the little boy. That was the one that really haunted him—how one of the guys doing this killed his own nephew. Decided he needed to snuff a kid, so somebody else went off and snatched him a kid. Brought the boy here, tossed him on the ground. The guy with the machete went right at him—just a boy with a bag over his head. It wasn't until the kid was dead that the guy started thinking, hey, that green football sweatshirt sure looks familiar.

But it's okay, you did right, the malignant thing inside him must have said. *This is what it takes to keep your world running.*

"Come on." Sofia reached up to rub his shoulder. "You're not doing yourself any good over here. Let's get back to the van so I can fix your makeup. Doesn't that sound like fun?"

"No," he said, like it was the silliest question she'd ever asked, and the exact right thing to do at the time, because it broke the spell. And he loved her for it. Loved her anyway, but sometimes it was good to be reminded of reasons.

They found that Sebastián and the photo team had decided where to take the shots. They had the *chacmool*—complete with the pig's heart now—set against a backdrop of gnarly scrub. Off to one side was a hummock of earth that, if they insisted it was a grave, the fans would say, oh, right, sure. A grave, still there after all this time. I totally buy that.

Olaf positioned them in different configurations, shuffled them around, with the sun dipping low enough that the natural light was coming in from the side. Morgan held the gold reflector to bounce the light back from the other side, give the scene a warm tinted glow, like the whole place was simmering.

Every few shots it was a different motivation. Look angry. Look disinterested. Look like you're grieving. Look hungry. Look dead. Anything but look like you're having fun. The only one of them enjoying the process was Sebastián. His idea, after all, the only one of them who could conceive of this. Who could think they could come here and evoke the spirits of this place where so much misery and evil were done, and then go away untouched.

Hector, though—Hector knew better. Once they'd unloaded the *chacmool* and got it set up, he was back in his SUV and hadn't left. Probably going to burn his shoes tonight because of what they'd touched, so he didn't track it into his home.

Be like Hector, Enrique told himself.

When they wrapped it up, packed it up, he'd never been more ready to leave a place. It was fitting that the last image he would take away from this little spot of Hell on earth was the heart of some poor pig, tossed aside now that they were through with it, left in the dirt for scavengers and blowflies.

Then they were in the SUV again, backtracking along the dirt road, halfway to the highway. He was slumped into the door with his head against the window when he perked up at the sight of something shooting out of a bush ahead of them. Thinking in that instant, holy shit, it was the biggest snake he'd ever seen, even though he knew that wasn't right.

An instant later came the sound of blowing tires, a double bang in front, another double bang in the rear. Enrique swiveled his head to follow the sound, and saw the not-snake slithering back into the bushes. No snake was triangular like that. No snake had spikes sticking up from its spine.

Hector was all instinct now, fighting the steering wheel and stomping the brake as the SUV slewed back and forth until he brought it to halt, skidding across the loose dirt as a churning cloud of dust caught up with them.

Just the worst feeling ever. Knowing, on one level, exactly what was happening, the rest of him denying it, no no no, this can't be real, Morgan's hand almost breaking his fingers she was squeezing them so hard, and he didn't even know when she'd grabbed him.

The driver's window blew inward and Hector's head went with it, a blizzard of glass and blood and brains and hair and bone and eyes spraying into the windshield. In the front passenger seat, Crispin got showered with some of it and had no idea what it was, turning with a look of pissed-off disgust on his face, like he was thinking what next, first the flat tires and now somebody had thrown a pot of stew at him, and the next dumb thing out of his mouth was going to be *Who's going to pay for this, do you have any idea how much this shirt cost?*

Outside, more guys than Enrique could count at once were converging from every direction, and he couldn't conceive of where they'd come from. This place was so poisoned that people like this came bursting out of the ground. If from the comfort of home he'd envisioned something like this, they would have been wearing masks. But they weren't. They had faces and didn't care who saw them, and that was the most frightening thing he could imagine.

They began yanking open the SUV's doors, and if they found one locked, would either aim through the window and scream until the person on the other side got the idea, or bash out the glass with the butt of a gun and reach in to unlock it themselves.

Everybody was vacating, stumbling out on their own or getting dragged. No say in it, Enrique hit the road hard and tasted a mouthful of hot, dry grit. A few feet away from him, Crispin was finally up to speed, groping for his pocket and pulling out his ID to flash like it was going to matter to someone: Oh, it's you, sorry for the mistake.

"*Americano!*" he screamed. "*Americano!*"

Nobody could've cared less. Nobody wanted to deal with him other than right then, right there, on the spot. They could just tell, the scariest judges of character in the world. You hear about someone getting blown out of his shoes and think no way, that's Hollywood bullshit. But it happened. Steps away, Crispin was hit with gunfire so hard he bounced off the fender and left a dent as he went down barefoot.

All Enrique could think of was Sofia, Sofia, because she'd gone out the other side and he couldn't see her any more. He'd forgotten how to pray, too, something about Santa Maria, but it wasn't there any more.

Santa Muerte, full of grace, was the only thing he had left. *You don't want us now.*

Vans came roaring up from the south, the direction of the highway, this entire operation going off with military precision. Someone's knee dropped into the center of his back and emptied his lungs with a whoosh. They twisted his arms behind his spine and he was so confused and paralyzed he let it happen, let some guy squat on top of him like a goblin and lash his wrists together with a nylon zip-tie before he realized that was happening too. Then everything went dark and stuffy when they yanked a black hood over his head, and now the world was reduced to bad sounds and worse sensations.

They hauled him upright, slinging him around like a bawling calf destined for a branding iron. Once his feet were under him, two pairs of hands rushed him stumbling toward whatever was waiting next. Then he was cargo, banging into the hard floor of a van as other bodies landed around him. Doors slammed, then the blackness shot into high-speed acceleration, and whenever any of them said anything somebody up front yelled for them to shut up, no talking, and it was a long bumpy ride before the last person was too tired to cry any more.

*   *   *

The only thing Enrique was sure of was that they hadn't gone north. Whatever was coming next, they hadn't been driven into Texas for it. No, they'd gone a long way south, or west, or both. The air felt dryer and hotter on his arms.

After hours of motion, the van finally stopped and guys hauled them out and rushed them across open ground, hardpacked earth under his wobbly boots. Then it was doorways and a fresh feeling of claustrophobia—a hallway. That opened into an expanded sense of space, the noise around them no longer confined. Wooden floors, he knew from the sound.

The ties were cut and the hoods came off and they were shoved forward. Behind them, doors slammed and locks turned. Then they were on their own in a big dark emptiness, still nothing to see because the night had followed them inside.

Head count: Sofia. Sebastián. Morgan. Olaf. Himself. In spite of the hours in the van, he hadn't been totally sure. Free to move, Sofia hugged him. Morgan hugged Olaf. Sebastián was on his own for the moment, and that wasn't right, so Enrique pulled him close and wrapped him up too. Everybody stank of sweat and fear, and he didn't care, he'd never been so glad to smell anything in his life.

They weren't alone. From the darkness came a sound of somebody stirring.

"Who's there?" he asked. "Who is that?"

"*Solamente nosotros los muertos. Acostúmbrate a la idea y cierra tu puta boca para que lo demás podamos dormir,*" came the sullen answer.

Just us dead people. Get used to the idea and shut the fuck up, so the rest of us can sleep.

*   *   *

They staked their claims in the floor, and if he could've folded himself all the way around Sofia like a fort, he would have.

The two of them had known each other too long to feel like anything other than brother and sister, but there were times he wondered, man, what if, huh? They'd come into each other's orbits as a couple of nerdy kids from bad neighborhoods, the kind it was easy to beat the shit out of, so that's what other kids did. The kids that listened to that thing inside, telling them, *This is what it takes to make your day more fun.*

They listened a lot, the cruel ones. Like they knew already, nothing had to tell them anything.

And keep at it, okay? There's a future in this. We got plans for you.

A couple of nerdy school band kids—they had targets on them early. It wasn't much of a band, and the instruments weren't much, either. Sofia liked to hit things, so they put her with a snare and a marching bass drum and a tom, but she never got to hit them as hard as she would've liked because she was scared of breaking a head, and then where would she be?

Enrique they'd fixed up with a leaky trumpet, but every spare moment he let the gravity of the out-of-tune piano in the corner pull him over to its yellowed keys. He could play more than one note at a time, plus if he held down the sustain pedal, he could pound them out and they'd keep ringing, a tapestry of overlapping noise that never had to end. The same thing he was doing now, just that with Los Hijos del Infierno he was doing it electronically, with synthesizers and sequencers and samplers, and it was way harder and louder and a lot more caustic.

So no, it wasn't much of a school band, and the instruments weren't much, but he always figured that without them, he and Sofia would be dead. Dead for real, or as good as dead, or wishing they were, or maybe worst of all, dead on the inside and not realizing it. There were all kinds of dead.

And Santa Muerte loved each and every one.

*   *   *

The dark bled out with the dawn.

He stirred awake at the first sign of it, sitting up in the floor so he could put an environment around them as things took shape. Get that much figured out, at least.

The first light came slanting in through windows set up high, near the roof. It lit up rough, bone-white walls and a gently peaked ceiling with wooden beams arching overhead, plus a few square pillars near the front and back. The windows on ground level started to brighten next. All of them were barred—no surprise.

It looked like it may have been an abandoned church or mission that had outlived its usefulness as anything but a prison, in some dusty little village where the good cops, if there were any to start with, were all dead. The mayor, dead. Anybody who'd ever said one wrong word, dead.

It was gutted of everything that might have marked it as a holy place. The pews were gone, the altar was gone, the font for holy water was gone. All that was left was a raised platform at the front where the altar would've been, and empty alcoves in the walls where statues of saints would've stood.

They shared the place with twenty-odd other people. Most were curled up on the floor, still asleep. A few others sat with their backs to the walls, looking ring-eyed and dazed, like they'd forgotten what sleep was. Men, mostly, gone grubby and unshaven. A couple of hard looking women.

"We don't belong here."

He turned and found Sebastián was awake now. He'd seen their singer looking this bad before, but it was only hangovers, or too many days speeding catching up with him. Nothing like this, like now he wasn't expecting to get better.

"This is cartel shit, man. We don't have anything to do with that. Why would they grab *us?*" Bas stopped a moment, getting a freshly horrified look on his face. "You don't think it has to do with the pictures during the show, do you?"

That was something new the past couple tours, since they'd put out the last album, *La máscara detrás de la cara.* They'd always gone for a projected multimedia assault whenever they played, and Sebastián had decided it was time to forget about the chaos of the world at large for their imagery and tap current events closer to home. All the photos of carnage you could want were a few clicks away online. The aftermath of massacres and assassinations and messages sent in buckets of blood splashed across pavement. Severed heads and arms hacked off at the elbows, and death sentence by blowtorch, and rows of butchered bodies hanging from train trestles. Film clips, too, that the anonymous murder teams had posted online. *This is who we are, this is what we do, this is what it takes to keep our world turning.*

He never knew how Sebastián could do it, comb through the ugliest shit in the world and arrange it in a sequence that whizzed by at four frames per second. From the audience perspective, there wasn't time to linger on any one thing, so you couldn't be sure what you'd just seen, you only knew it was terrible and probably real. Bas, though . . . he had to linger over it.

"No, I don't think it's got anything to do with that," Enrique said. "That's free advertising for them, is all."

He looked down at Sofia, still asleep, the kind of sleep that becomes the only self-defense you have left. Same with Morgan. Olaf too, only he looked like could just as easily be unconscious as asleep, all that dried blood down one side of his face and caked in his white-blond hair. He must've really taken a beating during the grab.

Sebastián was trying to look hopeful but it came off looking queasy. "Maybe they're gonna ransom us, that's what this is about. It's part of the business model now, you know."

He was right on that much. Used to, the people might see cartel crews rolling in their convoys of pickup trucks, and as long as everybody kept out of their way, they'd leave the people alone. Not anymore. Times were tougher, even for the cartels. Every time a boss got killed or captured, organizations fractured and the chaos ramped up. Plus anybody who said the Federal police and the American DEA weren't having an impact wasn't paying attention. Whenever they lost another tunnel to the north side, or another supply route, that was another fortune lost.

But all around them were people too scared to fight back. And people who loved those people. Some of them even had a little money to pay to get their loved ones back in more or less one piece. It wasn't drug-sized cash, but $40,000 for a few days of no-risk work wasn't a bad sideline.

Only Enrique wasn't seeing it. Not here.

"I don't know, Bas," he said. "They didn't have any interest in Hector. They didn't give him a chance. And Crispin, he was the one looking like he could buy his way out of anything."

Go back to the site now, what would be left? A lot of nothing. The SUV would've been towed to a chop shop in Matamoros or Reynosa. For Hector and Crispin, graves no one would ever discover, or maybe an acid bath.

"What I can't figure is how they knew where to find us at all. They shouldn't have known that. Nobody was following. Where would they have picked up on us?"

Oh god, that look on Sebastián's face—like his eyes were falling back inside the cold black emptiness of his head, and his skin was on too tight.

"What did you do, Bas? What the fuck did you do?"

It came from somewhere so far inside him he could barely squeeze out sound: "I sent out a tweet. Right after we got to the airport."

Enrique's breath left him all at once. Twitter. Sure, why not. Because Sebastián couldn't wait to get a jump on the image thing. Tell the whole world what lonely, godforsaken, evil place they were going to. Look at us, everybody, see how edgy we are. Never guessing who might be paying the wrong kind of attention.

"The airplane didn't kill us, so you figured you would?" Enrique whacked Sebastián across the face, open-handed but with heft behind it, to knock him off his ass and send him sprawling across the dingy wooden floor.

A few of the dead people, *los muertos*, looked up at the commotion, decided they'd seen it all before, and tuned them out again.

Near tears, Sebastián scuttled a few feet away and put his head between his knees. Sofia roused, coming awake, feeling the disturbance in the air.

"What?" she said, her tongue thick with morning, then she jolted into high alert as everything hit her all over again. "What's going on?"

"Nothing." He couldn't think of a single good result that could come from telling her. Not now. Later, if there was time for it to matter. "Just nerves."

She looked around, taking it all in and liking none of it. He noticed, for the first time, a pair of five-gallon plastic buckets in the farthest corner—the communal toilet. Currently in use.

Meanwhile, Sebastián had gotten brave enough to have a look out one of the barred front windows flanking the pair of main doors, big slabs of wood and iron that looked solid enough to withstand cannon fire.

Up. Sebastián was looking *up*.

He backed away from the window then, one slow foot after another, so tense his tendons were going to pop if he wasn't careful. His fingertips went to his lips and he stopped, something inside shutting down.

They took his place at the window.

Not far beyond the front doors was the biggest Santa Muerte he'd ever seen. She stood fifteen feet tall, easy. Her blue robes were voluminous, enough material there for a festival tent. She seemed too big to have found her a scythe that wouldn't look like a toy. Yet they had. Somebody must've made it just for her, a scythe big enough to cut the moon in half. And somehow . . .

somehow the skull was at scale.

"That can't be real," Sofia said.

No. It couldn't. It just looked real. The yellowing of age. The uneven teeth. The *missing* teeth, random gaps in the jaw. They'd had it made, that was all. Same props company that made the *chacmool*, maybe. Wouldn't that be a kick in the head.

A sight like this, the biggest thing around, your eyes would naturally go to it, linger on it. So it took awhile for them to notice the rest, the bits and pieces scattered around the hem of Santa Muerte's giant robe. Never mind the skull. *These* were real. Arms and legs, hands and feet and heads. They were as real as real got.

"Do me a favor," Sofia said, quiet as a butterfly. "If it looks like that's where I'm headed, kill me. If I ever got on your nerves and you wanted to break my neck, that would be a good time."

*   *   *

After everybody was awake and moving, there was only one person who would talk with them, a graying, droopy-jowled *viejo* who said he was a priest. Everybody else, Enrique figured it was like that guy in war movies— the tight-faced veteran with the thousand-yard stare who's been around the longest, and he doesn't want to get to know the new recruits transferring into the unit. Doesn't even want to know their names. They'll be dead in a week, so why bother.

"What's a priest have to do to get a cartel mad at him?" Enrique asked.

"Exorcisms," Padre Thiago said. "I cast out the devil from the ones who let him in but don't want him dwelling in them any longer. He doesn't like that, and neither do his servants." The old man looked out in the direction of the towering Santa Muerte, then grinned and spread his hands as if to bless his flock. "But you see how God works. He brings me here where prayers of liberation are needed most."

Enrique had all kinds of things he could've said then about God and deliverance and working in mysterious ways, but there would have been no upside to any of it. You choose your battles wisely. And you don't drive off your allies.

"Who are his servants here?" he said instead. "I don't know what this is about. I don't know who took us, or why."

"That group of men over there?" The priest pointed with discretion at a sullen cluster occupying the farthest corner opposite the toilet buckets. "They say they are with the Sinaloa Federation. This would probably make it the Zetas who have you."

"Just me," Enrique said. "Not you?"

"Wherever I am, I am only God's."

Knowing *who* still didn't explain why. The Sinaloa Federation controlled the northwest. The Zetas, once they'd turned against the Gulf Cartel, took control of the northeast and the coast all the way down to the Yucatan. There were others, but these two were the gorillas, fighting for as much turf as they could take, with strips of contested no-man's-land running down the center of the country.

"And there's that one, too." Padre Thiago meant a stocky man milling about on the Sinaloa periphery, as though he didn't belong but was allowed closer than most. "Do you recognize him?"

The man looked to be in his upper thirties, and like the rest of them, he'd been at least a week without a razor, so his beard was catching up with his moustache. Enrique gave it his best, trying to see who he was under the whiskers and the unruly, unwashed hair.

No," he had to admit. "Should I?"

"You don't recognize Miguel Cardenas? I thought one music person might know another, but what do I know."

Enrique never would have gotten it on his own, but now he had enough for the connections to link. Different music, different look, different everything. He knew the name, ignored the rest. Miguel Cardenas was a traditionalist, singing dusty songs for the provinces. Enrique could picture the man in his cowboy hat, holding an acoustic guitar, in front of a backup band of brass and accordion, tasteful drums and upright bass. He still wore a white dress shirt, dingy now, and black slacks with silver studs down the sides. What had they done—nabbed him after a show?

"I bet I can guess," Enrique said. "The idiot did a narco ballad about one of the bosses in the Federation."

Padre Thiago gave a sad nod. "If you seek favor by flattering one side, the other may not turn a deaf ear to it."

Enrique couldn't help but stare. He was looking at the deadest man in this room. A guy like that, there would be no ransom for him. He was an insult that couldn't be forgiven. He was the pet dog that got killed to make a point.

And it was one more reason why this didn't make sense. The three of them, Los Hijos del Infierno, weren't on anybody's side. They sang nobody's praises. It would've been like asking whose side you were on between lung cancer and heart disease. They were on the side of life, end of story.

That was the thing people never got about them. The look, the sound, the lyrics, the stage show . . . all of it left people who couldn't look or listen any deeper thinking they must've been on the side of death. What else could they be? Because look at them. Look at the freaks. Never once considering the band was another symptom, the world getting the art it deserved.

You only screamed that loud when dying was the last thing you wanted to do.

* * *

It was the middle of the day when they came for Olaf and Morgan.

A squad of armed guys burst in shouting for everyone to get on the far side of the room, and everybody else knew the drill already. It seemed to be the way the cartel guys handled everything here. They either brought what they wanted or took what they wanted, and did it at gunpoint with lots of yelling.

If you wanted to die quick, here was your chance. Whatever they said, do the opposite. Go straight at them, screaming for blood. It had to be a better end than you'd get under that giant Santa Muerte. There was every reason to believe whatever happened there would go a lot worse.

So why didn't anybody do it? Most of these people had been here for days or longer. Padre Thiago had been here over two weeks. They all knew what was going on.

The only thing that could've stopped them from rushing into gunfire was hope. They still hoped someone cared enough to buy their release. That's what kept them docile. That's what would keep them docile one day too long.

Then again? Forcing a quick end was easy to dream about, but when they came in that first time, all stormtrooping and chaos, the only thing Enrique could do was scuttle to the wall with everyone else and try to wrap the adobe around him. Ashamed, because the thing he wanted most in the world right then was to be invisible. Don't see me, don't pick me, don't act like you even know I'm here. He folded himself over Sofia and that was all the altruism he could muster. When he saw it was Olaf and Morgan they wanted, he'd never been more with disgusted with himself for feeling relief.

Olaf was still feisty. They had to pry Morgan from his arms and knock the wind out of him with the butt-end of an AK-47 to the gut. He dropped to his knees, gasping, then they dragged him by the shoulders. Morgan went easier, stumbling along with her eyes popped wide and her mouth open in a silent scream, like she'd hit a place of panic so overwhelming she froze there.

As quickly as they'd come, the extraction team was gone, and everyone unglued themselves from the wall. Enrique drifted up to the front window, forcing every step, because someone who knew them should bear witness. He would watch as long as he could.

Only they didn't reappear. Santa Muerte continued to stand alone.

That was life here, the terrible erratic rhythm of it. Long stretches of boredom and soul-eating dread, waiting for something to happen, and when it did, you shit yourself with fear.

Within hours, he and Bas and Sofia had become fixtures the same as the rest, subject to the same pecking orders and probing. Even in captivity, the Sinaloa guys had their own mini-cartel going. They'd been watching, taking the measure of the newcomers, and an hour or so after Morgan and Olaf were taken, one of them decided he wanted a woman and wanted one now, and made a move on Sofia.

Enrique went tense, ready to go off if needed, and he figured he would before it was over. One on one, though, the guy didn't have a chance. Sofia had been fending off grabby assholes for years. She'd gone through a phase when she cut her hair short and choppy, thinking it might discourage them, but it didn't, so she'd grown it out again and instead worked on preemptive strikes.

This one she kicked in the balls, and when he doubled over, gripped him by the curly ringlets of hair on the back of his head to steady him for a knee to the face. He was on the floor before his buddies saw it was going to happen. A few of them moved to step in, so Enrique came forward for the intercept.

He'd already guessed how they had him pegged. That they saw him as someone for whom size didn't matter, whose mass they could dismiss. He'd accepted years ago that he was always going to have the round, moonfaced look of some lumpen guy too big and slow to do anything other than let bad shit happen to him.

Sometimes it was good to leave the wrong impression. When all they saw was freaks with smudged, day-old makeup, you could do a lot of damage before they caught on.

The first one who got close, Enrique hooked a punch into the side of his neck that landed with the sound of meat slapping onto stone. It sent him staggering until he dropped a few steps away. The next, Enrique stomped a kick into his belly to fold him in half, then brought a hammer-fist down like an anvil to the back of his skull. Another he picked up and threw at two others, a carnival game of pins and balls. It took them by enough of a surprise that one of them stood there stupid, long enough to let Sofia break his wrist, and all at once they were backing away, changing their minds, no fresh pussy was worth this.

He'd have to sleep light from now on, but was probably going to anyway, if last night was any indication.

Awhile later, Olaf and Morgan were brought back, neither of them worse off than before. The cartel guys, Olaf said, had only sat them down and grilled them about who they were, what they did, where they came from, who did they know with money. Mainly it was about the money.

Nobody was more relieved to hear this than Sebastián. He turned giddy, going on how it was only a matter of time before somebody came through, somebody had to—they made other people money, didn't they? They were an investment somebody would want to protect. Bas couldn't wait to help their captors out, give them names. Manager, label people, promoters. They had fans, so maybe a Kickstarter, bring the whole world in on getting them home safely.

Sebastián was everything hope looked like when it came unhinged.

The longer the day went on with nobody asking them anything, the farther Bas fell again. By dusk, he was making such a fuss at the barred windows, shouting to anyone who'd listen how ready he was to talk, that Enrique dragged him back before someone decided they were sick of listening to him squall.

It wasn't happening.

Whatever they were here for, it was something other than money.

*   *   *

Later that night they got their first look at how things ultimately went here. It was just late enough for people to start getting drowsy, this holy prison filling with the sounds of people dropping off and snoring, one of them muttering from someplace deep inside a bad dream. Then reality intruded, as bad or worse, everybody roused by the extraction team as they burst in and went straight for one of the Sinaloa guys he'd scrapped with earlier and dragged him away screaming.

Straight to Santa Muerte.

Maybe they'd picked him because he'd outlived his usefulness. Or because it was a good time to grab him, since he was fucked up from earlier and couldn't struggle as well. Or because he'd lost a fight with a big chubby guy and this left him looking weak. Maybe it was random and there was no reasoning behind it at all.

Enrique's nerves were too shredded to settle on how he was supposed to feel about this. Relieved? One less enemy to worry about, after all. Hours earlier he could've killed the guy himself. He'd *wanted* him dead, wanted him humbled and suffering.

Just not like this.

Enrique was the only one at the window—everybody else must have seen it all before—until Sebastián joined him like it was the last place he wanted to be except for everyplace else here.

"Don't watch, boys," Padre Thiago called out to them. "Why would you watch?"

Good question. With that cartel snuff footage he'd combed through online, at least Sebastián was better equipped to handle it. As for himself? Could be he needed an unfiltered look at where this could end for them. All the motivation he would need to push the schedule and make it quicker, when the time came.

The crew had enough stark white lights burning out front that it wasn't hard to see. It took eight or nine guys to handle things—three to get the victim into place, the rest standing guard to enforce compliance if needed, then one more coming into view when the others parted and the light caught him.

"Oh shit," Sebastián breathed. "I know that one, I've seen him . . . seen him in pictures, I think."

This newest guy didn't need the machete in his hand to look like walking death. He had the part down already. Tall, thin as a broomstick and without a shirt, bone and ropy muscle standing out in equally sharp relief across his tattooed skin. They covered him, maybe 20% of his hide left uninked for contrast. The rest was monochrome designs in black and dark green, cheap ink. Or maybe he hated color.

"How can you be sure?" Enrique said.

"The ones on his face. I only ever saw one of them looking like that."

The skin around his eyes had been shaded into dark ovals. The sides of his nose were blacked out too, along with his lower cheeks and parts of his chin. His head was shaved. From a distance, and probably close-up, too, the effect was like a living, decorated skull.

"I think he's MS-13," Sebastián said. "They don't even try to blend."

Funny thing—he thought he was at rock bottom already. No more room left to feel worse about their chances. But hearing this was a reminder: There was always room to go lower.

Some may have been as bad, but nobody was worse than MS-13. Salvadorans from Los Angeles, originally, but over time they'd spread, exported, colonized, let others in. Worked with the cartels, some of them. Salvadoran, Mexican, Guatemalan . . . nationalities didn't matter as much when the big thing you had in common was the ability to bury your humanity so deep you could never find it again, leaving it to rot with the worms. When you could do what they did without feeling anything more than that it had to be done. That this was what it took to get business taken care of. No different than guys who clocked in at the meat plants. They all had two eyes, two ears, and a mouth, same as the pigs and cows, but were still the ones holding the chainsaws.

The Sinaloa guy was stripped to his boxer shorts, then stretched out flat on the ground as somebody stood on each arm to keep him there. The Skull started by taking off his hands. As somebody else moved in with a propane torch to cauterize the stumps, he picked up the hands and flicked the blood from them into the dirt as he carried them over to Santa Muerte. They hacked off his feet next and made offerings of those, too. The men weighting him down stepped off to let the guy roam at will because how far could he get now, down to four stumpy limbs, nothing but charred nubs at the ends.

They seemed to find it entertaining. Nothing funnier than watching a guy in that condition try to flop away.

The Skull opened a big wooden box then, pulling out every kind of knife there was: military knives, hunting knives, fish knives, kitchen cutlery. He took his time, sticking one in and leaving it in place like a plug, because pulling the blade out would free the wound to bleed, and the Skull didn't want that. Soft tissue, areas that wouldn't be immediately fatal—those were his targets, and he found them one by one.

There seemed no end to it, a harder thing to watch than the amputations because of the calm, casual progression, the guy on the receiving end mindlessly trying to wallow away every time another blade skewered him, until he could no longer manage even that much, and could only lie there and take it, more and more bristling like a porcupine. The only way Enrique was certain he was still alive was because of how the handles rose and fell with each ragged breath. Every now and then, his whole carcass shuddered.

Enrique wouldn't have thought so until now, but he found this ordeal worse to contemplate than coming apart at the joints. He had more soft tissue than anybody here, enough to keep the Skull busy for hours.

He watched when he could, turned away when he couldn't. But he never left the window. *This is what it takes to be glad to die.*

Sebastián, though, had checked out a long time ago, sliding down the wall and holding himself together with both arms wrapped around his knees. Maybe it was easier to watch when it was on video. Bas could always pretend it was special effects in a movie. All he had to do was turn off the sound.

Sound was the giveaway, he'd explained once, how you knew when something was real and when it was staged. Terrified people, dying people, people in agony, made sounds that nobody could get to under any other circumstances. Once you'd heard the difference, there could be no confusing the two.

Just as there were sights you couldn't unsee, there were sounds you couldn't unhear, and this poor fucker out there had made them all.

So when they finished it, the Skull tugging a wicked looking military knife free of the guy's groin and using it to saw off his head, the sound was more a part of it than anything Enrique could see. The angle was bad, too many bristling knife handles in the way. But he could hear it, that soul-shredding crescendo of mortality the guy had been holding in reserve.

Enrique didn't know when it happened, only that at some point Nietzsche's old warning came to mind: *If you gaze long into an abyss, the abyss will also gaze into you.* This was the feeling he got every time the Skull looked up from his work and peered straight at him in the window, as if making sure Enrique was still watching.

Good. You need to pay attention, the Skull seemed to be saying. *I know it's rough, but this is what it takes to get where we're going.*

*   *   *

He lost track of time, didn't know if it was an hour after the slaughter or an hour before sunrise. All he knew was that he was lying on the floor next to Sofia, their arms hooked around each other's at the elbow. He remembered seeing somewhere that otters slept this way, holding hands so they wouldn't drift apart on the river. If he had a next life coming, that was how he wanted to be reborn. Come back as an otter, sweet-faced and sleek and holding hands while he slept, and life would be simple.

"We should have never gone to Matamoros," Sofia said to him in the dark. "You and me, we should have voted Bas down. We should never have agreed to go to that ranch." She moved her head closer and kept her voice low, everything just between them. "It had us then. It reached out from the past and took us."

That was how it felt, yeah. They'd raised their heads high enough to be noticed by the dreadful thing that claimed this land, and it decided it wanted them. It opened its jaws to gobble them up and the cartel guys were its teeth.

"I was going to tell you earlier, when we were there, but I didn't want the place listening to me, you know?" she said. "Hearing about what happened at that ranch was my first memory. The first one I can pin down."

So much worse was going on around them, but this still hurt him straight to the heart. "That's awful."

"I was three," she went on. "Something like that, kidnapping, human sacrifice, you don't understand it when you're that little. And you shouldn't. You shouldn't ever have to understand it. At the time, it was more about the effect it had on my mother, and me seeing how she reacted. Not just to what they'd found, but what they hadn't, too, because there was talk of them maybe taking kids that never did turn up."

Lying there, he wished for an arm of iron that they could never break if they came in to drag Sofia away.

"I didn't understand it, but my mother did. I could see how much it scared her. How afraid she was for me. That there were people out there who would do these things. That's what came through. And I could tell, she was afraid she couldn't protect me, not from people like that. Because they had the devil behind them. Once that settled in, I don't know if I ever felt totally safe again."

"I'm sorry," he whispered, and meant it for everything he hadn't been able to do for her, then or now.

"I should have never stopped believing in the devil."

*   *   *

The next afternoon, at the height of the heat of the day, they came for Sebastián.

At first, weirdly enough, it was just an order, almost deferential compared to their usual methods, threat behind it but no force. When he didn't want any part of it, only then did things get rough, Bas taking a knee to the groin so hard it brought up his meager lunch. The bones went out of his legs, the fear so overwhelming every muscle went loose.

Sofia was screaming, reaching for Bas as they dragged him across the floor. It took both of Enrique's arms in wraparound to hold her back. Had it been just him and Bas, he would've done it, rushed them, made these savages shoot them both, let them bleed out quick from twenty bullet wounds apiece. But with Sofia here, he couldn't bring himself to do it, not as long as they didn't want her yet, and he hated himself for being like the rest of the docile herd, buying into the desperation: that as long as there was time, there was hope.

When they got Sebastián out the door, they surprised everybody by coming back for one more. Miguel Cardenas this time, the country balladeer who'd written one narco ballad too many, in his filthy white shirt and black pants with the silver studs down the sides. With him, there was no deference at all, the cartel team back to their usual routine of brutality first, orders later. Once he got over the shock, he begged all the way out the door.

You could follow their path outside by the sobbing. After Sofia hunkered on the floor with her hands squashed over her ears, Enrique forced himself to the window and saw two guys waiting near Santa Muerte, holding sledgehammers like firing squad riflemen waiting for the order to aim.

Both, as it turned out, were for Cardenas. They took out his knees first, and after he was down they smashed his elbows, then went to work on his hands and feet. They left him plenty alive, just nothing to crawl with, fight with, grab with, resist with. They reduced it all to pulp and compound fractures.

At the first couple of blows, Sebastián buckled to the ground as if he'd been hit too, going fetal as the hammers rose and fell. When the guys swinging the iron backed off, the Skull took over, squatting next to Sebastián, doing no worse than laying a hand on his shoulder, but Bas flinched anyway.

This was beyond figuring out, as long as he couldn't hear what the Skull was saying—and there *was* a conversation going on. One minute, two minutes, three. He wasn't treating Bas cruelly, only patting him on the shoulder a couple of times, as if telling him, *There, there, it'll be all right.*

Then the Skull had somebody bring his box of knives and it looked to be last night all over again. Until he took one for himself and gave another to Sebastián. He pointed at Cardenas and his pulverized joints, lying on his back and howling at the sky.

Enrique clutched the bars over the window as Bas began shaking his head, *no no no no*. The Skull went first, sinking his first knife to the hilt into Cardenas' thigh, then glaring at Sebastián: *Your turn.*

When he couldn't do it, the Skull's voice got louder, yelling now, discernible.

"You don't hate him? You don't hate his music, everything a hack like him stands for?" the Skull shouted. "Come on, man, you're ten times the singer he is. Let it out! You sing about hate all the time! Is that just an act? What good is the hate if you don't let it out!"

Sebastián gave Cardenas a half-hearted poke, sufficient to scratch the skin, but not good enough. The Skull badgered and threatened, then told him he'd better do it right this time or maybe Santa Muerte would get one of his eyes. He didn't need both eyes to sing. Didn't need either of them, for that matter.

It snapped him. Bas wailed from the ground and with a sob plunged the knife into Cardenas' belly.

Back and forth then. *One for you, one for me.* It came easier each time, Bas sticking in every subsequent blade with less hesitation and more resolve. *This is what it takes to crawl away.* It was like watching a little more of him going dead inside each round.

Ten or twelve knives later, the Skull called a break to confer, voices too low to hear again. He had somebody bring another wooden box—like a small, low crate—and hefted something out of it, treating it with obvious care. Enrique couldn't tell what it was, only that it looked flat and heavy and as black as outer space. It was lost from view as the Skull put it on the ground and the two of them hunched over it.

Minutes of this, while every so often, Cardenas wailed and moaned and tried to move in some way that his smashed parts wouldn't allow.

Until it was back to the knives. Just the Skull this time, looming over Sebastián in a posture of challenge, authority. Bas kept trying to back away but was too cracked to get anywhere, head hanging at the end of a neck gone limp as he used up the last of whatever he had in him to say no. Not that. Please no. Every time he did, the Skull merged another knife with some part of Miguel Cardenas.

"I can do this all day!" the Skull told him. "You gonna let that happen? Gonna let me keep doing this until I run out of knives? All you got to do is cut him once. It would be an act of mercy."

And that was how you broke somebody for good: made him do a thing like this.

"You tell me no one more time, the next thing you get to do is pick which one of your people you get to watch me gut in front of you. Your choice."

Took one piece of his soul at a time.

Bas must have quietly acquiesced. The Skull handed him a knife, one of the big, mean looking ones, maybe the same go-to blade he'd used to finish things last night. And the finish was the same. From this angle, Enrique couldn't see much, Sebastián in a kneeling position, his elbow pumping back and forth in a sawing motion. Two hideous screams. One ended quickly, the other one kept going. And going.

That was the impressive thing about Bas. He could hold a note for a long time.

Way past what for most people would be the breaking point.

* * *

It was hours before he could talk, another hour after that before anything intelligible came out. Until then, it was just Bas in a corner, huddled up like a whipped dog, catatonic sometimes, shaking when he wasn't, eyes focused on nothing. Sofia held him, rocked him, reported that he felt like he'd crawled out of a cold river. Morgan and Olaf hung close, ready to help if they could, but they couldn't.

"He wanted to know," Bas said, halting every few words, "about the last album."

La máscara detrás de la cara, that would've been. *The Mask Behind the Face.*

"What about it?"

"He wanted to know where it came from."

Enrique had to let this sink in, double-check to make sure Bas had it right. Even if it explained why they'd returned him alive, Enrique still couldn't believe it had come down to this: that they'd been taken by a fan who wanted to get close to the band.

"I didn't understand what he meant. I couldn't follow him. I didn't know what to tell him." Sebastián seemed unable to stop replaying everything in his mind, or stop shaking his head. "He made me look at a rock. He kept making me look at the rock. I couldn't see what he wanted me to. But he wouldn't let me look away from the rock."

It was about all they got out of him.

Things were quiet for the evening and the rest of the night, sitting in the dark with *los muertos*, the other dead. A whole new heavy black mood had settled in. Forced to butcher each other—this was an escalation nobody had seen coming, and now that it was here, how was anyone supposed to look at the person next to him without imagining which of them might end up forced to hold the knives?

None of them had overheard what Bas had said—it was too soft to hear unless you were right next to him—and Enrique wasn't going to tell the rest to ease their minds. *Go on, keep trusting one another, you're still in this together, because if it happens again, it'll only be me or Sofia holding the knife.* Yeah, that would go over great.

Just Olaf, just Morgan. He told them.

The rest? Let them live with it, the same fear they'd spent their lives inflicting on their neighbors. *This is what it takes to start paying for your sins.*

He listened in the dark as Padre Thiago ministered to the ones who decided they'd lived as wolves long enough and it was time to be lambs again. Time to let a priest pray over them, deliver them of the cruel devils that had taken them over to make them do such terrible things. If they were going to God soon, they wanted to go clean and pure and forgiven.

And there it was—the reason he'd never had much use for God. If he had to believe in a god at all, he wanted one who would really hold you to your life's choices.

*   *   *

When they came for him the next morning Enrique was ready for it, the only one in the room who didn't retreat to the far wall like the others. They were so used to it, these guys with their guns and their yelling, they didn't know what to make of him, that somebody would sit in the floor waiting for whatever came next. His passivity unnerved them, all eight guys peeking at each other like they didn't trust it and didn't know what to do next, afraid they were being suckered into the struggle of their lives.

"I'll go," Enrique said. "No big deal. When did fighting it ever work for anybody? I'll go."

They took him alone, him and nobody else. They escorted him around the side of the church, three days since he'd felt the ground beneath his boots and the open sky and the direct searing heat of the sun. At the end of it, the Skull was waiting, and behind him, that colossal likeness of Santa Muerte with her scythe, grim against the cloudless blue and gritting her ivory teeth at the horizon. Everything else looked baked to shades of brown.

Somebody shoved a foot into the back of one knee to drop him to the earth. He knew better than to get up. The guards backed off to give them space.

"I figured it was either you or Sebastián," the Skull told him. "Drummers, they're the heart, they're not usually the visionaries. They feel the pulse of the earth. They don't see through time. So it had to be you or him. And it wasn't him."

"I don't know what you're talking about."

"Yeah you do. You're just playing stupid."

From here, close up, it was like seeing this guy for the first time. He was more than a living skull now. Skulls didn't have eyebrows. Skulls didn't have lips. Enrique could see the way his skin moved over his actual bones, could discern the numbers and words, patterns and pictures, inked into his skin. He looked close to emaciated, either by genetics or by choice, or maybe he was an example of function creating form. He had only as much as a reaper needed, and no more.

"You keep playing stupid, I'll treat you like you're stupid. You'll make me do something to smarten you up. Is that what you want?"

"I want to be gone from here. Me and mine. That's what I want."

The Skull nodded as if this were one of many possibilities. "It could happen."

Three little words, so much hope. *It could happen.* But probably an illusion.

"Sebastián may be the one at the front of the stage, but he does what you tell him to. He's only got as much to work with as you give him. You're the architect of what you three do," the Skull said. "Tell me I'm wrong."

"It's more complicated than that. But you're not wrong."

"I get it. You need him and he needs you. You, you're not the kind of guy who'll ever be at the front of the stage. You don't have the look. But you got something better. You got the brains. You got the vision."

It was one of the more backhanded compliments anyone had given him. But under the circumstances? He'd take it.

"So . . . *The Mask Behind the Face.* I could tell, just from the title, here's someone who knows some things. Here's someone who sees. Then I listen and read the lyrics, and I think, here's someone who *understands.* How you did it, that's beyond me, I don't know how a studio works, but you managed to put together the electronics and all that other aggro shit with those ancient flutes and grinding stones and old drums, and made a sound not like anything I ever heard. An effect not like anything I ever felt. A sound, that's just noise unless you got an idea behind it. And you did. That was the thing that convinced me, whoever did this is some kind of shaman."

The Skull was pacing with the frantic movements of somebody who'd spent a long time looking for an elusive prize and was on the verge of finding it.

"It wasn't just the notes. Anybody can play the notes." He squatted, nose to tattooed nose with Enrique. "There's something in there *between* the notes, looking back out. I don't know how you captured that. But it's there. And it's a fucking monster." It was hard to tell if his eyes were desperate or insane. "How did you *know*?"

Slowly, Enrique shook his head. "I've got no answer for that. I wish I did."

"You don't leave here unless you give me better than that."

"I could make up a better lie. Is that what you want?"

The Skull peered at him from inches away, as if trying to see beneath the skin. "You got the look of the first people here. Maybe that explains it, why you and not Sebastián. You got the look of the conquered, not the conquistador. You got that blood memory in you, maybe."

He pulled back, squatting with his bony elbows on his pointy knees.

"And me, see, I know blood. I know sacrifice. I'm one of the ones they call when they really want to send a message, because I can do it and not blink." He motioned to the towering Santa Muerte, the body parts laid out before her. They buzzed with flies and gave off a stink like roadkill. "It's just another day's work to me. But that doesn't mean I don't ever think about what I'm doing. To me, it's nothing new. It's something that's come around again, part of something that goes way back. I can feel it in the knives. Their handles, man, they fucking hum."

His scrutiny turned puzzled, hungry for secrets he'd never been able to grab.

"A guy like you, you don't get your hands red the way I do. But you figured it out anyway. All I'm asking is how."

"It's just knowing some history, some myths, is all. Same shit, different century. It's just following where it leads."

The Skull nodded, eager, like they were getting somewhere. "You went straight to the oldest stories, I could tell. The people here, way before the Spaniards showed up, they had a good thing going. They had this teacher, maybe he was a god, or maybe he was something else and a god was the only thing they knew to call him. Kukulcan . . . Quetzalcoatl . . . whatever his real name was. He was teaching them everything they needed to know. These people, they were on their way *up*. The sun was theirs. And then the clouds came. It's what clouds do, right? Come in and wash things away."

The legends called him Tezcatlipoca—a dark, malevolent god who had come along and driven the teacher off.

Whatever the differences between them, he and the Skull could speak of this much like equals, at least.

These archaic figures, these events, had always felt to him like more than myth. More than his ancestors' way of trying to make sense of their failings, their hungers and thirsts, their savagery. Behind the stories was something hidden and true, and behind that, more truths that he couldn't begin to guess at. He just knew they were there.

Ever since he was a boy, seeing the world take shape around him, farther and farther from his mother's kitchen, it was hard to deny the sense that something had gone wrong here, in this land. Hundreds of years ago, or maybe thousands. Something had come down from above, or up from below, or in from outside, and convinced the people that it had a neverending need for their blood, shed in all kinds of ways. *You see those knives? You see those chests with the hearts beating inside them? You see those skins you can peel away and wear over your own until they fall apart? Get to it, and don't ever stop. This is what it takes now, so never forget.*

It was everything he knew and nothing he could prove. All he'd ever been able to do was turn up the volume and scream into the clouds.

"*Gracias*," the Skull whispered, and pushed up from his squat to stand tall again. "Thank you for letting me know I'm not the only one."

They'd been friendly enough that the anger began to override the fear. "Man, everything you asked is something you could've asked me through the band's web site. Or hit me up on Twitter. People got questions, we don't ignore them. We talk back, you know."

Images flickered like flash cards. Their driver Hector, killed at the wheel. Crispin, shot out of his shoes. Guys butchered outside the window, and forcing Bas to join in. They could let him go right now, and he would never unsee these last few days. For as long as he lived, he would be waking up from nightmares.

"Did it really have to take all this?"

And look. The Skull knew how to smile. "You think this little chat is it? No, this is us getting to know each other. The next part, that's the initiation. That's the important part."

He whistled and motioned toward their makeshift prison, and three guys came out escorting Padre Thiago. He'd chosen not to fight it either. Calmest face you ever saw. Like he expected God was going to take care of him on the spot. *There, there, my child, trust in me for deliverance.*

"Don't do this. Please don't do this." Enrique had sworn he wouldn't beg, and listen to him now. Everybody's got a plan until the knives come out. "Did I not treat you with respect? Didn't I take you seriously? What's the point of this? You think trying to turn us into you is gonna get you any closer to answers than you got already?"

The Skull was only half paying attention as he hauled over the box of knives and the compact crate from last night. The latter was the least among his props, and with every other nightmarish thing going on, Enrique had all but forgotten about it.

He made me look at a rock. He kept making me look at the rock.

The desperation was starting to eat deeper. "It wasn't any shaman that did that album, just three pissed-off people who like to make loud noises. I don't know shit, all I'm doing is asking the same questions as you."

I couldn't see what he wanted me to. But he wouldn't let me look away from the rock.

Padre Thiago passed him then, patted him on his big round shoulder, the cruelest thing the priest could've done—absolving him in advance. It was all Enrique could do to not scream at him. *Get your hand off me, old man. Don't you know where this is going? Don't you know what he's gonna make me do to you? I don't want you forgiving me for any of it.*

From the crate, the Skull removed the artifact from last night, flat and heavy. As black as outer space, he'd thought while seeing it from a distance, not knowing why he'd made the connection. Now he remembered reading about an astronaut who came back saying that, from out there in it, space looked shiny.

Obsidian, he realized, now that he saw the artifact close up. Volcanic glass. It was shaped like an irregular rectangle, scooped out but too shallow to be a bowl, too bulky to be a plate, and polished into a black mirror. The rim was threaded with gray-green veins marbled into the stone itself, seemingly random, but nagging him with a promise that if he stared long enough he would comprehend a hidden pattern, an intentional design the earth had woven in the chaos of fire and lava.

The outer edges were rougher, designs carved around the circumference, lines that thickened and thinned, swooped and jittered and curved back onto themselves. Not Aztec, not Mayan, not Olmec, not like any patterns he'd seen before.

As he looked at it, his gaze pulled by its peculiar gravity, it caught a reflection of lumpy clouds skimming overhead, the effect like smoke drifting across its gleaming black surface.

I know what this is . . .

Except when he looked up, there were no clouds.

The Smoking Mirror—it was another of their names for Tezcatlipoca, the dark god who had chased away their teacher. They hadn't called him that because of his eyes, his face, his demeanor. None of that. It wasn't poetics, it was practical. They'd called him that because of something he'd owned and used. He would gaze into it and see things—the far-away doings of gods and men, they said.

"Where did you get this?"

"A guy in Tampico," the Skull told him. "You kill enough people, you've seen everything they try to buy you off with. But this? This was a first. Where he got it, I don't know. I get the idea it's one of those things that doesn't stay in the same pair of hands for long. It keeps on the move. It's . . . restless."

Even Padre Thiago looked drawn to it, mesmerized, until the Skull lunged at him and clocked him across the jaw with his fist. The priest hit the ground before Enrique could scramble over on his knees to catch him, not wholly unconscious but not much good for anything else for a while.

The Skull pointed at him. "He tell you why he's here?"

"He said it was for doing exorcisms, and somebody didn't like it."

"Yeah? That's what he told you? Well, he's half right." The Skull squatted before him again, voice at a murmur. "I heard about him. This priest. Still God's warrior while the Church is losing people left and right to Santa Muerte. Still out there saving souls."

It took Enrique a moment to catch on: The Skull didn't want any of these other murderers listening to what he had to say.

"So I went to him, see what he could do for me. I thought maybe this thing inside, whatever it is that's got its hooks in me, I want it out, and he's the one who can do it. Most of the time I think it's just me. But that's the lie it feeds you. There's other times I can feel it moving. Like something else has got itself lined up with my eyes."

Or maybe *that* was the lie. Anything to believe it wasn't purely him all along.

The Skull glared at Thiago with scorn. "He didn't do shit for me. Isn't that the worst thing a priest can do? Leave you the same as he found you? But I don't know why I expected more. He's still got this Old World way of looking at things. What's he gonna do for me when he's stuck chasing after some pointy-tailed devil?"

The Skull patted the bony cage of his chest.

"So I figure as long as I'm stuck with it, I might as well go all in, make friends with it. And I got *that*." He hitched his thumb at the black stone, its shiny jet surface still drifting with billows and clouds. "Only it doesn't work for me. That's all it ever does. It won't show me shit."

I couldn't see what he wanted me to.

And now, *now*, Enrique understood why they were here.

But he wouldn't let me look away from the rock.

"You? You got the vision. You got the look, like your DNA never heard of Spain. You got as far as you did figuring some of these things out on your own," the Skull said. "So I got to wonder, how much farther could you get if we juice it up for you? How much farther can you get when there's blood?"

The Skull set the black stone, the smoking mirror, next to Padre Thiago, who still hadn't come to his senses. Then he chose a knife and tossed it over. Enrique stared at it, lying in front of him on the hard-packed dirt. He gauged the distance between himself and the Skull. Looked at the guys with guns, tuning in again now that the time for talking was over.

If he wanted a firing squad, the moment had come.

"You know what to do," the Skull said. "First one, that's always the hardest. Then it gets easier. It did for Sebastián."

Enrique glanced back at the church and saw Sofia in the window, fists wrapped around the bars and everything about her imploring him to live. She hadn't watched for Bas. But she was watching for him.

He picked up the knife. The blade was long, thin, with tiny serrations along its edge. A boning knife, it looked like. It would go in easy. The Skull had chosen it for that. Enrique wiped it clean on his pant leg. Pointless, maybe, but he did it anyway.

He made himself look at Padre Thiago, at the man's droopy, stubbled face as he rolled his head to the side, gaze meeting gaze. There was already blood, leaking from a split lip swollen like a bicycle tire about to burst. The priest was coming around again, peace in his eyes as he granted permission, stupid old man lying there ready to be a martyr. This is what it takes to be like Jesus.

Fuck these guys. He didn't want to give either one of them what they wanted.

Enrique didn't think about it. He just did it. Shoved it up the long black sleeve of his shirt, crusted with days of sweat and dirt, and slashed the blade across the meat of his forearm. It opened like a lipless mouth, red on the inside but nothing happening, just like he didn't feel anything yet, then all at once it hurt and welled up and spilled over hot.

"You stupid motherfucker! Why did you do that?" The Skull turned frenetic, diving toward him to snatch the knife and fling it out of reach. "Why would you *do* that?"

Somewhere behind him, Sofia was screaming too. A voice like that, maybe it should've been her at the front of the stage all along. And it was almost funny. This is what it takes to say I love you.

The Skull scrambled with him in the dirt and the blood, and he was strong, crazy strong, freakishly strong as he dragged the stone over and grabbed Enrique's arm to lay it across the shiny black surface. Because while it may have been the wrong blood, as long as it was flowing, might as well not waste it.

Black and red, red on black—it pulsed and spattered, and the Skull smeared it across the smooth glass like a kid starting on a finger painting. Enrique was already going lightheaded, maybe not so much from actual blood loss as the *idea* of losing it. He'd always been a wuss about that, seeing himself leak a reminder of those childhood beatings from guys like this, the kids who listened to the call.

Lightheaded—how else to explain what he was seeing? Stone didn't absorb blood. Sandstone, maybe, a little, but not obsidian. That wasn't how it worked. That wasn't how anything he knew about the world and rocks worked.

But the stone was a greedy thing, and it drank as if a million microscopic mouths opened wherever the blood pooled, and wanted more. His arm delivered. The Skull saw to that.

Whatever the black glass was showing him, clouds or smoke or steam, the billows and wisps began to drift apart. The space he saw waiting behind them looked shiny, shiny in a way that went beyond the glossiness of the surface. There was depth here, or a perfect illusion of it, the smooth black more like a porthole than a screen.

He couldn't tell if what he was seeing belonged to the infinite depths between worlds or the unplumbed recesses beneath the earth, only that whatever stirred there stirred alone. No, not stirred . . . *crawled*, all body and no limbs. His perspective was small, yet what stared back seemed vast, titanic in the way only something so pure and simple could be. When it raised its head, its blind face had the unfinished look of a worm.

The Skull was riding his back now, jamming his head next to Enrique's like they were both reading from the same engrossing book.

He thought of everything that lay between him and this monstrosity on the other side. He thought of altars, of ritual bowls and *chacmools*. He thought of killing fields and the steep, blood-slick steps descending the side of a pyramid. Channels and conduits, all. It didn't matter where this thing was—he sensed that much in his heart. Didn't matter how near or far away it dwelled. When blood was let, the flow found a way there. All spaces were one, a single point in time.

It drank him the same as it must have drunk millions before him, the thinnest visible drizzle falling on the flat, probing slug of its tongue. It then recoiled, as if it didn't like the taste of him. Blood was blood, you'd think, but maybe its palate was more refined than you'd expect. Maybe it could discern some difference in the flavor of him, his blood let by his own hand because he would rather do that than slaughter the man next to him.

And it spewed him from the cavern of its mouth.

The smoke billowed across the glass to obscure the gulf between once more, and the stone was only obsidian again, black glass and nothing more.

He thought it was a trick of the mind when a shadow seemed to dim the light on this patch of ground where he lay facedown and bleeding. That's what blood loss did. Made your world a dimmer place.

But did it make hardened killers, bored with watching men die, shout and run?

Did it make the ground shake under three ponderous footsteps?

Did it make a sound like an enormous scythe sweeping down from above to cut the air in two?

Beside him, Padre Thiago lifted off the ground, there one instant, then gone. It took the last effort Enrique could call on to roll over onto his back, where he saw the halves of the priest's body fly away to either side of the enormous blade, and beyond that, looming far above, the bone face of their Santa Muerte, the skull he'd always thought looked much too real.

A red rain showered them all.

*   *   *

He awoke to heat and stillness and the lazy buzzing of flies. There were flies in Hell, weren't there? Pesky, biting, pain-in-the-ass flies that never let up tormenting the sinners. So maybe he was okay. These were just hanging around, the same old everyday shit-eaters.

The inside of his left forearm burned, but that was his own fault. Enrique found it bandaged, and beneath that, stitched. The Skull and the rest of his crew—what were they, if not a unit gone to war? It made sense they'd have a medic around.

He lay on a thin mattress atop squeaky springs, staring at a ceiling scarred with peeling paint and plaster so cracked and crumbled he could see the wooden slats above it. Some rundown room in some other building that wasn't the church. He'd slept in worse places, actually, back when the band had to take whatever it could get. Never in clothes sticky with a priest's blood, though. There were all kinds of ways to hit a new low.

Except for the flies, he couldn't hear a sound. There was no sound *to* hear.

He got up from the bed—hung over from something they'd shot him up with, it felt like—and wandered to the window. Like waking up in a ghost town. Nothing out there to see but dust and corpses and pieces of corpses. None of it seemed real. He might as well be waking up in a video game. Wounded, not a clue, and next thing he was supposed to do was find a weapon and start killing anything that moved.

Only everything was dead already. Nothing outside was moving. Just him, once he got there.

Under the hot white eye of the sun, Enrique trudged toward the bodies. They'd really cleaned house before they'd abandoned the place, hadn't they? Finished what they'd started, wrapping it up in a hurry, then bugging out fast. Maybe this was normal for them, treating places like a landfill, and when the bodies piled up too high, they moved on.

Most were hanging by their ankles, like bloody laundry, from cables stretched between poles, more than he could count at a glance. Nobody had died easy. Some had just died harder than others. More blood for the vast grave worm that tunneled through their lives, their world, their existence. And sooner or later, all the flies found their way here.

He trembled like it was twenty degrees instead of a hundred. As he scanned the rows of the dead, he looked for clothing because he couldn't bring himself to look at faces, and was relieved to see there wasn't much black, and none of it meant for a stage.

Lots of black hair, though. Except for the blond guy. Except for Olaf. Olaf the photographer. Whose real name was Oliver, he'd learned in the church, the sort of thing that came out when you were sitting around killing time waiting to see who was next to be killed. Said he got more gigs as Olaf than he ever had as Oliver—a man who knew how the game was played.

Yet here he was.

Enrique checked for a smaller body, half of it hair, but Morgan wasn't among them. He was past deciding whether something was good or bad anymore. Maybe all that was left was bad right now, and bad deferred to later.

Like that empty spot where the towering Santa Muerte had stood. Did you just pack up a thing like that and move it? Was something like that really a priority? You'd need two strong guys just to carry the scythe.

Because no way had he seen what he thought he had there at the end. That priest had found some other way to get cut in half.

He turned his attention to the church. The pair of front doors was secured with a heavy, squared-off crossbar. Before he wrestled it from its brackets, he stooped to gather what was waiting, what had plainly been placed here for him to find. Three phones, plus a charger. When he tried his own, it was dead. When he tried the others, they were dead too.

But better the phones than Sofia and Sebastián.

He found them inside huddled along the far wall. Before they saw it was him, they scurried back farther, reacting only to the opening of the door, the way you learned to live in a place like this, where a few more millimeters might mean another second of life.

No sign of Morgan, though. She was just . . . gone.

When he went to Sofia and Bas, they felt real enough, sounded real enough, even if it felt like something was missing. Everybody too far gone at this point for a show of relief, let alone jubilation. How was he supposed to bring them back to themselves? How were they supposed to bring *him* back? There were no manuals for this. There was only standing. There was putting one foot after another. There was holding hands and holding close. There was making your way back into the sunshine, in spite of what it showed.

It would've been easier if the Skull had left a note, some validation of why they were still alive. But maybe the mere fact they were breathing was all the note he would ever need: *Keep doing what you're doing. Keep looking. Like skin, there's always another layer deeper to go.*

Yeah. Like he wanted any part of that. Like he didn't want to wipe his memory clean of everything about these past few days. Like he wouldn't do anything to hit the reset switch and go back a week.

No, longer than that—go back two years, take those first conceptual sketches for *La máscara detrás de la cara* and throw them out. Hope that some intuitive voice inside would tell him *stop right now, you don't want to start looking behind that succession of masks and faces*, and hope he'd have the balls to listen.

"How are we getting out of here?" Sofia said. "They could've at least left us one of the cars."

All they could do was charge one of the dead phones, try using it to get a fix on where they were, then relay the information to whoever they could raise. Sebastián had a GPS app on his, so they put him in charge of finding the nearest electrical outlet. They would've anyway, because if Bas didn't have something to do, he was going to keep falling apart a little more at a time.

Enrique knew the feeling. You couldn't stand around waiting. You had to do something, anything. He pointed to the church's open bell tower, said to Sofia come on, they should get up there, take the high ground and see if they could spot a landmark, more than they could see from down below.

They found the roof access tucked off a hallway inside, like a closet with a ladder affixed to the wall, stuffy as a chimney the higher they climbed. A trapdoor put them topside. The bell still hung mounted on a wooden headstock, no sign of the rope used for ringing it. Sofia gave it a rap with her knuckles to summon a sad, hollow clunk.

The bell sounded as dead as everything else looked, as far as he could see.

They were on an observation deck with nothing left to observe, a seared land scraped thin across a rocky world in a dozen shades of brown, barren of everything but scattered shacks and ruins. To the east, a line of green struggled to overcome, life trying to hang on beside an *arroyo*, maybe. He wished it well.

The sky, the blue of dreams, was the only vibrant thing to see. They hadn't killed the sky yet. Give them time, and enough guns and blades and poison, and they would find a way.

Sofia saw it first, pointing it out in the distance, nearly at the limits of his vision. His soul knew what it was before his mind let him believe his eyes. Even lost amid a simmering hellscape stretching for the horizon, it towered against the rugged desert hills, crossed gullies and washes in a single step, this striding colossus with bone for a face and a scythe in its hands and hunger in whatever passed for its heart.

She was, he realized, too terrible and too true not to have been real all along. And he feared she wouldn't stop until she'd visited every square inch of this land and gathered up her due.

Something had gone wrong here. Hundreds of years ago, or maybe thousands. No wonder it had always wanted their blood. That was where the memory lingered most.

They watched until its saint passed from view, beyond the farthest hills, then turned to each other again. Sofia touched his face like she'd never truly seen it before, and when he touched hers, the thing that hurt most was knowing that under the skin, the two of them looked more alike than not, and the same as everybody else.

AUTHOR'S STORY NOTE

After getting smacked in the face enough times with enough articles about kidnappings in Mexico, it settled over me that I should do a story about one. My Folder of Vague Intentions for it brooded on the hard drive for a few years, slowly attracting affiliates: the skyrocketing devotion to Santa Muerte; the rising rate of exorcisms in Mexico; the Matamoros cult killings of the 1980s; a few photos of MS-13 members, both alive and extremely dead.

The speed bump in the way was angle, direction. The prime mover behind most of these elements is the drug trade and cartel wars, and I didn't want to tread ground that authors like Don Winslow were always going to tread better.

Enter Hocico. Finally.

For the past 15 years, the hard-electro band Hocico has been a personal favorite—two guys who have made music their inflammation response to growing up in Mexico City.

I began thinking of a band very much in their mold; indeed, named after one of their early albums. What if they knew things? What if they managed to tap into a current of understanding that they themselves didn't understand? What if somebody from a world they want nothing to do with believed they knew things?

Once you have your victims and your motive, you have your crime. After that, it's just a matter of watching it play out and expecting the worst.

REPRISING HER ROLE

BRACKEN MACLEOD

From *Splatterpunk Zine* #8
Editor: Jack Bantry

gnacio thought the girl on the bed looked familiar, but then the glassy-eyed heroin slackness made them all look alike. Not that it mattered. She was a prop, not a performer.

He checked the setup again through the LCD monitor. The key light was too close; it washed out the scene and made the set look too clean. Not clean, exactly. The hardest part of Ignacio's job was making something dirty look even dirtier. Without looking directly at the girl, he stepped around the camera and pulled the light back to soften its glare and create deeper shadows that would add needed contrast to the scene. Otherwise, when he inserted the grain effect in post to simulate film instead of digital video, the actress' facial expressions would be lost in the noise. While the audience for this masterpiece would likely be looking elsewhere in the frame for most of the scene, he knew that her face was important. Her expressions sold what was happening, made it look real to a skeptical viewer. And "reality" was what people wanted. In the sense of a "real life" Alaskan trucker series or a pawn shop show. What they were filming couldn't look like a reenactment, but it had to have just enough doubt to let the viewer feel like they'd come within a safe distance of something terrifying. The people who bought Byron Blank's movies at conventions wanted them to look as real as possible, but not actually *be* real. They wanted the production to do the work of suspending disbelief for them so they could watch a couple of dudes tearing up a girl and at the end still feel like they hadn't been complicit in an *actual* atrocity. And that meant that it had to look just fake enough.

That was the problem.

"Vérité is context, not content," Byron liked to say. "What passes for authentic is what people *expect* reality to look like, not what it actually does." Ignacio's job was made easier and more difficult by the fact that people had their own opinions about what looked real, and those were almost always informed by entertainment instead of experience. Making something authentic look fake enough to convince people it was only almost real took work.

The men who'd dropped the girl on the bed a few minutes ago returned in wardrobe, wearing featureless white masks. A violent shiver rippled up Ignacio's spine. He worried that they noticed his discomfort. Detached aloofness to what happened on set was the only appropriate response from behind the production line.

Through the viewfinder, Ignacio studied the girl. He still couldn't place where he'd seen her before. She was pale as a corpse and as almost as still.

While the set depicted a nice, teen girl's bedroom, this girl didn't fit in it at all. Maybe once she might've, but not now. Not with the scar and the heroin dimness in her eyes. She looked like the person the girl who inhabited this room would become in the aftermath of what they were about to shoot.

"The fuck is wrong with her?" Byron shouted as he walked onto the set.

"She's so pumped full of slag she won't notice a thing. We're going to have to do ADR in post," Ignacio said.

"No dubbing!" Byron shifted his focus to the masked performers. "You two make sure she hits her lines, okay?" One thug gave a thumbs up; his other hand was occupied with the front of his trousers.

"And you. No fancy camera shit. Just what they pay for." Ignacio could have easily set up a three camera shoot and cut together the scene using the best footage from each angle. Really made something to be proud of. One camera, one take, one static shot. No artifice. "Vérité is context—"

"Not content," Ignacio finished. "Gotcha, Jefé. Hands off." *Whatever gets you through it,* he thought. *Detachment is self-deception, not distance.* The viewers wanted their brand of role-play porn looking a certain way. Most of the time Ignacio shot brother/sister or mother and step-son role play, and left the "forced" stuff to the Russians. But every once in a while, Byron wanted to wander outside of his demesne and go slumming.

Byron took his seat next to the camera and motioned for the men to stand ready. He looked at Ignacio who gave a weak nod. "Action!"

Ignacio leaned over the camera cupping his hands on either side of his eyes to better see the monitor, and wishing he still had *The Mic Drop* reality show gig. On the tiny screen he watched the men move toward the bed. The bigger of the two grasped the girl's ashy blonde hair, yanking her up from where she lay on the mattress. Her face remained slack except for lips peeled back in a grimace. The sound of the man's hand slapping her cracked in Ignacio's headphones. He flinched and feared bumping the camera. Resetting the shot was unacceptable. He could put in a false video defect so viewers could process the jump without being taken out of the narrative. *Thank you, David Fincher!* Too much of that and it started to look intentional. That kind of contrivance was the kind of thing that could cost him future gigs, and he had a food and rent habit he was unwilling to give up.

No edits. Stay cool. Stay pro.

The next hit was followed by a deep woof of air as a fist slammed into her stomach. But that was still it. No screams. Byron wanted screams.

A sound like tearing canvas crackled through the headphones; Ignacio leaned closer to get a look. Blood painted the woman's pale legs followed by a pile of intestine. He finally remembered the girl.

That can't be her. We killed her.

The smaller man took a step back. A smell of shit and bile rolled off the set like a fog over the bay. Ignacio stood confused and blinking. He hadn't worked an SFX film since he was a P.A. on the second unit crew for *Wicked Season*, and he'd gotten his fill of pig intestine on that shoot. Never again. But there wasn't a make-up creator on this shoot, and he sure as hell hadn't set up an effect. This wasn't even a real film. Just a porno scene. Something to sell to desperate men who thought that if it looked amateur enough, they were getting something unfiltered and forbidden.

The girl stood up, dropping the guts to the floor. She craned her neck around, leering at the camera like she expected Ignacio to zoom in for a close up glamour shot. Her teeth clacked in his headphones.

None of it was right. None of it was in the script.

Finally, a full-throated shriek broke the silence, crackling in Ignacio's headset. One of the performers stripped off his mask and clawed at the girl, trying to get her back on the bed. She wouldn't move. His partner screamed and fell to his knees, trying to gather up his intestines and shove them back in his stomach. The slick viscera kept spilling out over his hands; he fumbled at them, clumsily juggling himself as his tears dripped from beneath his mask, splashing in the spreading gore below. Ignacio heard the thug sobbing and ask for his mother.

Byron ran into frame and tried to grab the woman. Before he could think about what he was saying, Ignacio shouted at him to stop, that he was "ruining the shot." But everything was already ruined. Byron started to shout but his words were cut off before he got more than a word out. Ignacio stepped back and looked up from the monitor at the set to see the woman holding the director by his neck with a bony red hand. Ignacio tried to process what he was seeing; none of it made sense. The expression on her face and the light in her eyes was brighter and more focused than ever.

The full, unfiltered experience of the room settled down over him, the sights, the sounds, the smells. Everything he distanced himself from with the camera as mediator was right in front of him, exposed. The reality of the scene revealed itself like an opaque vinyl strip curtain being pulled back to reveal the cruelty of a charnel house. Byron pulled a pistol from inside his sport coat and aimed it at the woman's face. Instead of a shot, Ignacio heard a sound like he'd never heard before. It certainly wasn't like the stock sound effects he heard in the movies when an action hero broke the bad guy's neck. This sound was wetter. It popped and ground and a low aborted groan escaped Byron's throat. It sounded just like she had when he first saw her through his camera. It sounded like a person dying.

Ignacio ran tripping over cords and cables, getting caught up in them like a moth in a web. The camera and tripod clattered at his heels before getting caught in the doorway and tearing free from the headphone cable dangling from the clamshells still around his neck. He sprinted home, not caring about his equipment, car, or how people stopped and stared at the screaming man tearing up the street in the bright day light.

Ignacio slammed his apartment door, locked it, and doubting what he'd just done, unlocked it and threw the bolt again, just to make sure. He couldn't get a breath and his lungs burned, still, he raced to his bedroom and clawed out the false wall panel in the back of his closet. Dragging out a lockbox, he fumbled at the key pad until getting the code right on the third try and the lock clicked open. Inside, He found the fake Mexican passport his friend in the Art Department at TurnaЯound Films had made for him. It wasn't perfect, but he figured it'd be convincing enough with a couple of hundreds stuffed inside. And he never intended to use it—not unless what was on the flash drive underneath it got out.

Got out.

She can't get out.

He picked the memory stick out of the lockbox with trembling fingers and crept back to the living room. He stuck the thing into the port on the side of his sixty-inch television, and stepping back, pointed the remote at the TV. He hesitated, working up the will to click on the only file on the drive: CHKR.M4P.

The screen went black, replaced a second later with a view of the interior of a foreclosed house. A man in a black leather mask walked into the room and shoved a slender woman with ashy blonde hair onto the bed. After a few minutes of reluctant role-play bordering on the real thing, the actors seemed to pause as if unsure what to do next. Though the viewers didn't want that kind of intimacy, Ignacio had zoomed in on the woman's face. The man's thick white knuckles were visible below her jaw, his fingers white and her face purpling. The key light reflected in the tears that trembled at the edges of her eyelids. The image was real and terrifying and Ignacio was frozen, staring into them on his monitor. Something told him to look closer. Get her eyes on camera. Nothing said to him, nudge Byron. Get him to yell cut. Go over and stop it. Instead, he stared.

Standing in his living room, he remembered her now.

He stood, TV remote in hand and watched her lights go out. Again.

The image zoomed back and the scene blurred and swirled around as the lens pointed at the ceiling. Byron screamed in the background at the actor. The actor was hyperventilating, and crying, and then he threw up inside his mask. Ignacio recalled the competing smells of vomit and the woman's piss on the bed, and felt his own stomach churn. A minute later, the file ended and the TV screen returned to the menu.

The shoot wasn't supposed to go that way, but the girl was wasted and so was the other actor and she fought back a little too hard and that pissed him off and before anyone intervened she'd been . . . wasted.

They'd made an accidental snuff film.

They dressed the girl and dumped her body off a cliff into the ocean and went back to making low budget porn like nothing had happened. No one came looking for her because she was no one and only the three of them knew she'd ever been hired in the first place—and only Byron ever knew her name. Ignacio watched the local news for a solid year with his breath held for the first ten minutes of every broadcast. And then it really was like she never existed. Because she didn't anymore. The TV went dark and the scene began to replay. Ignacio pushed STOP on the remote and nothing happened. He did it again, and again, each time the scene continued to play out until her face filled the sixty-inch screen, and the scene paused. He threw the remote at his TV, and it bounced off, clattering in pieces to the floor, batteries rolling away under his futon. Despite the spider web cracks in the screen he could still see her face and on top of that, his reflection—watching himself watch her die . . . again.

"You can't come back," he said to the image on the screen. *Not after what we did to you.*

He unplugged the television and the broken screen went dark. He stumbled into the kitchen and grabbed a bottle of scotch down from the top of the refrigerator. He poured the amber liquid into a juice glass from beside the sink and quickly gulped it down. The whisky burned his throat and his stomach threatened rebellion. He answered the threat with another stinging blast of whisky straight from the bottle.

It's a gag. They are messing with me, doing some elaborate set up. Fake scar, fake guts, fake bitch. Fake!

A loud thump at the front door echoed through his apartment. Ignacio dropped his glass. It shattered and whiskey spread under his feet. He stood still, waiting for another knock.

None came.

He crept to the door, and peered through the fisheye peephole into the hallway on the other side of the door. It was empty but for a DV camera on a tripod.

My camera.

The red light lit up, recording.

His guts seized. He put his hands on the door to reassure himself that the barrier between him and the camera eye was solid, not an illusion. He checked the deadbolt again. Still locked. He let out a small breath of relief. It wasn't opening unless he opened it, and there was no way he was unlocking this door, not even to try to reclaim his camera.

A voice from over his shoulder whispered, "Action."
He fought to undo the lock.

AUTHOR'S STORY NOTE

I wrote the first draft of *Reprising Her Role* back in 2010. I'd taken a horror writing workshop at Grub Street in Boston and wrote the story as a part of that class. It was half as long then as it is now, but the basic structure was the same: a gormless cinematographer who took part in a snuff film in the past, recognizes something familiar about the actress in his latest project. Of the two stories I wrote there, I sold one, titled *Nullification*, to *Sex and Murder Magazine* (my very first story sale ever), and submitted *Reprising Her Role* at the same time to *Necrotic Tissue*. *Sex and Murder* snapped up *Nullification* and printed it. (For their next issue, they added a disclaimer they never had before to the front of the mag, and then promptly closed up shop.) In the mean time, the editors at *Necrotic Tissue* got back to me about *Reprising Her Role* saying that they'd love to buy the story, but their most recent issue was going to be their final issue. I resubmitted the story to another small magazine called *Grave Demand*, and the editor there loved it and wanted to buy it. But before we could sign a contract, he too closed his magazine. Though I am not superstitious, I put the story in a drawer, unpublished, thinking I had done enough damage with it.

Flash forward to 2017, and Jack Bantry got in touch with me asking if I had a story I might be willing to submit to him for the next issue of *Splatterpunk*. I didn't have anything appropriate for his magazine at that moment, but I assured him I could come up with something. And like the woman at the center of *Reprising Her Role*, the story came back, looking for me. I rewrote it from the first page to last, doubling the length and sanding off all the rough edges of my nascent style from seven years ago, and sent it to him, along with a warning: this story kills publishers. He liked it enough to risk the future of *Splatterpunk* by putting it in Issue 8. Fortunately, with two short anthologies from Jack since then and a short film adaptation of the story, titled -REPRISE-, by Killing Joke Films, the woman seems to be satisfied and I am done snuffing small presses with her.

Or am I?

THE WATCHER

DOUGLAS FORD

From *Infernal Ink Magazine Vol. 6, Issue 1*
Editor: Hydra M. Star

My failure to notice things in those days made me easy prey. I barely noticed the invasion of Iraq for one thing, and while my fellow students protested and fretted over how much a gallon of gas would cost, I spent my energy trying to keep Abby Sinclair from breaking up with me. If I could just keep the relationship intact through college, I thought, we would celebrate our graduation with a short engagement followed by a modestly sized wedding. Never mind the heated arguments, more and more frequent now, nor the obvious anxiety she had about introducing me to her parents, the source of her tuition and the weekly partying she could never afford otherwise. Her father, it turned out, would not approve of my brown skin, a prejudice she didn't reveal at first. It must have embarrassed her, I suppose, so she tried to hide it. But I put things together over time by decoding code words like "conservative" and "traditional."

"You mean he's not going to like imagining what his virgin white daughter does with someone who looks like me," I said during what became our penultimate break-up argument. This one happened on a weekend trip to Daytona Beach, a tense trip that finally came to a head in a crowded bar.

"Don't—" she started to say, but I'd have none of it.

"I get it. Daddy wants to keep you to himself." And then I said something my parents taught me never to say. *Jake, no matter what kind of stupid shit white people say about black people, never let the same kind of foolishness come out of your mouth.* But still, I said it. I said, "I get how white people are. Only way to keep it pure is to keep in the family."

That did it. We broke up for good.

After that, I could no longer count us a couple. It felt as if I had just pulled away the last fatal brick, and I could only watch helplessly as the entire tower collapsed. Saying little else, I left her in the bar where we had gathered with her friends, and knowing that I couldn't go back to the hotel room, I walked to the beach, thinking I would sleep near the water and take a bus back to campus in the morning. I had enough to drink that I felt drunk, and the way the moonlight rippled on the waves brought forth a rush of nausea. I sat down in the sand, my back to the lights of a hotel, and waited for the feeling to pass.

That's when the veteran came up to me.

I didn't see him until he appeared just a few feet away. "Hey bro, drink a beer with me," he said. He carried a six-pack, and despite the humidity, he wore a green army jacket. Normally, I wouldn't accept alcohol from a white stranger who crawled unbidden out of the darkness. All those survival warnings from my parents no longer mattered that night. Let him kill me,

I thought. So full of self loathing, I just didn't care.

I took the beer he offered and sipped it. It was warm. He opened one for himself and sat down in the sand near me.

"Just got back from the war," he said.

I had no reply, but the beer obligated me to say something.

"How was it?" I said.

"It was alright. Fucking nuts." As I struggled to untangle that contradiction, he went on. "Saw a woman giving birth in the street, right there during the Battle of Fallujah. Can you believe that shit?"

I took a sip from the bottle and said that no, I couldn't.

He said, "Things blowing up, and she was just lying there in the street, her legs spread open, screaming and shit." He paused to finish his beer in a single mighty chug. "I was running, but I had to stop because I couldn't believe it. You could see a head trying to come out and everything."

"Good thing you didn't get blown up," I said.

"Oh, I didn't but Gary Puett, that was another story. Gary was my buddy. I got my head together and started moving, but Gary, he was running behind me. He stopped where I stopped just a second before, his face all concerned and shit. 'We gotta keep going, come on,' I yelled to him, but he just stopped dead in his tracks, there with dirt flying up and shit. 'We gotta do something,' he yelled back, but I kept waving him on."

He took out another beer, twisted the top off, and chugged half of it. Then he looked at me. Suddenly, he thrust out his hand with his elbow cocked high. "Name's Dave, by the way."

I extended my hand, and he clasped it with his fingers up, not down, as if to say we were bros. His grip briefly cut off the blood in my hand. I told him my name.

"Good to know you, Jake," he said.

"So what happened to your friend?"

"You mean Gary? Shit." He sipped from his bottle and drew his knees up. "What do you think happened?" He reached inside his pocket and drew forth something red and compact—a pocket knife, I realized. He set the bottle down and began playing with it, opening and closing the blades inside.

The knife distracted me, sure, but now I wanted to hear the rest of the story.

"Did the woman make it out ok? Her baby?"

"No, she didn't make it out ok. Gary was my buddy. Did I tell you that? I went to his wedding. I was his best man. You want to know what old Gary did? He squatted down there in the middle of that exploding street and took out his knife. I'm not talking about a pig-sticker like this one. I'm talking about a real government-issue knife. I stood there trying to get him to run, but he just yelled, 'I gotta save the baby!' Don't ask me what gave him the idea. I mean, that motherfucker was no doctor. But know what he did? He took that knife and stuck it into that lady's stomach and started carving away, her screaming the whole time in Arabic, and before I knew it, he held it up in the air by the leg, like he'd just caught a grouper or something. The baby was covered in blood, but crying. That's when the mortar hit." Another chug from the bottle finished that one, and he tossed it toward the surf. "A big ole flame swallowed the three of them up. The woman died, probably because of Gary's nonexistent surgical skills. Holding the baby up saved that arm, at least. The rest of them—his other arm, his legs, everything else, blown off. The crazy thing is that his skin and the baby's—" Here, he made a gesture I didn't understand. "Like, fused together." He looked at me. "What do you think of that?"

I tried to return his gaze, but I had to turn away. The water looked black.

"It's fucked up," I said.

Then he said the thing that put me on edge. That has me on edge even today.

"I could cut you. Right now."

In the dark, the knife waited for me like the tip of a spider's leg. He said this as if he had to struggle to hold himself back.

The survival lessons of my parents come back to me in such moments, moments that force me to concede my stubborn belief that I lived in a world different from theirs. I did what they taught me to do. I smiled. "You don't want to cut me," I said. "I'm a nice guy."

We listened to the breaking waves as he seemed to consider my words.

"Yeah," he said, finally, "you seem like a nice guy. I won't cut you. Instead, I'm going to introduce you to someone. Someone fine. You like white girls?"

Trying not to think of Abby Sinclair, I said that I did.

He gestured to the hotel behind us, on the ground floor was a bar bright with lights and music. "She's in there. Hot as shit. She likes coloreds, too. Come on."

If the beer hadn't dulled my senses by then, I might have thought of a graceful way to avoid his company. Plus, fear of the knife made me more agreeable than sensible. Seeing the way he moved his crooked and gangly legs, I thought again of a spider, but as I walked next to him, I warmed to the idea of a girl's company. I didn't relish the thought of loneliness, and besides, a quick hook-up would help me forget Abby Sinclair and her racist father. The fact that my new friend referred to "coloreds," a term that would have enraged my parents, just meant he was a simpleton who hadn't been taught properly. The woman he promised to show me would erase all infractions. I genuinely believed this.

And at first, she did, with her skirt, her cleavage, even the slight space gap between her front two teeth. With a bumbling excitement that made him seem less dangerous, Dave the Veteran introduced me to her, and he surprised me by remembering my name. I learned her name—Brenda—and as she shook my hand, she raised her eyebrows and made sidewise glances at Dave to indicate she understood how crazy he was and that she would save me from him.

Somehow, she distracted him away from our conversation, at one point speaking to him out of earshot and apparently sending him off for some meaningless task. At one point, I glimpsed him talking to someone who looked like the manager, and it looked like an angry conversation. Knowing him well enough already, I assumed that he'd done something to get himself into trouble—probably taking his knife out again.

Because of Brenda, I didn't care what happened to him. She extended our handshake longer than necessary and touched me often. I tried not to stare at the way her breasts challenged the capacity of her shirt, squeezing together at the top to create a round, pale cleavage. I failed however, and she noticed.

"I just got a boob job," she said, as if to offer an invitation to look without embarrassment. I did so, quickly, and looked up to meet her smiling eyes. "What do you think?"

"They look very nice," I said.

"They feel real, too. Go on, touch them." I hesitated. I gazed around the bar, looking especially for Dave and his knife, but he'd disappeared, probably thrown out for some kind of misconduct. "Go on," she said. So I did, in drunken defiance of Abby Sinclair who no longer wanted me, not to mention my parents who constantly tried to protect me from a world they claimed would never accept me. I touched this strange woman's augmented breasts and felt their hardness, putting forth every effort not to look aroused or astonished, pretending that I had enough experience and knowledge that I could give her an expert opinion. I squinted one eye and furrowed my brow, causing her to laugh.

"They're nice," I said, although they had none of the softness found on Abby Sinclair's smaller chest, the only other breasts I had ever touched.

"*Nice*? Just *nice*?"

"Ok, spectacular," I said.

"So you say, so you say. I was thinking of letting you get a better look, but now, I don't know." She laughed, and once again I observed the gap in her front teeth. I wanted to kiss her very much. It made no sense that I had touched her breasts and not even kissed her yet. And I very much wanted to do so. "I had a top notch doctor," she said. "The kind my husband would've called military pay-grade, and trust me, he'd know. So you're damn right—they're fucking spectacular."

Husband. Thanks to my beer buzz, this information dampened my confidence just slightly, but enough to keep me from registering her verb tense.

"I think I recognize you," she said. "Are you on Adult Finder?"

"No," I said. "Are you?"

"Yep, I can give you contact info if you want. You could look me up. I'm under couples."

"You mentioned your husband. Is he—"

"Dead?" She laughed. "No, in fact, he's here. Don't worry though. We have an open relationship. You sure I don't know you?"

"Pretty sure." I struggled for a moment to think of something to add. "I wish I knew you better," I finally said.

"Well, come up then." She hooked her arm in mine, and she led me to the hotel's elevator. "I guess you just look like a lot of guys I've fucked." My groin stirred when she said that. "You're just my type."

"And what would that type be?"

Her eyes half closed, she licked her lips and brought her mouth close to mine. We began kissing as the elevator arrived. Her tongue probed my mouth as I felt the car begin to ascend, and I looked up, concerned because neither one of us had pressed the floor button. At that moment, I saw him.

Dave. He leaned against the wall of the elevator next to the panel of buttons. Watching.

"Don't mind me," he said.

"Dave doesn't like my boob job," Brenda said.

"I never said that. Just said you didn't need it."

Brenda kept her arms around me as if sensing my need to back away. I tried to keep Dave in my line of vision, not liking how he managed to slip aboard the elevator without me noticing. His eyes stayed fixed on Brenda. "I didn't know she was your wife," I said.

Brenda laughed while Dave frowned. "Man, we ain't married. I told you."

"He's definitely not my type," Brenda said.

Dave gestured at his crotch. "You'd love to hit this." Brenda held up a middle finger and laughed.

"Nah, you're a watcher." Brenda nibbled my ear lobe before whispering, "He's a watcher. Everyone's a watcher. You still want to see my tits, right?"

Drunk on beer and the promise of something forbidden, I said yes. The elevator stopped, but the door didn't open. Dave reached out with a hairy finger and started jabbing the open door button, mumbling about how he didn't like closed spaces. The door remained shut, and Dave kept pounding the button with a spidery finger so long and bent in more places than seemed possible, as if it bore too many joints for a normal human finger. He must've broken it and not set it properly, I thought. Brenda caressed and kissed me, but I felt my body go rigid with the fear that we would never get off this elevator, and this crazed veteran with PTSD would kill all of us.

But finally, the door opened.

"Our floor," he said, and walked out into the hallway. We followed.

We fell onto a bed covered with scattered laundry, her on top of me, kissing me and straddling me. The room smelled salty, worn, and smoky. Dave the veteran flopped down on the chair across from us, grunting like he'd just come home from a grueling day of work. I could feel him watching as he opened another beer, and thinking about what he had planned made me apprehensive. Did he expect to join us? I hoped not, but my mind hearkened back to something strange my dad said to me on the day of my high school graduation. Normally strict about how many glasses of wine he drank, he had one too many and sat me down in the corner away from the rest of his party, his expression signaling one of those you-need-to-know-this con-versations. *Son, everyone's going to want your dick*, he said, *and I'm not just talking about white girls, either. You'll see—white boys spend way too much time worrying about what's between our legs. Some of it's fear, but some of it's something else.* I wrote that off to my father's homophobia, something I could never claim—never wanted to, in fact, but as Brenda worked her way down my body, pulling up my shirt and unbuckling my pants, I could feel the gaze of someone else. My hands on top of her blond head, I watched as she took me inside her mouth, astonished as she seemed to swallow me up in a deeper way than Abby Sinclair ever could—or would. I might have exploded right away if not for the effects of the alcohol, as well as the uncomfortable feeling of being watched.

I avoided looking in Dave's direction. I didn't want to lose my concen-tration or risk losing the erection that opened the back of Brenda's throat. But I thought of his knife and the possibility that I had stumbled into some kind of scheme, a robbery maybe or an elaborate hate crime. I looked out of the corner of my eye. Dave, to my relief, kept his face turned in another direction, toward the door separating us from an adjoining room. He ap-peared anxious, worried.

Yet the feeling of being watched persisted. Brenda stopped sucking me so she could pull off her top. "You still want to see my new tits?" she said, and I said that I did, and she pressed their hard points into my face as she straddled me again, this time with all barriers removed—somehow she had taken off her shorts without me noticing—and I felt her wet slickness as she slid up and down on top of me.

As she shifted her position, I became aware of the closet on the other side of the room, the door slightly ajar.

My paranoia wouldn't go away. Now it seemed probable that somewhere inside that closet, a camera filmed everything. Maybe I'd fallen in with some cheap, low-life pornographers who didn't even have the ethics to ask me to sign a release statement. Still, I gripped Brenda's hips as she ground down on top of me with greater and greater urgency. I didn't even want to stop, even as I became more and more certain that the feeling of being watched came from something in there. Even the way she had positioned our bodies on the bed seemed like design, intended to provide the most gynecologically graphic view to the camera eye hidden within. As she continued to grind she pressed the palms of her hands down on my chest, and seemed close to climaxing, when we both heard it.

The sound caused her to stop her motion and look at me, as if seeing me for the first time. She looked different too, older than I at first realized. We stayed frozen like that, looking at each other, until she finally said, "Aw fuck," and dismounted in a way that made me feel like a horse.

The noise we heard sounded almost like a baby crying, but more raspy, like air escaping through the pipes of a broken commode.

Dave stood up at the same time she did, and he blocked her from the door leading to the other room.

"Nope," he said, "nope, nope, nope."

"Goddammit," she said. "I'll take care of it. Just let me by."

"You got something else to take care of. This is my responsibility. Mine. Your responsibility is there."

I propped myself up on my elbows, watching this exchange, unable to ignore the fact that when Dave said *responsibility*, he seemed to gesture not at me, but toward something further away.

Again, the closet.

He gave her a long look before opening the door just wide enough to let himself through, closing it behind him. The sound of a lock followed. Brenda returned to the bed, but she pushed my hand away when I reached for her. Instead of climbing back on top, she began rummaging through the clothes on the bed for clothes to dress herself with. "I'm done," she said.

"Listen—" Unsure of what I'd just witnessed, I didn't reach for her again.

"I don't need to listen to nothing," she said. "I do nothing but listen."

"That a baby?" I said. "In there? Your baby?"

"I don't have any baby," she said.

"I heard something," I said. I started to stand, feeling that the time to leave had come, but she wouldn't allow that. She stopped picking through the clothes and moved upon me with speed and anger.

I expected her to hit or to scratch, but instead she pushed me back onto the bed, swinging her legs around and sliding back down on top of me. "I know what you want," she said, "I know what all you fuckers want." Reaching between her legs, she slipped my dick back inside her, then leaned forward to bring her lips close to my ear. She pressed down and took me deep while she whispered. "This is all a show," she said, "but I'm done with it. I decided that tonight, down there in the bar while I was talking to you. Decided that I was going to smother him with a pillow." My dick softened, but she didn't seem to notice and continued to grind as she whispered. "You got a room, right? I'll fuck you in your room with no one watching. Just let me go there with you tonight."

I whispered back to her. I thought she didn't want Dave to hear from the other room. "A show, you said. For Dave? He makes you do this?"

"Not for Dave. Fuck Dave. For my husband. There's no other way for him to get off. Not anymore. You come yet?" She continued to grind against me even though I slipped out of her moments before. I lied to her, saying that yes, I had come. "Good. Help me do the thing with the pillow, and I'll fuck you again." When she spoke again, she spoke without the whisper. "That felt good. Now I have to pee." She kissed me without any passion and stood up. I watched the way she looked at the closet as she walked to the bathroom and closed the door behind her.

Still naked but now full of anger, I stood up and regarded the closet. I had no intention of helping her smother someone with a pillow. All this on film, too. She probably wanted to convince me to do it. Get it on film. I would take the cassette out of the camera, or better yet, I thought as I took the handle of the closet's louvered door, I'd take the camera itself. With that, I opened it.

I opened all the way and saw inside.

Clothes caught my attention first. The closet at first appeared to contain nothing but clothes, but unlike the piles of dirty laundry on the bed, these were neatly hanging suits, all black in color, many of them covered with clear plastic marked with the name of a dry cleaner. Hanging near one of them I found a mask with woolly hair, its cartoon visage molded to look like the caricature of an African warrior, complete with a bone through the nose. I reached out to touch it. At first I expected it to feel like rubber—a cheap Halloween mask—but I felt a momentary pang of fear that it would feel like real flesh, someone's skinned face.

Before I could touch it, I noticed what lay on the floor.

At first I thought it was a Halloween decoration, something like the mask.

Then, I realized that it was moving. It was alive.

The glinting thing I saw earlier was no camera. It was an eye, a human eye, attached to the stump of a scarred, ruined being. Whorled scars marked what remained of its flesh, and it bore only one arm, which it raised to me as if in supplication. That lone arm told me what I was seeing. I imagined the street erupting into flames as this once-whole person held up a baby freshly cut from its womb, the flesh of both bodies sizzling and blending so that someone had to cut them apart later. I knew then what lay beyond, in that other room, and I didn't want to see it, just as I didn't want to see the closet's occupant. I could free him, I thought—but then he smiled, and a gob of drool ran down his face. I realized what that meant and why they had positioned the door the way they had. All of this amounted to a show for the watcher in the closet.

The toilet flushed, and I knew I had to move fast.

He could read it in my face, my intention to run, and he opened his mouth as if to scream, but nothing came up. He lifted his raw, crooked arm as if he could stop me, but I rushed my clothes back on and made it to the door just as Brenda was coming back into the room, her arm lifting in a way that mirrored her husband inside the closet, her mouth opening with a word that had no time to get out as I stepped outside and closed the door behind me.

On the other side of the door, I used my weight to hold it closed as she pushed back from the other side. I could hear her curse and grunt as she struggled to get to me, and I no longer cared about what she wanted from me—to hurt me or to escape with me. Somehow I knew that if I let the door swing open, I would never again free myself of her. Strangely enough, I began to think of Abby Sinclair—how in all those fights we had, she secretly just wanted to get rid of me, but I'd become something she could never just banish on the other side of the door the way I'd just done to Brenda. I should have felt pity, I realized—pity not just for that trapped woman, but for the scarred wreck reduced to watching her fuck strangers in the closet.

It came back to me then, what she said about smothering him with a pillow.

I stopped holding the door, thinking it would fly open. I would go back inside and take all the pillows from the room. Take them all away so she couldn't hurt anyone.

But the pressure from the other side had stopped. From the other side came an awful silence.

I tried the door handle, but of course it didn't open. It locked automatically, and I had no key.

I tapped gently at first. Then I rapped harder. I called her name over and over.

When the door finally opened, Dave stood on the other side. He used his body to hold the door open as he dragged something toward the doorway.

"Help with this, will you?" he said.

I looked at what he dragged toward the threshold—a bag made of dirty white fabric. A laundry bag. What it held though made it difficult for him to lift.

"I said to help me, goddammit." He nodded toward the trash chute by the elevator.

When I still failed to move, he said, "Motherfucker, I fought for your freedom. Now, help me out. It's just laundry. Dirty clothes."

Together we struggled to pull the bag toward the latched door of the chute. Dave pulled it open, and together we managed to get the bag inside. I could feel the contours of what the bag held. It did have clothes—I could feel those—but it felt heavy, just too heavy.

"This isn't laundry, man," I said.

Dave didn't answer. He struggled to stuff the bag all the way in. Finally, it cleared the opening, and we both waited for the sound of it striking the bottom of the shaft below. I heard nothing, but maybe Dave did. He nodded, satisfied, at something I couldn't detect.

"That wasn't laundry," I said, again.

"Come back in and check," he said. "The bed's cleared off. All sent to the cleaners."

In the open door, Brenda reappeared. She leaned against the door jam, naked and smiling. Her left eye looked funny. It appeared puffy and red.

"Come on in and let me finish you off."

"No, thanks," I said.

"Suit yourself," she said.

"No, thanks," I repeated, but she had already disappeared inside the room.

"Not coming in then?" said Dave.

"No, thanks."

"Then, we need to settle up. You understand, right?"

At first, I didn't. When I said nothing, Dave brushed his thumb against his middle finger. Money. I owed him money.

I took out my wallet and began counting the little money I had left, only forty-eight dollars. As I held it out to him, the door opened again. Still naked, Brenda reassumed her position in the doorway.

But now she wore the mask I saw hanging in the closet. It had a grotesque red grin that held my gaze. I couldn't look away, even as Dave took the money from my hand and walked back to the door. She stood aside and let him by. Her hand went up and waved to me as she let the door close between us. It closed slowly, and she kept her face in sight, the grotesque grin that could have been made with blood. Eventually, the door closed all the way, finally removing her from my sight.

AUTHOR'S STORY NOTE

Although a work of fiction, elements of "The Watcher" really happened to me—though I was spared the more extreme moments of the story, fortunately. A chance encounter with a veteran behind a hotel in Daytona Beach actually occurred and left me shaken, but it took me several tries (and years) before I could find the right way to tell the story I needed to tell. Truth in fiction means something other than "true-to-life," and some "truth" about the experience kept eluding me in all those other attempts. The only way I could get within striking distance of it entailed making it a more extreme horror story. Since I am a writer of dark fiction, it should come as no surprise that this is where my truth often resides. My other obstacle involved finding the right voice for the narrator. Somewhere between my third and fourth attempt to write this story, he finally revealed to me that he was African American, and something finally clicked and allowed the pieces to fall into place. As for the actual veteran who threatened to kill me on the beach, I feel a great deal of pity for him—he had a hard road to travel, and I hope he survived his journey. I'm thankful to him for giving me this story, and I want to dedicate it to him, wherever he is.

SCRATCHING FROM THE OUTER DARKNESS

TIM CURRAN

From *Return Of The Old Ones: Apocalyptic Lovecraftian Horror*
Editor: Brian M. Sammons
Dark Regions Press

After two weeks of relative silence in which the pot of the world began to boil over, Simone Petrioux heard the scratching again. This time it came from within the walls. Sometimes it came from the shadows—particularly the shadows in the corners—and sometimes from behind her or the sky overhead. And sometimes from inside people.

* * *

"You have a marked hyper aural sensitivity," Dr. Wells explained to her. "A form of hyperacusis. It's not unusual with those without sight. When one sense fails, others are heightened."

"But it's beyond that," Simone told him with a singular note of desperation. "I hear . . . strange things. Things I should not hear."

"What sort of things?"

She swallowed. "Sounds . . . things echoing from another place. *Busy* sounds."

He told her that auditory hallucinations were known as paracusia. Sometimes they were signs of a very serious medical condition. He did not use the word schizophrenia, but she was certain he was thinking it.

"Just because you hear things others do not, does not necessarily mean there's anything there," he explained.

"And it doesn't mean anything *isn't* either," she told him. "Rocky hears it, too. How do you explain that?"

But he couldn't, of course. Dr. Wells was a good man, she thought, but this was beyond him. Ever since she was a child, she heard things others could not. It ran in the family. It was something of a Petrioux family curse—like the blindness—the ability to detect sounds in a frequency beyond that of ordinary human hearing. Simone had been blind since birth. Vision was an abstract concept to her. She could no more describe her acute hearing to Dr. Wells than he could describe sight to her. Stalemate.

Of course, it really didn't matter.

Things had gone far beyond that point now.

* * *

Feeling very alone and very vulnerable, she listened for it to start again because she knew it would. There had been the two-week reprieve, of course, but now the scratching was coming again and it was more frenzied and determined than ever. *Like someone's trying to get through,* she thought. *Trying to dig their way through a stone wall. Scritch, scritch, scrape, scrape.* That was the sound she kept hearing. It was worse at night. It was always worse at night.

Listen.

Yes, there it was again.

Scritch, scritch.

Rocky started to howl. Oh yes, he could hear it and he knew it was bad. Whatever was behind it, it was bad. "Come here, boy," she said, but he would not. She found him over by the wall, fixated on the sounds coming from the corner. She petted him, tried to hug him, but he would have none of it. Beneath his fur, he was a rigid mass of bunched cables. "It's okay, my big boy, it'll be okay," she said, but he knew better and so did she.

The scratching sounded like an animal digging, claws scraping against a door, the sound of tunneling, determined tunneling. She cried out involuntarily. She couldn't bear it any more. Her greatest fear was that whatever was doing it, might get through.

Get through from where?

But she didn't know. She just didn't know.

Night—another abstract concept to the sightless—was a time she had always enjoyed the most. The noise of the city diminished and she could really hear the world. The gurgling of pipes in the ceiling. The gentle breeze playing at the eaves. Bats squeaking as they chased bugs around streetlights. Mr. Astano rocking in his chair on the third floor. The young couple—Jenna and Josh Ryan—at the end of the corridor making love, trying to be quiet because their bed was so terribly creaky (through the furnace duct she always heard them giggling in their intimacy).

But that had changed now, hadn't it?

Yes, everything had changed. These past few weeks, the night breeze was contaminated by a sweet evil stench like nothing she had ever smelled before. Mr. Astano no longer rocked in his chair; now he sobbed through the dark watches of night. For three nights running she had heard whippoorwills shrilling in the park, growing louder and louder in a diabolic chorus. Rocky howled and whined, sniffing around the baseboards almost constantly. And the Ryans . . . they no longer made love or giggled, now they whispered in low, secretive voices, reading jibberish to one another out of books. Last night, Simone had clearly heard Josh Ryan's voice echoing through the furnace duct, *"There are names one must not pronounce and those that should never be called."*

The scratching was persistently loud tonight and no one could ever convince her it was hallucinatory. It came from outside, not within. Her nerves frayed, a frost lying over her skin that made her shiver uncontrollably, Simone turned on the TV. She turned it on *loud*. The voices on CNN were initially comforting but soon enough disturbing. There had been a mass suicide in Central Park. By starlight, two thousand gatherers had (according to witnesses) simultaneously slit their left wrists, using the gushing blood to paint an odd symbol on their foreheads, something like a stem with five branches. The police were saying they were members of a fringe religious sect known as the Church of Starry Wisdom. In Scotland, there had been arrests of a group—the Chorazos Cult—in Caithness who had gathered on the bleak moorland at a prehistoric megalithic site known as the Hill of Broken Stones. Apparently, they had ritually sacrificed several children, offering them to a pagan god known as "The Lord of Many Skins." In Africa, there were numerous atrocities committed, the most appalling of which seemed to be that hundreds of people had congregated at a place known as the Mountain of the Black Wind in Kenya and cut their own tongues out so that they would not, in their religious ecstasy, speak the forbidden name of their holy avatar. There were rumors that the offered tongues were then boiled and eaten in some execrable rite known as the Festival of the Flies which dated from antiquity.

Madness, she thought. *Madness on every front.*

Christians called it Armageddon and began feverishly quoting from the Book of Revelation as, all across North America and Europe, they flung themselves off the tallest buildings they could find, smashing to pulp far below, so that the Lord could wash his feet in the blood of the faithful as he walked the streets of men during the Second Coming.

It was falling apart.

It was all falling apart now.

There was mass insanity, religious frenzy, mob violence, murder, and genocide coming from every corner of the world.

Simone finally shut the TV off. The world was unraveling, but there seemed to be no root cause. At least none a sane mind would even consider.

* * *

The whippoorwills resumed their eerie rhythmic piping in the park, growing louder and louder, their cries coming faster and more strident as if they were possessed of some rising mania. Rocky began to whine in a pathetic puppy-like tone. At the windows, Simone heard what sounded like hundreds of insects buzzing. It all seemed to be building towards something and she was more afraid than she had ever been in her life. Now there were screams out in the street, hysterical and rising, becoming something like dozens of cackling voices reaching an almost hypersonic crescendo of sheer dementia. They resonated through her, riding her bones and making her nerve endings ring out. There was a power to them, some nameless, menacing cabalism that filled her head with alien thoughts and impulses. Now the walls . . . oh dear God, the walls were vibrating, keeping time with the voices and the whippoorwills.

Not out in the streets, not out in the streets, but from within the walls.

Yes, echoing voices from some terribly distant place and as she listened, she could not be certain they were of human origin . . . guttural croakings, discordant shrieking, bleatings and hissings and vile trumpeting, a reverberating lunatic chanting, hollow noises as of storm winds rushing through subterranean channels.

Dear God, what did it mean?

What did any of it mean?

There was a sour taste on her tongue and a foul stench of graveyards.

Feeling dizzy and weak, her stomach bubbling with a cold nauseous jelly, Simone fell to the floor, cupping her hands over her ears as the blood rushed and roared in her head, making it feel as if her brain was boiling in her skull. The sounds were getting louder and louder, the floorboards shuddering, the room seeming to quiver and quake like pudding. There were smacking and slurping sounds, the cries of humans and animals, of things that were neither . . . all of it lorded over now by a cacophonous buzzing that made her bones rattle and her teeth chatter. It sounded like some monstrous insect descending from the sky on droning membranous wings.

Then it stopped.

All of it ended simultaneously and there was only a great, unearthly silence broken by her own gasping and Rocky's whimpering. Other than that, nothing. Nothing at all. A voice in Simone's head said, *it was close that time. Very, very close, they almost got through. The barrier between here and there is wearing very thin.* But she had no idea what any of it meant. Between here and where?

"Stop it, stop it," she told herself. "You're losing your mind."

She pulled herself up from the floor, barely able to maintain her balance. The silence was immense. It was a great soundless black vacuum of the sort she always imagined existed beyond the rim of the universe.

She made it to the sofa and collapsed on it, wiping a dew of sweat from her face. With a trembling hand, she turned the TV on because she needed to hear voices, music, anything to break that wall of morbid silence.

On CNN, there were voices, yes, but they spoke of the most awful things, things that only amplified her psychosis . . . because it must have been a psychosis, she couldn't be hearing these things, these awful sounds like the veneer of reality was ripping open.

It was reported that several million people had made a pilgrimage to Calcutta to await the appearance of a dark-skinned prophet at the Temple of the Long Shadow whom they referred to simply as "The Messenger." Border skirmishes had broken out in Asia and the Middle East. There was pestilence in Indochina, bloodshed on the Gaza Strip, immense swarms of locusts blackening the skies over Ethiopia, and the Iranians had fully admitted that they were in possession of several dozen hydrogen bombs, each of which were equivalent to fifty million tons of TNT. With them, they would soon "ascend to heaven in the black arms of destiny" via a synchronized nuclear detonation which would bring about what they referred to as the symbolic "Eye of Azathoth." In Eastern Europe, a terror organization calling itself either the Black Brotherhood or the Al-Shaggog Brigade had been burning Christian churches, Jewish synagogues, and Muslim mosques, calling them "places of utter blasphemy which must be eradicated so that the way be purified before the king could descend from the Dark Star and the Great Father rise from his sunken tomb . . ."

"Kooks, Rocky," Simone said. "This world is full of kooks."

The idea made her smile thinly. Was it at all possible that the human race was losing its collective mind at the same time? That instead of sporadic outbreaks of insanity there was a global lunacy at work here? She told herself it was highly unlikely—but she didn't believe herself.

*   *   *

That afternoon, the UPS man came to her door, knocking gently, announcing that he carried a parcel that had to be signed for. It was perfectly innocuous. He was delivering her new laptop with screenreader software . . . yet, as she made to open the door, a sense of fright and loathing swept through her as if what was out there was something hideous beyond imagining. But she did open the door and right away she was gripped by a manic paranoia and a mounting claustrophobia.

"Package for you," the man said, his voice cheerful enough. But it was a façade, an awful façade . . . for there was something sinister and lurking just beneath his skin and she knew if she reached out to touch his face it would be pebbly like the flesh of a toad. Right away, she heard that dire scratching coming from inside him like rats pawing and chewing. In her mind, she sensed a spiraling limitless abyss waiting to open like a black funnel. A voice—his own, but ragged and wizened—whispered in her skull, *has she . . . has she . . . has she linked? Have the angles shown her the gray void? Has she seen the black man with the horn?* The voice kept echoing in her head until she felt a cool, sour sweat run down her face.

"Are you okay, ma'am?" asked the UPS man.

"Yes," she breathed, taking the parcel from him with strained, shaking fingers. "Yes, fine."

"Okay, if you're sure."

But deep within her, perhaps at some subconscious level of atavistic fright, she could sense a godless vortexual darkness opening up inside him, and a noxious stench like seared porcine flesh blew into her face and that dry, windy voice whispered once again, *show her, show her, it has been promised in the* Ghorl Nigral *as such . . . let her gaze into the moon-lens and gape upon the Black Goat of the forest with a thousand squirming young . . . let her . . . let her . . . find communion with the writhing dark on the other side . . .*

"Listen, are you sure you're all right?"

"Yes . . . please, I'm fine."

But she was not fine. She was blind and alone and a ravening outer darkness was spilling from this man in diseased rivers of slime. She felt scalding winds and dust blowing in her face, a fetid odor enveloping her that was no single stench but dozens breathing hot in her face with a fungous, gangrenous, nearly palpable odor.

He reached out to steady her, clutching her wrist with a flabby, leprous claw.

She screamed.

She could not help herself.

She slammed the door in his face, ignoring the whining and growling of Rocky. Physical waves of disgust and utter repulsion nearly paralyzed her, but she managed to reach the toilet as the vomit came out of her in a frothing expulsion. And crouching there on the bathroom floor, shuddering, drooling, her mouth wide in a silent scream, she could still hear that voice whispering from unknown gulfs: *eh, even now at the threshold, the veneer of the Great White Space weakens as the time of the pushing and the birthing draws near—*

*   *   *

Enough, by God, it was enough.

She went into the kitchen and made sure Rocky had enough food and water. He had touched neither all day. He was hiding under the kitchen table, trembling. When she reached out to comfort him, he snapped at her. *Even my dog, even my dog.* Feeling depressed and defenseless and without a friend in the world, Simone climbed into bed and tried to sleep. After a desperate round of tossing and turning, she did just that.

Her dreams began right away.

Twisted, unreal phantasms of limitless spaces closing in on her. Immense and shaggy forms brushing against her. Monstrous pulpous, undimensioned things moving past her. Crawling up winding staircases that led into nothingness and being hunted through shattered thoroughfares of wriggling weeds and monolithic towers that felt like smooth, hot glass under her fingertips. And a world, an anti-world, of shifting surface angles where everything was soft and slimy to the touch like the spongy, mucid tissue of a corpse. And through it all, she heard a voice, a booming and commanding voice asking her to make communion with the beautiful, cunning darkness that awaits us all in the end.

A sinister, malign sort of melody was ever-playing in the background, at first soft and silky then building to a harsh feverish pitch, an immense ear-splitting dissonant noise of bat-like squeaking and shrill creaking, bone grinding against bone, thunderous booming, saw blades biting into steel plate, chainsaws whirring and jagged-toothed files scraping over the strings of violins and cellos . . . all of it combining, creating a deranged jarring cacophony of disharmonic noise, filling her head, melting her nerves like hot wires, cracking open her skull like an eggshell until she came awake screaming in the deathly silence of her bedroom—

* * *

Soaked with sweat, shaking like a wet dog, she forced herself to calm down. She was awake and she *knew* she was awake, but the terror and anxiety bunched in her chest did not lessen; it constricted tighter. Her brain was sending a steady current of electricity to her nerves and the result was that her entire body was jittery and trembling. She had the most awful sense that she was not alone in the room, that another stood by her . . . breathing. She could hear a low, rasping respiration, a coarse, vulgar sort of sound like that a beast might make.

"Rocky?" she said in a weak, barely existent voice. *"Rocky?"*

Her voice reverberated around her oddly. The sound waves it created seemed to make the air around her vibrate. Her words bounced off the walls and came back at her like ripples she could feel on her skin.

She could still hear the breathing.

Terrified, she swung her legs out of bed and stood, instantly recoiling because the floor was not the floor but something almost gelatinous, a cool burning mud that was crawling with squirming things that began to slink up her legs. *Dreaming, dreaming, you're still dreaming.* But she couldn't convince herself of that. She reached out for the bed but it was no longer there. Panting, she stumbled towards the door and felt an immense momentary relief when it was still there. Something had happened. A pipe had burst or something and she was wading through shit, yet there was no odor save a dank, subterranean smell. She was in the short hallway that led into the living room. She pushed on through the slopping ooze. She reached out and could find no walls. The hallway seemed to have no end and no beginning.

"ROCKY!" she screamed in desperation.

Again, her words bounced around, becoming waves crashing ashore on an alien beach and striking her with force in their reverberations. The air . . . warm, thick, almost congested . . . trembled like jelly. She kept moving, reaching out in every direction but there was nothing, absolutely nothing to touch. That awful, degenerate breathing kept pace with her but its owner made no sound as it glided along with her. Her head was throbbing, her temples pumping. A headache was gathering steam, its pain funneling out from the back of her brain to some excruciating white-hot spot in her forehead. There was an explosion of brilliance in her mind that left her reeling, it blazed like white phosphorus, igniting her thoughts into a firestorm of luminosity.

What?

What?

What is this?

Being blind since birth, she did not know sight. She could not conceptualize it. It was perfectly abstract in all ways to her. Even her dreams were of sounds, smells, tactile sensations . . . but not this. She saw for the first time in her life . . . a multitude of colors and images and forms like thousands of bright fireflies filling the night sky. And then, then she saw—if only for the briefest of moments—what stood breathing behind her. A man, a very tall man in a tattered cloak that crept with leggy vermin. He was staring down at her. His face was black, not African, but something like smooth shiny onyx. A living carved mask. Two brilliant yellow eyes, huge and glossy like egg yolks watched her. And then it was gone. Whatever had opened in her head had closed and she nearly passed out.

The dark man gripped her with fingers like crawling roots and she let out a scream, one that seemed to echo from a distant room. Her hands, unbidden, reached out to him as they had done so many times in her life, finding a face that was greasy and soft like a gently pulsating mushroom. She cringed, but her fingers continued exploring despite the abhorrence that made her viscera hang in warm, pale loops. Beneath her fingertips, nodules rose and from each something worming slinked free. They crawled over the backs of her hands. One of them licked at a cut on her pinkie. Another suckled her thumb. Whatever they were, they came out of him in hot geysers, vermiform fleshy nightmares that gushed over her hands and brought a stench of death—old death and new death—that made her want to weep in her revulsion. Her fingers, seemingly magnetized to the face, continued exploring until they found something like a muscular, phallic optic stem growing from his forehead. It held a great, swollen, juicy eye that her index finger slid into like an over-ripened plum soft with rot.

And a voice, a gurgling slopping voice that sounded as if it was spoken through mush, said, "*So thou might see and thou might make communion with the beautiful, cunning darkness that waits for all . . .*"

* * *

When Simone was next aware, she was sitting on the couch. She had no memory of getting there. She was in bed, she had nightmares, now she was on the couch. Her sense of smell, heightened beyond normal ken, gave her a sampling of the oily, sweaty, fetid odors that seeped from her pores in toxic rivulets.

The TV was on.

It was on the public access channel. She never listened to public access, but here it was. A man's voice was droning endlessly in great dry detail about the cult of the Magna Mater, Cybele-worshipping Romans, and the depravity of Phrygian priests. Little of it made much sense, from the dark secrets of alchemy to the thaumaturgical arts and necromantic rites, from Etruscan fertility cults worshipping the Great Father of Insects to nameless miscegenations that did not walk but crawled within the slime of the honeycombed subterranean passages of Salem. "Was it not foretold?" the voice asked. "Did not Cotton Mather warn of it? Did not his sermons of those cursed of God, born of the tainted blood of those from outside, serve as an omen of worse things to come? Yes, but we did not listen! Was it not known to the mad Arab and his disciples? The time of the shearing and the opening is it hand, is it not? In *Al-Azif*—thus named for the sounds of night insects, some say, but in truth a cipher that prophesied the coming of Ghor-Gothra, the Great Father Insect—did he not tell us that Yog-Sothoth was the key just as the mad faceless god was The Messenger? *Yes!* Just as he hinted at the blasphemies of the Father Insect who was the needle that would open the seams of this world to let the Old Ones through!" He ranted on about something known as the *Pnakotic Manuscripts* and the Angles of Tagh-Clatur and the Eltdown Shards. Becoming positively hysterical as he discussed *De Vermis Mysteriis* and the dread *Liber Ibonis*. "It was all there! All there!"

Simone wanted to turn the channel because these public access stations were always infested with half-baked religious fanatics, but she did not. There was something here, something important. The voice told her that in 1913 there appeared a novel by Reginald Pyenick called *The Ravening of Outer Slith,* which quickly disappeared from bookshelves because of its horrendous nature detailing a fertility cult worshipping a pagan insect deity. It was basically a retelling of the ancient German saga, *Das Summen,* which was hinted at in the grand, grim witch-book, *Unaussprechlichen Kulten,* and written about in detail by the deranged Austrian nobleman Jozef Graf Regula in his banned tome, *Cultis Vermis . . .* the very volume which detailed the history of the Ghor-Gothra cult and the coming age of the Old Ones. Regula was convicted of witchcraft and sorcery for writing it and was drawn-and-quartered in 1723. No matter, despite the suppressed knowledge of the cult, fragments of knowledge persisted in Verdin's *Unspeakable Survivals* and in the poem "Gathering of the Witch Swarm" which was to be found in *Azathoth and Other Horrors* by Edward Derby. "It was there—prophesy of the ages! Now *He* comes from the Black Mist to usurp our world and let the others in and we, yes, *we,* shall tremble in the shadow of the true progenitors of the dark cosmos that shivers in their wake. The 13th Equation is on the lips of the many and soon comes the Communion of Locusts, the buzzing, the buzzing, *the buzzing . . .*"

Simone shut the TV off before she lost what was left of her mind.

*   *   *

She was hallucinating, she was paranoid, she was delirious. And listening to the ravings of mad men was not going to help her.

Do something! You must do something! The time draws closer! It is now!

Frustrated, scared, quivering in her own skin, she called good friends—Reese and Carolyn—but they didn't answer. She called friends she hadn't seen in months—Frank and Darien and Seth and Marion—nothing. No one was answering their phones. Why was no one answering? *Because they're gathering now in secret places, on hilltops and misty glens and lonesome fields to wait the coming of—*

That was insane.

Wiping sweat from her face, Simone called her mother. Mom was at the Brighton Coombs Medical Care Facility, a nursing home. Half the time, she did not even recognize her daughter's voice and when she did, she laid out a heavy guilt trip. *You shouldn't be living in the city alone. Terrible things can happen in those places. Your father would roll over in his grave if he knew.* The line was answered and thirty seconds later, her mom was on the phone.

"Mother . . . how are you?" Simone said, trying to keep from choking up.

"Oh, Simone, my darling. I'm fine. How are you? You sound stressed. Are you eating enough? Do you have a boyfriend yet?"

Jesus.

"I'm okay. Just lonely."

"Ah, loneliness is a way of life as the years pile up."

But Simone didn't want to get into that. "I'd like to come see you."

"Oh! That would be just fine. I wish you were here now. We're all sitting in the sun room, waiting for the big event."

Simone felt a cold chill envelope her. "What . . . what event?"

Her mother laughed. "Why, the stars will soon align and *they* will come through. The seas will boil and the sky will crack open. Cthulhu shall rise from the corpse city of R'lyeh and Tsathoggua shall descend on the moon-ladder from the caverns of N'Kai when the planets roll in the heavens and the stars wink out one by one. Those of true faith will be numbered and heretics shall be named . . . you are not an unbeliever, are you, dear?"

Sobbing, Simone slammed the phone down. When something furry brushed against her hand, she nearly screamed. But it was only Rocky. It had to be Rocky . . . then it moved beneath her hand with the undulating motion of an immense worm and now she did scream. She launched herself off the couch as that thing moved around her, making a slobbering, hungry sound.

She was hallucinating.

She had to be hallucinating.

Through the furnace ducts she could hear Josh Ryan saying, *"She crawls because she cannot walk, she hears but she cannot see. The sign . . . she does not bear the sign."*

Simone pulled herself up the wall, standing on shaking legs. She heard the scratching again . . . but this time, it was in her own head like claws and blades and nails scraped along the inside of her skull.

Scritch, scratch, SCRIIIIIITCH, SCRAAAAAATCH.

The apartment was filled with a hot slaughterhouse stench of viscera, cold meat, and buckets of drainage. She could hear the buzzing of flies, what seemed hundreds if not thousands of them. And the scratching. It was very, very loud now, like giant buzzsaws in the walls and echoing through her brain.

The barrier was coming apart.

Shifting, tearing, fragmenting, realigning itself. She pressed a hand against the wall and felt a huge jagged crack open up beneath her fingertips. She touched something that pulsed within it—something busy and squirming like grave worms wriggling in some peristaltic nest. The buzzing was so loud now she could no longer think. Insects filled the room. They crawled over her arms and up the back of her neck. They tangled in her hair and lighted off her face, sucking the salt from her lips.

She stumbled from the living room and into the hallway as that great furry worm searched for her. Things touched her. They might have been hands, but they were puffy and soft with decay. Worming feelers came from the walls and embraced her, squirming over her face to touch her and know her as she had done so many times with so many others. A mammoth rugose trunk brushed her arm and her fingers slid through a heaving mass of spiky fur. She pulled away, trying to find the wall and succeeding only in finding a wet pelt hanging there that she knew instinctively belonged to Rocky. Her screams could barely be heard over the constant sawing, scratching noise and something like a great tolling bell.

Sobbing and shuddering, she fell to the floor and her knees sank into the floorboards as if they were nothing but warm, malleable putty. This was not her apartment; this was the known universe gutted and turned inside out, merging with another anti-world. She heard the roaring of monstrous locomotive mouths blowing burning clouds of irradiated steam. They shrilled like air raid sirens as the barrier weakened and the bleeding wound of this world split its seams and the nuclear blizzard of the void rushed in to fill its spaces. Her fingers touched snaking loops of crystalline flesh and things like hundreds of desiccated moths and mummified corpse flies rained down over her head. There was a stink like hot neon, shadows falling over her whose touch burned like acid. *The elder sign, child, you must make the elder sign, reveal the Sign of Kish.* Yes, yes, she knew it but did not know it as the air reverberated around her with a scraping, dusty cackling.

Though she could not see, she was granted a vision of the world to come. It filled her brain in waves of charnel imagery that made her scream, made blood run from her nose and her eyes roll back white in her head. Yes, the world was a tomb blown by the hissing radioactive secretions of the Old Ones who walked where man once walked, the skeletons of heretics crunching beneath their stride. The blood of innocents filled the gutters and putrefied bodies swollen to green carrion decayed to pools of slime. The world was a slag heap, a smoldering pyre of bones, and no stars shone above, only an immense multi-dimensional blackness that would have burned the eyes of men from their sockets if they were to look upon it.

Then the vision was gone.

But she could still see.

The crack in the wall was an immense fissure in the world, splitting open reality as she knew it . . . and through the gaping chasm, through some freakish curvature of time and space, she saw strobing, polychromatic images of a misty, distorted realm and some chitinous, and truly monstrous form striding in her direction with countless marching legs. Something that was first the size of a truck, then a house, then what seemed a two-story building. She heard the nightmarish whirring and buzzing of its colossal membranous wings. It looked almost like some grotesque mantis with a jagged, incandescent exoskeleton. It was filling the fissure. Not only filling it, but widening it, its droning mouthparts and needlelike mandibles unstitching the seams of creation.

AL-AZIF, AL-AZIF, AL-AZIF, she could hear voices crying.

Hysterical and completely demented, she tried to escape it but one of the insect's vibrating skeletal limbs reached out for her and she was stuck to it like flypaper. Then it had her, flying off through trans-galactic gulfs, through shrieking vortexual holes in the time/space continuum.

She was dropped.

She fell headlong through a dimensional whirlpooling funnel of matter where slinking geometric shapes hopped and squirmed and then—

Her sight was stripped of meat, her soul a sinewy thing desperate for survival in some godless chaos. She crawled, slinked, crept through the bubbling brown mud and pitted marrow of some new, phantasmal unreality.

Hungry insectile mouths suckled her, licking sweet drops of red milk, glutting themselves on what she had left. All around her, unseen, but felt, were crawling things and throbbing things and sinuous forms, mewling with hunger. She crept forward, razored webs snapping, cobweb clusters of meaty eggs dripping their sap upon her. She was trapped in the soft machinery of something alive, some cyclopean abomination, a gigantic creeping biological mass born in the night-black pits of some malefic anti-universe. She was crawling over its rotten fish-smelling jellied flesh, sliding through its oily pelt, a speck of animate dust on a loathsome unimaginable life form that dwarfed her world and filled the sky with coiling black tendrils that she could not see but could feel crowding her mind and poisoning the blood of the cosmos.

She was not alone.

Just one of many colonial parasites that crawled through the mire of the beast's life-jelly, swam its brine and foul secretions and oozing sap, her atoms flying apart in a storm of anti-matter and energized particles.

And then—

And then, it ended. A rehearsal, perhaps, for what was yet to come. She lay on the living room floor, drooling and gibbering, numb and mindless, giggling in her delirium. She wished only for night to come when prophecy would be realized and the stars would be right. There was a knob on her forehead, the bud of an optic stem that would let her see the time of the separating and the time of the joining, the rending and the sowing, the communion of this world and the next, as the Old Ones inherited the Earth and the Great Father Insect left his ethereal mansion of cosmic depravity with a swarm of luminous insects and took to the skies on membranous wings.

As spasms knifed her brain in white-hot shards, the stem pulsated and pushed free, opening like a hothouse orchid so it could show her what was coming: that holiest of nights when the world of men became a graveyard and the cities, tombs.

FOREIGN BODIES

ADAM HOWE

From *Chopping Block Party: An Anthology of Suburban Terror*
Editors: Brendan Deneen & David G. Barnett
Necro Publications

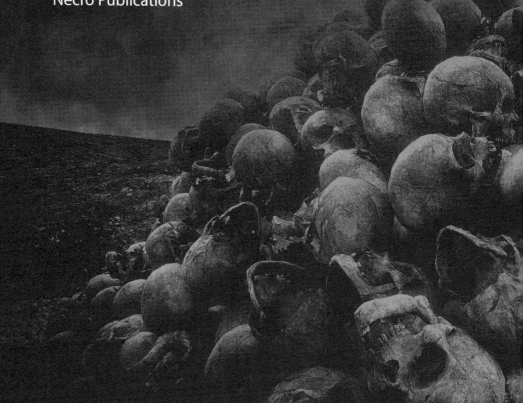

I flew in on the red eye, arriving at dawn at the address in the burbs that the panicked voice on the phone had given me. Climbing from my hire car, with the satchel containing my tools of the trade, I crept up the concrete walk to the door of #141, and rang the buzzer. A man's shrill voice called my name faintly from somewhere inside. With a glance at the neighbors' places, satisfying myself no early bird snoopers were watching from the windows, I went into the hall.

It was quiet; in the movies, they called this kinda quiet, *too* quiet. The hell was everybody? This was supposed to be a family home. According to my intel, my client had been staying here with his son since he checked out of rehab.

"Buddy?" My voice echoed in the stillness of the house.

"Up—upstairs . . ." The voice cracked with fatigue.

I padded upstairs to the landing, put my palm to the door of the master bedroom, steeling myself for whatever I might find on the other side.

In my line of work, about the only thing you can count on, it's never pretty.

Pushing the door open, I entered the shadowy bedroom, blindly treading on a rubber cock that stiffened beneath my shoe with an angry squeak and scared the bejesus out of me. The dildo was just one of an orgy of sex toys erupting from the open suitcase at the foot of the bed, and scattered across the carpeted floor.

The client was sprawled facedown on the bed. I'd never seen the old man without his rug before. The toupee was curled on the pillow beside him like a glossy chestnut-brown lapdog. Without his hairpiece, the wizened old man looked like the lovechild of Don Rickles and Zelda from the *Poltergeist* movies. He was otherwise naked, too, which was bad news for a lot of reasons, not least his shabby shape, and coarse pelt of back hair. In a pitiful attempt to preserve his last shred of dignity, he'd swaddled a silk tiger print robe around his lower back and upper thighs. Sadly, this only drew more attention to the cardboard postal tube jutting up like a periscope from between his bare buttocks.

On the nightstand was an empty bottle of Jack, and a small mound of coke that'd probably been bigger when he'd called me for help; a tub of lube and a vial of amyl nitrate, which explained the wince-worthy depth of the tube in his ass, if not the tube itself; plus a framed photo portrait of his son, daughter-in-law, and six-year old granddaughter. The family seemed to be grinning in unanimous approval.

Perched on a chair in the corner of the room was Scamp McRascal.

Wearing shitkicker dungarees and clodhoppers, with his fire-engine-red thatch of hair, jug ears, freckled face, the puppet looked like the bastard offspring of Howdy Doody and Chucky from the *Child's Play* movies. Grinning his famous gap-toothed grin, Scamp sat watching the scene on the bed like a cheerily cuckolded husband jacking off while some gigolo bones his old lady.

On the side table was a wire cage for a small animal. The cage was bedded with sawdust and a nest of shredded tissue paper. It had a running wheel, water dispenser, a little bowl filled with nuts, and a gnawed toilet paper tube, almost like a scale model of the postal tube jutting from my client's ass. Attached to the front of the cage was a child's lovingly hand-painted sign. The sign said, GERRY. The R's were written backwards; either the kid was Russian, or it was a damning indictment of the education system. Then I suddenly realized—

There was no sign of Gerry inside the cage.

My heart started hammering and I broke into a cold sweat.

This was worse than I'd feared.

*   *   *

There comes a time in every puppeteer's career, all those years with his hand up inside a puppet, he starts to wonder—how would it feel, the shoe was on the other foot?

So to speak.

For beloved children's entertainer Buddy Mortimer aka Uncle Buddy aka Mr. Family Entertainment, it started with small items, at first. For years the cast and crew of *Scamp McRascal's Playhouse* had innocently believed Uncle Buddy was a closet kleptomaniac, and a glutton when it came to certain phallic foodstuffs from craft services—whole carrots, cucumbers, and kielbasas. Forgivable sins for a star of his magnitude. Easily swept under the rug. Visitors to the set were discreetly warned to keep any pocket-sized valuables on their person, lest they vanish around Buddy. What no one suspected, least of all the parents of the children of America, who for thirty years of Saturday mornings, had entrusted their brats to Uncle Buddy and his puppet, Scamp McRascal, was that Mr. Family Entertainment was caching an Aladdin's cave of contraband up his keister.

Six months ago, Buddy had been outed when airport security detained him with what appeared to be an improvised explosive device in his colon. A tense cavity search—bomb squad, dogs, *Short Circuit*-style robot, the works—followed by a painful, and humiliating extraction, revealed the 'IED' to be nothing more harmful than a ladies' wristwatch.

But the damage it did to Buddy's career was quite explosive.

The watch was linked back to a pro named Ramona, nee Ramon, a she-he who specialized in fisting. Ramona's current whereabouts were unknown. She'd missed out on cashing in her fifteen minutes of fame, perhaps living the high life on the hush money Buddy paid her. But according to Ramona's pimp, who sold his story to the scandal rags, she had last been employed in the service of 'Uncle' Buddy Mortimer. It was never established if Buddy was unaware the watch had disengaged in his ass, or if he'd been sporting it there as a perverse trophy.

In the aftermath of the airport bust, not to mention the Ramona/Ramon revelations, Buddy's career as a children's entertainer was over; he'd burned down *Scamp McRascal's Playhouse*. But despite the scandal, even now, he played his cards right and a comeback of sorts was still a possibility. Why the hell not? We forgave Pee Wee Herman. Eventually.

The past six months, Buddy had been rehabbing for pick-an-addiction, hiding out from the tabloids until the shitstorm blew over and the muck-rakers found their next piñata. Now he was out, supposedly cured, sin-free and sorry as hell, eager to start his dishonor lap of the talk shows. He'd turn on the waterworks, feed 'em the whole 'tears of a clown' bit, and most important of all, plug his upcoming autobiography.

All he had to do was stay out of trouble.

That's where I came in.

Joe Conklin: Joseph Conklin Solutions, Ltd.

The A-list gets Ray Donovan; the lower end of the alphabet gets me.

'Course, there's only so much a fixer can fix.

* * *

I glanced between the empty small animal cage and the cardboard tube in Buddy's ass.

Buddy forced a sheepish smile. "It's not what it looks like, Joe."

"Glad to hear it," I said. "Because all the signs are pointing to you having Gerry the Whatever-the-fuck up your ass."

Buddy wet his lips with a nervous flick of his tongue.

"Alright. So maybe it is what it looks like. What I meant was, I can explain."

I could see him thinking how best he could sugarcoat it.

Much as a man can sugarcoat the rodent in his ass.

He glanced at Scamp in the corner of the room.

I said, "If you even *think* about blaming that puppet—!"

Buddy blew out a sigh. "Alright, so maybe I can't explain either."

"Chrissakes, Buddy . . ." I paced the room, stepping on the squeaky cock once more and kicking it angrily away from me. It ricocheted off the closed door of the en-suite bathroom like a rubber bullet. "You had *one* job! Don't stick anything up your ass until after the talk show tour! Was that really so hard!"

"It just happened, Joe."

"No! Things like this don't 'just happen!'"

"After six months of rehab, I thought I was on top of this anal fixation thing . . ."

Buddy shook his head ruefully.

"I mean—sheesh, Joe—*you* think *you're* surprised!"

"You came here to stay with the kid to stay out of trouble," I reminded him. Gestured to the photo of Buddy's son on the nightstand. "After everything you've put him through, that kid's gotta be a fucking saint letting you anywhere near his family . . . And *this* is how you repay him?"

Buddy's eyes welled with tears. He bowed his head in shame.

It occurred to me again how quiet the house was.

"Where is everybody anyway?"

"Erin's mother got sick."

According to my intel, Erin was the daughter-in-law. The smiling, plump blonde in the family photo. Old-fashioned floral dress, crucifix necklace. The wholesome churchgoing type.

"They left last night for Florida," Buddy said. "And for what it's worth, they hadn't left me on my own, none of this would have happened."

"So it's their fault?"

"It takes two to tango is all I'm saying."

"When are you expecting them back?"

"Tonight."

"So time is of the essence?"

"You could say that, yeah."

I considered the problem before me.

"What are we dealing with here? What is . . . Gerry?"

Buddy cast his eyes down, and in a hoarse voice, said, "Gerry's a gerbil, Joe."

I glanced at the lovingly hand-painted sign on Gerry's cage, and the photo of Buddy's granddaughter on the nightstand.

Buddy choked down a sob. "She can never find out."

It was all I could do just to shake my head at him.

"You gotta understand, Joe. It's this *Wake Up, America* spot. I been climbing the walls, I'm so nervous about it—"

Wake Up, America was the first stop on Buddy's comeback tour. Major network. National exposure. Buddy aced *Wake Up, America*, charmed the anchor Wendy Wang, and the gravy train was back on the rails and rolling again.

"I needed something to take the edge off," he went on, "so I called for a masseuse."

"This masseuse," I said, "he in the book?"

"Not exactly," Buddy said. "But that's all I wanted. Just a backrub, I swear.

"Well, the kid shows up. 'Course, he recognizes me. Says he used to watch the show every Saturday morning. A fan, y' know. He knows the Scamp McRascal Secret Handshake and everything. Nice kid. He tells me he's sorry for my recent troubles. I think he's being sincere. Why wouldn't I?

"Then he says, casual-like, 'I see you got a gerbil next door.' Not knowing where he's going with this, thinking the kid's just making polite, I say, 'My granddaughter's, yeah.' Then he says, still casual-like, 'You ever tried it with a gerbil before?' I says to him—and now I'm starting to get a funny feeling about the kid's line of questioning—I says, 'Tried what?' He says, 'C'mon.' Like I'm shining him on. 'You know. Like that actor. Used to be married to Claudia Schiffer.' He's got the actor's wife wrong, but I knew the guy he meant. I says, 'I don't do that kinda stuff no more, kid.' Forceful-like. You woulda been proud of me, Joe. I says, 'All I want is a backrub. Nothing else.' Firm.

"But the kid—*that fucking kid*—he's planted the seed in my mind, and now he starts watering it . . . Describing how it feels: The tiny claws, the bushy tail brushing the walls of my colon, the whiskers tickling my prostate . . ."

Buddy swallowed hard.

"I'm telling you, Joe, the way the kid sold it, even you woulda been tempted!"

"I sincerely fucking doubt that."

"After that, it all happened so fast. We're knocking 'em back, we're snorting blow. Next thing I know, I got this tube up my ass and a gerbil inside me. And I won't lie to you, Joe, it's everything the kid said it would be, only better. I'm in heaven. Then there's this flashing light, and suddenly I'm in hell, cuz now the kid's got a camera in his hands, and he's telling me he wants fifty gees, else he's taking the pictures to the tabloids."

I closed my eyes, pinched the bridge of my nose between my forefinger and thumb, and let out a long sigh. *Fucking celebrities . . .*

"This kid," I said, "where is he now?"

"Forget about the kid," Buddy told me, "I took care of it—"

"Have you even got fifty gees?" I guessed it was possible he could've squirreled away a little rainy day money; I don't have to tell you where.

"The kid's not the issue, Joe."

"No?"

"In all the commotion, Gerry must've panicked. He started burrowing up into my guts like something from *Alien*. Now, I got a high pain threshold, as you know—"

"No shit."

"But jeez . . ." Buddy winced at the memory, "this was something else. The pain was so bad I almost called for an ambulance. Luckily common sense prevailed."

"Common sense, right . . ."

"I'm gonna go to the hospital with a gerbil up my ass? I'm not sure my insurance even covers that . . . So instead of the ambulance, I called you, Mr. Fixit." He buttered me up with a *you're-my-hero* grin. "And I haven't moved from this bed since. I knew you'd know what to do."

I wasn't sure if I should be flattered or insulted.

I said, "Is—is it even still alive?"

"I been lying here so long, my whole lower body's gone numb, I can't feel nothing from the waist down—"

He jerked his head back at the tube in his ass. "Was hoping you could tell me."

And to think, there'd once been a time when I'd thought working for a star like 'Uncle' Buddy Mortimer was a glamour gig. The pay was better than my regular fixit work for Z-list celebrities . . . But man, it sure came at a price.

I took a wary step towards the bed—and caught a violent whiff of ass, and pet store, wafting from the open end of the tube. I staggered back, swatting at the air and retching, shaking my head like a prizefighter trying to shake off a knockdown punch. "Nope," I said. "Forget it. This ain't what I do. This ain't burying a news story or making a DWI go away. I didn't sign up for this."

"But you gotta help me here, Joe! I can't go on *Wake Up, America* like this!"

"Maybe you should've thought about that before you stuck a gerbil up your ass."

"I'm begging you, please! Name your price!"

My price . . . Of course I had one; I'm not proud. But what was the going rate for extracting a gerbil from a man's ass?

"The fifty gees you paid the kid," I said. "I assume, when we're done here, you expect me to get it back."

"Well, sure. But first things first, huh?"

"When I do, the money's mine."

I'd expected him to haggle. But he must have realized that under the circumstances, the last thing he could afford was to be a tight ass. "Done."

"I'd shake your hand," I told him, "but . . ."

He nodded he understood.

I peeled off my jacket, slung it over the grinning puppet in the corner.

"Hey!" Buddy cried, "Careful of Scamp!"

"You might like an audience," I said, "I don't."

I rooted through my satchel for a penlight and a pair of latex gloves—tools of the trade. Then I clamped a handkerchief over my nose and mouth like a surgical mask cum breathing apparatus, and started taking tentative steps towards the bed. The penlight shook in my hand as I shone the beam down the tube. Eyes watering in disgust, I forced myself to peer into the black depths of Buddy's alimentary canal. What was it Nietzsche said about gazing into the abyss?

"See anything?" Buddy said over his shoulder.

"Too much," I said, turning off the penlight. "But no gerbil." I went and opened a window for some fresh air, wishing I could bleach my eyeballs.

"Damn it," Buddy said. "Sonofabitch must be dug in like an Alabama tick . . ."

"You're sure it's in there, right?"

I didn't put it past the sick fuck that this was some perverted sex game, that he'd lured me to the house under false pretenses, and was getting his rocks off while I performed my makeshift colonoscopy.

Buddy bristled in offence.

"I'm a lot of things, Joe. But I'm not a liar."

"Alright . . ." I tried to think; mostly I tried not to puke. "You're gonna have to turn on your side."

"I told you, I can't move."

"I'm gonna roll you."

"Just mind you don't crush Gerry inside me."

"It's a little late to start worrying about Gerry's welfare."

I climbed onto the bed behind Buddy, gripped his shoulders, and rolled him onto his side, until the length of the tube in his ass extended towards me across the mattress. "Cover yourself, would you?" He fetched his toupee off the pillow and covered his genitals, the rug like a glossy chestnut-brown modesty patch.

I climbed off the bed, kneeled down beside it, facing the open end of the tube.

Then, what the hell else could I do, I whistled for Gerry and called his name in a high-pitched voice.

Buddy looked at me sharply over his shoulder. "It's not a dog, Joe. It's not gonna come to heel." He shook his head. "Didn't you have pets as a kid?"

"Well, yeah, sure. A goldfish." I added defensively, "My mother had allergies."

"Go down to the kitchen," Buddy said. "There's cheese in the refrigerator."

"All this time in your ass, you really think Gerry's gonna have an appetite?"

After getting that whiff from the tube, I wasn't sure I'd ever eat again.

Buddy said, "And bring a couple slices of bread and some ham, too."

I frowned. "You want I should fix him a sandwich?"

"The sandwich is for me."

I just looked at him.

"I been lying here half the night," he shrugged, "I got my blood-sugar to consider."

As I went downstairs, of course I considered just fleeing that madhouse. The only thing keeping me there was Buddy's promise of the fifty gees. I told myself I'd remove the gerbil from his ass (like that was gonna be a cakewalk), retrieve the incriminating photo and the money from the 'masseuse' (as if that'd be any easier), and then Buddy and me were done.

In the kitchen, I was about to open the refrigerator when I saw the child's crayon drawing pinned to the door with a Scamp McRascal magnet. The drawing showed Uncle Buddy and Scamp, the puppet with his stepchild-red thatch of hair and gappy grin, the old man with his rat's-nest toupee. GRAMPA + SCAMP was scrawled in childish hand beside the two figures. The R in GRAMPA was written backwards, like the R's on the sign on Gerry's cage. Uncle Buddy and Scamp were leaning from the window of a tree house that I guessed was supposed to be Scamp McRascal's Playhouse. They were waving down at an angelic little blonde girl with ME! scrawled next to her. The little angel was proudly holding up her pet gerbil for GRAMPA to see.

My heart sank.

"Joe!"

I startled at Buddy's screeching voice.

"What's wrong?" I called back to him.

"Mustard! For the sandwich!"

Cursing him under my breath, I fetched a saran-wrapped chunk of cheddar off the shelf. Then, with a last despairing glance at the drawing on the fridge, I trudged back upstairs.

Buddy said, "Where's my sandwich?"

"Stick your sandwich up your—" I didn't finish the sentence. "I'm not here as your personal chef, Buddy."

I unwrapped the cheese, and placed it on the bed at the open end of the tube.

Then I backed away to the wall, slid down it to the floor, and sat there to wait.

Buddy said, "You mind if I rehearse my *Wake Up, America* apology?"

It was a rhetorical question.

As Buddy droned on, I zoned out his voice, and gazed at the family portrait on the nightstand. The forgiving son. The devoted daughter-in-law.

The adoring granddaughter. The little girl's innocent blue eyes bored into me, gnawing at my conscience like Gerry gnawing at Buddy's guts. The kid's parents couldn't have told her about the shame GRAMPA had brought upon the family. *That* was a conversation I didn't envy them. Birds and bees was one thing, keistering quite another. Of course, it was only a matter of time before the other kids at her school spilled the sordid beans and her innocence was shattered. And what about all the other children whose trust 'Uncle' Buddy had betrayed? For an entire generation, their happy memories of Saturday morning television were irrevocably tainted.

I couldn't bear the little girl looking at me a second longer.

"Turn that picture down, would you?"

Buddy started reaching for the portrait—

Suddenly he screamed, and then started to convulse, as if the tube in his ass was a live cattle prod. "Yaaaaaaaaaaargh! For the luvva Christ! Make it stop!" He thrashed his hands as if to fend off the pain. The family portrait was knocked to the floor and shattered.

I scrambled to my feet. "What is it?" I pictured the gerbil chewing through Buddy's colon like a rat chewing through a sardine tin.

"Guh—guh—Gerry! Huh—he—he's . . . MOVING!"

"North or South?"

"Nuh—nuh—north!"

"Pucker up," I cried, "pucker up!"

Buddy tensed his sphincter, clenched his colon, gritting his teeth with effort.

"I—I think I got him!" he gasped, tears leaking from his eyes.

"Alright," I said, rolling up my shirtsleeves, "no more screwing around."

I told Buddy what I needed.

"Are you fucking nuts?" said the guy with the gerbil in his ass.

"You got any better suggestions?"

He told me where to find what I'd asked for.

"Hurry!" Buddy said, sweat streaming down his face. "I can't hold him like this much longer."

I returned to the room lugging a Henry Hoover.

Buddy cried out in horror as he saw the cheery eyes and lunatic smile painted on the red tub of the Henry's body. The Henry's vacuum hose nose snaked across the carpet in my wake.

I fitted the slimmest attachment to the vacuum hose. Then I started feeding it slowly into the tube in Buddy's ass, careful as a model ship enthusiast raising the sails of a ship in a bottle, trying not to panic Gerry more than he already was. As I fed the Henry's nose deeper into Buddy's ass, I glanced back at the grinning face painted on the Hoover's red tub body. Whoever thought to anthropomorphize a fucking vacuum cleaner, had they ever envisioned a scenario like this?

The Henry's nose reached its end; Buddy flinched and let out a whimper.

"Now," I said, "when I hit this switch, you gotta push—"

"Let's think this thing through a second, Joe—"

I flicked the switch.

The Henry roared to life.

Buddy screamed.

I yelled, "Push, goddamn you!"

Buddy bit down on his pillow, pushing and straining, his face flushing red, the tendons cording his neck, the pillow muffling his screams. The vacuum hose bucked in my hands as the Henry snorted something weighty through the tube. A gerbil, I hoped, and not one of Buddy's vital organs. There was a muffled thump as it was sucked into the red tub of the Henry's body. I yanked the Henry's plug from the wall, silencing the roaring vacuum.

Buddy teetered from the bed, clutching the nightstand for balance, the tube in his ass waggling like a cardboard tail. Squatting awkwardly, he reached between his legs, gripped the tube, and then wrenched it from his rectum like Arthur freeing Excalibur from the Stone. He dropped the tube to the floor and crumpled to his knees, sobbing with relief as he dragged his tiger print robe around him.

I tore the Henry's body open and ripped the vacuum bag apart with my hands. A blinding cloud of dust billowed out, choking the bedroom. A shit-smeared gerbil thudded lifelessly to the carpet. I pumped Gerry's chest with my fingertips, trying to jumpstart his tiny heart. Even if he *hadn't* spent the night stuck in Buddy's ass, *wasn't* caked in shit, I drew the line at giving a gerbil mouth to mouth. I bowed my head. "I'm calling it . . . He's gone."

Buddy said, "Gerry's dead?"

I glared at him. "The hell did you expect?" Peeling off my gloves, I started towards the en-suite to wash my hands. Thoroughly.

Buddy called out, "Joe, wait—"

But I'd already opened the door.

A young man wearing a white PVC masseuse's smock was sprawled inside the bathtub. The leather flails of a cat whip were coiled around his throat. His neck was bruised and swollen, his face flushed purple. His bloodshot eyes bugged from his face, staring at me lifelessly.

I wheeled around.

Buddy stood blocking the door.

In his hand was a .38 snub, the barrel pointed at my chest.

I showed him my palms. "Whoa! Easy now, Buddy."

"I didn't mean for you to see this, Joe. I was gonna fix this one myself."

I nodded my head towards the body in the tub.

"It wasn't blackmail, was it?" Which meant—*shit*—there was no fifty gees.

Buddy didn't answer.

"And Ramona?" I said.

This explained her—his—mysterious disappearance.

"Jesus, Buddy . . . How many have there been? How many others?"

His lips teased into a smirk. Something terrible glinted in his eyes. I may have removed the gerbil from his ass, but there was another animal inside Buddy Mortimer, a wild beast with sharp fangs and insatiable appetites.

"You gotta understand, Joe. I need these things. All the happiness and joy I've brought to people through the years, it's not too much to ask. Hell, I deserve them! Is the world really gonna miss trash like this?"

He wrinkled his nose, shook his head prissily.

"Now," he said, "are you gonna help me fix this?"

I glanced at the gun in his hand.

"Whatever you say, Buddy."

"Go fetch a hatchet, a saw and some garbage bags from the garage."

He considered the body in the tub. "Four oughta do it."

But it turned out three were all we needed.

By the time I was finished, no one would've guessed the bathroom was a murder scene. The place was spotless, every tile gleaming white. The tools I'd used to hack and saw the masseuse into pieces had been scrubbed clean and set to dry. The three bulging garbage bags were placed neatly next to the door.

I laid Gerry to rest inside a Ritz cracker box casket. Vacuumed the bedroom carpet, made the bed with fresh sheets. Buddy cleaned the booze and blow from the nightstand, and packed his sex toys back into his suitcase, including that damn squeaky cock, and the cat whip he'd strangled the kid with. Throughout it all, Scamp McRascal smiled from his perch in the corner, a silent accomplice.

We drove my hire car to a spot in the woods Buddy knew. Dumped the kid's remains in the river. As we watched the garbage bags sink, I wondered how many other times Buddy had been to this spot; maybe every time he visited his family?

"Now . . ." Buddy said, "There's just one last thing to fix."

He turned towards me with the gun in his hand.

I'd already resigned myself to how this was going to end.

But instead of plugging me, he said, "Gerry."

I frowned. "But—Gerry's dead."

Buddy grinned. "My granddaughter's only six-years old. You really think she'll know the difference between one fucking gerbil and another?"

*   *   *

Buddy waited in the car while I went inside the pet store alone. He didn't want to run the risk of being star-spotted buying a gerbil. People might leap to the correct conclusion. He took my cellphone before letting me out of his sight. "Wouldn't want you calling the cops." Or the men in white coats with the butterfly nets, I thought. But he needn't have worried. After hoovering Gerry from Buddy's ass, I was hardly thinking straight to begin with; dismembering the masseuse had pushed me right over the edge, driven me blood simple.

I returned from the store carrying a small box with a perforated lid. I climbed back in the car and gave Buddy the box. He prized up the lid, peered inside and grinned. "Any problems?"

I lied and told him, no.

We drove in silence back to Golden Elm Lane. I pulled up outside #141. "You done good today, Joe." He made it sound like I'd passed an audition. And maybe I had. "About that fifty grand we talked about—"

I dredged up my voice, "Forget about the money."

He frowned at me.

"All I want is out," I told him.

"Out?" He looked at me in stark surprise. "You mean, leave showbiz?"

I nodded.

He drummed his fingers thoughtfully on the lid of the gerbil box.

"You wouldn't ratfuck me now, would you, Joe?"

I glanced at the box in his lap and shook my head.

"Because I go down, I'm taking you with me. You think people will believe you only ever helped me dump one body?"

"I understand."

"Fine. You want out, you've earned it, I guess." He studied my glazed expression with something like grandfatherly concern. "Give it a few days, Joe. All this'll seem like nothing but a bad dream." He winked at me. "You'll see."

He started climbing from the car. "Buddy?" I said.

He glanced back at me.

"Break a leg on *Wake Up, America.*"

He grinned. "You know I will, kid. Don't forget to tune in."

Oh, I wouldn't miss it for the world . . .

*   *   *

The next morning, slumped at the bar in the airport lounge, waiting for my flight home, I necked my beer, ordered another, and thought about the run of bad luck and worse life choices that'd led me to work for a monster like 'Uncle' Buddy Mortimer. I wondered about my other celebrity clients;

what skeletons were they hiding in their closets, what dirty secrets were they keeping from their own fixer? I glanced at my haunted reflection in the back-bar mirror. Was I doing the right thing not calling the cops? Then I remembered my visit to the pet store . . .

It clearly wasn't the first time the storekeeper had been complicit in the cover-up of a deceased pet. Like me, she was a fixer. She'd peered inside Gerry's Ritz cracker box casket, recoiled slightly at the stench, but to her credit, let it slide without comment. "One brown female gerbil." She went to find a ringer.

Before I could tell her I believed Gerry had originally been white—I suddenly registered what she'd said. "Female?"

"And by the looks of her," the woman said, "very recently pregnant."

Nursing the dregs of my beer, I stared intently at the airport lounge's TV screen.

Wendy Wang was welcoming Buddy and Scamp to the *Wake Up, America* couch. Buddy took a seat, perching Scamp on his lap. Buddy's autobiography was displayed prominently on the coffee table. The old man's voice cracked with emotion as he described to Wendy Wang the living hell of his secret life as a keisterer. As Buddy recalled his time in rehab, and his painful journey towards self-enlightenment, Scamp reached up a spindly arm and a brushed a tear from his master's cheek. Even Wendy Wang choked down the lump in her throat.

"Do you have anything to say to the children of America?" she coaxed him.

Buddy took a deep breath. "Yes, Wendy, yes, I do."

The old man cleared his throat, staring soulfully into camera, steeling himself to deliver the heartfelt apology that would win him America's forgiveness—

Then he suddenly sat bolt upright, the color bleeding from his face. Scamp's jaw dropped open, his glass eyes rolling spastically back in his head. Buddy shuddered on the couch, wild-eyed, breaking into a sweat that soaked through his snazzy suit. His lips trembled as he cut a long foghorn of gas.

Wendy frowned in concern. "Uncle Buddy? Is everything—?"

Buddy clutched his gut and bellowed in pain. Then he sprang to his feet and flung Scamp from his wrist, the puppet flopping lifelessly across the coffee table. Screaming, Buddy started yanking at his clothes, tearing his pants down, ripping off his underwear. Wendy Wang cried out in horror as Buddy nakedly squatted and shat a shower of hairless pink baby gerbils into every home in America—

The live TV transmission cut to static. Then a PLEASE STAND BY card appeared. Muzak played. A crowd of people thronged the airport lounge bar around me, staring at the TV in shocked silence.

I raised my glass to Gerry aka Geraldine, and said:

"Come back from *that*, Buddy, you sonofabitch."

AUTHOR'S STORY NOTE

Writers are often encouraged to "write what you know," something which may alarm readers of Foreign Bodies, my story about a Z-list Hollywood fixer, a sleazy children's TV entertainer with a dark secret, and a gerbil named Gerry. The basic idea came to me while watching Ray Donovan. I remembered the urban legend about Richard Gere and the gerbil and I wondered how Ray would handle the situation if the gerbil became ... stuck. Regular readers of my work will know that I do not shirk when it comes to research. They have come to expect a certain gritty realism from titles such as Jesus in a Dog's Ass, Damn Dirty Apes, and Tijuana Donkey Showdown. So how far did I take my research this time? Sadly, not as far as I would have liked; as a consequence of researching those stories, I have found myself banned from my local pet store, blacklisted by my veterinarian, and forbidden from keeping small animals. But I'm a stubborn SOB, not easily discouraged. I considered improvising with one of my baby daughter's plush toys. She has a miniature chimpanzee that I estimated to be approximately the size of Gerry the Gerbil. Then I remembered the advice Sir Laurence Olivier gave to method-actor Dustin Hoffman on the set of Marathon Man: "Why don't you try acting, dear boy?" The plush toy was spared. I used my imagination ... or did I? Because that's something else about writers—you can't believe a damn word we say.

ADRAMELECH

SEAN PATRICK HAZLETT

From *L. Ron Hubbard Presents Writers of the Future*
Editor: David Farland
Galaxy Press

dreamt of a peacock. Not the majestic fowl in all its pomp and beauty, but a twisted and perverted chimera. Blackened, burnt, and torn plumage radiated from its serpentine form. Jaundiced eyes, both human and animal, infested its spotted feathers. Each eye shone with what struck me as a keen and malevolent intelligence.

I woke to find myself scribbling arcane symbols in my daily ledger—strange, indecipherable glyphs. Though executed by my own hand, the writing was more precise and beautiful than mine. It was so small, I considered using a magnifying glass to make out the wedge-shaped marks. My phantom hand had filled all two hundred pages with this inscrutable script in the course of one night.

As I turned the pages to marvel at this prodigious effort, I stumbled upon several revolting illustrations. Children boiling in kettle pots, inverted crucifixions, and the dismemberment of babes—these were but a few of the horrors I witnessed on the ledger's sacrilegious sheets.

As I leafed through the tome, a crushing sense of melancholy suffocated me. It was as if a sickly film of somber gray had occluded my vision. After turning the book's profane pages, it took all the energy I had to rise from my bed.

I should've burnt the accursed book on the spot, but its artisanal quality was unrivaled. Despite its corruption, it had a dark beauty that made it impossible for me to feed it to the flame.

The urge to destroy the blasphemous text waned, while my curiosity about its contents waxed. So I wrapped the book in burlap and brought it to my dear friend, Alastair Moorcock, Professor of Hebrew and Semitic Languages at the University of Glasgow.

A Christ-fearing man, I had never resorted to outright deception before, but I feared Moorcock would name me a madman if I'd told him the truth. So instead, I concocted a story about how I'd uncovered the ledger in some flea-bitten apothecary shop in West London.

Surrounded by dusty books lining his walls or arranged on the floor in haphazard piles, Moorcock cultivated an aura of aristocratic intellectualism. With a keen eye and a strong sentimentality for the past, he refused modern conveniences, preferring the illumination of candlelight to one of Edison's incandescent light bulbs.

"Where did you really find this?" he demanded, his waxed whiskers vibrating as he stared intensely at me from his cramped study.

"What do you mean?" I said, playing coy.

"This text is written in Sumerian cuneiform, in ink, and on a modern ledger, not chiseled on a stone tablet."

"That is rather unnerving," I admitted.

"If I may ask," Moorcock continued, "which apothecary shop sold you this forgery? I should very much like to meet the shopkeeper. He seems to be an exceptionally well-educated man. Only a handful of academics possess the scholarship to identify these glyphs; even fewer know enough to translate, let alone write them."

I lowered my head, embarrassed. If I continued this charade, Moorcock would summarily expose my lie. Then I'd get no help from him at all. So I confessed. "My deepest apologies, Professor Moorcock. I didn't find this at an apothecary shop. I composed it last night. The truth is so preposterous I reasoned you'd more likely accept the lie. Regardless of the text's origin, I very much require your expertise."

His eyebrow arched. His jaw tightened. "Mr. Brooks, how is it you're incapable of reading something you wrote?"

He had a point. So I tried a different approach. "It matters not how this ledger came to be in my possession. What's important is that we decipher its contents. You're the first and only person I've sought for guidance, because I'm convinced that your curiosity will outweigh your concerns about how I acquired this book."

Moorcock cupped his chin in his hand in what appeared to be a moment of consideration. "You didn't steal it, did you?" he asked in a manner suggesting that's exactly how he thought I'd come by it.

I smiled and shook my head. "Of course not."

"Very well then. Let's have a look," he said, rolling up his sleeves. He opened the tome and squinted at the first page.

"Here," I said, handing him my magnifying glass.

He took it without saying a word and began his examination. He traced his index finger across the page in a steady hand. As he read, his eyes widened.

Then they rolled back into his head until I saw nothing but their whites. He raised his head, turning away from the ledger. He smiled in a most unsettling manner.

"And so it begins," he cackled. "For your assistance in this life and for your eternal servitude once you pass beyond death's veil, I will grant you the power to inhabit the bodies of others. What say you to my offer?"

Moorcock's transformation was so strange and so abrupt that I hesitated, unable to formulate anything resembling a coherent response to this rather unnerving query.

"I'm sorry, Professor Moorcock, I don't understand."

"Not Moorcock," it said, "Something else. Something far older. What say you to my offer?"

"No," I said without wavering.

When I tried to elaborate, I found my ability to draw breath thwarted. I struggled for air, desperately opening and closing my mouth like a herring flailing on the slick deck of a trawler.

"What about now?" it said, grinning.

I fought and I prayed and I panicked and I tried to weep. But nothing would bring me air. As patches of hazy blackness obscured my vision, I nodded in submission.

With that, Moorcock collapsed. Shaking his head like a befuddled drunkard, he slowly rose back to his feet. "My God," he said, "you must burn that tome, immediately."

I shuddered at his suggestion. Once more, I couldn't bear to contemplate the ledger's destruction. The book was a foul thing, but one of exquisite splendor, and it hinted of shuttered secrets I despaired to learn. There were still too many unanswered questions. What had possessed Moorcock? With whom or what had I made a bargain? Could it be undone?

"No, I can't. We can't. There's still much to learn from this text," I pleaded.

Moorcock scowled. He lifted the foul ledger from his desk and held it over a candle's open flame.

"No!" I yelled. Then, from Moorcock's own eyes I watched my body collapse. I yanked the book away from the flame and placed it on the floor next to my still-breathing human husk. I sat in Moorcock's chair. Then I returned to my own body and snatched the ledger before standing.

Moorcock regarded me with an expression that straddled the thin line between awe and horror. "What have you done, sir?"

"You have no right to destroy my property," I replied.

Pointing at the tome, Moorcock said, "That thing is an abomination. You saw what it did to me."

I tried to ignore his outrage. "Please, tell me what you learned. I must understand what just happened," I begged.

He brooded behind his desk. "Get that thing out of my sight and never come here again."

"Done," I said. "But please, for the love of God, help me understand what knowledge you gleaned from your brief reading."

Moorcock paused, then said, "Return to London and call on Sir Willard Hilton. Show him your ledger and inquire about the *Dictionnaire Infernal*. Good day, Mr. Brooks."

With that, I grabbed the ledger, left his study, and returned to London by rail.

*   *   *

I was to meet Sir Willard Hilton in a modest pub about half a block away from the electric adverts illuminating Piccadilly Circus's thoroughfare. I entered the establishment, happy to find shelter from the cold and rainy night.

It was always night for me. Since I'd birthed the ledger, I'd become a nocturnal thing, preferring the solace of shadow to the loud and arrogant face of the sun. Even the moon, whose source of light was the sun's reflection, was something I shunned.

I collapsed my umbrella and removed my bowler hat, taking in the tiny pub's ambience. The establishment was little more than an alcove, carved into the bone and sinew of London's West End. The tables were roughhewn and discolored, pitted oak slabs from years of use and neglect.

"What'll it be, sir?" the portly barkeep said.

"I'm just here to see someone," I replied.

"Best you be seeing them elsewhere," the man said, leering at me. "Only have space for paying customers."

I balled my fists. Fantasies of ripping out the man's throat filled my mind's eye. I had to blink twice before I was able to regain my composure. "Fine," I said. "A glass of whiskey will do."

"What kind?" the man said.

"The kind that is cheapest," I said, annoyed.

He harrumphed and poured my drink.

"Do you happen to know if a Sir Willard Hilton frequents this pub?" I asked.

He answered with a scowl. "You? Here to see Sir Willard?"

"What? Were you expecting someone different?" I said, insulted.

He rolled his eyes and then pointed to a table in the pub's back left nook. I followed his arm to find a wiry-thin man with curly black hair that receded into a widow's peak. He vibrated with nervous energy while he chatted up a curvaceous blonde. He clutched an overflowing pint of ale.

I grabbed my cheap whiskey and made my way to his table, interrupting him in midsentence. "Excuse me, Sir Willard, may I have a quick word?"

Sir Willard ignored me, sipping his drink.

I cleared my throat. "Excuse me, Sir Willard . . ."

He held up his hand, never taking his eyes off the woman. "Piss off."

"But Sir Willard, this can't wait. It's a matter of life and death."

His head swiveled toward me. "I said: Piss. Off."

Sir Willard's stern tone and a glint of violence in his eyes told me that if I didn't back off, the world-renowned explorer would very likely do me harm.

So I took my whiskey and sat at the bar, where I brooded. I had to get Sir Willard's attention, but I couldn't compete with his companion. Then I had a curious idea. There was no need for me to compete with her for Sir

Willard's notice at all.

My head slumped onto the table. In an instant, I was staring at Sir Willard from across a common table.

"C'mon, luv. My flat's only a few blocks away. We can have a nightcap there," Sir Willard said, winking at me.

I felt awkward inside this woman's body. So I got straight to the point: "Sir Willard, I need your help. Professor Alastair Moorcock recommended that I seek your assistance about the *Dictionnaire Infernal*."

Sir Willard's jawed dropped. His eyes shifted past my feminine host and stared at my empty human husk.

"What are you?" he said.

I gestured toward my original vessel. "I'm the chap over there you wouldn't speak to."

He stood up and backed away from me, nearly stumbling over his chair. "No," he said with a hint of panic in his voice. "What kind of thing are you?"

"I'm a man, just like you," I said in a woman's voice and without any trace of irony.

"But . . . but only demons are capable of soul displacement."

And with that one sentence, I learned more about my predicament than I had in the last month.

"Tell me more," I said.

"Not here. And not until you release your hold over Victoria's body."

"If I do, will you help me?"

He nodded, so I released her.

"Adramelech is its name," Sir Willard whispered, paging through the ledger. Candlelight flickered in his dank cellar study. His mahogany bureau was firmly rooted in the middle of the room like a citadel anchoring its power in the center of a far-reaching kingdom. The floor beneath and the walls surrounding the bureau had a complex series of circular and triangular warding sigils scrawled in chalk.

"Whose name?" I asked.

"The entity that holds your contract."

"What entity?" I said.

"The thing called Adramelech. According to the *Dictionnaire Infernal*, references to Adramelech pre-date the founding of Christianity. They point to its origin as a Mesopotamian deity. According to the lore, worshippers appeased Adramelech through ritualistic human sacrifice. It is said that Adramelech's acolytes frequently offered it burning children."

I shuddered at Sir Willard's words. What had I done? Then my thoughts became more urgent, more focused on solving my immediate dilemma.

"And contract? What contract?"

"Your immortal essence for the ability to project your soul into others," he said.

"But . . . but, I was coerced," I stammered. "I had no choice."

"We always have a choice. You could have chosen death."

I bowed my head in resignation. There had to be a glimmer of hope, a way out. "Is there any way that I can break this pact?"

He fixed his gray eyes on mine. "Tell me one thing: did you summon Adramelech or did it seek you?"

"The latter," I said almost too quickly, my desperation roiling beneath a thin veneer of calm.

"I see," he said. "Then, according to this tome, there's still hope."

"Thank the Lord," I said. "Tell me what I must do."

Procuring the hollowed-out bronze statue required a fair bit of archival work and logistical meandering, but the request was harmless enough.

After paying Sir Willard a princely sum to recover the artifact, he returned with word that his expedition had unearthed the item and loaded it on a steamship in the Levant. He'd promised that the artifact would arrive in London within the month.

When it arrived at my flat, enshrouded in black, I couldn't help but experience a sense of deep foreboding and woe. The hidden statue had an uncanny aura that invoked dread in its beholders.

I had the deliverymen lower it into my cellar. They used a complex system of levers and pulleys. The hemp groaned and creaked with the effort. I scarcely believed the relic would make the passage without snapping the ropes that held its colossal heft at bay.

After they departed, and despite my trepidation, I removed the statue's dark shroud. I trembled as I beheld the image of my nightmare cast in bronze—all those menacing eyes glaring at me, boring into the pit of my soul.

I immediately covered the statue back in its shadowy veil before the ghastly figure befouled my mind with more sinister visions.

And there it sat, awaiting Adramelech and whatever sordid purpose the fiend had intended for it.

The next several years passed at a glacial pace. Serving as Sir Willard's acolyte, I dedicated my life to uncovering the esoteric mysteries of the obscene tome I'd transcribed in my youth.

Even with the meticulous warding in Sir Willard's cellar, the book exacted a punishing toll on my constitution. Darkness became my permanent abode, and I a thing of midnight.

Each year, on the anniversary of my contract, Adramelech summoned me on pain of death, compelling me to scour the barrows for the corpse of an orphaned child. It was a gruesome task, digging into the loamy earth and exhuming the tiny coffin.

On one such night, I passed under the moon's glowing crescent, its reflected sunlight scarring the blue-black sky like a cicatrix on unblemished skin. The light it cast revolted me—no doubt a consequence of the corruption festering in my spirit.

My method for selecting which body to disinter was a simple one. Before my nighttime jaunts, I would pore over the obituaries of rural newspapers for the names of recently deceased orphan children. On this particular year, my research led me to Bocking Cemetery in Braintree, Essex.

Stalking the lichyard in the service of my master, I meandered through a maze of tombstones and mausoleums without the aid of lantern light. There, I sought the grave of the Jameson boy. The ground was still muddy from the rainstorm that had soaked the land earlier that day.

It didn't take long for me to locate the Jameson plot with its freshly turned dirt. Hoisting my spade, I began to dig.

A faint light glimmered through the distant hedges and oak trees. I ceased digging, fearful my illicit activity might garner unwanted attention.

The light grew brighter and drew closer. My heart pounded. Sweat slithered down my brow. To avoid discovery, I hid behind a gravestone and lay on my stomach.

The silhouette of a man passed through the trees. He shined a lantern in my direction. I held my breath, cowering.

He approached slowly.

I hugged the earth, clutching clumps of mud in a futile attempt to avoid detection.

A light blinded me from above. "What the bloody hell are you doing here?" a gruff voice said.

I held my hands before my face, trying to blot out the glaring light. As my eyes adjusted, I saw the night watchman, his countenance grimacing in disgust.

"Stand up!" he commanded, waving a baton.

This was the end. If he turned me over to the authorities, I would be forever severed from that spellbinding tome. I couldn't bear the thought of it. There was a way out, but it terrified me. I'd promised myself never to use that dreadful power again.

Now I had no choice. I locked my eyes on his.

In an instant, I watched my body slump to the ground. Wearing the night watchman's skin, I sprinted back toward the tree line, my lantern swaying like a chaotic pendulum scything through darkness.

In moments, I'd passed through the oaks and hedges, and into Essex's flat fields, running until the night watchman's heart felt as if it were on the verge of bursting. My mind raced. It would take me hours to get him far enough away from the cemetery so I'd have enough time to unearth the body.

But I didn't have hours. I had only until daybreak.

Then I stumbled upon my redemption.

It was no more than a black speck on the horizon. As I drew closer, the stone well jutted from the earth like a broken tooth. When I reached it, breathless, I stared down fifty feet into its gaping maw.

It was either his soul or mine.

I leapt into the well.

In half a breath, I was back in my own skin. I grabbed my spade and dug with a fury, using guilt as my fuel. I tried not to imagine the man's frantic effort to keep his head above water in that black well. Despite my rationalizations, what I had done was unforgivable. But what choice did I have?

Hours later, I placed the muddy coffin onto a dolly and wheeled it to the midnight-blue Ford Model T waiting on the side of the country road. There, I loaded the small coffin into the backseat, covered it with an olive drab tarp, and then motored back to London.

With shame, I carried the coffin to my flat, removed the corpse of a freckled boy with strawberry-blonde hair, and placed it inside the repulsive statue. Then I positioned a brazier heaping with coals behind it, where I presented the burnt offering to my demented overseer.

I know not why Adramelech forced me to repeat this grim ritual year after year. It was as if through these unspeakable acts, the demon was honing my instincts and inuring my conscience to prepare me for something far worse.

I yearned to sever my contract, devoting every waking hour to study of the diabolical tome, scrutinizing it for a loophole. Sir Willard assured me from his extensive scholarship that the brazen statue was a crucial element of the remedy. Yet the puzzle remained.

Despite my wretched nocturnal existence, I resolved never to use my unnatural ability again, fearing that each use only served to spread Adramelech's infestation of my immortal soul.

But through the toilsome years, I knew only failure and regret, until I convinced myself that the only way out was by the fiend's own hand.

There was something troubling about the boy's voice. Both haunting and familiar, it rumbled above the din of the boisterous pub like an echo in the crag lands. Under the guise of youth, it carried the weight of eternity on sonorous and ethereal wings. Of love and of loss twisted with a sense of despair in some cruel and arcane concoction not birthed of the natural world.

The pub's denizens made merry, drowning their earthly worries in the false mirth of fermented barley. Each year, I came here to think, to reflect on the bargain. For thirty years I had come to commemorate the anniversary, finding solace that I still had more time. But today was different. Today, I sensed that the butcher's bill was due.

"Logan," the man-child said, the ken of my name betraying his deception of innocence. There was power in the knowing of names, but that power had long been lost to the kindred of men.

A storm was brewing outside. The smell presaging the coming of rain wafted into the pub each time another poor soul entered the establishment. If you were old like me, you could feel it in the hollows of your knees. The void of the space betwixt flesh and bone coupled with the creaking pain of age. The hackles on my narrow neck rose in warning to the gathering maelstrom.

What most didn't know or realize was that another tempest was brewing. It had been building for three decades. And tonight, it would discharge its vast malevolence.

Girding for the inevitable, I swigged my whiskey in one last pathetic attempt to preserve my mortality. I then turned to regard my night caller.

"Can't say I'm pleased to see you, Adramelech, but I'm sure you understand why."

The child nodded in a manner unlike a child. Its smile taunted and tore at my soul. I could feel it rattle inside me like a rat caught in a cage with a serpent.

"Logan, let us speak of less unpleasant things. It's true that your soul is now mine to rend. But you still have free will. What if I were to offer you a way to repay your debt that would free you of your obligation?"

I knew with every fiber of my being not to trust this spawn of the abyss. But hope was a powerful thing. As the autumn of my life fast approached, the horror of harvesting the rotten fruit of a dying tree had become more real.

"Say on," I said.

Adramelech smiled, his eyes conveying an unsettling malice. "All I require is one final task. After that, I will consider your debt paid in full."

I took a deep breath, downed my whiskey, and said, "Tell me more."

I didn't understand why this infernal thing wanted to be encased in the statue, but I was only too happy to oblige. If I could broil the beast inside the boy by burning the boy, I wouldn't hesitate, especially to save my own soul.

So, as instructed, I hoisted the child who was not a child into the bronze statue and sealed it. I placed the brazier behind the statue, loaded it with coals, and heated it.

I thought about my freedom as the heat began to rise and fill the air with the scent of steaming charcoal. I wondered if this doom would forever be my shadow, stalking me to the grave in a life that ultimately offered neither freedom nor security. Would I ever escape Adramelech's choking grasp?

I stepped backward as the process of thermal conduction radiated heat throughout the hollow statue.

The child screamed.

My gut lurched. A wave of guilt flooded my consciousness, blotting out the influence of my rational mind. Instinct told me Adramelech no longer enthralled the boy, but I couldn't be sure. And was it really worth my immortal soul?

I panicked. The entity had made me its agent of evil. This child would suffer and die because of me.

Wind swirled in the draftless room. I shivered. Ink-dark, the smoky essence slithered through the dank air and hovered before me.

Adramelech was here.

A vision of the perverted peacock appeared in my mind's eye. The thing cackled at me. It had subverted my free will, twisting it to its own maleficent ends.

"So much for free will," Adramelech whispered from the space in-between life and death, from a twilight realm where entities beyond the ken of humanity dwelled.

The child's earsplitting shrieks became more urgent. The strangely sweet smell of burning flesh made my mouth water, evoking an unsettling feeling as I listened to him howl inside the statue.

"Do you recognize the child?" Adramelech hissed from the ether.

I shook my head.

"He is the orphaned son of the man you threw in the well."

What had I done? What kind of a monster had I become?

And then the idea came to me, a spark of salvation in a sea of suffering. Adramelech had never taken away the power it had granted me.

So I possessed the boy, shouldering his agony in one final defiant display of free will, completing the circle—master becomes boy, boy becomes master, and master becomes boy again.

A serpent swallowing its own tail.

And so I burn.

AUTHOR'S STORY NOTE

"Adramelech" is based on a Mesopotamian sun god akin to Moloch. In its various incarnations, Adramelech has often been depicted as having a human body, a mule's head, and a peacock's tail. The demon has been associated with human sacrifice, specifically the practice of burning children in sacrificial rites. Adramelech has appeared in two major catalogs of demons including *The Lesser Key of Solomon* and *The Dictionnaire Infernal*. The former was an anonymous grimoire compiled in the mid-seventeenth century from sources several centuries older and consists of five volumes. The first of these, the *Ars Goetia*, includes descriptions of seventy-two distinct demons. The latter tome is *The Dictionnaire Infernal*, a book on demonology composed by Jacques Auguste Simon Collin de Plancy and published in 1818. References to Adramelech have also appeared in the Bible (2 Kings 17:31) and John Milton's *Paradise Lost*.

In crafting this story, I fused many of Adramelech's attributes referenced in this source material with some of my own additions, particularly Adramelech's ability to possess others and to grant that power to others. This story is ultimately about whether we truly possess free will and, if so, what one man would be willing to sacrifice in order to preserve it.

ULTRA
DANIEL MARC CHANT

From *The Offering:*
Daniel Marc Chant & J.R. Park
Sinister Horror Company

'**D**eath or glory!' bellowed the Sergeant Major, a square-jawed, barrel-chested brick outhouse of a man whose volume level never fell below eleven. He was in Wilbur Edgar's face, filling his vision with tombstone teeth and eyes that bulged so much they looked ready to pop. 'Ain't no way you're coming back from this one, Private Edgar, but at least you'll die a man.'

'With all due respect, Sergeant Major,' Wilbur responded. 'I *will* come back. I always do.'

The world dissolved into something resembling multicoloured water being sucked into a vortex. When it had sorted itself out, Wilbur was lying on his stomach, surrounded by rubble and burning buildings.

Like a penitent sinner, Captain Allen, clasping at his abdomen in a desperate attempt to keep his guts from spilling through a shrapnel wound that had condemned him to a painful and certain death, dropped to his knees in front of Wilbur.'

'It's up to you now, Private. You, me and the Sergeant Major are all that's left of the regiment. We've come a long way together, and though I'll always be superior to you—as an officer and a man of better breeding—I think of you as a friend. Sort of.' The Captain had a coughing fit. A fine aerosol of blood sprayed from his mouth. 'Can we rely on you, soldier?'

'Sir!' Wilbur saluted smartly. 'Yes, sir!'

The Sergeant Major wept openly. 'God damn it! That's why Jerry can't win. You can't keep a good Englishman down.'

Wilbur checked his weapon. He had six clips of ammo in his pockets, a half dozen hand grenades and an abiding hatred of Nazis. 'Let me at 'em!'

Without further ado, he came out of hiding, machine gun blazing.

The enemy spotted him straight away. Lethal lead whistled past his ears. He was buffeted by explosions that caused rubble to rain down on him.

The dirty bastards were out to kill him. Well he'd show them.

A glint of sunlight on a Mauser betrayed the presence of a sniper in the upper floor of what was left of a warehouse. In a move he had practiced a thousand times, he simultaneously dived for cover and fired. There was a satisfying scream as the sniper tumbled from the building clutching at his chest.

Wilbur celebrated by jumping to his feet and letting rip with a single shot that caught an advancing Nazi on the forehead, causing his head to explode.

With a whoop, Wilbur leaped onto the burnt-out shell of an armoured troop carrier and fired with wild abandon. To his left, he caught a glimpse of helmet. A second later, the helmet and the head it was supposed to protect were shredded by his expert gunfire.

'Englischer Schweinehund!' One of Hitler's finest broke cover and came charging at Wilbur. He was blond and blue eyed, aged about fourteen and armed with a broom handle. Wilbur took great delight in cutting him down.

A whistling sound warned Wilbur that a mortar bomb was headed his way. Instinctively, he somersaulted off the troop carrier and dashed through the door of a ruined house. A split second later, the troop carrier exploded.

The concussion knocked him against a wall. Briefly, he was stunned, but quickly recovered. He tasted blood in his mouth and was impressed by how real it tasted.

Machine gun fire raked the wall. A piece of debris hit the back of his hand, numbing it and causing it to bleed. The pain was brief but intense.

Luckily his trigger finger was unaffected. He could still kill Nazis.

One came running in through the door. Wilbur shot him in the eye.

The Nazi's companion wasn't about to make the same mistake and lobbed a grenade into the room. Wilbur thought briefly about picking it up and throwing it back, but decided not to take the risk. He ran into the adjacent room and immediately spotted a set of wooden stairs leading to a cellar. As he began descending, the grenade went off. His ears rang from the concussion but he was otherwise unscathed.

He stood still and listened. There were no footsteps, nor anything else to suggest he was still being pursued. The enemy must have assumed the grenade had got him and were no doubt hurrying back to their bolt holes.

He would deal with them later, but right now he was hungry. Hundreds of hours of urban fighting had taught him an important lesson. Namely that when cities are besieged, the occupants have a habit of stashing their food and other valuables in the cellar. With luck he could score at least a chunk of cheese and maybe even some ham.

Half the cellar wall and the ground beside it had been blown away, allowing daylight into the cellar. A group of German civilians cowered in the corner, arms round one another, eyes wide with fear.

Wilbur trained his machine gun on them.

There were three of them: a woman, a boy who couldn't have been much older than six and a teenage girl. Almost certainly a mother and her children.

The little boy began to cry. His mother babbled in German. She dropped to her knees, hands clasped before her. 'Barmherzigkeit!'

Wilbur recognised the German word for *mercy* and was outraged.

Mercy? How dare she ask for mercy when her people had reduced half of Europe to a wasteland and murdered millions along the way? He'd give her mercy all right. The same sort of mercy she and her kind liked to dish out.

He stepped towards the Germans, hands raised and open to show he meant no harm. He made shushing noises and even managed a smile. Then, when he was close enough to the German Frau to smell her fear, he whisked out his knife and cut her throat.

The daughter grabbed her as she fell and was rewarded for her efforts by being sprayed with blood. Horrified, she let go of her dead mother.

That was the cue for the boy to start screaming hysterically. A moment later, the knife that had slit his mother's throat ripped open his stomach, and he screamed no more.

Wilbur pushed the boy's body aside with his foot and eyed the girl. Although the deprivations of war had hardened her, she was remarkably pretty and had a face that belied the evil in her Nazi heart. She was clearly in shock. Wilbur doubted she'd put up any sort of resistance, no matter what he did to her now. He was going to kill her, of that he had no doubt, but first he would teach her just who was the Master Race around here.

As he reached for his flies, he was suddenly hit by a wave of self-loathing. What was he thinking?

I'm not an animal, he told himself. *I'm better than that.*

Eager to rid himself of temptation, he despatched the girl in the same way he'd despatched her mother.

The rattle of machine gun fire and the sound of jackboots on rubble told him he was under attack once more. He checked his watch to see if he had time to kill a few more Nazis and reluctantly decided he didn't. His boss had already spoken to him about his time keeping and warned that the next time he was late would be his last.

Muttering an oath, he placed his gun against his head and pulled the trigger.

Everything went dark. The machine guns fell silent. He could no longer taste blood in his mouth.

Wilbur took off his VR helmet and sat still as his mind adjusted to the transition back to reality. As always when he came out of a session of *Nazi Hunter*, he was pumped up. The temptation to go back in and renew the slaughter was all but irresistible.

Stay strong, he told himself, taking deep, steady breaths to help bring himself down. His heart seemed to be throwing itself about like a trapped animal. A bead of sweat rolled down the side of his nose and came to rest just above his mouth.

Reluctantly, he pushed his chair away from the desk and placed the VR helmet beside his computer. It was time to go to work.

* * *

'You got to try it. There ain't never been anything like it. I tell you, it makes every other game seem like—well, like a game. Because, you see, *Slut Slayer*

is just so damn real. It's even better than cocaine. Better than anything.'
Mickey Stratton was babbling like he'd just swallowed a whole handful of
amphetamines. 'I tell you, if I didn't need the money, I'd tell the suits where
they can stick their job and spend all my time playing *Slut Slayer*. It's the
only thing in my life that matters a damn to me.'

Wilbur tried to ignore him, but as they were sitting at adjacent desks,
there was no way he could. He would just have to soldier on as best he could
and hope Mickey would quickly run out of steam as he always did.

'You know how many prostitutes I've killed in the last two days?' Mickey
went on. 'Twelve crack whores. Nine streetwalkers. Four brothel madams.
Sixteen—no, seventeen—call girls. And a couple of slavic sex slaves—one
of whom turned out to be a transvestite, would you believe it?'

Isabella Holder plunked herself into her seat at the desk on the other
side of Mickey. Having just made it into work on time, she was flustered.
'You been hanging about in dodgy sex bars again?'

'No, no.' Mickey shook his head. 'I don't do that shit no more. Found
something way better.'

'Not religion, I hope.'

'*Slut Slayer*,' said Wilbur.

'Beg pardon?'

'The game. He's been playing it.'

Isabella's lip curled in disgust. 'I thought it was banned.'

'Oh yeah, sure.' Mickey wiped his nose on his shirtsleeve. 'Like they
can ban anything these days! Once it's on the Net, that's it—the genie is
out of the bottle.'

'Look at you! You've not shaved. Your clothes need a wash. And you
stink like a dog fart.'

'I bet you say that to all the boys.'

'Seriously, Mickey. You need to sort yourself out before it's too late.'

'Oh, here we go. Little Miss Goody Two Shoes is lecturing me again.'

'She's right,' Wilbur interjected. 'You need help, Mickey. And you need
it fast.'

'Go blow it out your arse.'

Further conversation was curtailed by a klaxon blasting out a one-minute
warning. The forty or so people in the office stopped what they were doing
and turned their attention to their computer screens. Chairs were adjusted.
Bottoms shifted. Mouses were reached for.

The screens came alive, displaying a digital countdown. *50... 49... 48...*

When the countdown reached 10, everyone in the office joined in, shouting out each number as it came up. *10... 9... 8... 7... 6... 5... 4... 3... 2... 1... Go!*

Each screen was suddenly filled with charts and graphs. Between the graphics, numbers fluctuated up and down.

Wilbur soaked up the information in front of him at a prodigious rate. His well-trained mind assessed what the figures were telling him and he made his first sale of the day—100,000 shares in Rio Tinto at 13 pence a share. He watched to see how the market responded and five seconds later bought the shares back at 14 pence a pop.

A nice start to the day but scarcely earth shattering.

Sensing that coffee beans were on the rise, he invested a million pounds of his employer's money on a futures option. Now he was seriously motoring.

The morning went by swiftly. Wilbur was on his best form. Every prediction he made about every market he poked about in proved to be spot on. When he broke off for lunch, he had added a little more than six and a half million pounds to the vast coffers of Arthur and Lawrence.

That night, Wilbur firebombed Dresden.

'You've got a bloody nerve,' said Raymond Arthur. He didn't so much speak as grind the words through his perfect white teeth. Rising from behind his mahogany desk, he skewered Wilbur with a steely gaze. 'A pay rise? In this economic climate? This country's been out of recession for barely two years and here you are, holding out your grasping little hand, going *gimme, gimme, gimme.* Who the buggery bollocks do you think you are, Edgar?'

I'm the schmuck who labours day in, day out, thought Wilbur, *to keep you and your cronies in yachts and stately homes.* Out loud, he said, 'I'm only asking for a fair—'

'Fair!' Arthur looked like he'd been shot while simultaneously swallowing a wasp. 'This is business, not the boy scouts! We don't do fair. That's for sissies.' He strode over to the picture window. 'Come here, you worthless little squib. Let me show you something.'

Wondering what the Hell he'd let himself in for, Wilbur did as he was told and stood beside his boss.

The multi-billionaire threw an arm around Wilbur's shoulders. 'Take a look out there and tell me what you see.'

They were fifty floors up. Wilbur could see a lot. 'Buildings, mostly,' he said. 'Some trees and the River Thames.'

'That's London, that is. Greatest city in the world, with real estate worth billions upon billions. And this company happens to own 3.728 percent of it. Now that's an awful lot of real estate, I'm sure you'll agree. And if you think we got that by being fair, you're even more stupid than you look.' Arthur pointed. 'You see that on that horizon? That grotty concrete monstrosity? Do you recognise it? Yes, of course you do. You bloody well live there, you poor little drone, you. And I'll let you into a secret, shall I?' Arthur lowered his voice to a whisper. 'I own that entire building, every last concrete inch of it, and if you ask me for a pay rise again, I will have it demolished within twenty-four hours and see to it that you spend the rest of your life living on the street. *Comprendez, mi amigo?*'

Wilbur comprendezed big time. He was in the presence of a genuine, A1, 24 carat, out and out arsehole. *Is this what we fought the Nazis for?* he asked himself. *Just to have our faces ground into the dirt by a different kind of jackboot?*

As Arthur's arm decoupled itself from his shoulders, he realised he'd been holding his breath as if to protect himself against the stench of his boss's greed.

Arthur drifted back to his desk. As he didn't give Wilbur any indication as to what to do next, Wilbur stayed where he was and turned from the window.

'You recently applied for a place on the company's Executive Training Program.'

'Yes, sir.'

'And I bet you're wondering why you weren't selected.'

'Frankly, yes. I scored high on the intelligence tests. I demonstrated initiative and showed I could think on my feet. There was no way I should have been turned down.'

'You never stood a snowball's chance in Hell. And do you know why? It's because you're nice, and *nice* is not a quality we value here. If you want to get on in the world of high finance, you have to be a sociopath. The only thing that should matter to you is you.' Arthur nodded in the direction of the window. 'You have, of course, noticed the balcony and are aware that it was from that very spot that my late, benighted brother supposedly jumped to his death, leaving me sole heir to the Arthur fortune.'

'I'm sorry for your loss,' Wilbur toned automatically.

'Loss? What fnugging loss? I hated the douche bag every bit as much as he hated me. And I'll let you into a little secret, shall I?' Arthur smiled the smuggest smile Wilbur had seen in a long time. His eyes sparkled with mischief. 'He didn't jump. I pushed him.'

For a moment, Wilbur grasped futilely at the straw that he must have misheard, but he clearly hadn't. The fact that Arthur had killed his own brother came as no great surprise; the fact that he had openly admitted it—now that was a real jaw dropper.

Arthur laughed. 'You should see your face, Edgar. It's a picture.' Composing himself, he sat forward and propped his elbows on the desk. 'You can tell whoever you like what I just said. It doesn't matter. Now get out.'

Acknowledging to himself that he had been played by an expert in mind games, Wilbur headed for the door on legs that felt like jelly. But Arthur wasn't finished with him yet.

'Incidentally, Edgar. Mickey Stratton has left the company. His replacement starts at noon.'

Wilbur arrived at his desk minutes before trading was due to begin. For once, Isabella Holder was ahead of him. She sat at her desk clutching a cup of Starbucks coffee.

'You hear about Mickey?' she asked. 'Went mad, he did. The police are after him.'

'What?' Wilbur dropped into his seat.

'The police are after him.'

'No shit.'

'He attacked one of the girls from the typing pool. Tried to rape her.'

'Double no shit.'

'I'm not surprised. Last week, he put his hand up my skirt.'

'Did you report him?'

'In this place? Are you kidding? Report someone for sexual harassment here and they're liable to get a pay rise.'

Finding the topic of conversation uncomfortable, Wilbur tried to change it. 'Do you know Raymond Arthur murdered his own brother?'

'Sure I do. Everyone does. So what?'

Wilbur eyed what had until recently been Mickey Stratton's desk. In spite of the company's clear desk policy, it was littered with used napkins, well-chewed pencils, coffee cups, sweet wrappers, a half-eaten sandwich and a USB stick.

'Wonder what's on this,' he said, grabbing the stick and dropping it into his shirt pocket.

'Porn,' said Isabella. 'I'll give you any odds you like on that one.'

It wasn't porn.

When he got home that evening, Wilbur fired up the software.

Installing Slut Slayer, said the splash screen. *Please wait.*

A *ping* told Wilbur his microwave pizza was ready. He went to the kitchen, served the pizza up on a plate, cracked open a can of Pepsi and returned to his living room. Now the splash screen was telling him *Special Edition.*

Wilbur crammed a piece of pizza into his mouth and sat down. The pizza was too hot; he took a swig of Pepsi to save his palette from blistering. Then he put on his VR headset and waited for the game to finish loading.

He didn't have to wait long. After only a few seconds, he found himself in a subterranean public toilet. To judge from the state of its walls and the fact that every urinal was a repository for brown water, old tissues and other detritus, it hadn't been used for its original purpose in quite some time.

Now it was an armoury.

On a row of wooden tables was laid out a variety of knives, swords, garottes, handguns, knuckledusters, thumb screws, nipple clamps, bicycle chains, coshes, cattle prods, semi-automatics and sundry other weapons and instruments of torture.

An oriental gentleman dressed like an English butler complete with bowler hat stood behind the tables. 'Welcome to Secret Emporium of Fu Chan,' he said with a faux-Chinese accent. 'You want to kill ladies, you come to right place.'

Wilbur was having second thoughts, and he was glad to be doing so. It showed he hadn't lost his perspective. He wasn't the new Mickey Stratton, nor did he intend to be.

He was here only out of curiosity and intended to stay just long enough to find out for himself if *Slut Slayer* deserved it's reputation as the vilest, most evil game on the planet. And then no more. As soon as he got back to reality, the USB stick was going straight down the toilet where it belonged.

Wilbur picked up a knuckleduster.

Fu Chan smiled his approval. 'That good choice for beginner. You gonna be real great at killing ladies. Fu Chan can always tell.'

'How much?'

'Special one time offer: ten pounds.'

'I'll take it.'

Fu Chan clicked his fingers. A *ker-ching* sound told Wilbur his bank account had just been debited by the agreed amount. 'Enjoy.'

Wilbur came into work the next day feeling he'd just met himself for the first time in ages and wasn't at all how he remembered. *Who*, he wondered as he took his seat in the office, *was that last night? Not me, that's for sure.*

No wonder Mickey Stratton had gone over the edge.

I can't let that happen to me. He patted his jacket to reassure himself that the USB stick was still in his pocket. The first chance he got, he was going to destroy the accursed thing.

'It's only a game.' Mickey Stratton's replacement sat down next to Wilbur. Like every new employee, he was bursting with enthusiasm. It wouldn't last.

'What's only a game?' Wilbur replied with undisguised hostility. He had a horrible feeling that he'd been rumbled, that the new guy knew what he'd been up to last night.

The new guy waved his hand in the direction of his screen. 'All this. Playing the markets.'

'A game? Say that to someone in senior management and count the seconds before your arse meets the pavement.'

'OK. I know it's not really a game. It's way more serious than that. What I mean is that you've got to treat it like a game. Otherwise you'll go mad.'

Wilbur felt bile rise in his throat and blamed the new guy with his youthful exuberance and unrelenting naivety. He'd been in the job six years now; he didn't need some punk barely out of nappies telling him how to do his job.

He might have given voice to his disgust had Isabella Holder not chosen that moment to arrive. With no thought for decorum or etiquette, she rapidly opened and closed her umbrella, spraying Wilbur and the new guy with water. 'Sorry about that,' she said, sounding not sorry at all. 'Got caught in the rain. Why does it always happen to me?'

Isabella threw the umbrella under her desk and took off her coat, which had not been wholly successful in protecting her from the rain. Her damp blouse clung to her bosom, revealing the outline of a black bra.

Wilbur pictured his hand down that bra. In his mind, his other hand was clamped over Isabella's mouth while she struggled helplessly.

Isabella sat down. 'Why are you looking at me like that?'

'Like what?' But Wilbur knew. He felt his cheeks flush. He pointedly looked away and stared at his blank screen.

'That's the way Mickey used to look at me. Like I was a piece of meat. And I can't say I like it.'

Wilbur squirmed inwardly. He was saved from further discomfort by the screens coming to life. 50... 49... 48... 47...

'By the way,' said the new guy. 'We didn't get introduced yesterday. My name's Martin.'

Wilbur and Isabella responded in unison. 'Fuck off, Martin.'

The girl lay dead at Wilbur's feet. He wiped the blood from the blade that had killed her and slipped the knife back in its sheath. Then he dragged her by one leg until he had her under the streetlight and could see her face.

Even in death, it was a pretty face and he was glad he hadn't bruised it too much.

If only it hadn't been so easy to kill her. For a while now, Wilbur had been nursing the suspicion that he was getting too good for *Slut Slayer*. The first time he'd tried it, his intended victim had managed to get away unscathed. His next target put up a hell of a fight and for a while it had seemed all too possible that she would get the better of him.

After that, he'd been more careful and planned his attacks in advance. He knew how to sneak up on his victims, how to charm them, how to talk them into going to isolated spots with him, how to drug them, how to evade the police, how to stop them screaming. In fact, now that he'd played the game nigh on a hundred times, it seemed to him he was now the perfect slut slayer, which was a problem.

How long, he wondered, before the game ceased to entertain him? What would he do then? Move on to a better, more extreme game? Something that stretched his abilities and offered greater rewards than the slaughter of fallen women?

Did such a game even exist? He doubted it.

Determined to get his money's worth, Wilbur reached for his knife only to find it gone. A quick forage in his pockets confirmed that his knuckle-duster had also disappeared.

He could only watch in grim acceptance as the dead girl faded into nothingness.

It should have been his cue to exit the game and step back to reality, but he wasn't about to do that just yet. Not until his cravings had been satisfied.

He was going to have to get new weapons.

One of the magical things about the world of *Slut Slayer* was that the armoury was never far away. All Wilbur had to do was picture the place and step through the nearest door.

'Ah, Mr. Wilbur,' said Fu Chan, bowing deeply. 'How nice to see you again. I trust you have had most enjoyable experience.'

Wilbur saw that the wooden tables that were usually piled high with weaponry were bare. 'I need weapons,' he said. 'A knife. An axe. Anything!'

'And how would you pay for such a thing?'

'Just take the money from my account like you usually do.'

Fu Chan gave a sad shake of his head. 'Such a thing not possible, Mr. Wilbur, sir. For there is no money in your account to be taken.'

'Yes, there is.' Wilbur laughed a brittle laugh. Not so long ago, he'd received a small inheritance from an obscure relative he'd never met. Surely he couldn't have used it all up just yet?

The truth of the matter though was that Wilbur hadn't checked his bank balance of late. Part of him knew he was getting through money far faster than he was earning it, but his addict part didn't want to know.

'It's OK,' he said, frantically clutching at straws. 'I can apply online for an overdraft. It shouldn't take more than a minute to come through.'

But that hope was quickly squashed by Fu Chan. 'You already exceed overdraft allowance. Bank will lend no more.'

'Please. I'm begging you!'

'I run business, not charity. Goodbye, Mr. Wilbur, sir.'

Before Wilbur could respond, he found himself standing in the middle of a road getting soaked by a rain shower which he had no doubt was a deliberate act of malice. Dazed by his sudden reversal of fortune, he looked around for some form of solace.

It was night as it always was in the world of *Slut Slayer*. A rectangle of light lay on the pavement ahead, indicating the possibility of at least being able to get in out of the rain. Head down, he ran towards the light and discovered it was falling out of the window of an all-night cafe.

Once inside, Wilbur was immediately dry again.

'She didn't put up much of a fight, did she?' said a voice Wilbur recognised. 'Bloody disappointing when that happens.' Mickey Stratton sat in a booth, nursing a cup of coffee. He was dressed in black leather and a U-Boat captain's cap. 'You should ask for your money back.'

'Mickey? Is that you?'

'Nah. It's the Pope.'

'What are you doing here?'

'Waiting for you. You want tea? Coffee? Something stronger?'

'Coffee. White. Two sugars,' Wilbur and Mickey were the only customers. There was no sign of any staff. Nonetheless, when Wilbur sat opposite Mickey, there was a cup of white coffee waiting for him on the table. A quick sip told him it was exactly how he liked it. 'Are you still on the run from the police?'

'Yes. And no. It depends on your point of view. But that's not really the question you should be asking, is it?'

'I guess not.'

'So go on then—ask. Don't worry about my feelings.'

'OK. Are you real.'

'Again: Yes. And no. If the question is: am I the real Mickey Sutton or a cybernetic simulacrum, I'd have to say I really don't know. If I can trust my memory, then I most definitely am Mickey Sutton and I'm sitting out there in Realityville jacked into this game having a whale of a time. On the other hand, I might just be a collection of 1s and 0s programmed to believe I'm an actual human being.'

'How did you get here?'

'I plugged myself in, the same as you.'

'That's not what I mean. I mean how did you get here—' Wilbur stabbed the table with his finger to drive home his point. '—inside my computer. I have firewalls to stop this sort of thing happening.'

Mickey snorted his derision. 'Firewalls? I laugh in the face of firewalls. When you loaded *Slut Slayer*, you left yourself wide open to me. I just had to stroll in. It was a doddle.'

'And you waited for me in this cafe?'

'Don't be an arse, Wilbur. Nobody comes to Slutland just to sit on their lonesome drinking piss-poor tea. If you really must know, I've been spying on you—watching you at work, as it were.'

'Why?'

'To see if you could make the grade.' Mickey took a packet of cigarettes from his pocket and broke the seal. 'People like you and me, Wilbur—we're the future. We're the people who make the world go round.'

'I don't follow you.'

'You ever hear of Project MKUltra?'

'I heard you mention it in the office once. You kept wittering on about the CIA and illegal experiments and stuff, but I wasn't really listening.'

Mickey had a lit cigarette in his hand. Wilbur hadn't seen him remove it from the packet or light it, but that was virtual reality for you. Disjoints happened all the time. 'A pity. Because if, just for once, you'd extracted your head from between your arse cheeks and paid attention, you'd have learned something worthwhile and be much more prepared for what I'm about to tell you.' Mickey took a drag on his cigarette and blew a smoke ring. 'It all began in the 1950s when the CIA decided it would be beneficial for them to control people's minds. Using their own people as guinea pigs, they discovered and refined ways to modify human behaviour in quite extreme ways. Some of their techniques involved drugs; some relied on torture; others were more subtle but equally as effective. And by *effective*, I mean *ineffective*.

'It turned out they couldn't tamper with a person's mind without all but destroying it. You want a robot, a robot is what you get—and not much else.'

Wilbur felt a mixture of boredom and frustration he associated with bad parties and people trying to interest him in things he couldn't give a toss about. 'I'm sorry, Mickey. I haven't got time for this. I need to get to work.'

'Work can wait. I'm just about to tell you everything you need to know to sort your life out.'

'Bollocks.'

'Bollocks? Seriously?'

'I know you, Mickey. Bullshit is your first language. I'm out of here.'

'Off you go then.'

Wilbur rolled up his sleeve and tapped his wristwatch three times to signal that he wanted to quit the game.

Nothing happen.

Wilbur tried again. And still nothing happened.

He wasn't freaked out. At least not yet. But he could feel the first tendrils of panic as he got up and headed for the door. He turned the handle and yanked. The door didn't budge.

Behind him, Mickey laughed.

'Shut up, Mickey. Or so help me—' Wilbur grabbed a chair and threw it at the plate glass window. The chair bounced off the window and left the glass intact.

'You want out of here,' said Mickey, 'you have to do what I say. This is my world, Wilbur. In this little froth of bubbling binary notation, I am God.'

'Screw you.'

'Well, that's an option, but let's put it to one side for now.'

'Let me out or—'

'Or what? You'll kill me? Here in virtual reality? What would be the point?' Mickey got up and tossed aside his cigarette. It vanished in midflight. 'Look. Forget MKUltra for the moment. We'll come back to that later. You're in no mood to listen right now. Too tense. Too uptight.'

'I'm uptight because you're keeping me here against my will.'

'You're uptight because you need a fix. So why don't you go slaughter a couple of cuties and then perhaps you'll be more co-operative?'

'I don't have any weapons.'

'Here.' Mickey pointed to the serving hatch. It had been bare a moment ago, but now it sported a machete and a knuckleduster. 'These do you?'

Wilbur snatched the weapons and slipped the knuckleduster over his fingers. Mickey slapped him on the back. 'OK. Let's go hunting.'

They were a mother and daughter, aged mid-40s and early-20s respectively. It hadn't been easy killing them, but it had been fun.

His head buzzing with the thrill of it all, Wilbur sat down on the settee and wiped blood from his eyes. 'Man, those bitches sure put up a fight.'

'Didn't they just?' said Mickey, who was standing between the dead bodies. 'Once or twice, I thought I might have to intervene to save your sorry hide, but you did just fine on your own. In fact, you were magnificent.'

'They're different though, aren't they? To the others, I mean.'

'Meet Mrs. Lucinda Barron and her lovely daughter Krystal. If you hadn't been so keen to kill them, I would have given you their full biog.'

'Well, do so now.'

'Mrs. Barron is recently divorced. She is well-educated and has—or rather had—a good job at a bank. Young Krystal is a virgin. She recently got engaged and was looking forward to a big church wedding.'

'Not sluts then?'

'No more skankers for you, Wilbur. From now on, you only get to murder nice people.'

'I don't know if I want to murder nice people.'

'Go back to killing whores if you like, but it won't be the same and you know it.'

'The other women I killed all deserved it.'

'And that's why killing them has stopped being fun. You sensed the goodness in these people and it had the same effect on you that catnip has on a cat.'

'My god,' said Wilbur, feeling a blanket of despair falling over him. 'What have I become?'

'What you were always meant to be.'

'This is MKUltra, isn't it? That mind control thing you were on about.'

'Very astute, Wilbur, my boy. Once upon a time, MKUltra was dead in the water but then along came the Internet and with it came video games and virtual reality. So now our Lords and Masters have the technology to manipulate the hordes in ways that would give Hitler a hard-on and they're not shy about using it.

'Games like *Slut Slayer* and *Nazi Hunter* contain subliminal messages designed to break down what the advertising industry call sales resistance. It temporarily paralyses the part of our brain that questions authority, and simultaneously weakens our sense of right and wrong.

'Was a time when the only thing you got to shoot at in a video game was a collection of pixels shuffling across a computer screen. Hardly what you'd call the stuff of nightmares. But gradually the games got more realistic and more violent and here we are.

'This game we're in doesn't stand alone. There's a whole barrage of media out there—film, television, music—that's been hijacked by the powers that be. Day in, day out, we get a steady drip feed of violence and deviant behaviour. What used to be unacceptable is accepted. Perversity is the norm.

'The human race has been reprogrammed. As to why and by whom, that's for you to work out.'

Mickey held out a bottle of gin and Wilbur took it almost without thinking. For something that wasn't real, it sure had a kick—and a much needed one at that. 'It was no accident I got hold of *Slut Slayer*, was it? You made sure I did.'

'Guilty as charged,' said Mickey.

'Why me?'

'Because somebody at Arthur and Lawrence saw the potential in you.' Mickey clapped Wilbur on the shoulder and disappeared.

A moment later, Wilbur removed his VR headset. The first rays of a new day were pouring in through the window, filling the room with light that seemed both unnatural and unpleasant.

He stood and stretched and yawned. Then he hurried off to the bathroom and threw up.

This was the end. The end of everything Wilbur had worked for.

'You lying bitch!' he yelled. 'I didn't touch you!'

'Calm down,' said Raymond Arthur from behind his desk. 'Just tell me your side of the story.'

Wilbur felt like a trapped animal. For only the second time in his life, he was in Raymond Arthur's office and the outcome this time looked set to be even worse than the last. His job was hanging by a thread. 'I swear she's making this up.'

'You're a liar, Wilbur.' Isabella Holder's voice was soft and childlike. There was a tremor in it that indicated fear, or at the very least shock. She was sitting on a leather sofa by the picture window, her face streaked with mascara and tears. 'You grabbed my breast. You tried to kiss me.'

'Oh, come off it. I didn't do anything you didn't want me to. Coming on to me like that! You women are all the same. You tease, tease, tease and then you back out at the last minute.'

'I've seen the CCTV footage,' said Raymond Arthur, speaking in the grave tones of a judge about to deliver sentence. 'It's even worse than she says, Edgar. The camera shows you undoing your zip. You were going to rape her.'

And I bloody well wish I had, thought Wilbur. Attacking Isabella in the lift had been an impulsive act, in no way premeditated. At the time, he'd felt a twinge of guilt, but not now that she'd dropped him right in it.

'The company,' Raymond Arthur went on, 'takes this sort of thing very seriously, Edgar—not least because Miss Holder is in a very good position to sue us. I'm left with no choice but to fire you. Also, we'll be passing the CCTV footage to the police who will no doubt see to it that you end up in prison where you belong.'

Anger, raw and red, ripped through Wilbur. The injustice of it all! To think that a bit of fun should cost him so much.

It wasn't fair.

'You slut!' Wilbur stormed towards Isabella. Seeing what was coming, she just had enough time to get to her feet before his hands wrapped themselves around her throat. 'You lying, malicious slag! Who would want to rape a skinny rat like you?'

Wilbur let fly with an obscenity. It felt good, so he uttered another. And then another. And another. Each time he swore, he tightened his grip.

Isabella went limp.

Wilbur's anger evaporated as the enormity of what he was doing struck home. Only now did he feel the sting from where Isabella's nails had raked his cheek.

Shocked to find himself holding onto a human being as unresponsive as a rag doll, he let go. Isabella hit the floor with a sickening thud.

Wilbur stepped away. 'Oh God! What have I done?'

A smattering of applause caused him to spin on his heel.

'Well done,' said Mickey Stratton, walking into the room from a door behind Raymond Arthur's desk. 'That was most entertaining.'

'Great fun to watch,' agreed Raymond Arthur. 'But it ain't over yet.'

Isabella coughed. Her hand grabbed weakly at Wilbur's ankle. Although barely conscious and barely able to move, she wasn't quite dead.

Arthur handed a silver paper knife to Mickey. 'We at Arthur and Lawrence believe in finishing what we've started. We don't tolerate half measures.'

Smiling grimly, Mickey brought the knife over to Wilbur. He held it up to allow its viciously sharp blade to catch the sun. 'If she leaves here alive, you're finished. It's her or you.'

Wilbur was unable to deny the logic of the choice being offered him. He took the knife and knelt beside Isabella. It pleased him that he could still look her in the eye. 'Nothing personal. It's just business.'

For old times' sake, he killed her quickly. If it had been anyone else, he would have prolonged their suffering, but he still considered Isabella to be a friend despite her trying to ruin his life.

When he was finished, he sat on the leather sofa, looking down at her dead body. 'OK. So now what?'

'Now,' said Raymond Arthur, 'your real training begins. Welcome to the Arthur and Lawrence Executive Training Program.'

AUTHOR'S STORY NOTE

Despite rapidly approaching my forties I'm still an avid gamer, I always loved gaming ever since my youth when I was first introduced to its wonders via the Commodore VIC 20, and then throughout each successive generation. As the years passed and the technology grew I saw the wide-eyed amazement of gaming being replaced, or overrun, with an odd sense of entitlement and impatience. Parts of gaming had become (and sadly still are) a seething corner of misogyny and racism. I then recalled the famous MK ULTRA program (where the story takes its name, I'm a master of subtlety I know!) where the Soviets were experimenting with mind control in the early fifties. I wondered what would that look like today, how would and could it be used to control or brainwash the youth of today? And also how would it be utilised in today's modern dog-eats-dog corporate world? I wouldn't say I tried to answer that question with this story, more make the reader think about it. And hopefully you did.

TREE HUGGERS

NATHAN ROBINSON

From *Shadows And Teeth Volume 3*
Editor: R. Perez de Pereda
Darkwater Syndicate, Inc.

*F*eeling *a brave defiance, the group swallowed the keys in unison. Then, seconds later, in an act of grotesque irony from the great and knowing universe, what they thought was a meteor blazed overhead, landing upon the lake behind them with little sound, the elongated obsidian form gliding beneath the surface like a dart, sending ripples to every shore. It travelled deep, the sharpened point sticking deep into the mud at the bottom, sending ancient silt billowing up into the clear, moonlit waters. Fish fled as the dark diamond fell apart and a shape emerged from a flurry of bubbles.*

It waited a moment, testing its surroundings, taking stock of where it was, using this cautious pause to gauge whether or not any predators waited in the glossy darkness. It detected nothing, then broke for the surface.

*   *   *

"What the fuck was that?" Jake Conroy announced as he felt the key slide down the depth of his throat; cold, hard and alien.

Beside him, his girlfriend Katy Mace smiled and looked at the skies above. "It looked like a meteor. I don't think I've seen anything so beautiful."

"Wow." Ziggy Moonstone grinned from the next tree, his perfect teeth somehow gleaming despite the lack of light. "I think it's a sign from the universe. It's telling us that what we're doing is right. We're on the right path."

Jake looked across to his friend Phil Barlow, who was chained to the same tree as Georgina Bainbridge, Katy's lifelong friend. Phil rolled his eyes and mouthed something to Jake along the lines of *"Bullshit."*

"It was a meteor all right," Johan Loft confirmed with assumed authority. "I've never seen them fall like that before. It was too slow. I would've expected more of a bang. I'm glad I was here with you guys to experience it." Johan was chained to the final tree with his wife Clementine. She smiled and grasped his hand tightly, looking up at his statuesque six-four frame adoringly. Jake had never seen an older couple so in love. It made him a little sick at how saccharine they were.

Ziggy was grinning dopily at Johan, lapping up every word he said.

"Why didn't it fucking explode?" said Lola Mace, Katy's younger, and far more foul-mouthed sister. "Meteors move much faster than that."

"The lake," said Georgina, "It must have landed in the lake. Remember last summer, Katy? We went swimming."

Katy smiled as he she reminisced. "It was a beautiful day. I remember."

"Actually, we were more than swimming, girls." Ziggy grinned. "The three of us were skinny dipping if I remember correctly."

"Ziggy!" Katy chided. "Not in front of my sister!"

Ziggy's smile widened. Jake had told her that her ex looked moronic,

259

with his beads, and his man bun, his stupid goat-like beard and open shirt exposing shaved pectorals.

"I'm sorry Katy, it's just a treasured memory of mine."

Katy looked to her new beau beside her.

Daggers from Jake. Big fucking daggers. But he still smiled. Because he wanted to make it work with her, even if her ex insisted on coming along to help save the Abcastle Oaks, he had to be friendly. Katy reached down and took his hand in hers, squeezing it to reassure his delicate, masculine ego that they were cool and still very much an item.

"And you lost your shorts," Georgina added with a giggle.

Ziggy held his hands out, the moronic smile beaming bright in the light of the torches. *Guilty as charged.*

Katy had told Jake why she and Ziggy broke up. He was going to India for a year travelling, so they both agreed that a break was the best option. They could always hook up later if they wanted. Time had passed, and now she was going out with Jake. But now Ziggy was back, tanned by foreign climes and chiseled by volunteer work; and it appeared he wanted back in Katy's knickers. Her relationship with Jake was the only thing stopping him. Now he was sniffing around her like a dog at a lamppost, as Jake had said. He'd invited her to this Save the Fucking Abcastle Oaks thing that the Lofts had organised, and she jumped at the chance. Not because she still had feelings for him, but because she enjoyed his company in the platonic sense. He was funny, sweet and genuinely a nice guy, but a bit too much of a free spirit for her liking. She had the feeling that Jake had come along purely because he wanted to keep an eye on her. Clearly he felt threatened that Ziggy was perhaps the kind of guy to find chaining himself to a beautiful woman in the darkest woods imaginable to be quite romantic. And to be fair, he probably did. Her sister Lola was here because she was grounded, but their parents were away, so Katy was burdened with her for the weekend. Jake had invited his best friend Phil to act as moral support as he didn't really know the others, plus Phil fancied the pants off of Katy's friend Georgina, so there was that.

So here they were, chained to a tree as an act of protest, because supposedly the bulldozers and chainsaws were coming in to clear the land to make room for an exclusive housing estate by the lake. Not only had they chained themselves to the tree, they'd tethered themselves to the chain with a smaller, second chain, then swallowed the keys to show that they really meant business. That had been Ziggy's idea (who else's? He, the hipster generation's answer to Captain Planet) and Jake, eager to impress his new girlfriend, he had swallowed that cold, jagged, tiny lump of steel to show he meant business as well. They all followed suit, regardless of whether or not the alien object they'd ingested would tear their insides before they shat it out. She fancied Jake a little more for going along with it. He was making an effort. Brownie point for him.

But that anxiety vanished when the "meteor" or whatever the hell it was flashed overhead with a strange blue tinge, almost the second after the last of them had swallowed their keys. It didn't blaze through the sky as if it intended on travelling into the earth itself, but moved about as fast a glider, just as silent, and with the same swooping grace. The blue fire it exuded was almost the colour of a summer sky, giving their faces a glowing azure hue as it moved over the trees ahead. Faces of peace and wonderment. Then it was gone.

*   *   *

The solid constant cold of space had kept it preserved for aeons, but this newfound cold was pleasurable, playful. It touched every inch of its surface, sleekly washing off the fug that plagued it upon rousing.

It felt refreshed, eager, anew; but a new notion niggled within, an emptiness, a void that felt wider than the space it had travelled through to get to its new home. An urge that must be acted upon immediately before sleep or coitus or anything.

HUNGER.

It stretched out a clawed limb to its full extent, its rear claws kicking out, giving it propulsion through the cool liquid that held its weight, guiding itself forward until it touched something soft and pliable that the claw sank into. It used this new material, digging in with one foot-claw, then another, then another, pulling itself forward, limbs digging and heaving until whatever buoyancy it held over the liquid started to fade and it was forced to hold its own weight.

It moved forward, the liquid sliding off from its hard carapace with a pleasant, tinkling noise.

It was cool.

It was dark.

It was ashore.

*   *   *

"Figures," Lola said in her usual glum, doom-laden teenager tone. "Out in the fucking sticks without one bar. Thanks sis."

"Relax. It's one night. I'm sure your *Facebook* friends can do without you for one night," Katy replied.

"Actually, I was going to tag us here," Lola defended. "Start a hashtag to help your cause. I won't bother now."

"We'll get that tomorrow," said Johan. "What I really want to see is the contractors' faces in the morning. It's going to be priceless! They'll call the cops, then the media will turn up. It'll all work in our favour."

Ziggy clapped, much like an excited seal. She felt Jake sending more daggers beside her. She could practically hear his eyes rolling.

"Wait," Phil said, raising a hand as if in class. "Cops?"

"Yes, they usually turn up," Johan replied. "To keep the peace."

"Could we get arrested?" he asked, getting worried.

"Possibly," Johan grinned.

"Would they hurt us?" Jake asked, genuinely concerned for his precious skin.

"They might pepper spray us. That's about as bad as it can get Jakey boy."

Clementine faux-punched the old man on the arm, then tugged his wispy beard to further the light punishment. "Don't tease the poor boy. Don't listen to him. The police only resort to violence if we get violent."

"I kinda hope that's true," Phil replied.

"Speaking of cops, shouldn't we phone them about the comet thing we just saw?" Jake was checking his phone, holding it up towards the moon. Georgina and Phil did the same. Lola was already aware of the distinct lack of signal. Ziggy didn't own a phone, because mobile phones *cause cancer and infertility,* and *"end up owning you,"* as he'd already told Jake earlier. Jake had yawned, but Katy was sure he hadn't meant it.

"No signal," Georgina said.

"Ditto," Phil added.

"We're in a valley, you'd have to move away from the lake to get closer to the transmitters on the edge of Abcastle," Johan informed them.

Phil and Georgina looked at the chains around their waists that committed them to the cause as well as the trees they were trying to save. Jake jangled his chains, sighing at the sudden futility he felt. It was tight around his middle, tighter than his hips, so he couldn't pull the links down, nor could he wriggle his arms through and lift it over his head.

"Hey, relax," Katy soothed. He stopped tugging the chains.

They were all here until someone cut them loose or they passed the keys out naturally. Katy hadn't thought about ablutions, or whether they'd be able to sleep or not. They'd brought blankets, and they had enough slack on the main chain to lie down and sleep until morning when the contractors arrived. Ziggy had brought an axe and chopped up some fallen branches, constructing a small fire lined by rocks in the centre of their little triangle to give them a measure of warmth and comfort throughout the night. They also had torches and lanterns so they wouldn't get scared in the dark, and to hopefully keep the wildlife at bay.

Hopefully.

*   *   *

The heat of sustenance. The sense of it glowing brighter than its taller surroundings. It was close and stationary, a collection ripe for plucking.

Something above twitched, something closer.

Easier prey.

Smaller.

Sensing the smaller prey was less of a threat, it decided that this would be its first meal. An appetiser to welcome it to its new abode. It reached out and grabbed onto the rough object that extended skyward, and began to climb until it was within a metre of its intended prey.

It sensed that it was sleeping, so it reached out with an elongated limb that folded out from its body and ended in a three-pronged claw. Rising above the prey, it paused, to see if it responded to the sight of something new in the night.

It didn't.

Without further hesitation, the tri-claw surged forward, clasping onto the small furry object, clamping hard with a breaking of brittle bones. It fought back, scratching and biting at the hard shell to no avail. From the centre of the tri-claw, a dart-like tongue surged forward, piercing the oh-so-soft flesh of the little creature. A sphincter opened up, and the pressure changed within the little creature. Within five torturous seconds, its blood, organs and a few bones had been sucked through and masticated by a tube of grinding teeth before being fed straight into its stomach, churning with eager acid.

It had been sated some, but not enough. It looked back over in direction of the other pack of prey that would surely sate this overwhelming hunger.

They hadn't moved. But something else alerted its senses and made it cautious of approaching too brashly.

Light.

Regardless of the threat, it moved forward, neglecting the forest floor, but choosing instead to move through the trees at this newfound higher vantage point. It still needed to feed.

* * *

Katy shared the tree with Jake and her younger sister Lola.

Phil and Georgina were paired up at theirs. Judging by the grin on her friend's face, Katy could tell Phil was happy about this coupling, as he was eager to perhaps take things further. Katy knew for a fact that Phil wasn't Georgina's type. He didn't have a beard for a start.

Ziggy had been shackled to Johan and Clementine. As far as Katy knew, the couple had never had any children. Had they ever managed to bring a child into the world, she imagined that Ziggy would be the kind of son they'd dream of, and Katy the ideal daughter-in-law.

She was aware of their fantasy that Ziggy and she would settle down one day, as they thought that they made a cute couple. But Ziggy had made his choice when he went travelling and she had made hers with dating Jake.

Discussion about the meteor and the possibility of a police beating had passed. Now Johan was talking to Ziggy about a falafel recipe, Clementine adding odd little techniques and facts about herbs throughout the conversation.

Georgina was rolling her eyes at another of Phil's puerile jokes. Meanwhile, her sister was content playing with her phone, despite the lack of signal.

"Say, do you fancy the cinema tomorrow night?" Jake kept his voice a whisper in her ear. "There's that new Ryan Gosling film you wanted to see."

"I might still be here tomorrow Jakey," she replied. "You can go if you like."

"It kinda defeats the object if I go by myself. I'm not as much of a Ryan Gosling fan as you."

"Ha, cute. Sorry I'll still be here. I'm dedicated to the cause."

"Oh."

"But if we do manage to get the contractors to delay, I've already arranged to go out for a meal with the others."

"Georgina?"

"Yep."

"Johan and Clem?"

"Uh huh."

"The Zigster?"

"Yeah, why?"

"So you can't go on a date with me but you can go out with your ex?"

"No, it's not like that. The others will be there."

"Yeah, for how long though?"

"Zig's my ex. It's over. We were friends before. We just wanted to have a meal before he goes travelling again."

"Am I invited?" Jake's voice raised in tone. The others looked over, quietening their own conversations.

"If you really want to come, fine. Come. I don't want you being paranoid in this relationship."

"I'm not paranoid, it's just . . ."

Lola harrumphed before she interrupted. "Listen numbnuts, my sister fancies you. She's fucking beautiful and kind, and yet she's chosen you. You should be honoured that she ever spoke to you. I've never met a nicer person and I'd trust her with my life. If she ever cheated on you, which I highly doubt, it would be because you would've had to have cheated on her first!"

Jake's cheeks flared red in the firelight. He had no words.

Everyone else in the group was looking their way.

"Is everything okay, brother?" Ziggy asked. "Would you like to talk about it? I would never come between Katy and you. We're just friends. Well, now we are."

Ziggy was far too amicable. He was a bit of a dick at times, but he wasn't an arsehole.

"It's okay Ziggy, I'm just . . ." Jake paused, his eyes fixing on a branch above Ziggy's head. Katy followed his alerted gaze. Even in the light of the fire and the torches, it appeared darker than the rest and looked to be slowly descending with a sinister slowness towards the trio sitting at the bottom. They watched as the angle of it moved, twisting towards the tree and group. If it fell, it would land on all three of them. Was it a rotting branch that was slowly bending towards the ground? No, it had too many angles in it, the branch seemed to adjust and bend at different points along its length.

Ziggy saw that Jake's and Katy's gaze had shifted above his head and turned to face the strange branch as it suddenly lurched forward.

"Move!" Jake barked, and Ziggy did as he was told, ducking to the ground as instinct took over. The dark branch shot over his head, catching Johan in the left side of his neck, disappearing deep. He squealed, gurgled, then was lifted up and off the floor of the forest as easily as one would lift a newborn from a crib. The old man's legs kicked against the tree, drumming out a sudden and deranged tattoo. They all watched helplessly as the branch retreated upwards, taking Johan with it until the chain met the end of its slack, halting him from being lifted farther, but still, the thing tugged on the old man.

Clementine turned to where her husband had once been, only to see the back of his feet frantically kicking notches out of the bark. Screaming, she recoiled backwards, jangling her own chains as she tried to pull away.

The others watched as Clementine grabbed at her husband's flailing ankles and tried to pull him back to earth, getting a kick in her teeth for her troubles. She lurched back with a high yelp.

Ziggy looked up at Johan, his teeth bared in fear, wanting to help, but being ultimately powerless to do anything. He jumped up and wrapped his sculpted arms around Johan's kicking legs, then dropped his own, leaning on his heels and using his weight to pull the old man back down.

All the while, Johan was screaming. They could see that the black branch (or whatever the fuck it was) was lodged in his neck, the stubby ends moving in an almost repetitive pulse.

All of the girls screamed along with Johan. Even Phil was making a panicked *uhhhhh* noise as his only response to the unfolding horror he was witnessing, giving the once silent forest a peculiar soundtrack.

After a few liquid gasps, Johan stopped screaming. A loud, wet farting sound resonated from Johan's mouth, then deepened to the gurgle of a blocked drain being emptied.

The sound was involuntary, but forced like a rude child draining the last drips from a juice carton. He legs were shaking violently, kicking out as if a deadly current circulated throughout his body. Unable to hang on any longer, Ziggy released his grip. Fearing for his own safety now, he lunged toward the forest floor and picked up the small hand axe he'd used to chop kindling for the fire. He ducked and lay down as far from Johan as he could, the axe held up to his cheek, elbow bent and ready to retaliate.

Whatever had gotten hold of the old man gave up and let go. Johan dropped down, landing on top of Ziggy. Katy didn't watch him fall, instead she watched the strange length of angled blackness retreat behind the tree. She thought she saw something else.

A shadow.

A body.

Lola and Georgina were screaming hysterically. Gasping in deep breaths of air that seemingly weren't enough to calm them, then screamed again, replenishing and depleting, replenish and deplete.

Katy's eyes flicked down to Johan. He was dead. Or at least he looked dead. If his brain somehow still fired electrons inside that papery skull of his, it would be both a miracle and a tragedy.

Johan had crumpled on top of Ziggy, his limbs folding at inexplicable angles as if broken and bent like a discarded puppet. His clothes now hung loosely from his frame. The whole process had taken less than a minute.

The real horror of it all was in Johan's face. His skin was white, almost translucent, sagging away from the skull beneath it like his clothes loosely hanging from his body. Before, he was charmingly wrinkled and wise-looking, but now the laughter lines were folded over and the mouth was a slack and perverted orifice that gaped with twisted jaw behind puckered lips that sloped to one side. Blood had bubbled from his lips, giving a dark crimson circle to the beard around his mouth. But the eyes, the eyes were the worst. Now broken windows to a lifeless soul. They'd sunk inwards and deflated, the whites had gone, the liquid of the irises had burst, making them sad little sacks of milky greyness. The centres of twin blackness staring not at Katy, but straight at Jake, with the twisted mouth caught in an airless whistle, as if singing to him . . .

This is about as bad as it gets Jakey boy . . .

*   *   *

The liquefied innards and blood of Johan Loft were already being digested as he was breathing his last. Even as his brain was being sucked through the tight little circle at the base of his skull it was still receiving pain messages from the nerves that hadn't yet snapped and pinged off towards their fate. Moments of his life had flashed before his eyes, he'd felt the urge to evacuate his bowels and bladder, but these were already gone, and the creature had zero concern for that of its prey. It had fed, but still it hungered. It moved back for more.

Moving around to the other side of the tree, it unfolded a whelk-like proboscis. Sensing the heat of food, it jabbed forward with the intention of immediately hunting its next course. The sensory organ at the end of its feeding implement felt flesh then hard bone. Its tri-claws gripped tight, breaking the skin and the weak skeleton in one vice-like motion. Three thin tongues wormed into the break in the skin, inflating as they pulsed forward, creating room to manoeuvre its food sack. Valves opened deep within its elongated carapace, forcing out air from within, creating a vacuum. Once pressurised, sphincters opened along its trio of tongues and the evacuation of its latest meal began.

As it began feeding then a new sensation shook the entirety of its being, something new that alarmingly altered its pressures without warning. It tried to repressurise the expanse of its stomach, but it wouldn't take. Instead it lost what it had just taken.

The pain wouldn't leave the end of its proboscis. Danger flared, it was an uncommon feeling, but erring on the side of caution, it retreated up the tree, outstretching its limbs, fleeing away from the light.

Light meant danger. It had learnt a lesson.

* * *

The thing had come back, on Clementine's side of the tree this time, punching that long dark limb into her rib cage with a horrible crack that chilled the others left watching. From this new angle, Katy could see more of it. The limb was attached to something else hidden behind the tree, a larger body. It wasn't a tree branch, but an actual *thing*.

Clementine gave a terrified yelp as she was stabbed. Ziggy had the axe poised and didn't waste a moment in launching into hero mode. He raised the blade, pushed Clementine flat against the tree and swooped the axe down on the intruding attacker. It took him four swipes, until finally the great angled limb cracked like a crab claw and pulled back up into the tree above, spewing blood and yellow bile like a garden hose.

Clem collapsed to the ground, the remnant of the axed-off proboscis still embedded in her torso like a spear. She gave a few short shrieks. Georgina gave one long, ear-bleeding scream.

"Stop fucking screaming!" Jake blurted, his hands over his ears. No one took any notice of his request.

Katy grabbed her sister and clung onto her for dear life after the inexplicable horror they'd witnessed.

"Stay close," she whispered to Lola.

Georgina's scream faded to a croaking hiss, her hands clasped to her face in an attempt to block out the images before her. Phil was tugging desperately at his chains, trying to wiggle it past his belt and ignoring the others.

Clementine fell into Ziggy's arms, blood pumping freely from the obscene open tap that stuck out beneath her right breast. She gasped for air, bubbling blood and god knows what else from her mouth. Her insides had been churned. They could all smell odours that they'd rather not smell.

"I'm sorry, Clem. I'm so sorry. It shouldn't be like this . . ." Ziggy wittered.

"What the fuck is that thing?" Jake half-screamed. "What the hell are you?" he asked the silent darkness, dreading the devil's response.

All that answered were the whimpers and sounds of the dying that were louder than anything else.

It was Lola who spoke next, uttering the only thing that made sense. "The meteorite. It has to be the meteor."

Yes, that was it. Whatever it was, it was a fucking alien. That was the only explanation, they all realised in a grim unison.

Katy's thoughts on the matter became diverted when Phil suddenly jumped away from his tree, shaking the chains from his ankles. He'd dropped his trousers and squeezed the chains down his legs then simply stepped out of his bonds, then pulled his trousers back up.

"I'm sorry, Jake. I'll go get help. Gimme your keys."

"What? Help us get out you fuck!"

"I'm out, I can get a phone signal, I can get help, now give your keys!"

"For fuck's sake, Phil," Jake chided, then dug into his pocket, fished out his car keys and tossed them to Phil.

Phil caught them one-handed, turned and ran through the darkness towards the gravel lane where they'd all parked their cars.

They watched as Phil disappeared deeper into the darkness, wondering if he even knew the way. His silhouette faded until it melted into the shadowy forest.

"Do you think that . . ." Lola started to speak, when above them the branches creaked with movement.

Twigs fell.

Leaves fluttered.

The five of them looked skyward, each shivering back towards their own respective tree.

Much of the detail was lost in the darkness, but between the glow from their torches, the fire, and the moonlight descending from the skies above, the outline of the creature could be made out as it pulled itself from branch to branch with a multitude of spindly limbs. It was earwig-shaped, elongated with overly long limbs and god knows what other appendages. It moved swiftly through the trees with a frightening deftness, following the direction Phil had fled.

"Oh shit, oh Phil, oh no," Jake muttered before he started screaming his friend's name.

"Jesus Christ, Phil, don't stop! Keep running!"

Inspired by Phil's abrupt escape, Georgina had dropped her jeans, revealing a tiny pair of lacy panties. With her thumbs tucked into the chain, she attempted to push her bonds down her body, but as with her plentiful breasts, Georgina was also blessed in the buttocks department. The unrelenting metal dug into the skin around her hips and rump, bulging the flesh, but refusing to budge any further down her legs. Still she tried, desperate to free her bonds.

Sometimes it was hard to be a woman.

A masculine scream echoed from the darkness and through the trees, probably Phil. The scream lasted for just a few seconds, enough time for one last breath before the cry ceased. They all thought they could hear other accompanying noises, and each of them strained to listen with dire intensity that saddened them with each passing moment as the reality sank in.

Ziggy lay the deceased Clementine down and stood up.

"Katy, I'm going to get us out of here," Ziggy said, then picked up the small hand axe and began to chop notches out of his own tree.

Katy looked at her phone again. "Everybody check your phones, let's see if we can get signal. We need to call for help."

"Fuck all," Lola spat grimly. No one else responded with a positive.

"We need to try our chains at least," Jake suggested. "Pants down."

He dropped his trousers and tried the same trick that had worked for skinny Phil but failed Georgina. He couldn't get the chains past his hips; he'd strung it too tight around his waist. Katy tried without removing her jeans, but gave up almost instantly on realizing she'd never work the chain past her wide, childbearing hips.

Lola didn't even try. She was young. She still had an abundance of puppy fat that hadn't been burnt away by hormones and the pressure of modern beauty norms.

"Shit! Fuck!" Jake cursed, pulling his trousers back up. "Ziggy, give me the axe."

The ancient oak tree Ziggy was hacking at was roughly two feet in diameter; it would take him hours to get through.

"Why?" he replied without pausing.

"There are three of us on this tree. We should be given the chance to escape first."

Lola looked up at Jake with part awe, part amazement at his selfishness.

"Yeah, he's right. There's three of us," she said, nodding. "Plus, I'm younger. I deserve to survive."

Ziggy stopped. He glanced at them, but wouldn't look them in the eye. "I'm faster with the axe. It's our best chance."

He continued chopping. Nobody else said anything. Ziggy had chosen for them.

*　　*　　*

The fire in the centre had started to dwindle, so Lola, being the closest to the pile of logs between her and her sister, grabbed a few and tossed them onto the glowing embers, soon stoking the flames and creating a warmth that brought little comfort.

"Holy shit!" Georgina yelped, startling the group, who readied themselves for another attack.

"What?" Katy asked.

"The keys, why didn't I think of this before?" Georgina dropped to her knees, jabbed two fingers into her mouth and began to dry heave as she tickled her gag reflex.

"Holy fuck, she's right!" Lola exclaimed, then followed with fingers to the throat.

Jake looked at Katy and they both shrugged at one another with a "*if you can't beat them, join them*" attitude. Then they both began to gag themselves with fingers down their throats. Apart from Ziggy, who continued his determined chop with the axe, they made a chorus of gut-wrenching noises as they tried to vomit up the keys to their escape.

Georgina was the first to succeed. A heavy gob of bright yellow bile left her mouth. She spat again in effort to remove the bitter, stinging taste from her mouth.

"I've . . . got it . . ." her fingers searched the forest floor detritus and carroty chunks of stomach lining for the glimmer of silver she'd evacuated along with the thin river of fresh vomit.

She found it, and wiped the clinging muck off on her jeans when something flew past her head and crashed into the small fire, sending the embers sparking off like stray fireworks.

The shock of the sudden arrival made her drop the key.

They all tensed, silently alert, until their eyes locked onto the abhorrence that had skidded through the fire. It was a twisted and saggy mess, like a wet bag of bones, but somehow familiar. It took them a second for recognition to set in, but after the moment of shock and horror had passed, they realised that the sad sack was wearing Phil's clothes, which was now starting to smoulder and smoke.

The fire had been knocked out, taking the majority of the light with it. They still had their individual torches and the few islands of embers cast about, but now darkness was clamouring for the advantage.

Now the darkness held more teeth than ever.

Georgina started to laugh, a loud, insane cackle inapposite to their situation. Her eyes were wide and white, trying to take in as much light from the destroyed fire, trying to comprehend what had happened to Phil who was now nothing more than a deflated-skin sack of bones, already trying to expel the memory as it was burnt onto her retinas.

Then she remembered the dropped key, and the fact that her survival was pretty damn important.

She was laughing.

She was crying.

She was jibbering words that didn't even make sense to her, but for the soundtrack of the situation, they made perfect sense.

Dreading the same fate as poor Phil, the desperate trio of Jake, Katy and Lola began with fingers in throats again. Ziggy continued with his axing, confident that his way was the only route to safety.

Georgina searched the forest floor for her lost key. Within seconds, she was holding it up for the others to see.

"Found it!" she mumbled to herself as she jabbed the key into her padlock and began to twiddle with the mechanism. The padlock dropped just as something inhuman and not of this world in the slightest crashed through the branches with the breaking of twigs and a shower of leaves.

She took a step forward, the chains dropping in the same moment as her body suddenly tensed in spasm. She screamed. Not the kind of scream you get in the horror movies, but one that went quickly high-pitched before it curdled to a gurgle in the sudden wetness of her throat.

With the scream chilling their blood, the trio looked up, Ziggy did not, furiously focused on his act of the killing the tree that he was so intent on saving at the start of this debacle.

The alien creature was in the tree above, emerging from the thick limbs. Some of its thin, insectile appendages descended from the camouflage of branches. One poised behind Georgina's back, just above her left hip, another planted firmly on top of her scalp, the tri-claws embedded deep, both twitching as they sucked hungrily.

Georgina's eyes were on the others, arms out stretched, yearning for a helpful embrace.

But they couldn't look at her.

Their eyes were drawn to it, the thing, the unnamable evil that plagued them all, in all of its grotesque glory despite the lack of light. They could see its long, earwig shape with a thick ridge of armour down its back. The spindly, multitude of limbs that seemed to melt into the maze of branches and its armoured, flat face. There was no mouth. Just a single, curved plate, which sat below two gauzy, light blue eyes which seemed to entrance those that stared into them, with their calm, arctic coolness.

The thin limbs quivered as they effortlessly drained the life from Georgina Bainbridge, her body shaking as each litre of her innards was stolen from her body. Her now pendulous breasts shrank into old, deflated balloons, leaving her bra hanging loose like an abandoned hammock. With her skin slackening further, her features became gaunt and drooped from her skull as the musculature beneath was drawn away. Katy was reminded of stop-motion effects from some gruesome eighties horror film as Georgina's form and structure changed before their very eyes. The creature lifted her from the ground, her head taking her weight, causing her thrapple to protrude unnaturally as every ounce of fluid drained away from within.

Katy wanted to scream, but her mouth was dry. Screaming achieved nothing in the eyes of this unrelenting beast.

Beside her, Lola jammed her fingers as far down her throat as she could, choking, gagging and retching as she clawed the back of her mouth. Her cheeks, wet with tears, were flushed a bright cherry as revulsion from her stomach fought to keep its contents.

It lost.

Lola retched wetly and then her own key was in her hand. She shook off the sticky contents of her stomach that clung to it and unlocked her padlock.

"Give me your car keys!" she demanded of her sister.

Katy paused from her attempts at purging, rummaged in her purse that was by her side and passed the keys to her sister.

"You're not leaving us, are you?" Katy asked, wiping spittle from her lips.

"I'm coming back. There's something in your car I need. Keep that fucking thing busy!"

"Busy? Fuck off, Lola!"

Then her sister ran off into the darkness as the creature discarded the depleted remains of Georgina beside Phil's, like an old coat, the two of them becoming a couple in death. The creature turned its attentions to the remaining split trio, those cold blue eyes sizing up its options, seemingly calculating its next move with an unnerving intelligence that one shouldn't see in an insect.

But this was no normal insect.

Indeed, it wasn't even an insect.

Ziggy ceased chopping at the tree and readied the axe.

"I'm going to give you more time, Katy. I love you. Try to escape. Live a good, long life. Have babies."

"Ziggy, wait!"

"Katy, get your key," he barked.

Ziggy waved the axe at the creature, then shouted: "Come over here, you ugly fuck!" in an effort to sway its next choice.

Unfortunately for Ziggy, the creature took him up on his invitation, grasping hold of a branch in the tree above.

"No!" Katy protested, but the creature still advanced. Ziggy beckoned the beast with his blade, as Jake continued to wretch. The creature, the tree hugger as it were, reached out with another limb, positioning itself.

Katy couldn't reach Ziggy to aid his battle, but she could throw something. She reached out for a thick branch from the pile of logs and threw it at the monster. It glanced off its back, causing zero concern.

"Leave it, Katy, it's okay," Ziggy reassured. "Get your key and get out of here."

She couldn't. She was dry. She'd tried, but her stomach had refused to give up its contents. She loved her food far too much.

The creature had descended fully from the tree, and now stalked painfully slowly towards Ziggy with its hellish, calculated skitter. Its front end reared up, moving with a mantis-like sway as its multitude of legs changed weights, feigning left and right as Ziggy slashed out with the axe.

The creature raised one of its tri-claws directly above Ziggy.

It had the advantage of reach.

With a single downward sweep of the limb, the giant insect imbedded the claw deep into Ziggy's skull, splitting his head open like a soft Halloween pumpkin in late November. His face opened up, his eyes rolling in different directions, but one focusing on Katy, his twisted, sloped smile meant for her as he dribbled blood and broken teeth over a protruding tongue that hung out further than it should have, a perverse scroll speaking words of death. A cascade of gore soon hid all of this as the creature began to feed noisily on what it needed.

Katy Mace screamed at the sight of her ex-boyfriend being slurped like a juice carton. His body shook perversely, jittering out a final jig as he was consumed from the inside. His hand swung the axe at his side, then with a palsied spasm, the weapon dropped to the forest floor with a soft thud. His knees buckled and he knelt before his death god in submission. She realised that she still loved him and she screamed again as the fear flocked out from her in fluttering waves. A deeper darkness bled into her vision as she realised that she was next.

It turned her stomach and then with no real effort at all, Katy Mace vomited over herself, but mostly down the crease between her breasts.

She collapsed as the last ounce of hope left her. Here she was; shackled to a tree, covered in vomit and about to be eaten alive by a creature that had devoured her friends.

It was over.

Then she saw the key on the forest floor, amongst the splatter of her half-digested last supper, still glinting despite its surroundings and meagre light. She picked it up and with shaking fingers, managed to undo her padlock.

She was free!

Jake was still retching but with no luck and gazed upon the key as if it were fabled treasure.

"Katy . . ."

"I'm sorry, Jake. I think it might be over."

Katy shouldered her chains and picked up a log from the pile.

The creature had finished with Ziggy, dropping his empty corpse as useless litter. His death hadn't been in vain. He'd bought her time as a last act of his love for her.

Katy turned and threw the log. It hit the beast along its flank and it turned, making a guttural snarl, those deadly blue eyes searching for its next victim. It saw only Jake, for Katy had vanished behind the tree.

Jake was sitting bait.

*   *   *

Unperturbed, the creature approached the meal, not in the slightest curious as to where the other had gone. Perhaps it had fled. It didn't matter. Food was food. It would find more.

The meal was making noise, screaming. They'd all done this. It was a minor annoyance, but the sound did nothing to ruin the feast.

It approached and struck down with one of its feeder arms, plunging it into the throat of its food. The scream became wet, then stopped altogether. It began to feed in silence.

Something struck it from behind, nudging it forward, but it paid no heed. It was feeding, that was all that mattered.

*   *   *

Jake had been a sacrifice. Without his key, he was doomed either way. Katy chose to use his imminent death to her advantage, hiding behind the tree as the beast fed on him then circling back around, shoulder barging the beast and using her own chain and padlock to fasten it around its carapace to the chains where she once stood.

She winced as she pricked herself on the sharp ridges of its back, but determined, she worked through the pain and stepped away, the padlock secure.

Unless it removed several of its legs, the thing would be stuck fast.

She backed away and picked up Ziggy's fallen axe, ready to strike, when a shape emerged back into the trio of oak trees.

Katy readied the axe, expecting another monster from the darkness, but relented when she saw it was her sister.

"Wait! I've got this!" Katy looked at what her sister held. It was a five-litre fuel can. She recognised it as the one that she kept in the back of her car, ever paranoid that she'd run out of fuel one day.

"I got a signal and managed to call the cops. Let's smoke this mother-fucker."

Katy swapped the axe for the fuel can, but as she unscrewed the top, the monstrosity managed a half turn and jabbed a claw at Katy. It wasn't one of the feeder ones, but a simple curved spike it used to cling. Regardless, it hurt as it twisted between the skin of her collarbone and ribcage. She fell to her knees before it hoisted her up, bringing her closer to its feeder claws, ready to drink her insides like a smoothie.

Katy held onto the claw with one hand, taking her weight so it didn't tear any more than necessary.

She screamed as she felt the claw move and chafe against the bones inside, the unnaturalness of it strangely exhilarating to her as it scratched and reverberated within.

Below her, Lola screamed her name but the sound meant nothing as the claw ground against bone and the blood rushed past her ears.

The surge of adrenalin was preparing her for death. Her body was readying for the pain of what was to come.

"I'll give you a drink, have one on me," she growled and then began tipping the contents of the fuel can over the thing's eyes before tossing it at the creature's flank. It skidded across the underside of its carapace, dropping next to the tree with a dull *thunk*, glugging its contents at the beast's multitude of legs.

"Light it up!" Katy bellowed.

The creature hissed, drew the claw back and flung Katy away as if she had become poisonous to touch.

Sensing the opportunity, Lola swiftly dipped low and used the blade of the axe to shovel up a glowing ember from the scattered fire.

The creature removed its claws as it abruptly finished feeding on Jake, dropping his half-empty corpse so it hung limp and folded over the chains, leaking guts and gore from a ragged hole in the top of his skull.

It wheeled around, its blue eyes half-blind but still searching for new food to quench its blood-thirst. It lunged, coming to a jarring halt as the chains held it back. It raised its numerous feeder arms, blood frothing angrily from the strange mouths.

Lola tossed the axe upward. The ember left the blade and landed with precision beneath the monstrosity.

A moment of agonising nothingness was followed by an eruption of light as a fireball erupted from the ground and engulfed the creature wholly.

Lola ran to her sister and helped her up, leaving the dark creature to suffer the hungry flames, its flailing limbs sending strange shadows flickering up around them as they fled.

The creature made a noise that sounded like a scream, but they knew that it wasn't for it had no true mouth.

It was the blood and everything else boiling within.

* * *

They reached the road and embraced, sobbing into one another despite the filth that covered them.

They watched the dying light beyond the trees, which grew in intensity as the flames took hold of the dry forest, burning up everything else around the creature's remains. The fire was spreading with frightening hunger, and they both hoped that the destruction was worth it.

In silent reverence, the gravel crunched underfoot as they made their way back to the cars. They smiled as the flash and awe of police lights approached in the distance.

They watched as streaks of blue light scored through the sky above, hundreds, if not thousands of them.

And they lost their smiles, forever.

AUTHOR'S STORY NOTE

I've had the idea for Tree Huggers for a while now, a tale of environmentalist besieged by an actual tree hugger, giving full irony to the title. I wanted a fun, gory, 80's creature type movie that near enough jumps straight into the action with minimal set up.

I recently listened to an audio version of the story, and was struck by how filmic it was. I'm currently working on adapted Tree Huggers into a film script.

THE DOGS

SCOTT SMITH

From *Dark Cities*
Editor: Christopher Golden
Titan Books

Her real name wasn't Rose—that was just what she used when she met guys on Craigslist: Rose or Rosa or Rosemary or even Rosaline (but mostly Rose). She'd always liked names that came from flowers. When she was six, she'd had a set of dolls, four of them, dressed like little cowgirls, and she'd named them Rose, Daisy, Petunia, and Tulip. Rose had been her favorite, though, the one she'd slept with every night.

There was a way you could phrase your post on Craigslist so it was clear what you wanted—or what you were offering—without being too explicit. Rose's go-to headline was: "Gorgeous Young Girl Searching For Generous Older Gent." She didn't think of herself as a prostitute because she never took money from the men. Or only one time, with that Egyptian guy, and then just because it would've felt awkward to refuse it—the wad of bills he'd slid into her jacket pocket as they kissed goodbye at the door. It was a thick wad, but mostly tens and fives (even a couple of singles), so it seemed like it ought to have been more than it actually turned out to be. Rose ended up feeling disappointed when she finally had a chance to count it, in a bathroom stall at Penn Station, waiting to board the 8:37 AM train back to her mother's house. She hadn't eaten, and she was coming down from whatever the pink pills were that she and the Egyptian had taken together, so her hands were shaking, and she kept dropping the bills onto the bathroom's dirty floor, kept dropping them and picking them up, and each time she did this she lost count and needed to start all over again. She never managed to arrive at a consistent number—it was one hundred and twelve dollars, or maybe one hundred and seventeen—a weird number either way, and small enough to make Rose feel cheap and whorish rather than classy like she'd hoped.

Money was never the point. It was the sense of adventure, the feeling of power, and the thrill of the places where the men took her, places Rose never would've been able to go on her own—expensive restaurants, clubs, and hotels . . . even their own apartments sometimes. Rose spent a night in a penthouse once, overlooking the East River, with a Christmas tree on the terrace. The guy she was with turned on the tree's little white lights for her. Rose wanted to take a photo with her phone, but the guy wouldn't let her. He was worried she'd post the picture online somewhere, and that his wife might see it. The wife was in Anguilla with the children, who were out of school for the holidays.

Rose lived at her mother's house, in New Jersey, an hour's train ride west of Penn Station. She had a room in the basement. This wasn't as depressing as it might sound. Rose had her own shower and toilet down there, her own entrance; the only reason she ever needed to venture upstairs was if she wanted to use the kitchen—which she didn't, mostly. She had a mini-fridge beside her bed, and a hot plate she never used, and there was a pizza place a short walk down the road, so who needed a kitchen? Rose was nineteen, but believed she looked older. She'd bought a fake Ohio driver's license online two years ago; it listed her age as twenty-three, and no bouncer or bartender had ever questioned it. Rose had gotten her GED the previous summer, and then had taken a few classes in dental hygiene before dropping out (she told anyone who asked that she planned to go back, but she didn't really believe it). Now she worked part-time at a beauty salon in downtown Dunellen, massaging shampoo into the scalps of elderly women and sweeping up the cut hair. On the first of every month, she paid her mother seventy-five dollars cash for the room in the basement (her mother called this "a symbolic gesture").

Her mother didn't know about her Craigslist dates. Rose would tell her she was going to spend the night in the city with friends—with Holly or Carrie—and this always covered things. Her mother didn't know that Holly had moved with her boyfriend to Buffalo, or that Carrie had gotten mono and then hepatitis and then some sort of intestinal disorder, and now she was living in Alabama with a Pentecostal aunt and uncle, who were trying to cure her with prayer (so Rose didn't really have anyone left in her life you could properly call a friend).

Enough people had told Rose she was pretty in the past decade that she'd come to believe it, too. She was self-conscious about her teeth (she had a slight overbite; if she wasn't careful, it could make her lisp), and she wished her hair had more body to it, and always in the back of her mind was the comment a boy had made in tenth grade (that she had a rabbity, white-trash aura about her), but generally Rose could keep all of this at bay, and feel almost beautiful—especially at night, especially if she'd been drinking. Long blond hair, blue eyes, skinny hips, softball-sized breasts: sometimes on Craigslist she'd describe herself as "a young Britney," and no one she'd met had ever challenged her on this.

*   *   *

He said his name was Patrick, but he didn't seem like a Patrick to Rose. In Rose's mind, "Patrick" implied an Irish look—tall and fair-haired and blue-eyed, rather than short and dark and fidgety, the latter quality so pronounced in this case that Rose thought maybe he'd fortified himself for the date with a bump or two of coke. She didn't care what his real name was. Most of the men she met were lying about one thing or another, just like her—names were the least of it. He took her to dinner at a sushi place in the Meat Packing district, and then escorted her across the street to a bar where it was too loud to talk. They ended up making out for five minutes in the little hallway that led to the bathrooms, and when she refused to follow him into the men's room, Patrick told her he wanted to take her home.

He'd said he was thirty, but Rose guessed he must be closer to forty, if not already safely across the line. She thought he probably wore glasses in his normal life, because his eyes had a blurred, watery look when he talked to her, as if he couldn't quite bring her into focus. His face was round, and slightly flushed, like the baby angels she'd seen in old paintings. Rose was certain she'd known the name for these creatures once, but she couldn't remember it now—sometimes this would happen to her. Right after they'd sat down for dinner, he'd announced that he was a lawyer, and Rose had no reason to doubt him, but if he was saying it merely to impress her, he was aiming in the wrong direction.

He kissed her again in the cab uptown, his mouth tasting of sushi and sake, and then he cupped her breasts in his hands, first the right, then the left, giving each a gentle squeeze: Rose had a brief memory of her mother, in the produce section at Safeway, testing oranges for ripeness. She was half-splayed across Patrick's lap, and she could feel his erection through his pants—the bulk and heat of it. When she pressed down with her leg, Patrick groaned, then bit her ear.

His apartment was on the Upper West Side, somewhere beyond Lincoln Center, but before the Apple Store, a prewar building, with no doorman. The elevator was tiny, almost phone-booth size—they rode it to the seventh floor—and then there was a long, dimly lit hallway, a door with three separate locks. The door was dark gray, and had two black numbers painted at eye level: 78. Patrick looked nervous suddenly. He undid the first lock, dropped his keys, undid the second lock, dropped the keys again. Rose was accustomed to this by now, the terror some men appeared to feel when there was no longer any question of what was about to happen. It always seemed odd to her, since this was precisely the moment when she began to feel most calm: no one needed to think anymore, they were in the chute, all of the necessary decisions had already been made, and now gravity could take command. Other people's anxiety had a way of unsettling Rose—as if it were contagious—and she felt an urge to soothe Patrick. She lifted her hand to caress the nape of his neck; she was close enough to feel that buzzy sensation another person's skin can radiate an instant before you touch it, when the barking began. Rose jumped at the sound, then laughed, and the final lock was undone, and the door was swinging open, and there they were: three dogs, one big and black and shaggy, one small and white and fluffy, and the last of them lean and brown with a white patch over its eye, like the hero in a children's picture book.

Rose managed only a brief impression of the apartment. It had a dorm room feel: linoleum on the floor, a glimpse of what appeared to be a plastic lawn chair through the archway to the darkened living room. There was a flurry of panting and licking from the dogs, along with much wagging of tails, and some leaping and yapping by the fluffy white one, and then Patrick was leading Rose across the little entranceway, kicking off his shoes, dragging his shirt over his head, pulling her down the hall to the bedroom. He pushed her onto the bed, and started to undo his belt, while all three dogs watched from the doorway. The dogs stayed there while she and Patrick fucked; every time Rose glanced in their direction, she saw them staring. Rose was too drunk to enjoy the sex—it felt hazy and faraway, and the bed kept threatening to start spinning—but none of this was Patrick's fault. He was surprisingly gentlemanly in his efforts; he seemed to want her pleasure almost as much as he desired his own, and Rose was grateful for this—grateful, too, for the glass of water he fetched afterward, grateful for what felt to her like clean sheets, and grateful most of all that Patrick showed no appetite for post-coital conversation. Sometimes guys wanted to talk. In Rose's experience, it was never a good idea.

The last thing Patrick said to her was the dogs' names.

Jack was the taut, brown, intelligent-looking fellow with the patch over his eye—a mix of whippet and Lab.

Zeus was the big, black, shaggy one . . . a Bernese mountain dog.

Millie was the tiny, fluffy, white one: a Bichon Frise, which Patrick assured Rose meant French bitch.

"For real?" Rose asked.

Patrick laughed, and something about the sound jarred loose the word she'd been searching for earlier. It just popped into her mind—sometimes that could happen, too.

Cherub.

A moment later, with the lights still on, they were both asleep.

*   *   *

"The most difficult part is right here: believing this is happening. If you can manage that, you can manage everything."

Rose was still half-asleep when she heard the voice—a male voice, calmer than Patrick's, deep and slow. There was an air of authority to the words, of command; Rose sensed it was the slowness that accounted for this quality (one further tap of the brakes, and the voice would've slipped into a drawl). She opened her eyes. Patrick wasn't in the room—she could hear the shower running. Jack, the tan dog with the eye patch, was sitting beside the bed, staring at her, and she knew without a moment's doubt that it was his voice she was hearing.

"He'll come back from the shower in another minute, and he'll suggest you have sex again. He'll pressure you to try on a pair of handcuffs. Then he's going to kill you."

Rose lifted her head from the pillow. She could still feel the alcohol from last night, a sloshing sensation inside her brain, as if she might spill out of herself were she to move too quickly. Zeus, the big black dog, was lying on the floor by the closet. Millie, the little white one, was on the armchair by the window. They were both watching her.

Jack's voice continued: "Other girls have decided this was a dream. I hope you won't make the same mistake."

Over on the chair, Millie began to wag her tail. Rose's clothes were scattered across the floor. She was thinking about how much effort it would take to pick them up and pull them on, and how unpleasant it would be to rush out of the apartment without washing her face or emptying her bladder or rinsing her mouth, when she heard the shower shut off.

Jack walked toward the armchair, his nails making a clicking sound on the linoleum. There was a square of sunlight beneath the window, and he lay down in its center. He didn't move his mouth when he spoke—it wasn't like that. Rose just heard the words inside her head, and she knew they were his. "The knife is in the night table drawer," he said. "All you need to do is get there first."

Then he shut his eyes. So did Zeus and Millie. From one second to the next, the three dogs went from staring at her to what looked like the deepest sort of sleep. Then Patrick was in the doorway, smiling down at her, naked, rubbing his hair with a towel. His penis was edging its way toward an erection, both stiff and floppy all at once. "Wanna try something fun?" he asked. He moved toward the closet, without waiting for a reply.

Rose was about to tell him that she'd just had the weirdest dream, that his dog was speaking to her in it, telling her that—

But then Patrick turned from the closet, his penis all the way erect now, a deep purple. He was moving toward her, holding a pair of handcuffs, bending to reach for her wrist.

She lunged for the night table, and all three dogs began to bark.

*　*　*

Afterward—maybe an hour, maybe two, Rose wouldn't have been able to say for certain—she was sitting on a bench, five or six blocks away, on the edge of Riverside Park. The panic was starting to ease now, but this didn't mean she was feeling calm, not remotely. Numb would be the better description, though even this adjective would imply a degree of equanimity that was completely lacking. It was more like the absence of sensation that comes with extreme cold, as frostbite starts to set in: Rose knew there was a lot going on inside her head, but it had reached a point of extremity beyond which she could no longer feel anything specific, just a generalized, deeply subterranean hum of distress.

It was early April, and the wind off the river retained a wintry bite, but the trees didn't seem to mind: they were beginning to bud. Nannies pushed strollers; squirrels made darting forays across the still-not-quite-green grass. Rose's nose was running. She didn't know if it was the wind or an early bout of allergies or maybe just some physiological response to what had happened—to what she'd done. Could terror cause your nose to run? She kept wiping the snot on her sleeve, her leg jiggling with leftover adrenaline, while she tried to decide what she ought to do.

She'd gotten the drawer open, and there was indeed a knife inside, a large knife, the kind a soldier might carry in a sheath on his ankle, though there wasn't any sheath for this one, just the knife, its blade forged from some sort of black metal, its grip feeling slightly sticky in Rose's hand. The next few moments might not have unfolded so easily for her had it not been for the dogs. All three were leaping and barking, and in the midst of this tumult, Zeus made contact with enough force to knock Patrick off balance. Rose wasn't trying to stab him in any particular place; she was just swinging the blade, and the dogs were leaping, and Patrick was rushing toward her—stumbling, really, and then falling—and that was how the blade ended up piercing his throat, sinking deep, all the way to the hilt. Patrick dropped to the bed, and the knife came out of his body with a sucking sound, like a stick yanked from a muddy yard, and there was blood everywhere, an immense amount of it, fountaining upward, hitting the wall beside the bed and splattering to the floor with a lawn-sprinkler sound, and Patrick was gurgling and frothing and trying impotently to rise, and Rose dropped the knife, gathered up her clothes, and ran from the room. Her arms and face and chest were covered with blood. At first, she'd feared it might be hers, but when she washed it off in the kitchen sink, she couldn't find any wounds, and finally she decided it all had to be Patrick's. Standing at the sink, still naked, searching for a towel to dry her body, there was a moment when she thought she was going to call 911. It seemed like the obvious path, and if there'd been a landline in the apartment, she might've gone ahead and dialed the number—it would've been so easy, just three quick taps of her finger, and then other people would be making the decisions for her. But there wasn't a landline, and Rose's phone was still in her purse, and her purse was still in the bedroom, which was where Patrick was, along with the three dogs, so Rose found a tablecloth to dry herself, and she crouched to pee into a drinking glass, and emptied the glass into the sink, and then she was shivering, so she pulled on her clothes, and suddenly it seemed like maybe the easiest thing to do was leave, just leave, walk across the little entranceway to the front door, undo its three locks, and flee.

Sitting on the park bench, Rose tried to imagine what she must look like to the people passing by. It was a shock to realize she probably seemed perfectly fine; it made the whole situation feel that much stranger. A horrifying, desperate thing had happened to her, and none of these strangers who saw Rose here, sitting in the sun, wiping her nose on her sleeve, jiggling her leg, none of them would ever be able to guess.

Not one. Not ever.

She'd made mistakes. Jesus fucking Christ: it appalled her to think how many.

If she were still planning to call 911 (and she was, wasn't she?), she should never have left the apartment—she shouldn't even have left the room, shouldn't have washed herself at the kitchen sink, shouldn't have pulled on her clothes. She should've scrambled for her cell phone, should've called for an ambulance right there, standing beside the bed, bent over Patrick, balling up the sheet and pressing it against the jagged wound in his throat.

Jesus, Jesus, Jesus. She'd fucked this up.

Now, when she dialed 911, the police would want to know why she'd left, why she'd waited so long to call. And what was she supposed to tell them, anyway? That she'd stabbed a near stranger in the throat because his dog had warned her the guy was planning to kill her? How well was this story going to play for her? Rose didn't have any wounds, not even a bruise—Patrick hadn't managed to touch her.

And the *dog* . . . well, she had to think through that part of the morning's events, didn't she? It had seemed so obvious when she was there in the room, half-awake, hearing his voice.

But now?

Oh, for fuck's sake. She'd had one of those weird early morning dreams, hadn't she? She'd mistaken it for real, and she'd killed a guy.

But what about the handcuffs? And how had she known there was a knife in that drawer? And *why* was there a knife in that drawer?

Rose thought of Doctor Dolittle. She thought of Son of Sam. Neither model seemed especially helpful.

She'd left her purse in the apartment. Her phone. Her wallet. And that was just the easy stuff. There would be fingerprints. Hair. Saliva. Vaginal fluid. Tiny flakes of dead skin. There would be other stuff, too—there had to be—stuff she'd probably never be able to think of.

Rose had no idea what she was going to do, but one thing seemed unavoidable: she needed to go back.

* * *

The street door was locked.

Rose hadn't thought of this, and it made her angry with herself—there was so much she wasn't thinking of, so much she was getting wrong. She tried the knob; she pushed at the door with her shoulder. There was a buzzer system, with buttons for the different apartments. In movies, people were always using this sort of thing to gain illicit access to buildings. They'd push a button, claim to be a UPS deliveryman, and some too-trusting tenant would buzz them in. Rose didn't think this strategy would work for her, but she also didn't think she had much to lose in trying: she started with the top floor, pressed the button, waited long enough to realize there wasn't going to be a response, then tried the next apartment down the line. She was on her fifth button before she got an answer. What sounded like a very old man's voice said: "Hello . . .?"

Rose put her mouth up against the speaker: "UPS."

There was a long pause—too long, it seemed to Rose—maybe there was a camera? Or maybe the old man was coming downstairs to sign for the supposed package? Or maybe he'd seen all of those movies Rose had seen, and he was calling the police right now, so she'd have one more inexplicable thing to explain to them when they finally showed up? Or maybe—

The door buzzed, and she jumped forward, pushing it open.

The building had fifteen stories. Rose got into the elevator and pressed buttons for the ninth, tenth, eleventh, twelfth, and fourteenth floors. That way, if the old man had stepped out into the hallway and was watching the elevator, he wouldn't know which floor Rose was going to. She rode to nine, then crept along the hall to the stairs, and tiptoed back down to the seventh floor.

Apartment 78. The gray door, with its three (not locked) locks.

Rose felt an impulse to ring the bell (which she resisted), and then— once she'd pushed open the door and stepped into the apartment—she had an even stronger urge to call out Patrick's name (which she also resisted). From the entranceway, you could see into the kitchen. The tablecloth Rose had used as a towel lay in a damp mound on the linoleum in front of the refrigerator. To the right of the kitchen, a short hallway led to the bedroom. Beyond the bedroom, the hallway turned to the left—Rose assumed this must be where the bathroom was.

She made her way to the bedroom. Part of her was hoping that none of it had happened—that it had all been a dream, not just the talking dog: everything. Patrick would still be asleep in the bed, or else awake now, drinking coffee, wondering where Rose had run off to so abruptly, and why. The sight of the bloody sheets cured Rose of this fantasy: the blood on the wall above the bed, the blood pooling on the floor. There was no sign of Patrick, so Rose assumed he must've slipped off the mattress, that he must be sprawled on the floor now, hidden by the bed's bulk. But when she edged her way into the room, angling toward the armchair by the window, where her purse awaited her, and inside her purse, her cell phone, and through the magic of the cell phone, the police . . . when she cleared the foot of bed and forced herself to look, there was more blood, there was the knife lying in the center of that blood, and there were paw prints—dozens of them—around the margins of the mess, but there was no Patrick.

He must've crawled under the bed as he bled himself out. It gave Rose a shivery feeling to imagine this.

She crouched, bent to peer into the darkness. Down low like that, just an inch or two above the puddle, the raw-steak smell of the blood hit Rose with extra vigor, and for an instant she thought she might vomit. The sensation passed as quickly as it came. She could see nothing under the bed but dust bunnies and clumps of shed dog hair.

Which meant . . . Patrick was alive?

Such an outcome seemed impossible to Rose, but even as she thought this, she was stepping into the pool of blood, and reaching for the knife. It was the purest sort of reflex, fear-driven, from the base of her spine. Part of her was saying: *Couldn't this be a good thing?* And another part—the stronger part, the part that had never intended to call 911, that had known all along the only way through this was to bury what needed to be buried, and run away from the rest—*that* part was shaking its head, and saying: *No, no, no, no, no . . .*

Rose didn't see any blood on the linoleum in the hallway, and this puzzled her. She couldn't imagine how Patrick had been able to escape the bedroom—crawling or staggering—without leaving some sort of trail behind. Then she reached the bathroom, and came upon Millie. The hallway was dim, and Rose's first impression was of a soccer-ball sized clot of white fur, tensely vibrating. It took her a moment to realize that Millie was licking the floor, with a frenzied aura of purpose. The dog swung its tiny body toward Rose; she stared up at her for a half-second, her muzzle stained dark-red. Then she pivoted away, lowered her head to the floor again and resumed her licking, audibly panting with the effort. Beyond her, Rose could see that the linoleum was smeared with blood. The trail led to a shut door at the end of the hall, fifteen feet past the bathroom.

Rose could hear something making a shuffling sound on the other side of the door, and . . . was that a grunt? She took a step forward, and called out: "Patrick?"

The sound stopped.

"Patrick . . .?"

Jack seemed to materialize from the center of the door. Rose flinched, almost dropped the knife. Then she realized there was a swinging panel cut into the wood—a dog door. Jack had pushed his way through it, and he was standing there now, in the dim light, his front paws in the hall, his back paws still on the other side of the door. His muzzle, like Millie's, was stained with blood. There was a strong odor coming from the room; Rose couldn't identify it—all she knew was that it was unpleasant. Jack stared at her. She could feel him looking at her face, then at the knife in her hand, then back at her face. She heard his voice in her head again. "Why don't you go wait in the kitchen? Get yourself something to drink. I'll be out in a minute, and we can talk this through."

And then, without waiting for Rose to respond, he ducked back through the tiny door.

*   *   *

The strangest part wasn't that the dog could speak. It was that—while it was happening, at least—Rose didn't find it strange at all.

The first thing Jack said when he came into the kitchen was: "Would you mind freshening the water in the bowl?"

There was a dog bowl sitting on a mat beside the refrigerator, half-full of water. Rose took it to the sink, rinsed it out, refilled it, and set it back on the mat. Then she sat in her chair again and watched Jack lap at the water. When he was finished, he lay down beside the bowl, facing her. He'd managed to clean most of the blood from his muzzle, and Rose was thankful for this. She'd found a Diet Coke in the otherwise almost completely empty refrigerator, and she sat clutching the can in her hands, feeling grateful for the chill against her palms—there was something soothing about the sensation, something grounding. She'd been sitting here for the past five minutes, waiting for the dog to appear, and wishing that she'd never posted her ad on Craigslist, wishing this, and then wishing it again, and then again, which was a pointless expenditure of energy, she knew, and a stupid thing to waste a wish on.

"Where do you live?" Jack asked.

"In New Jersey," Rose said.

"With roommates?"

Rose shook her head. "At my mother's. In her basement."

"That's good," Jack said. "That's very good. So moving in here won't be a problem?"

Rose just stared at him. *I'm talking to a dog,* she thought. *I killed a man, and now I'm talking to his dog.* She felt exhausted suddenly, and dizzy to the point of nausea. She thought she was about to faint, so she bent forward and placed her head between her knees. It helped, but not a lot.

Jack made a noise—it sounded like a sigh. "I know this is probably quite confusing for you, but if we can just focus on the basics, I'm confident you'll soon find your bearings."

"How do you know how to speak?" Rose asked, without raising her head.

Jack ignored the question. "It might feel uncomfortable for you to acknowledge this, but you're not really in a position of power here. And the sooner you come to grips with that fact, the sooner we'll sort everything out. There's a body in the back room. A body with a knife wound to the throat. Your fingerprints are on the knife. Are you with me this far?"

Rose could feel the dog watching her, waiting for her to lift her head and look at him. She didn't move.

Jack seemed to take her silence as an affirmation. "Would you like to know what would happen if you were to run away? Zeus and Millie and I would eventually get hungry. We'd start to bark and whimper and howl, and soon enough one of the neighbors would call the landlord, and the landlord would call the police, and the door would be broken down. And the body would be found. And the knife. And your fingerprints. And inside the back room? Other bodies. I think you'd be startled to learn how many. Now, you could certainly try to tell the police: 'I didn't kill those girls. Daniel did.' But then they'll ask how you came to know this. And you'll say that his dog—"

Rose lifted her head from her lap. "Who's Daniel?"

"The young man you stabbed in the throat."

"He said his name was Patrick."

"What did you tell him your name was?"

Rose dropped her head back between her knees.

"You're a Jersey girl," Jack said. "Isn't this what you've always dreamed of? A Manhattan apartment?"

"How can you talk?" Rose asked again.

Once more Jack ignored the question. "You don't have to worry about the body. Zeus and I are taking care of it. Millie will handle the blood on the floor and walls—I think you'll be surprised at how clean she can get things with that tiny tongue of hers. The mattress and pillows are lined with plastic—Millie will lick them as good as new. It's really only the sheets that are ever a problem. Daniel used to tie them up in a Hefty bag—double bag it. There's a chute beside the elevator; it leads straight down to the building's incinerator. Just drop the bags in, and it will be like he never even existed."

Rose lifted her head again. "What about his family? His friends?"

"Daniel was a guy who spent the past seven months luring young women to his apartment, so that he could handcuff them to his bed, and kill them. Does that sound like someone with a close-knit social network?"

Rose was silent. She was thinking about all the people Daniel must've come into contact with as he moved through his days: his boss, his—

Jack seemed to guess her chain of thought: "He worked at a copy shop in midtown. They'll call once, maybe twice. When they don't get an answer, they'll hire someone new. In three weeks, they'll have forgotten Daniel's name."

"He said he was a lawyer."

Rose wouldn't have guessed a dog could smile, but that was what Jack did now. Not with his lips, of course—it was just an upward slant of his tail, a tilt of his head, and the way his ears lifted slightly—but it communicated the same amusement that a smile would have. It was a funny thing to see a dog do—almost more extraordinary than his talking. "You'll find new sheets in the hall closet," he said. "Daniel bought them in bulk. The keys are on a hook by the door, along with the leashes. Zeus and I usually like to go out first thing in the morning—around eight or so. Millie sleeps late; she goes out around noon, and then again together with me at six PM—that's when you'll take us to the dog run, over by the river. The last walk is for Zeus and Millie, around midnight. How does that sound?"

Rose shook her head. "I can't—"

"Of course you can. You don't have a choice."

Jack got up and walked over to Rose. He rested his head on her knee. He could talk, but he was still a dog. He looked up at her with that adorable white patch over his eye, and gave a slow wag of his tail. Rose's hand lifted toward him, reflexively; she only stopped herself from petting him at the last instant. Jack offered her another one of his smiles. "I know it must be a lot to absorb. We're asking you to change your whole life. But consider this: maybe it will be a change for the better. There's a bankcard on the table by the front door. The code is six-three-eight-four. I don't know what the exact balance is at the moment, but it should be enough to live on for quite some time, if you're frugal. You could take a course or two, if you liked. Lay the groundwork for a career. You'd have the freedom to do that, living here. It can be a win-win situation, if you only embrace it with the right attitude."

Rose tried to imagine the life he was proposing. Four walks a day with the dogs. A bankcard that wasn't hers. Resuming her dental hygiene studies. Nights spent sleeping in the bed where she'd killed Patrick. Or Daniel, rather. And where Daniel had killed some as-yet-unknowable number of young women. Whose bones, Rose assumed, must be lying in the back room, picked clean by the—

"What should we call you?" Jack asked.

"Rose." She spoke without thinking, and she realized as soon as she'd said the word that it implied a degree of consent.

"You can't imagine how tired we were of him, Rose."

"Who?"

"Daniel. The cologne . . . did you smell the cologne? We asked him to stop with it—again and again, we asked. But he wouldn't listen. And Millie, well—you'll see what I mean soon enough—Millie can be difficult in her way. But Daniel had no patience with her. He started to lock her in the hall closet for long periods, and we couldn't accept that sort of behavior, could we? So we decided to find a replacement. And as soon as you walked through the door, we were certain you were the one. You have a kind smile. Has anyone ever told you this? And you smell nice. Do you eat bacon, Rose? Because there's a bacon-y smell to your skin. We all noticed it, right from the start."

Rose stared down at the dog. Her hand kept wanting to touch his head, and finally she surrendered to the temptation. She scratched him behind the ears. Jack shut his eyes with pleasure. "How can you talk?" she asked again.

"It's something with the apartment. Out on the street, we're just like any other dogs."

"But your vocabulary? The phrases you use? Like 'win-win'? How do you know that?'

It wasn't just smiling; Jack could shrug too—a lift of his shoulder, a downward tilt of his head. He did it now. "We watch a lot of TV."

"The others can talk, too?"

"Zeus doesn't like to. But he can, if he wants."

"And Millie?"

"You'll see. She likes it maybe a little too much."

Rose could still call the police. She could walk back to the bedroom, fetch her cell phone, and dial 911. She considered doing this for a few seconds, and then found herself thinking about the bankcard Jack had mentioned. It was difficult to keep from wondering how much money might be in the account.

"One step at a time," Jack said. "That's always the easiest way, isn't it? Start with the sheets. Bag them, throw them out. Then take Zeus and me for a quick walk. By the time we get back, Millie will have cleaned the mattress. You can put fresh sheets on the bed. And then, well, you'll see. It will start to feel like home in no time."

* * *

There was still a lot of blood on the bedroom floor, so Rose spent the first night on the couch in the little family room, just off the kitchen. She kept waking and staring into the darkness, at the shadowy skeleton of the plastic lawn chair across the room, at the TV hanging on the wall, and the empty bookshelf beside it, and wondering where she was—wondering and then remembering, not just where she was, but what had happened. In the morning, her back hurt from the couch's lumpy cushions, and she showered until her fingertips started to wrinkle, and she thought: *I can't do this, I'm going home, I don't care what happens.* But when she climbed out of the shower, Jack was sitting on the mat beside the tub, and Zeus was in the hallway, pacing back and forth, and she realized that they needed to go outside for their morning walk, so she dressed, and leashed the two dogs, and took them around the block. And then she was hungry, but there wasn't any food in the apartment, and she only had four dollars in her wallet, so she took the bankcard from the table beside the front door, and went to the bank on the corner, and punched in six-three-eight-four at the ATM. The card had a woman's name on it: Tabitha O'Rourke. Rose didn't want to wonder too long who this woman might be, or how Jack had come to know the PIN for her account, which had a balance of . . . *whoa* . . . just over nineteen thousand dollars.

Rose withdrew twenty dollars, then immediately thought better of this sum, reinserted the bankcard, and took out two hundred more. She bought some groceries at Fairway and carried them back to the apartment. She made a grilled cheese sandwich, and ate an apple, and took Millie out, and then she came back and sat on the couch with Jack at her feet, and it wasn't that bad, really, not at all. And Rose thought to herself: *Okay, maybe one more night.*

Jack looked up at her from his place on the rug, and he did that thing that was just like a smile.

The next day, Rose took a train out to New Jersey and brought back a suitcase's worth of clothes. She left a note for her mother on the kitchen table, saying she was going to be in the city for a while, dog-sitting for a friend. She spent the evening cleaning the kitchen, and then she used the bankcard to withdraw another hundred dollars, and she bought more food and filled the fridge with it.

A week passed.

Millie finished licking up all the blood in the bedroom—Jack was right; she did a remarkable job—and Rose took to sleeping there. It wasn't nearly as creepy to spend the night in the bed as she'd feared, and the mattress was much more comfortable than the couch's misshapen cushions.

Jack and Millie liked to watch TV in the evening. Rose would sit on the couch with the two dogs, one on either side. Jack often dozed, only half-attending to the screen, but Millie watched with a tense alertness that Rose found a little unsettling. Zeus never took part in these evenings. He spent most of his time hidden in the rear room. He would emerge for his two walks every day, and then trot back down the hallway as soon as they returned, squeezing his big body through the swinging panel that had been cut into the door. All three of the dogs slept in the back room. Rose assumed there still must be some meat left on Daniel's body, and that this was what the dogs were sustaining themselves on, because Jack would prod her to refresh the water bowl, but he hadn't asked her to buy them any food yet. She kept waiting for him to do this.

One morning, Rose woke early, just before dawn, with a full bladder, and after she used the toilet, she crept down the hall to the rear room, and crouched in front of the door, and quietly pushed open the wooden panel, and tried to peek inside. The room was very dim—there didn't appear to be a window—and she could sense more than see the three dogs. It was hard to tell what else was inside the room. There was that smell again: a not-good smell. Rose had a vague sense of tumbled objects—bones, she supposed, though she couldn't be certain—and then she heard the beginning of a growl, low and threatening, as much vibration as actual sound, and she dropped the panel back into place, and retreated quickly to her bedroom.

Rose assumed it must've been Zeus who'd done the growling, because Zeus didn't appear to like her very much. He had a sullen and aloof demeanor; perhaps it was just Rose's impression, but he seemed to make a conscious effort to avoid her gaze. Millie was the opposite—it was difficult to get away from her. And, unlike Zeus, she talked. Jesus, how she talked: she never seemed to shut up. Her days were a continuous outpouring of substance-less chatter. She had obsessions, and she shared them liberally. There were TV shows she'd seen over the years, repetitively, and now she liked to recount their plotlines, complete not only with long excerpts of dialogue, but also with Millie's elaborate analyses of their characters' actions. *Friday Night Lights. The Brady Bunch. Melrose Place* (the original—Rose made the mistake of mentioning the remake, and the next seven hours were consumed by Millie's criticisms of it). *As the World Turns. Sex and the City. The Flintstones. Seinfeld. Gilligan's Island.* The list appeared to be endless. Rose wouldn't have thought it would be possible to fill entire days talking about this sort of thing, but apparently it was quite easy. She took to carrying her iPod around the house, to block out Millie's voice.

And Jack? Jack was her favorite.

In the mornings, before Millie was awake, and with Zeus still hiding in the back room, Rose and Jack would have the apartment to themselves. Jack would curl up on the couch beside Rose while she drank her first cup of coffee, or he'd lie on the mat beside the tub while she showered, or he'd sit on the still unmade bed and watch as she dressed. He called her "Girl." As in: "You need a new pair of tennis shoes, Girl. Those are completely worn out." Or: "You realize what time it is, Girl? Aren't you going to be late?" Or: "Let Millie choose the channel, Girl." Outside the apartment, walking around the neighborhood, he was just a normal dog. But what a beauty! With his lean, muscular frame, his silky coat, and that white patch over his eye . . . people would turn to watch them pass. They called out to Rose:

"Gorgeous dog!" And whenever this happened—almost every afternoon, in other words—Rose would wish that it was just her and Jack living together in New York, that there was no Zeus, and no Millie, and no back room full of bones. She'd wish, too, that Jack couldn't talk, and that she hadn't stabbed Daniel, and that she didn't have to lie awake at night and wonder what had happened to Tabitha O'Rourke. But what she'd wish more than anything else—what she'd wish, and then wish again, and then wish once more, three times for luck—was that her life didn't feel so much like a bomb, ticking its way down toward *boom.*

One morning, in the shower, she thought of something that she probably should've considered much earlier. "What about the rent?" she asked.

Jack was in his usual spot, on the mat beside the tub, licking his paws clean. "What about it?"

"Don't I need to pay it?"

"It's deducted from the bank every month—automatically."

Rose wiped the water from her eyes, stuck her head out from behind the shower curtain, and peered down at the dog. There was a lot of money in Tabitha O'Rourke's account, but not so much that a New York rent wouldn't rapidly erode its balance. "From the same account as the bankcard?"

It wasn't just smiling and shrugging; Jack knew how to shake his head, too. This particular gesture he managed just like a human would. He did it now. "A different one."

"Daniel's?"

Another shake of that bony skull: "It belongs to someone who lived here before Daniel."

Rose ducked her head back behind the curtain, immersed it under the showerhead's torrent of warm water. She didn't ask: *Who?* Because then, when she'd received an answer, she'd need to ask: *What happened to her?* And Rose didn't want to ask that question.

There was something pleasantly narcotizing about her daily routine in the apartment. She woke just after seven, and made herself a cup of coffee, and showered, and dressed, and took Jack and Zeus for their morning walk. Then she ate breakfast, and ran whatever errands needed to be run, and came back around noon to take Millie for her first walk of the day. Sometimes, if the weather was nice, she'd sit on a bench alongside the park, with Millie in her lap—enjoying the silence that came from being outside the mysterious domain of the apartment, and wondering if the words still filled Millie's tiny head even as they sat there in such blissful quiet, if the dog was sifting through the hundred and fifty episodes of *The Twilight Zone* that she'd memorized, or analyzing the strengths and weaknesses of the various guest stars who'd appeared on *Fantasy Island* over the years. Then it was home for lunch, and sometimes a nap, or sometimes—when Rose was feeling ambitious—a yoga class at the tiny gym just down the block. At six PM, she took Jack and Millie to the dog park. This was her favorite part of the day. She'd throw a tennis ball for Jack, and Jack would fetch the ball, then drop it at her feet, and wait for her to throw it again, and again, and again, his body quivering with pleasure in this activity, again, and again, and again, until Rose's shoulder began to ache with the exertion. That was when things could feel almost normal to Rose, at dusk in the dog park, with the ball bouncing down the gentle incline toward the river, and Jack sprinting away in pursuit.

At some point, of course, the money was going to run out.

At some point, Rose would have to deal with the back room. She'd need to break down the door. She'd need to think of a way to dispose of the piled bones.

Mostly, though, Rose did her best not to think too far beyond the present moment. This was what Jack advised her to do. He assured her it was how Buddhists lived—and quite happily, too. Rose liked to believe she was getting pretty good at it.

After the dog park, she'd fix dinner, do the dishes, retire with Jack and Millie to the living room for the nightly dose of TV. Then she'd take Millie and Zeus out for their midnight walk, and brush her teeth, and wash her face, and pull on her pajamas, and climb into bed. As easily as that another day was done.

And another.

And another

Sitting on a bench at the dog run one evening, Rose thought of what Jack had said that first morning: *It can be a win-win situation, if you only embrace it with the right attitude.* She'd finished with the ball throwing for the evening; Jack was lying at her feet, panting from his exercise. Millie was perched on the bench beside her, watching the other dogs play. This was in the middle of May, and the air smelled heavy with pollen. Rose shut her eyes, breathed deep: *win-win.*

* * *

It was only a day or two later, a little after midnight, that Jack said: "Just a heads-up? Your rent's due tomorrow."

Rose was in the bathroom, brushing her teeth. She leaned, spit the toothpaste into the sink, twisted off the water, then turned to look at Jack. He was sitting in the bathroom doorway. "I thought it was withdrawn from the bank account," she said.

"Not the apartment's rent. *Your* rent. As a subletter."

"I have to pay rent?"

"Nothing in life comes for free, Girl."

Rose considered that for a moment, then shook the water from her toothbrush, set it in the glass beside the faucet. "How much?"

"It's not about money."

"It's not?"

Jack shook his head. "It's about keeping us fed—Millie and Zeus and me."

Rose turned the water back on, waited for it to get warm enough for her to wash her face. "You want me to buy some dog food?"

"We want you to bring someone home with you."

Rose was bending toward the sink, cupping water in her hands, but she stopped at this, pivoted to look at Jack again. She knew what he meant, but she didn't want to know, and this desire was strong enough so that, for a moment at least, it almost felt as if she actually *didn't* know. "I don't understand."

Jack gave her his exactly-like-a-smile thing, with his tail and head and ears. "Yes, you do," he said.

Then he stood and walked off down the hall. She heard the dog door creak as he nudged it open and vanished into the rear room for the night.

*   *   *

In the morning, sitting on the couch, drinking the day's first, pre-shower, pre-walk cup of coffee, she told Jack she wasn't going to do it—not now, not ever.

"You're acting as if you have a choice here," Jack said. "This situation would unfold so much more smoothly, if you accepted that you don't."

"It's not that I won't do it," Rose said, hating the hesitancy in her voice, how it made her sound as if she were attempting to negotiate, rather than issuing an ultimatum, which was her intention. "It's that I can't."

"You've already done it once."

"That was self-defense. That was panic. That was—"

"Exactly. Think how much easier it will be now. When you know what you're doing."

"I'll cook you whatever you want. Chicken. Steak. Fish. Do you like—"

"Remember when you asked how we can talk? And I said it was the apartment? That was only half the answer. It's also what we eat. What we've been fed."

"So stop fucking talking! Eat normal food and become a normal dog. Would that be such a terrible thing? What's so great about speaking, anyway?"

"You bring someone home. You have sex with this person. And then you kill them. That's your rent."

"I have *sex* with them?"

Jack nodded.

"Why do I need to have sex with them?"

"It tenderizes the meat."

"You're kidding, right? This is some sort of joke?"

"There's a ticking clock here, Girl. Just so you're warned."

"Meaning?"

"You won't like Zeus when he's hungry."

Rose had finished her coffee by now. She stood up, started for the kitchen. "Fuck Zeus," she said, as she left the room. "Fuck Millie. And fuck you. I'm not going to do it."

She meant this, too. Or at least she thought she did. Because Jack was right: Rose still believed she had a choice in the matter. She brought home two packages of chicken breasts that afternoon, three cans of cream of chicken soup, a bag of potatoes, a bundle of carrots, an onion, and some bouillon cubes, and she spent the evening making her mother's chicken stew. She ladled out a dish of it and set it down beside the dog's water bowl.

Let them smell it, she thought. *Let them taste it.*

But the dogs ignored her offering. By the following afternoon, the stew was starting to have an odd, jelly-like appearance, so she threw it out, and washed the dish, and ladled in a fresh serving, and placed this beside their water.

She'd cooked enough to get through four days of this ritual, and when the stew ran out, she bought two sirloin steaks. She grilled one and set it on a plate beside their water, and when the dogs ignored this, too, she took the second steak out of the fridge and set it down uncooked, and on the seventh day, when they'd ignored this, too, she ordered Szechuan beef from a Chinese restaurant, and tried that. She could sense they were hungry—they were growing short-tempered and listless. Jack had stopped chasing the ball when they went to the dog park; one of the other owners even asked Rose if there was something wrong with him. She was certain she just had to persist, that eventually they'd relent. They'd begin to eat, and once they began, it would be difficult for them to stop. Rose didn't know how long it would take for them to lose their ability to talk, but once they did, she could force open the door to the rear room and clean out the bones. And once she'd cleaned out the bones, she could leave the apartment—she could go back to her old life. She'd have to figure out what to do about the dogs, of course, but this shouldn't be that difficult. She could take Zeus and Millie to the pound, and maybe keep Jack for herself, bring him with her back to—

She was at the kitchen sink, washing her dinner plates, when she heard a noise behind her, and she turned to find Zeus entering the kitchen. He shuffled toward the bowl of Szechuan beef, and Rose felt her heart rate jump—the throb of blood in her veins, urgent and hopeful. She watched Zeus sniff the bowl. He turned and looked at her.

"Go on," she said. "Try it."

Zeus gave the bowl a sharp smack with his paw, sending it skittering to the far side of the kitchen, the Szechuan beef spilling over the linoleum.

"Bad dog . . .!" Rose shouted. "Bad dog . . .!"

Zeus crouched, began to empty his bladder, staring at Rose the entire time. Then he turned and walked slowly out of the kitchen, an immense puddle of urine spreading across the floor behind him, mixing with the spilled food. Jack was watching from the doorway. "You're a week late now, Girl," he said. "Which means you'll have to pay a penalty."

Rose ignored him. She grabbed a roll of paper towels, began to sop up the mess. Did Jack really think that Zeus peeing in the kitchen was such a terrible thing? That it would pressure her into bringing a stranger home for them to eat? A stranger she'd need to fuck first, to "tenderize" his "meat?" Because if that was what he really thought . . . well, he had another thing coming.

*   *   *

But that wasn't what Jack thought—not at all, as it turned out.

*   *   *

It happened later that night. Much later.

Rose was asleep. She was lying on her stomach. The room was dark, and someone was on top of her, holding her down. Someone else was roughly yanking at her underwear. Rose was waking up—not slowly, but all at once—and the person on top of her wasn't a person, it was Zeus, and the person yanking at her underwear wasn't a person, it was Millie, and Jack was there, too, standing beside the bed, watching, and she heard a voice, but it wasn't Jack's and it wasn't Millie's, and she knew it had to be Zeus's, a deep, angry voice, that said: "You bitch. You fucking bitch."

Millie got Rose's underwear down, and Zeus was thrusting at her— growling and thrusting—no, that wasn't it, that wasn't it at all, he wasn't thrusting *at* her . . . he was thrusting *into* her.

Rose screamed.

"You bitch," Zeus said. "You fucking bitch."

He kept saying these words, over and over, in rhythm with his thrusts. This went on for a full minute, maybe two, an excruciatingly long stretch of time, and finally Rose felt the dog come inside her. Then he leaned down, growling again, and bit her left shoulder. He clamped into her with his teeth and he twisted and tugged, and twisted and tugged, and then he tore a hunk of flesh from her body.

Rose was still screaming.

Her right arm was trapped under her torso, but she was swinging with the left one, trying to land a blow, flailing, open-handed, and then something grabbed at her, arresting the arm's motion. There was a snapping sound, like a branch breaking. This last part happened so quickly that it was finished before Rose could even register the full horror: Jack had caught her hand in his mouth . . . Jack had bitten off her pinkie. The pain took a long moment to arrive. Rose was fumbling for the lamp, turning it on, blood running down her back from the wound on her shoulder, blood spigotting from her hand, Zeus's semen spilling out between her legs.

Oh my god oh my god oh my god . . .

Jack and Zeus had already vanished from the room. Only Millie remained, scurrying about on the floor beside the bed, frantically licking at the spilt blood.

*   *   *

Rose sat for three hours in the Mount Sinai Emergency Room (a towel wrapped around her hand, another towel clamped to her shoulder) before a nurse finally called her name. She was led into an examination room, told to take off her clothes and put on one of those hospital robes that tie in the back, and then she waited for another forty-five minutes before a tired-looking Indian woman entered. This woman introduced herself as Dr. Cheema. She started to set out a collection of medical supplies on a metal tray, and she asked Rose what had happened.

"I was attacked by a dog. Three, actually."

Dr. Cheema pursed her lips and clucked her tongue, but didn't seem especially interested or impressed. "Do you know if they've been vaccinated for rabies?"

"I think so."

"Can you find out for certain?"

"I can ask them."

"The owners?"

Rose thought to herself: *No, the dogs.* But she didn't say these words; she just nodded.

Dr. Cheema picked up a syringe, inserted it into a small ampule, pulled back on the plunger. "Okay, then. Shall we start with your hand?"

If the doctor had probed even a little further, Rose believed she would've told her everything. She would've told her about the apartment, and Daniel—she would've even tried to explain the talking-dogs part of the story. She didn't care; she was past caring. But Dr. Cheema didn't probe. She focused on Rose's wounds, flushing them clean, stitching them up. The shadows under the doctor's eyes were so dark they looked like tattoos, and Rose could sense her fighting a repetitive impulse to yawn—the involuntary inhalation, the stiffening of her body, the clenching of her jaw. It was six in the morning, and a man was shouting somewhere down the hall, telling someone to fuck off, to get their fucking hands off him, shouting this—screaming, really—and then suddenly falling silent. Rose didn't want to picture what was happening—not to the man, and not to herself, either. Dr. Cheema was standing behind her, willing her body not to yawn, and she'd injected something into Rose's shoulder so that Rose no longer felt any pain, just a tugging sensation each time the doctor stapled another suture across the wound. Rose was given a bottle of antibiotics, a bottle of painkillers, and a slip of paper with a surgeon's name on it: Dr. Thomas Hawthorne. She was supposed to call this man later that day and make an appointment so that Dr. Hawthorne could address the damage to Rose's hand, which looked like a paw now—a polar bear's paw—encased in its white wrapping.

They sent her home.

Rose didn't have enough money with her for another cab, so she dry-swallowed two of the painkillers and started walking west, into Central Park. The sun had risen, and the joggers were out. Rose tried to imagine what life must be like for these people, up early before work, pulling on their brightly colored outfits, tying the laces on their shoes, heading out into the dawn, the sweat rising on their skin, the shower afterward, the healthy breakfast, and then onward into the well-oiled machinery of their days. Even at the best of times, Rose could feel an aversion to people like this. But now, with Zeus's semen still leaking out of her, dampening her underwear, with the pain in her hand and shoulder both there and not there (the pills were keeping it at bay, but Rose could feel how weak they were, how quickly they'd fade from her system, and how restive the pain was, waiting for its moment), with her sense of fatigue like a companion, limping along at her side, leaning more and more heavily upon her with every step, what she felt for these strangers running past was something closer to hatred. She would never be like them. She would never even know people like them. She thought of the young men who showed up at shopping malls with loaded rifles, and she believed she understood why.

Her hand was beginning to throb. At some point very soon it was going to become unbearable. And yet Rose would have to find a way to bear it, because that was what it meant to be alive. She wasn't going to return to the apartment. Her body decided this before her mind: she realized she was walking south through the park, rather than west. Rose didn't have money for a train ticket, but this didn't matter. She could get on the train and then, when the conductor came to punch her ticket, she could pretend to have lost her wallet. She knew that if she looked distressed enough—*and what could be easier today?*—the conductor would end up comforting instead of scolding her. She'd have to get off the train in Newark, but then she could just catch the next one coming through, and repeat the pantomime. And so on, station by station, all the way home. It would take a lot longer to reach her destination, but she'd get there in the end. She'd done this once before, a year ago, after she'd been pickpocketed, dancing at Cielo. When she got to the Dunellen stop, she could call her mother collect from the station's payphone, and beg her to come and pick her up. If she cried—*and what could be easier today?*—she was certain she could get her mother to do it.

And then?

She supposed it would all play out exactly as Jack had originally threatened. The dogs would bark and whimper and howl until a neighbor took notice. The neighbor would call the landlord. The landlord would contact the police. The police would break down the door—not just the door to the apartment, but also the door to the rear room. They'd find the bones there, and the apartment would become a crime scene. Neighbors would describe Rose to the police; the techs would find her fingerprints, her DNA. Rose didn't know how long all of this would take, but she knew it wouldn't be long enough to count as a respite. Soon enough, she'd be in a jail cell. But she didn't care; she'd been past caring in the Emergency Room, and now she was even past the point of not caring, past the point of thinking at all—she was just walking, with her fatigue shuffling along beside her, and her hand throbbing in rhythm with her heart, and her underwear like a damp hand fondling her groin.

She was near the Reservoir when the first dog lunged at her. It was a little terrier mix, twenty pounds of clenched muscle on the taut end of a leash, growling and barking and snapping its jaws as Rose moved by, the owner staring in surprise, saying: "JoJo! Stop it! What's gotten into you?"

And then, just a little further down the path, a black Lab, carrying a tennis ball in its mouth, loping along with a happy-go-lucky air; the dog dropped the ball, and leapt toward Rose as she drew near, growling and slathering and pawing at the dirt, and its owner had the same startled reaction as the terrier's, straining to hold the Lab back, saying: "Ichabod! What the fuck . . .?"

A third dog, then a fourth, then three chihuahuas on the same leash, all of them straining toward Rose in a state of fury, teeth bared, and Rose realized in a muddy sort of way what must be happening. If she was right—and she was certain she was—then the park was the wrong place for her to be, the wrong place entirely. After all Rose had been through, she wouldn't have thought she had the energy to run, but she was scared, so adrenaline was in the fuel mix, and run she did: east now, toward the Metropolitan Museum, toward Fifth Avenue. If she could just get to the exit, if she could just—

She heard a man shout: "Bo . . .!"

And then she heard the barking—deeper than the Labrador's barking, and the terrier's, and the chihuahuas'—deep enough to force Rose to
glance back over her shoulder. Bo was a pit bull. He was fifteen yards away,
sprinting toward her, his leash bouncing along behind him in the dirt. He'd
broken free of his owner's grip.

"Bo . . .!"

The owner was running, too, but the owner was overweight and out of
shape, and still forty yards away.

"Bo . . .!"

Bo hit Rose in the chest with both front paws, knocking her onto her
back. She was trying to push him away, but he was far too strong.

"Bo . . .!"

Rose felt the dog's breath for an instant, the damp heat of it against her
face, and then he had his jaws around her throat, pressing her downward,
cutting off her air. *I'll go back,* she thought, screaming the words inside her
head. Somehow, she knew this was the key that would free her: *I'll go back!
I'll go back! I'll go back!*

Instantly, Bo let her go.

The owner was there—panting, flushed, sweaty. "I'm so sorry. I'm so
sorry." He grabbed Bo's leash, gave it an angry, belated tug, his hands visibly
shaking. The dog was cowering, hunch-shouldered. A crowd had gathered,
a little clot of wide-eyed bystanders, staring at Rose, at Bo, at Bo's owner,
who kept giving those angry tugs to Bo's leash: "He's never . . . Jesus . . . I'm
so sorry . . . Are you—?"

But Rose was on her feet now. She was in motion again, and she didn't
look back when Bo's owner called after her. She was running with her
wounded hand cradled protectively against her chest—running west, running for the apartment.

*   *   *

The dogs were sleeping in the back room when Rose returned. She took a
hot bath, scrubbing one-handed at her vagina, her wounded hand tied up
in a plastic bag, to keep the bandages dry. After her bath, she swallowed
another of the painkillers and dropped into a drug-heavy sleep on the couch.
The sun reached the living room window in the early afternoon, and it fell
on Rose with enough vigor to rouse her into a murky half-consciousness.
She thought to herself: *Maybe I can kill them.* She wasn't confident she
could manage it with the knife—especially not when it came to Zeus. But
what about a gun? Shouldn't she be able to buy a pistol somewhere? Take
a train outside the city, get off in one of those small, NRA-friendly towns
upstate, find a—

"You realize we can sense what you're thinking, right?"

Rose lifted her head. Jack was lying under the window, watching her.

"If there were a way to avoid doing what you need to do, don't you think Daniel would've thought of it?"

Rose lowered her head back onto the couch's cushion, shut her eyes. She might've slept some more then, or maybe not—it was hard to tell—but Jack's voice kept coming, and either she was dreaming it, or it was real. Some part of Rose's mind was struggling to decide if it mattered which was true, dream or reality; a little engine inside her brain was assiduously chipping away at this question, but somehow never managing to reach a conclusion. Dream or reality, Jack was offering Rose arguments she could use, if arguments were what she needed.

"Would you kill a cow for us? Because that's what you did when you put those steaks down on the floor. There was a dead cow in the pipeline that led to that particular moment, and you bore some responsibility for it, didn't you? And if that's okay, doesn't it seem like it should be okay to *actually* kill the cow—with your own hands? Not only okay, but maybe also more honest? And if it's okay to kill that cow with your own hands, why isn't it okay to kill a human? Doesn't that seem like a slightly self-serving moral scale you folks have developed for yourselves? And can you understand how from *our* perspective—Millie's and Zeus's and mine—there's no difference whatsoever?"

Rose could smell urine, and she realized she hadn't taken the dogs out since the previous evening. Now the day was slipping away from her, the sunlight shifting slowly across the floor, then departing altogether. Without the sun, the room grew chilly. Rose thought of moving to the bedroom, burrowing under the covers, but this would necessitate finding sufficient energy to rise and walk, and she worried her legs might not cooperate in such an endeavor, so she just rolled over instead, pressing her body up against the back of the couch, feeling as if she were about to start shivering, but then not shivering, not yet.

"We saved your life. Have you factored that into the equation? If we hadn't warned you, Daniel would've cut your throat. And now? When it's time to pay us back? Look how you're acting. You're a week late, Girl. A week and a day. You don't see a problem with this?"

There was a noise behind her, a creak in the floor, and she rolled over to find Zeus standing beside the couch, his huge shaggy head only a few inches from her face. Rose tried to tell herself this part was definitely a dream, but she could smell the big dog's breath—a rotten-tooth heaviness in the air—and was that really the sort of detail that occurred in a dream? She stared at the dog, waiting to see what he was going to do, and feeling too weak to thwart whatever it might be; then the floor creaked again, and Zeus turned and walked from the room, taking his smell with him.

"Think of someone hateful. That usually helps with the first one. Someone you'd *like* to stab."

Rose was hungry. She had to pee. Her hand felt as if a great weight were lying upon it: an immense slab of steel, vibrating slightly.

"Come on, Girl. Everyone hates someone."

A terribly cold slab of steel—or maybe terribly hot? Rose couldn't decide which; she knew only that it was one extreme or another. And not vibrating: it was bouncing. Or no, not bouncing either: it was *hammering*. Her painkillers were in her purse, and her purse was on the far side of the room. She stared at it, trying to will it closer, but it didn't work.

"If you can't think of someone hateful, think of someone weak."

The room was dark when Rose finally forced herself into a sitting position. It was almost eight o'clock. From sitting to standing, from standing to walking—each transition posed its own challenges. She brought her purse into the kitchen and filled a glass of water at the tap and drank the water, swallowing another painkiller in the process. She was only supposed to have one pill every twelve hours, and this was already her fourth. She supposed it was probably a bad idea, but she also knew this wasn't the worst thing happening in her life right now. She wished it were.

If she didn't do anything to stop them, the dogs were going to attack her again that night. Rose was certain of this.

She ate a peanut butter sandwich and drank a glass of milk and changed her clothes, and by the time she left the apartment, a little after nine, she had something almost like a plan in mind—or no, maybe not a plan, but a destination at least, which felt like the next best thing.

*   *   *

Rose had gone through a six-month stretch, just after she turned eighteen, when she'd thought she might like girls as much as boys. While exploring this question, she'd stumbled into an on-again, off-again entanglement with a friend of hers named Rhonda. And it was Rhonda who had first taken her to a lesbian bar in the village called the Cubbyhole.

Even without her wounded hand, Rose had worried about bringing a guy home. She wasn't strong—she was skinny, and physically timid—and the idea of engaging in a life-or-death struggle with a man filled her with dread. She'd have the knife, of course, and she'd have the element of surprise, but it still didn't seem like enough to guarantee success. So her plan, if you could call it that, was to sit in the Cubbyhole, and hope a woman would decide to pick her up—a petite woman, preferably—the smaller, the better.

If you can't think of someone hateful, think of someone weak.

Rose sat on a stool at the bar, sipping a tequila-and-soda, which started out seeming like a brilliant choice, but then began to feel more and more misguided with every sip, and twenty-five minutes passed in a slow drip, and she thought to herself: *This isn't going to work.* She'd go back to the apartment unaccompanied, and Zeus would rape her again, and Jack would bite off another finger, and Millie would scurry about on the bedroom floor, licking up the blood, and Dr. Cheema would stare at her with those tired eyes and purse her lips and cluck her tongue and stitch her back up again, and Bo would be waiting in the park—

"Is this stool taken?"

The baited hook, the cast line, the long, drowsy wait . . . and then that sudden thrill when the fish strikes.

Her name was Amber. She was too tall, too lean, too fit—a beautiful girl, in her early twenties, with a full mouth, and green eyes, and red hair down to the middle of her back. She was dressed in jeans, cowboy boots, a sky blue hoodie. She had a tiny stud in her nose—it looked like a diamond—and Rose had to will herself consciously not to stare at it.

When Amber asked about her bandaged hand, Rose told her she'd caught it in a car door. Amber winced and leaned forward to touch Rose's wrist. "You poor thing," she said, and she was looking at Rose, *truly* looking. Rose tried to remember the last time someone had offered her this gift. The doctor hadn't looked at her, not really, and her Craigslist dates had never ventured it, and her mother—

"Another round?" the bartender asked.

Rose didn't resist when Amber offered to pay. She twisted on her stool to get a better look at this stranger. Amber's hair wasn't just red, it was thick and curly; maybe it had something to do with the painkillers and the tequila, but Rose wanted to touch it, wanted to take big handfuls of it and press them against her face. The two of them held eyes for a long moment, and then Amber started to laugh. "You're an odd one, aren't you?" she asked.

Rose took a swallow from her drink, draining half of it, and then she leaned forward and kissed Amber, and Amber didn't flinch: Amber kissed her back. Her mouth tasted of cinnamon. Rose buried her un-bandaged hand into that luscious red hair; she grabbed a fistful and held on tight, feeling lonely and frightened and sad. She never would've imagined herself to be a terrible person, but it turned out that she was, because just look at the unforgivable thing she was about to do. This girl wasn't hateful. And she probably wasn't weak. But she was kind—and Rose despised herself for sensing that this might be enough.

She pulled away from the kiss, leaned to whisper into Amber's ear: "Will you come home with me?"

* * *

The gray door, the three locks, the panting, whimpering dogs . . .

"Holy shit," Amber said. "Look at these guys! You didn't tell me you had dogs. I *love* dogs." She crouched to pet them, bending to let Millie lick her face.

"Oh, Girl," Jack said. "She's perfect. We knew you'd come through."

Rose remembered Daniel, his sense of urgency that night, his nerves, the way he'd hurried her down the hallway to the bedroom, just like she was hurrying Amber now, kicking free of her shoes, pulling off her clothes, tumbling the girl onto the bed. Amber laughed: "Easy there, hustler."

It wasn't just her mouth that tasted of cinnamon; her skin did, too. Her vagina was freshly waxed, and for a moment Rose couldn't stop herself from thinking of the dolls she'd owned as a child, the hairless fold between the legs. She was drunk, and overmedicated, and she only half-knew what she was attempting—just enough to be certain that she was being too rough, and too fast, doing everything to Amber that she'd hated when guys had done it to her, and Amber kept grabbing her hand and trying to guide her, and Millie was right beside the bed, panting and pacing, and saying: "Fuck her! Fuck her good! Use your mouth!"

"Is she okay?" Amber asked.

Rose stopped what she was doing, lifted her head: "What do you mean?"

"That panting and pacing. Is she hungry? That's what my sister's dog does when she's really hungry."

Rose heard Jack give a little laugh. He and Zeus were in the doorway to the room, watching. "She's all right," Rose said. "She's always like that."

"Stop talking!" Millie's voice had taken on a pleading, whining quality inside Rose's head. "Keep fucking. Fuck the bitch! Fuck her good!"

Afterward, once Amber had come, maybe for real, and Rose had done her best to fake it, and they were lying there in each other's arms, Rose arrived at a decision: she couldn't do it—she *wouldn't* do it. Her hand had stopped hurting for a bit, but now it was making up for this dereliction with a compensatory vengeance. Rose plucked the pill bottle off the night table, took another painkiller.

"What are those?" Amber asked.

"Oxy," Rose said. "For the pain." And she held out the bottle. "*Mi casa, su casa.*"

Amber laughed again—she had a pretty laugh. "I *knew* I liked you." She presented her palm, and Rose tapped a pill into it.

This had been part of Rose's almost-a-plan, which she was now certain—or nearly certain—she couldn't (wouldn't) follow through on.

They turned out the light.

Rose counted to sixty in her head, and then she told Amber that she needed to use the bathroom. This, too, had been part of the plan that she couldn't (wouldn't) follow through on: she would go to the bathroom and wait for the girl to fall asleep, and when she came back, she'd quietly ease open the night table drawer, lift out the knife, and do what needed to be done.

Rose tiptoed from the darkened room and headed down the hall. Millie followed her, panting ever more heavily: "Where are you going? Get the knife! Stab her! Cut her up!"

Rose shut the bathroom door on the little dog. She sat on the closed lid of the toilet and tried not to feel the pain in her hand, tried not to feel anything at all, in fact, thinking *couldn't* and *wouldn't*, and *can't* and *won't*. At some point, she began to lose track of time. Her head kept dipping— she'd drunk too much tequila, swallowed too many pills. It seemed as if she must've waited long enough by now: Amber ought to be asleep. Not that this mattered, of course (because of *couldn't* and *wouldn't*, because of *can't* and *won't*).

Rose pulled open the door, stepped quietly into the hall. Millie was gone; she'd returned to the bedroom. The light was on in there again, and Amber—inexplicably—was still wide-awake, sitting against the headboard, staring at Rose, who stood in the doorway, hesitating. Millie was dozing in the armchair. Zeus was asleep at the base of the bed. Jack was beside him, his head on his paws, his eyes shut. It was odd: the dogs were never all asleep—not out here, at least, away from the back room, especially not Zeus.

Thinking this, Rose knew what was about to happen.

She should've turned and sprinted for the door. It was all reflex from this point on, though, and Rose's reflexes had never been the best part of her.

The dogs began to bark even before she was in motion.

She was running for the bedside drawer.

But Amber—kind, green-eyed Amber, with her long red curls, her cinnamon-flavored skin, her Barbie doll vagina—Amber, that lovely girl . . . she got there first.

AUTHOR BIOS

NATHAN BALLINGRUD: I was born in Massachusetts in 1970, but spent most of my life in the South. I studied literature at the University of North Carolina at Chapel Hill and at the University of New Orleans. Among other things, I've been a cook on oil rigs and barges, a bouncer at a strip club, and a bartender in New Orleans. My first book—*North American Lake Monsters: stories,* from Small Beer Press—won the Shirley Jackson Award, and was shortlisted for the World Fantasy, British Fantasy, and Bram Stoker Awards. Now I live in Asheville, NC, with my daughter in an apartment across from the French Broad River. Freight trains pass by my window at night.

DANI BROWN: Born in Oxford, UK but raised in Massachusetts, USA, Dani Brown is the author of *Dark Roast* and *Reptile* out from JEA. She is also the author of *My Lovely Wife, Middle Age Rae of Fucking Sunshine, Toenails*, and *Welcome to New Edge Hill* out from Morbidbooks. She's the person responsible for the baby blood bath that is *Stara* out from Azoth Khem Publishing. She has written various short stories across a range of publications. There's always more coming soon. Upcoming releases to include "Night of the Penguins" and the first in the *Stef and Tucker* series. She's a bit of a party girl, which is weird because she isn't much of a people person, but her adventures often end up with her at a party doing something stupid. Cats aren't very fun at parties. Cats are better than people. If something sparkles, she loves it, unless it is a vampire. Her jealous, spiteful cat sometimes wears a sparkly collar. She tries her best to be a Placebo fan girl, but fails at it, somewhat miserably.

OCTAVIA CADE has sold stories to *Clarkesworld, Shimmer,* and *Asimov's,* amongst others. Her creepy novella, *The Convergence of Fairy Tales*, was published by The Book Smugglers and won best novella at the Sir Julius Vogel awards, and her food and horror columns have recently been published as a collection. She attended Clarion West 2016.

DANIEL MARC CHANT is an author of strange fiction. His passion for H. P. Lovecraft & the films of John Carpenter inspired him to produce intense, cinematic stories with a sinister edge. Daniel launched his début *Burning House* in 2015, swiftly following with the Lovecraft-inspired *Maldición*. His most recent books *Mr. Robespierre, Aimee Bancroft and The Singularity Storm* and *Into Fear* have garnered universal praise. He has been featured in the anthology collections *Cthulhu Lies Dreaming* from Ghostwoods Books, *Death By Chocolate* from KnightsWatch Press, *VS.* from Shadow Work Publishing,

Bah! Humbug! from Matt Shaw Publishing, and *The Stars at My Door* from April Moon Books. Daniel also created *The Black Room Manuscripts*, a charity horror anthology & is a founder of UK independent genre publisher The Sinister Horror Company. You can find him amongst the nameless ones on twitter @ danielmarcchant, and at facebook/danielmarcchant. He doesn't bite. Much.

TIM CURRAN lives in Michigan and is the author of the novels *Skin Medicine, Hive, Dead Sea, and Skull Moon.* Upcoming projects include the novels Resurrection, *The Devil Next Door*, and *Hive 2*, as well as *The Corpse King*, a novella from Cemetery Dance, and *Four Rode Out*, a collection of four weird-western novellas by Curran, Tim Lebbon, Brian Keene, and Steve Vernon. His short stories have appeared in such magazines as City Slab, *Flesh&Blood, Book of Dark Wisdom*, and *Inhuman*, as well as anthologies such as *Flesh Feast, Shivers IV, High Seas Cthulhu*, and, *Vile Things*. Find him on the web at: www.corpseking.com

DOUGLAS FORD lives and works on the west coast of Florida, just off an exit made famous by a Jack Ketchum short story. His weird, dark fiction has appeared in *Dark Moon Digest, The Horror Zine, and DarkFuse Magazine*, as well as other small press publications. He lives with his wife who gives him loving support and four cats who merely tolerate him.

GLENN GRAY's stories have appeared in a wide range of online and print magazines and anthologies. His story collection, *The Little Boy Inside and Other Stories* was published by Concord ePress. Apart from his writing, Glenn is a physician specializing in Radiology. He lives in New York.

RYAN HARDING is the author of *Genital Grinder* and co-author of *Reincarnage* with Jason Taverner, both from Deadite Press, and co-author of *Header 3* with Edward Lee. He contributed to the multi-author collaborations *Sixty-Five Stirrup Iron Road* and *The Devil's Guests.* His stories have also appeared in the anthologies *Masters of Horror, DOA 3, Into Painfreak, In Laymon's Terms*, and *Excitable Boys;* the chapbooks *Partners in Chyme* (with Edward Lee), *A Darker Dawning* and *A Darker Dawning 2: Reign in Black*; and the magazines *Splatterpunk* and *The Magazine of Bizarro Fiction*. Upcoming projects include a novel with Bryan Smith and the sequel to *Reincarnage* with Jason Taverner. Amazon author page: https://www.amazon.com/-/e/B01N1HSDZ5

SEAN PATRICK HAZLETT: I am a technology analyst and Army veteran living in the San Francisco Bay Area, where I consider writing fiction as therapy that pays for itself. My fiction has appeared in *Writers of the Future: Volume 33, Abyss & Apex, Grimdark Magazine, Sci Phi Journal, Unnerving Magazine, Weirdbook, Speculate!, Fictionvale Magazine, Perihelion, The Overcast, Plasma*

Frequency Magazine, Stupefying Stories, NewMyths.com, Kasma SF, Mad Scientist Journal, Outposts of Beyond, Digital Fiction, and *The Colored Lens.* Others are scheduled to appear in *Galaxy's Edge, among others.*

BRIAN HODGE is one of those people who always has to be making something. So far, he's made eleven novels, over 125 shorter works, and five full-length collections. Recent and upcoming titles include his latest novel, *Dawn of Heresies*; *I'll Bring You the Birds From Out of the Sky*, a novella of cosmic horror paired with folk art illustrations; and his next collection, *The Immaculate Void*, coming in early 2018. Two recent Lovecraftian novelettes have been optioned for feature film and a TV series. He lives in Colorado, where he also likes to make music and photographs; loves everything about organic gardening except the thieving squirrels; and trains in Krav Maga and kickboxing, which are of no use at all against the squirrels. Connect through his web site (www.brianhodge.net), Twitter (@BHodgeAuthor), or Facebook (www.facebook.com/brianhodgewriter).

ADAM HOWE writes the twisted fiction your mother warned you about. He lives in London with his partner, their daughter, and a hellhound named Gino. Writing as Garrett Addams, his short story "Jumper" was chosen by Stephen King as the winner of the international *On Writing* contest, and published in the paperback/digital editions of King's book. His short fiction has appeared in places like Nightmare Magazine, Thuglit, and Mythic Delirium. He is the author of *Black Cat Mojo, Die Dog or Eat the Hatchet,* and *Tijuana Donkey Showdown*. His Honey Badger Press publishing label recently released *Wrestle Maniacs*, an anthology of dark wrestling fiction featuring a murderer's row of today's best indie writers. Up next: *Scapegoat*, an occult thriller co-written with James Newman . . . Stalk him at Goodreads, on Facebook, and Twitter @Adam_G_Howe

ROBERT LEVY is an author of unsettling stories and plays whose work has been seen Off-Broadway. A Harvard graduate subsequently trained as a forensic psychologist, his work has been called "frank and funny" (Time Magazine), "idiosyncratic and disarming" (The New York Times), "ambitious and clever" (Variety), "smart" (The Magazine of Fantasy & Science Fiction) and "bloody brave" (the UK's SFX Magazine). His first novel, the contemporary dark fairy tale *The Glittering World* (Gallery/Simon & Schuster) was a finalist for both the Lambda Literary Award and the Shirley Jackson Award. Shorter work has appeared in *Black Static, Shadows & Tall Trees*, and *The Best Horror of the Year*, among others. Robert lives in his native Brooklyn near a toxic canal, where he is awaiting his mutant powers to develop any day now. He can also be found at TheRobertLevy.com.

BRACKEN MACLEOD has survived car crashes, a near drowning, being shot at, a parachute malfunction, and the bar exam. So far, the only incident that has resulted in persistent nightmares is the bar exam. He is the author of the novels *Mountain Home*, *Come to Dust*, and *Stranded*, which was a finalist for the Bram Stoker Award, and a collection of short fiction, *13 Views of the Suicide Woods*. He lives outside of Boston with his wife and son, where he is at work on his next novel.

LUCIANO MARANO is a newspaper reporter, photographer and author. His award-winning journalism, both written and photographic, has appeared in a number of regional and national publications. His short fiction has also been featured in several digital, print and audio outlets. A U.S. Navy veteran, he enjoys running, craft beer, movies (especially horror and documentary films), traveling to new places and oldies music. His favorite book is *Something Wicked This Way Comes*. His favorite movie is *Point Break*. If he could have any superpower, he'd choose Wolverine-style healing abilities (or maybe just the ability to grow Wolverine-style sideburns). He lives near Seattle, Washington. Get to know him better at www.luciano-marano.com, or visit citmyway101.wordpress.com where he blogs, albeit sporadically.

ANNIE NEUGEBAUER is a short story author, novelist, and poet with work appearing and forthcoming in more than a hundred publications such as *Cemetery Dance*, *Apex*, and *Black Static*. She's a member of the Horror Writers Association and a columnist for Writer Unboxed and LitReactor. She lives in Texas with two crazy cute cats and a husband who's exceptionally well-prepared for the zombie apocalypse. You can visit her at www.AnnieNeugebauer.com for news, blogs, organizational tools for writers, and more.

RAMIRO PEREZ DE PEREDA: Born in Cuba in 1941, Ramiro Perez de Pereda has seen it all. Growing up in a time when then-democratic Cuba was experiencing unprecedented foreign investment, he was exposed to the U.S. pop culture items of the day. Among them: pulp fiction magazines, which young Ramiro avidly read and collected. Far and away, his favorites were the Conan the Barbarian stories by Robert E. Howard. Ramiro, now retired from the corporate life, is a grandfather of five. He devotes himself to his family, his writing, and the occasional pen-and-ink sketch. He writes poetry and short fiction under the name R. Perez de Pereda. He serves Darkwater Syndicate as its Head Acquisitions Editor—he heads the department, he does not collect heads, which is a point he has grown quite fond of making. Indeed, it's one reason he likes his job so much.

NATHAN ROBINSON lives in Scunthorpe, England. He's contributed to over twenty different anthologies so far, with lots more on the horizon. His crime thriller 'Top of the Heap' was adapted in a podcast by www.pseudopod.org to rave reviews. *Starers*, released by Severed Press in 2012 gained much praise, with fans hungry for a sequel. He is currently completing four collections of his own work, the first entitled *Devil Let Me Go* which was released in 2013. His novella *Ketchup on Everything* was released in 2014 to rave reviews. His novella *Midway* was released by Severed Press in 2015, followed by *Caldera* in 2016. For news, updates and releases check out www.facebook.com/NathanRobinsonWrites

MATT SHAW is the published author of over 100 titles—all readily available on AMAZON. He is one of the United Kingdom's leading—and most prolific—horror authors, regularly breaking the top ten in the chart for Amazon's Most Popular Horror Authors. With work sometimes compared to Stephen King, Richard Laymon and Edward Lee, Shaw is best known for his extreme horror novels (The infamous Black Cover Range), Shaw has also dabbled in other genres with much success; including romance, thrillers, erotica and dramas. Despite primarily being a horror author, Shaw is a huge fan of Roald Dahl—even having a tattoo of the man on his arm; something he looks to whenever he needs a kick up the bum or inspiration to continue working! As well as pushing to release a book a month, Shaw's work is currently being translated for the Korean market and he is currently working hard to produce his own feature length film. And speaking of films . . . Several film options have been sold with features in the very early stages of development. Matt Shaw lives in Southampton (United Kingdom) but is looking to move in with you in the near future. He also thinks someone called Donnie is an idiot.

SCOTT SMITH is the author of two novels, *A Simple Plan* and *The Ruins*.

TIM WAGGONER has published close to forty novels and three collections of short stories. He writes original dark fantasy and horror, as well as media tie-ins, and his articles on writing have appeared in numerous publications. He's won the Bram Stoker Award, been a finalist for the Shirley Jackson Award and the Scribe Award, his fiction has received numerous Honorable Mentions in volumes of *Best Horror of the Year*, and he's twice had stories selected for inclusion in volumes of *Year's Best Hardcore Horror*. He's also a full-time tenured professor who teaches creative writing and composition at Sinclair College in Dayton, Ohio.

ACKNOWLEDGEMENTS

"So Sings The Siren" © Annie Neugebauer, From *Apex Magazine #101*, Editor: Jason Sizemore, Publisher: Apex Publications (September 2017)

"Junk" © Ryan Harding, From *DOA III*, Editors: Marc Ciccarone & Andrea Dawn, Publisher: Blood Bound Books (May 2017)

"The Cenacle" © Robert Levy, From *Shadows and Tall Trees Vol. 7*, Editor: Michael Kelly, Publisher: Undertow Publications (April 2017)

"The Maw" © Nathan Ballingrud, From *Dark Cities*, Editor: Christopher Golden, Publisher: Titan Books (May 2017)

"Burnt" © Luciano Marano, From *DOA III*, Editor: Marc Ciccarone & Andrea Dawn, Publisher: Blood Bound Books (May 2017)

"The Better Part Of Drowning" © Octavia Cade, From *The Dark Magazine,* Editors: Silvia Moreno-Garcia & Sean Wallace, Publisher: Prime Books (November 2017)

"Til Death" © Tim Waggoner, From *Never Fear: The Apocalypse*, Publisher: 13Thirty Books LLC. (April 2017)

"Letter From Hell" © Matt Shaw, Published by Matt Shaw (May 2017)

"Theatrum Mortuum" © Dani Brown, From *VS:X: US vs UK Extreme Horror*, Editor: Dawn Cano, Publisher: Shadow Wrok Publishing (December 2017)

"Break" © Glenn Gray, From *Hard Sentences: Crime Fiction Inspired by Alcatraz*, Editor: David James Keaton, Publisher: Broken River Books (July 2017)

"Bernadette" © R. Perez de Pereda, From *Shadows And Teeth Volume 3*, Editor: R. Perez de Pereda, Publisher: Darkwater Syndicate, Inc. (June 2017)

"West Of Matamoros, North Of Hell" © Brian Hodge, From *Dark Screams Volume Seven*, Editors: Brian James Freeman & Richard Chizmar, Publisher: Hydra/Random House (July 2017)

"Reprising Her Role" © Bracken Macleod, From *Splatterpunk Zine #8*, Editor: Jack Bantry (April 2017)

Made in the USA
San Bernardino, CA
19 June 2020